THE MOON GODDESS'S SMILE

A NOVEL

THE MOON GODDESS'S SMILE

CATHERINE C. WU

Cover and Typesetting by Autumn Skye
Edited by Mike Fleming

Library of Congress Control Number: 2025908038

Paperback ISBN-13: 979-8-9927912-0-4
Hardcover ISBN-13: 979-8-9927912-1-1
Ebook ISBN-13: 979-8-9927912-2-8
Audiobook ISBN-13: 979-8-9927912-3-5

First edition 2025

CRANE BRIDGE **PUBLISHERS**
ONE PAGE AT A TIME

"It will take me a while to 'recover' from this gripping, powerful, and heartbreaking tale... We readers...witness history from Mei's personal perspective as we journey into her and her family's past. Readers, take the trip Catherine Wu has created with her amazing pen and stay on the road, be it twisted or straight. You will learn so much about China you may never have learned in school."

~Patricia Daly-Lipe, PhD, award-winning author,
artist, philosopher, and historian

"Catherine Wu guides the reader through a journey of cultural clashes between her protagonist's Chinese family's traditional ways, present-day Chinese society, and her adoptive America's mores. This is one of those books that makes you feel more intelligent after reading it. I'm looking forward to her next books."

~Dr. Edward Mickolus, fellow author

"This soulful and beautifully written story invites readers to contemplate fate and the unforeseen forces shaping our lives. . . Catherine C. Wu creates an outstanding story that explores cultural heritage and its relevance in modern life. Mei's return becomes a journey of self-discovery. . . As she reconnects with her past, the rising of the full moon enables her to view an unexpected revelation during her trip with clarity. One line from the book that resonated with me is: "Is it good fortune, or a bad omen?" I highly recommend this novel to readers who appreciate fascinating stories on Chinese history and culture, multigenerational family dynamics, and immigrant experiences."

~Maalin O, Readers' Favorite

". . . we spend less than a week as Mei travels to her childhood home to help. . .her cousin. . . But in those few days, we accompany her ancestors through generations of fascinating family history – a history that includes war, resistance, betrayal. . . Along the way, we learn about Chinese art, politics, and culture while experiencing a romantic triangle that keeps us guessing right up until the final, startling revelation that changes everything Mei believes about her marriage and her future. . ."

~ Darlyn Finch Kuhn, author of *Red Wax Rose,*
Sewing Holes, and Three Houses

For my father

In paradise there are no stories, because there are no journeys. It's loss and regret and misery and yearning that drive the story forward, along its twisted road.

— Margaret Atwood, *The Blind Assassin*

The length of the journey has to be borne with, for every moment is necessary.

— Georg Wilhelm Friedrich Hegel,
The Phenomenology of Spirit

梅花香自苦寒來

The winter plum blossom's fragrance comes from the bitter cold.

— Chinese idiom

(Mei in Chinese is 梅花, the winter plum blossom. It is a symbol for resilience and perseverance in the face of adversity—because it often blooms most vibrantly amidst the harsh winter snow.)

TABLE OF CONTENTS

The Hong Family Tree

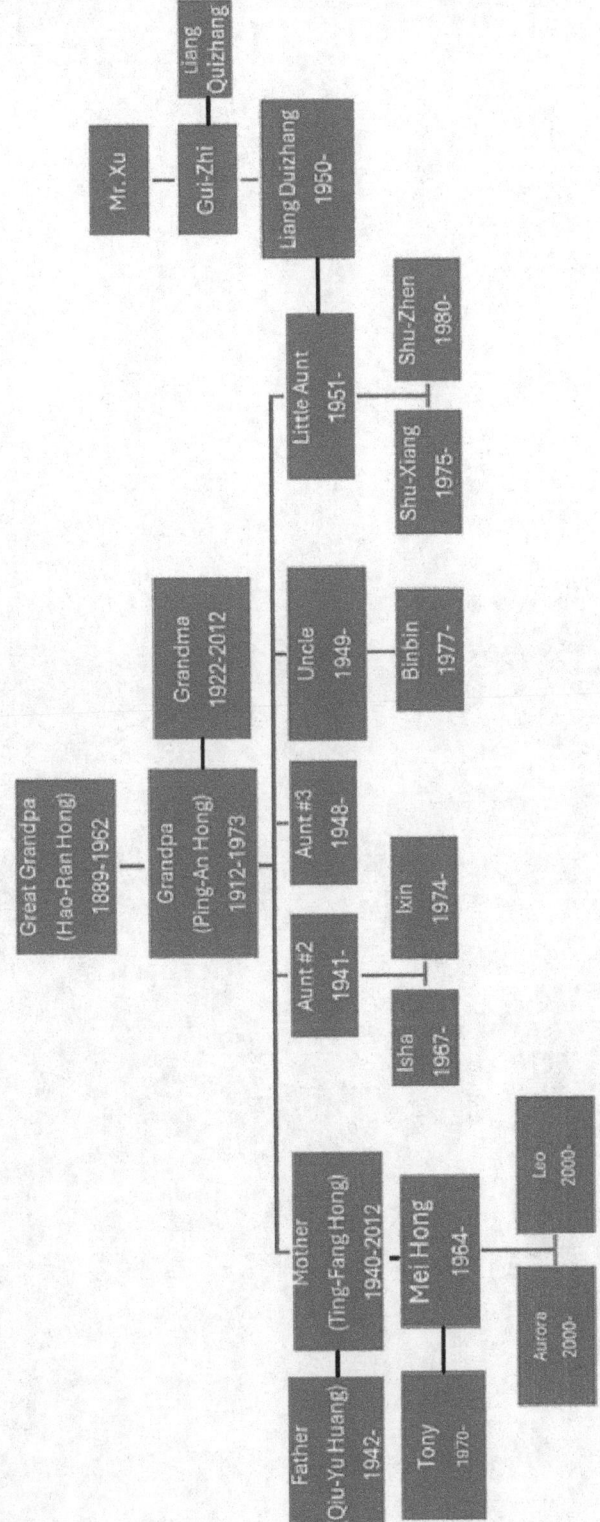

THE HONG CLAN'S
EXISTENTIAL CRISIS

Three weeks before, Aunt No. 2 had phoned me from China, needling my conscience.

As a rule, I shunned distractions at all costs during my experiments. But I made an exception that day because calls from Aunt No. 2 were as rare as total lunar eclipses, and I knew she wouldn't quit redialing until my cellphone battery drained.

Technically, I should call her Aunt No. 1 because my late mother was the firstborn. Yet, my mother had insisted I call her the same way as all my cousins did— "to avoid confusion at our family gatherings," she said. But seriously, confusion? Even Cousin Binbin, cute-but-clueless, whom we protected like an endangered panda, could figure it out from the context. Nevertheless, Aunt No. 1 had become Aunt No. 2 to me; by implication, Mother demoted herself to her sister's place.

Aunt No. 2 announced, "Mei, Grandma passed away two weeks ago, peacefully." Before I could gasp, she chirped, "Her funeral was a huge success—three hundred people attended."

"Ohh . . ." My vocal cords constricted, unable to squeeze out another word. *Why didn't you call me earlier?*

"Don't be upset. Grandma had a good, long life. Now, the reason I'm calling today pertains to a waiver I've mailed to you," she said matter-of-factly. "Please sign it when you receive it."

"What kind of waiver?" I said, collecting myself to wipe down a spreading puddle on my stainless-steel counter. Regrettably, I had spilled a sticky cocktail mixed for my precious transgenic mice.

"It's for Binbin. Poor thing, he is getting married in a month, for real."

As soon as she mentioned Binbin, I sighed. No need to broach the obvious topic. We had all pretended not to notice it, the giant, black thundercloud hovering overhead. Binbin was our last hope.

The year before, Aunt No. 2 had become our de facto matriarch, following in the footsteps of her dying big sister. Our succession order mirrored not only members' seniority, but also meritocracy. Aunt No. 2 had spent more time with my senile grandma than her younger sisters combined. Of course, nobody would expect my retired uncle, the honorary tribal head, to provide any kind of elder care. He had accomplished his mission in life—as the donor of a successful sperm with the crucial Y chromosome. As far as our clan was concerned, he could be put out to pasture.

According to a five-hundred-year-old genealogy map, our branch of the Hong House had dwindled alarmingly in the past three generations, with only one flag-bearer to carry on the family name. My poor grandma had attempted six times—three girls and three miscarriages—until she finally gave birth to my uncle. For insurance, she struggled for a second son. Little Aunt was born instead, to everyone's disappointment.

Here was an irony: by the time of my uncle's arrival, there was hardly anything left to inherit. Our prime real estate in Nanjing had been donated to the Communist government long before, along with productive land in the countryside. That left the chipped Ming Dynasty jars used for storage of salt, sugar, and detergent; some mismatched dinner plates and bowls from the Jiaqing period; and seven marble-inlaid rosewood chairs with rickety legs.

Yet without a male heir-apparent, our colony would collapse. By the mid-seventies, the government had strictly enforced the "One-Child Policy." As a result, when my uncle's wife became pregnant, our entire family traveled to a once-famous-but-now-defunct temple outside Nanjing for blessing. We burned incense, knelt, and prayed to gilded statues with missing heads; we stashed rolled-up paper bills—as charitable as we could be—in a hole on Guanyin's clay toe.

When Cousin Binbin was born, we all sighed with collective relief. The fertility goddess must have been pleased with our offerings, or perhaps my uncle was a super sharpshooter.

For the past ten years, it had been Binbin's turn to pass the baton to the next generation. From an early age, we all understood his destiny: before exhaling his last breath, Bibin must produce a male progeny against all odds. Sometimes I wondered if he could hear the stationary marching band playing in our heads.

In a rapid clip—a habit of a well-organized penny-pincher—Aunt No. 2 briefed me, by now an uninitiated foreigner, on the customary prerequisite for marriage in China: an apartment in town, a car, and a certain amount of gold jewelry or cash equivalent for the bride. Forget about the dowry of the Dark Ages. In a country with a shortage of marriageable females, girls called the shots now.

Binbin, expanding in all directions except height in his third decade of life, had a residual cuteness with his sad, reverse-slanted eyes, puffy cheeks, and chubby chin. With a dead-end HR job in a local glove factory, he'd accumulated modest savings by living under my uncle's roof. He didn't mind the teasing he got for his five-year-old Volkswagen beetle: the pink car was a bargain when its previous owner, his pregnant boss, outgrew it. Nevertheless, one hurdle had remained: since the reforms in the nineties, a flat in any first- or second-tier city had become a piping-hot commodity, with a shelf life of an undisturbed seventy years. Like a swimmer struggling against the current,

Binbin had been watching his goal fade further beyond the horizon year after year.

"Everyone has to chip in to help Binbin," Aunt No. 2 declared. "His fiancée this time is very promising."

"What's so special about her?"

"Between you and me," she whispered, "she isn't a looker, thin as a bamboo stick. But, she's the *only girl* in her family of the past three generations."

Before I could wedge in a word to correct her misconception about reproduction, she had shifted topics again, unfolding drama after drama.

Five weeks before, my ninety-year-old grandma, who had slipped into the twilight of Alzheimer's, regained a sudden spurt of mental clarity. She insisted on traveling to Shanghai to see her "ailing" daughter, my late mother. Unfortunately, Aunt No. 2 had coerced us into withholding the truth from her, "on account of her delicate heart!"

The delay-and-distract strategy backfired. No match for my strong-willed grandma, Aunt No. 2 eventually coughed up the old news.

"How dare you!" Grandma shouted, stomping the floor with her four-prong cane, her cloudy eyes burned with blistering fury. "Deceiving me like I'm a fool!"

Surprisingly, Grandma didn't shed a single tear for her first-born. She refused to talk to Aunt No. 2. That night, her bitter, delicate heart stopped altogether.

Unapologetic for withholding information from me also, Aunt No. 2 insisted, "Mei, I did it to protect you."

I could see her logic—I was close to Grandma. Although my heart had never been delicate, it did skip a beat upon hearing about her passing. Rearranging test tubes into a neat row on a rack, I mumbled hoarsely, "I . . . I appreciate your concern."

"We had a family meeting after the funeral," Aunt No. 2 continued. "As you can imagine, we unanimously bequeathed Grandma's apartment to Binbin."

Yet, much to the surprise of my family, the local government denied their joint petition to pass their inheritance shares to

Binbin. The head clerk had insisted, "According to our records, Hong Ping-An is still alive. What could a photo of his tombstone prove? Show me his death certificate."

Upon hearing that part, I interrupted. "Grandpa's death certificate is stored in a tin box in my mother's mahogany chest. Just ask my father."

"I did. *Twice.*" Aunt No. 2 enunciated each syllable with icy mockery. "He said, 'It's gone.'"

"Gone where?"

"Never mind him," she said curtly, probably raising her queenly palm on the other side of the globe.

Since our future generations would otherwise be stuck in limbo, Aunt No. 2 hefted the burden onto her rounded shoulders. She embarked on an odyssey of calling on all relevant authorities, hoping to find a stub or carbon copy of the death certificate in a dusty cabinet somewhere. No such luck. Unfortunately, Grandpa died on a train ride during the chaotic Cultural Revolution. And no jurisdiction would issue a retrospective death certificate.

Then, a young clerk in the Deed Office took pity on tearful Aunt No. 2. "Ahem," he said, coughing into his fist, "there is still a backdoor approach."

First, every potential beneficiary must sign a notarized waiver, he explained. After public notices for three consecutive weeks and a grace period of three months, Binbin could apply for a temporary permit. "Once your nephew inhabits the apartment for some yet-to-be-determined period, he could file a petition in a legal proceeding." Winking, the clerk joked, "The immortal Grandpa would never jump out of his grave to object, I assume?"

Thanking the clerk profusely, Aunt No. 2's eyes moistened again.

"Mei, I have everyone else's notarized waiver now." Aunt No. 2 wrapped up her call with a demand, "Please hurry. The girl's parents are getting impatient with Binbin."

"Yes, Aunty No. 2," I said eagerly, then scooped an extra helping of fresh frozen coconut chips to reward the jittery mice scratching their cage.

Alas, a few days later, Aunt No. 2 phoned me again, catching me in my kitchen, zesting an orange with a peeler.

"Thanks for sending your waiver by FedEx International." She said, then cried out, "But it's no good! Now they say the waiver must be notarized within our municipality." She pleaded, "Mei, please, come to Nanjing ASAP!"

Outrageous! I pitched my dulled vegetable peeler into the trash can, silently cursing the Byzantine rules of a backwater province. Must I drop everything in my life to grace some sleepy denizens in a smoky office with my distinguished face?

On second thought, Aunt No. 2 had just bestowed upon me a starring role in an epic saga—to stretch the thin but tenacious line of the Hong clan to yet another generation. Dramatic music began to crescendo in my ears, clamoring for a heroine.

Then, I remembered my ancient pledge to my grandpa—on my seventh birthday. Sighing, I bent over the trash and fumbled among coils of orange peels to retrieve the tossed peeler. Then I said to Aunt No. 2, "All right, I'm coming."

THE CRYING MOON GODDESS AND THE NASTY MOONCAKES

As soon as I hung up the call with Aunt No. 2, my husband burst into the kitchen with an armful of brown bags. I stared at him, tongue-tied. *Shoot, I'm in trouble.*

With our upcoming vacation to Disneyland, I would have exhausted all my "flexible time off" for this miserable year, a year of back-to-back catastrophes, a year of an inexhaustible well of grief. I harbored no illusions. Begging my boss for special treatment would be suicidal—I was valuable but not indispensable to our pharmaceutical startup in Cambridge.

Tony plopped down the Chinese takeout on the counter, then shoved a six-pack into the cramped fridge. *Bingo,* an idea emerged.

"Hey, I've just realized something: this year's Mid-Autumn Festival will fall on our vacation. Why limit us to the lousy, overpriced food in Disneyland? Let's trim off a few days with Mickey and eat like royals in China—we would be halfway there anyway."

"What's going on?" Tony said, wrinkling his forehead.

I explained my predicament, then pleaded to the outdoorsman in him. "After feasting with my folks, we can even throw in a short hiking trip to boot!"

He rubbed his chin and regarded me.

I cajoled in my most convincing voice, "Lately, the twins are losing their Chinese vocabulary fast. So, this modified trip will be like killing three birds with one stone."

"Changing our plan at the last minute to please your aunt? You must be kidding!"

I shook my head miserably.

Raking his wavy hair in exasperation, Tony said, "Do you know you're a hopeless sucker?"

"Ouch," I objected. But was it even possible to explain to any non-Chinese the ingrained sense of family obligation?

In the backyard, our twins were dribbling a soccer ball on a patch of crabgrass. I offered them freshly squeezed orange juice. While they happily gulped down my token bribe, I lectured, "Remember the word *Wei-Ji* that you learned in your Chinese school? *Crisis* literally means 'dangerous opportunities.' Today, your dad and I have decided to turn a family crisis into an opportunity for a cultural enrichment trip."

Their mouths gaped. So, I amped up the fun factor to lure them on board. To compensate for the truncated Disneyland trip, I enticed them with a bonus hike to a UNESCO World Heritage site. "Yellow Mountain is more challenging than the Mount Monadnock trails. But the views are unbelievable. Oh, there's a famous tree there—the greeting pine of China. Imagine this lonely pine," I said, swaying my outstretched arms for the visual effect, "clinging to a rocky cliff for thousands of years. Its gnarled trunk has yielded to the prevailing wind; its graceful boughs are shrouded in mist."

The kids exchanged dubious glances.

Oops, I overkilled with the lyricism. But their hardly concealed smirks nudged me to try harder. I pressed on, pitching like a desperate tour operator at the end of a dismal season. "The portrait of this iconic tree, this symbol of resilience, is hung in the Great Hall of China. We can see it up close and—"

"You mean, it's a Chinese version of the Lone Cypress in Monterey?" Cut in Aurora, my twelve-going-on-twenty-year-old daughter.

"Well, it's much older," I countered. "And more majestic."

She lifted the bottom of her damp T-shirt to wipe her face; her acne looked fierce. This new itinerary would eliminate her favorite Universal Studio tour. Ignoring her thinly veiled hostility, I stood my ground. "Anyway, kids, you're long overdue for your Chinese immersion trip."

Wordlessly, the twins resumed their soccer practice. Holding their emptied glasses, I tried another tactic. "If we don't go, your Chinese grandpa will be all by himself for the Mid-Autumn Festival."

Cocking her head and narrowing her eyes, Aurora said, "Who gives a crap about this Chinese holiday?"

"Wait, is it that silly holiday about a crying woman? And the nasty mooncakes?" Leonardo chuckled, stealing the resting ball from under Aurora's sole.

Just then, Tony brought out the reheated takeout. Trays in both hands, he intercepted the rolling ball with his foot and said, "Guys, guys, be respectful to your elders."

Nodding at Tony, I said firmly, "Time to double down on your Chinese practice. Like it or not, we're going."

Leonardo's face fell.

A sulking second later, Aurora turned to her twin brother. "Do you think this counts for that lame assignment, you know, for social studies?"

"Good thinking," I said, beaming my brightest smile. "Other kids would have to fight for slots in exchange programs to gain this kind of experience. Lucky you!"

For years, I had tried to instill Chinese heritage in my children. Rain or shine, I shuttled them to the Chinese school in Newton every Sunday. I fancied gifting them the bicultural perspective—something like bifocal, or, even better, progressive lenses for vision.

When the twins turned five, I took them to the Museum of Fine Arts in Boston. In the Asian wing, I pointed out a porcelain bowl on display. Two vivacious dragons were chasing a ball on the celadon-glazed surface. With swelling pride, I said, "Mommy used to have a special bowl just like that. Hmm, maybe slightly smaller." But my remote life in China was as relatable to them as *The Arabian Nights*. Before I could elaborate on the story of my bowl, they had trotted toward the red-faced Tibetan Demon near the exit.

Undaunted, when they turned six, I took them to visit China. Sadly, all they could remember about that trip was the novelty of mung-bean-and-peanut popsicles that my mother bought for them in Yu Garden.

Mother had also attempted to teach the twins Chinese for many summers. But she always abdicated her temporary throne to return to Shanghai at the end of each August. When the kids bid cheerful goodbye to their *popo* (the maternal grandmother in the Nanjing dialect), I could sense her inner wince at their butchered pronunciations. Despite her repeated corrections, the twins could never master the second tone in the first character and the fourth tone in the second.

The "silly holiday" that Leonardo referred to happened four autumns ago.

On that crystal indigo night, a full moon bathed Pleasure Bay. Under its silver sheen, even the grapevines choking our neighbor's chain-link fence looked as if being plucked out of a Zen master's garden. Arranging mooncakes, persimmons, and pomelos on our picnic table, I deliberated whether to tell my children a peculiar myth. After all, they already had three years of schooling in Chinese, plus my mother's diligent tutoring. *They should be ready*, I decided. So, I proceeded with an abbreviated version of a story I'd learned from Grandpa.

"A long, long time ago, one day, nine tandem suns rose to the sky. Soon, rivers dried up, the earth was scorched, crops withered, and livestock dropped dead from thirst.

"Yes, I guess you could say it was a global warming crisis during a prehistoric period.

"A brave archer named Ho Yi stepped up. Aiming at the sky with his powerful bow, one by one, he shot down the eight extra suns.

Leonardo interrupted me again, "You mean, he used a rocket?"

"Tsk, tsk," I clicked my tongue, "don't distract me with the technical details. That's not the point. Anyway, for his good deed, the gods rewarded Yi with a vial of the ambrosia of immortality.

"Yes, he could have lived forever had he drunk it right on the spot. But he didn't. Why? Ah, he decided to gather his people to witness the event, to celebrate him becoming a god on an auspicious day.

"While Yi was preparing for his farewell speech, another disaster struck. The sky opened, and torrential rain flooded the Middle Kingdom. Elders knelt before Yi, begging him to dam the ravaging river and stop the deluge. With a sigh, our hero locked up the vial, entrusted the key to his wife for safekeeping, and left in a hurry on another impossible mission.

"And, guess what? Curiosity often clouds one's judgment. Holding the key, Chang'e—the wife—paced at home for days. Finally, she gave in to the temptation. *Just a tiny drop, for a taste,* she thought.

"But as soon as the droplet of elixir hit her tongue, Chang'e felt giddy. Next thing she knew, she'd finished the entire vial, hiccuping and laughing.

"Remember, kids, just like any drug, once you start, you can't stop.

"Soon, the room swirled around her, and she lifted off from the floor like a hot-air balloon. Yes, Leo, maybe the elixir generated helium. Anyway, to avoid hitting the ceiling, she grabbed the windowsill. Instead, her body shot out. In a panic, she grasped a willow branch in front of her house, screaming for help. Then, the branch broke off. But, instead of hitting the ground, she reversed her fall in midair. Up and up, she spiraled, cartwheeling into the sky. From below, people watched with goggled eyes and wide-open mouths.

"Eventually, Chang'e tumbled down and crashed onto a giant boulder. When she woke up, she thought she was hallucinating. She rubbed a painful bump on her head, but a silver palace shimmered in front of her.

"The grand palace was empty. 'Hello?' She said tentatively but heard no response. Then, a white rabbit jumped out of nowhere. Following its hop, she limped into a lush garden perfumed with sweet, exotic blooms. A sweaty lumberjack was hacking at a laurel tree with an ax. But as soon as he straightened his back, the fresh cut would close on its own.

"'Ha, ha, ha. . .' The rabbit laughed, widening its split lip. Then it whispered to the bewildered Chang'e, 'Don't pity him. He is serving his sentence here for having offended the gods. The rightful owner of the Moon Palace is—drum rolls here please—you!'

"So that's how Chang'e, a beautiful but ordinary housewife, became the Moon Goddess.

"However, ever since that day, the Moon Goddess had been crying her heart out, night after night, in her cold, lonely Moon Palace."

After finishing the story, I showed my family an image of the accidental goddess on my Samsung. Tony, with three China trips under his belt, peered at the teary beauty and frowned, "Isn't that Guang Yin, the Goddess of Compassion?"

"All Asian women ae still look-alikes to you, after you are married to me for fourteen years!" I said with annoyance, "Nope. Chang'e is an indigenous goddess, way before Buddhism was imported from India." After a moment of reflection, I admitted, "Well, since the Chinese only worship her once a year, perhaps she isn't as powerful as Guang Yin."

"Oh, I see," he said, his voice laced with a trace of disappointment.

My children weren't impressed with the crying goddess, either. After blowing a chewing gum bubble as big as a rice bowl toward the distant bay, Aurora ruthlessly jeered, "What a retarded story! She totally deserves to be left alone in the cold— for stealing from her husband."

"Imagine her flying?" Leonardo faked a shrill, his spread arms wobbled like an out-of-control aircraft. "Help! Oh, no, oh, no! Oh, no, no, no, no!"

"Ha, ha, ha . . ." Aurora giggled.

Tony tilted his face away, grinning at a rumbling FedEx cargo plane flying over the moon.

"Cut it out, all of you! Have you ever heard of the word *empathy*?" I was appalled. Something must be terribly wrong with my rendition of the tale. Dejected, I took out a knife and quartered the mooncakes. "Help yourself. Lotus seeds, red beans, pine nuts, and duck eggs," I said, pointing out the four traditional varieties. I'd steered clear from cakes with smoked ham and durian fruit in a Chinatown bakery.

Aurora spat out the orange duck yolk onto the grass. "Yuck, do Chinese consider this salty thing a *dessert*?"

My stomach sank. Perhaps we had picked the wrong name for our daughter. Aurora—the goddess of dawn. Conflict of interest with the moon?

"Nasty!" Leonardo chimed in.

"Well, salted duck egg is an acquired taste for adults," I relented. "Try the one with red beans."

But Tony, the adult in my audience, scrunched up his face.

"What's wrong?" I was alarmed.

"Toothache. What's in this red bean paste?"

"Sugar and shortening. All empty calories," I snapped, "just like the Italian cookies you grew up with!" Then it crossed my mind: *Did he bite into a piece of accidental gravel?* But I was in too foul a mood to inquire. Instead, I resolutely gazed at the moon, touching the image of Chang'e engraved on a jade pendant on my chest, and sending a silent blessing to my other family half a world over.

The day after the fiasco, I ate the leftover mooncakes—for breakfast, lunch, and dinner. Ultimately, my heritage pride gained me nothing but three extra pounds around my waist. The mooncakes were only two pounds—another mystery in life.

Stubbornly, I wrote down the tale of the Moon Goddess. Black words on white paper, I thought, ought to carry more weight than the ineffectual sounds that had fizzled out of my lips.

Then, reading my draft, I saw the root cause of my children's mockery: I couldn't articulate the story's meaning.

Nevertheless, the writing itself comforted me inexplicably. Soon, my writing expanded to Grandpa's other memorable tales, then stories of the storyteller himself, and eventually the entire family. Someday, I hoped, I could present the collection to my mature children.

I'd mentioned my amateurish project to no one. In fact, I also had another hidden agenda about this China trip: I needed to clarify a few fuzzy details about Nanjing, my hometown.

To economize our vacation, I had to tweak it into forked multi-segments. In the end, like all compromises in life, our trip looked preposterous. Yet, to my surprise, Tony agreed to the revision without further persuasion. "Do they serve decent Kung Pao Chicken in Shanghai?" He chuckled good-naturedly. "You know, that dish."

That dish was an inside joke between us. Noticing a long-absent twinkle in his eyes, my heart bloomed with joy. "Absolutely!" I cried out. "And I could take a refresher course."

Smiles lingered on our lips as we basked in that warm amber memory of our courtship days.

3

MY FATHER'S APARTMENT

A wall of evening fog surged, barring our exit from Pudong International Airport. The worn windshield wipers squealed like an injured puppy. Over the radio, a high-pitched male voice cheerfully glossed over the traffic casualties. "Multiple accidents on all major highways..." No longer so familiar with the Shanghai dialect, for a split second, I mistook the numbers for the raffle prizes given out at numerous shopping malls that had mushroomed during my self-imposed exile.

"Visibility is less than ten meters," my father shook his silver hair and muttered as our taxi crawled toward his apartment. Then he turned to me with an expectant smile, "Did you spot anything new on the Boeing Dreamliner, Mei?"

"Well, everything on our plane looks brand-new." Yawning behind my palm, I tried to describe the dimmable windows, a cutting-edge feature that might intrigue an engineer.

"Ah, they finally made it into the commercial fleet!" he exclaimed. Eyes sparkling behind his thick glasses, he couldn't resist explaining this feat of engineering: sandwiching a special gel of electrochromic material between two pieces of glass, adjusting the opacity by controlling the conductivity...

Before I could don my own scientist's hat to contribute to this scintillating topic, I yawned again, far more discreetly this time.

My father noticed, nevertheless. Pushing up his sliding glasses, he asked, "So, when will Tony and the twins arrive?"

"In four days. We'll rendezvous here after my trip to Nanjing." In my email to him, I had only outlined our ambitious itinerary. So, I added warily, "I'm leaving tomorrow afternoon."

To spare him from any guilt, I skipped the implied "to finish the business with Mother's family." My complex trip wouldn't have been necessary had he not misplaced Grandpa's death certificate.

He brightened. "Perfect. The Mid-Autumn Festival is in four days. I'll make a dinner reservation then."

His words were almost verbatim what I had imagined, yet my stomach tightened another knot. Celebrating a family reunion festival with a new widower couldn't be fun. And this dreadful holiday would be our first since I left China decades before.

Worse, I had left Boston with my own house still in disarray, hoping that this last-minute trip would work its magic. *A change of scenery is like pressing a RESET button. Everything will work out.* I inhaled a lungful of humid Shanghai air. The tang of burning rubber stung my nostrils like a punishment.

An ear-piercing screech—our heads lurched forward as a refrigerated truck materialized before us. "*Xiangwunin!*" Our cabbie pumped his fist on the steering wheel three times in rapid succession. "That idiot almost got us killed!"

With inches of clearance to spare, the rogue truck jockeyed for the exit ramp. In the company logo on its back, a crab with red claws appeared to be wiping slanting tears of condensation.

"This year's *dazhaxie* crab harvest is terrible," my father mumbled.

"No shit!" agreed the irate cabbie. "This festival is expensive as hell."

I nodded my sympathy—no feast for this holiday would be proper without mitten crabs and mooncakes.

"Global warming," my father commiserated, lamenting about algal blooms that had decimated the crab population in the nearby lakes. His voice quivered as if he were personally responsible.

The sour-faced cabbie darted him a dirty look through the rear-view mirror.

Finally, we emerged from the milky half-light and arrived at my father's apartment, the one he and my late mother had shared for over two decades. I instantly noticed the open kitchen. It hadn't existed six months before—when I stayed here to visit my dying mother. After a brief hesitation in front of the shoe rack, my father ushered me in without changing into his slippers. While I was laying down my carry-on, he said, pointing to the fridge, "Your favorite, the Nanxiang soup dumpling, is in there. Best to microwave on 'low' for three minutes."

"Great," I said, a little perplexed. *Shouldn't he dive into the kitchen to prepare my welcome-home dinner?* I had imagined that we would talk and re-bond under the intimate pools of the pendant lights. Instead, following his gesturing, I found myself staring at a yellow energy-efficiency label still attached to the fridge door.

"Sleep in as late as you want. Let's have brunch at a new dim sum place. Here," he handed me his key chain, then turned toward the door and said gently, "Call me tomorrow. Good night, Mei."

"Wait, wait," I said, blinking. "Where are you going?"

"I'm staying at Aunty Tian's tonight." He flashed me another sheepish smile. "You look tired. Why don't we save the talk for tomorrow?"

"Aunty Tian's?" My jetlagged brain churned sluggishly after the fifteen-hour flight. Instead of registering his words, it only picked up a whiff of a sharp odor in the apartment.

"Oh. Aunty Tian and I got married, hmm, five months ago," he volunteered. "Just a piece of paper from the city hall. That's all."

"What?" I gaped at him stupidly. "Who's this Aunty Tian?"

Fixing his gaze at the good-luck charm on the door, he said, "She's—she was my co-worker. You met her before—at your mother's funeral."

Unbelievable! So he remarried just a month after the funeral, yet procrastinated until the last possible minute to announce this vital information. Unsure whether I should laugh or cry, I managed to click back my dislocated jaw to demand, "Why didn't you tell me earlier?"

His face flushed under the dim hallway light. Or was this one of the optical illusions he mentioned so often? An excruciating second later, he mumbled, "I meant to. But . . . it slipped my mind."

"Aha!"

He shuddered. The cutting word must have sounded as if it came from my late mother's lips. People had told me before, *"You two were cast from the same mold."*

Hand still gripping the doorknob, he consulted his watch awkwardly. "Look, it's half past nine already. See you tomorrow." Then he hurried away, flying down the corridor.

Staring at his receding back, I vaguely remembered this Tian woman: a petite, impeccably dyed brunette with a squirrel face, a Shanghainese woman whom nobody would take a second glance at on any crowded street. At the funeral, embarrassingly, I had mistaken her for one of my mother's acquaintances. In fact, I only remembered her because of her unique voice—like the squeaky sound of someone scratching glass with coarse granules. Yes, granules of Sweet'n Low.

"My deepest condolences," she had said in that grating, artificial tone, her tiny, bony hands clasping mine for three beats too long, inclining her pointy chin and drilling me with her prolonged, meaningless smile. Perhaps she was attempting to tell me something via telepathy, but the enormous cemetery swallowed her message. The memory of that chilly spring morning sprang back to me now, and that repulsive sensation of being seized by a rodent's claws.

The sound of my father's fleeing footsteps gradually faded away in the staircase. *Ridiculous!* I thought, scoffing at his absurdity. What did he imagine his adult daughter might do if he'd waited for the elevator? Cling to his sleeves, stomp her feet, flop and howl on the floor? Even as a child, I could never throw a tantrum at him, though I'd fantasized about it, yearning for closeness to him by any means.

A sudden LED light shot out as I squeezed his keychain.

I slammed the metal door. The red fringe of the lucky charm swung back and forth on the peel-off hook like a pendulum. The entry hall suddenly spun. My vision blurred; cold sweat poured out of every pore. Leaning against the wall, I slid down and landed on a pile of lumpy slippers.

I'd never been the type of fragile damsel who is prone to faint. But I was famished. Hours earlier, anticipating a feast with my father, I had barely nibbled the enticing spaghetti and meatballs served on the Dreamliner. Remembering the airline candies I'd hoarded, I fumbled in my pockets. A handful of melting peppermints delivered on its promise of being lifesavers.

Yet a dull, throbbing headache lingered, shading my mood a notch darker. Massaging my temples with clammy fingers, I caught the sorry sight of a middle-aged woman in the hall mirror, her tousled hair as wretched as soggy ramen noodles. I winced. Then, I grabbed the shoe rack and hoisted myself up with a grunt.

In the revamped bathroom, I cranked the shower setting to the " Maximum Hot." At once, hundreds of mini-cannonballs fired from all directions. Gritting my teeth, I counted the seconds that I could endure. Soon, the burning and pounding sensations gave way to an invigorating endorphin rush. White vapors transformed the glass stall into a comforting cocoon, transporting me back to my home in South Boston. For a confusing minute, I thought about cooking a hearty dinner for my children. After their most recent growth spurt, they could wolf down an entire rotisserie chicken plus the aluminum tray.

Tenderness swelled in my chest. Only eighteen hours had passed since I hugged them goodbye at Logan Airport, but I already missed their goofy banters, their annoying groans, and the scent of Axe deodorant.

I stepped out of the shower with dripping hair and a growling stomach. But instead of foraging for food, I roamed around the apartment, searching for a tin box.

At one point, pine-nut candies had filled the round box. I could visualize a slight dent at seven o'clock on the lid, which depicted a wholesome-looking girl, bearing a glinting overbite, brandishing a badminton racket. When Grandpa presented the box to me on my seventh birthday, he pinched my dimpled cheeks and said, "Whoa, you look just like that happy girl!"

Two years later, the candies were long gone, and so was my grandpa. Mother repurposed the tin box for her essential documents, including Grandpa's death certificate.

Despite my father's claim, I still cradled a microscopic hope of finding the supposedly missing tin box. Part of my childhood resided there, too.

Mother had always tucked the box inside the top drawer of an antique chest. The tall mahogany chest, with hand-carved scrolls and ball-and-claw feet, was the only surviving piece of my grandmother's dowry. Mother had wanted to pass it down, but I declined—the overseas shipping was too much of a hassle.

To my dismay, the chest was gone, too. Worse, I could not recognize a single piece of furniture in this apartment.

Granted, I hadn't grown up here. I was living in New York when my parents bought this flat. That was in the early nineties, a dramatic era when housing became a commodity instead of an employee benefit administrated by the government; the Oriental Pearl TV tower—Shanghai's new landmark—was just beginning to emerge from the reedy marshes near the East China Sea.

I surveyed my surroundings: a stainless-steel kitchen. A laminated table with a centerpiece of a polyester rose in a bud vase—all from IKEA? Two identical bedrooms, one theme-painted spring pastel, the other earthy brown. Stacked cans of leftover paint in an otherwise empty closet. An abstract print hung askew on the beige wall above a sofa bed. Mother would have had a fit over such sloppiness.

Something else was off. There wasn't a single photo here—of my parents, of me (their only offspring), of my twins, or of anything living except a kitten wearing an expression of suspicion.

Disoriented, I felt like an anonymous guest, perhaps someone testing a new Airbnb rental.

Ah, that familiar feeling of being a guest in a different, silent apartment. My armpits turned damp again; my core began to freeze up. Layer by layer, the ice block grew, its weight crushing me into that eight-year-old I once was, a girl longing for a big, warm hand that would brush away the stray hair from her teary eyes and the inevitable teasing: *Now, now. What's wrong, Meimei?*

With well-practiced effort, I snapped out of the trance. To escape an insufferable formaldehyde smell, I stepped toward the balcony. Near the sliding door, a heart-shaped water stain on the slightly warped wood floor glared at me. Oh yes, I was the guilty culprit. On that drizzly spring evening six months earlier, I had rushed to the hospital after a nurse's call, forgetting to close the sliding door. Now, these imperfections were the only preserved artifacts in this transformed apartment.

A shadow flickered under a strangely placed shower curtain in the far corner of the balcony. I tensed up. A burglar? Steeling myself, I inched toward the flitting curtain. Then, I saw the pair of claws peeking from the darkness underneath. With a racing heart, I yanked off the curtain.

At last, the mahogany chest! Thousands of dust motes danced in the misty light filtering through the glass door. I sneezed uncontrollably: *Achoo, achoo, achoo.* Tears rushed down my cheeks.

The once-a-statement piece, lovingly polished by my mother in the past, now looked shabby. Its rich burgundy varnish was coated with mold speckles, twinkling as if from a painting of a starry night. Where a brass handle was missing, a rusty screw stuck out.

One by one, I pulled out the sticky drawers. The dovetail joints threatened to fall apart. No tin box anywhere. All I uncovered were wire hangers, wooden clothespins, cleaning supplies, rags, and newspapers dated five months earlier. The rags looked familiar. I felt a stab in my chest when I recognized them—my mother's torn-up pajamas.

No wonder my father couldn't find Grandpa's death certificate. Did he toss away Mother's too, along with our family photos, during his big purge?

Ч

MY MOTHER'S RIDDLE

I called Tony and left a voicemail announcing my safe arrival in Shanghai. Then, I logged into my ancient Yahoo mail account (because Google had exited China two years before.) The last email was a week old—from my father confirming our meeting point at the airport. Seeing it, I snickered. A family reunion, a festival feast. What a farce!

I turned off the bedside light. Tossing and turning in the spring-themed bedroom, I was furious. Why bother bringing my own family here to celebrate the holiday with my defector father? Unable to sleep, I drank some water, then walked to the balcony.

Aha, Aunty Tian! Now I remembered that woman with a distinctive, grating voice. She had insisted on talking to my father six or seven summers earlier while my parents were visiting us in Boston!

My face burned in the cool, damp Shanghai night. I couldn't believe it had taken me this long to connect the glaring dots.

At first, we ignored the call. Then, three minutes later, the phone rang again, and my father started to fidget with his napkin.

"The telemarketers," I assured him in Mandarin. "Always these obnoxious people around dinner time."

"I see. Should I check the caller ID anyway?"

"No, no. I will." I got up grudgingly. Seeing the flashing number 011 and a Shanghai area code, I answered the phone. In a honeyed, raspy voice, the caller identified herself as my father's secretary.

I handed my father the cordless phone, and he carried it to the farthest corner of the adjacent living area. I only heard his whispered "yes," "um," and "okay." Meanwhile, my mother poked at the wrinkly, over-blanched string beans.

"Problem at work?" I asked when my father retook his seat.

"Not really." Dabbing his sweaty nose with his napkin, he repeated in English for everyone to hear, "Nothing serious."

"Then, tell your secretary not to disturb our dinner with frivolous calls," I snapped. Somehow, I instinctively detested that woman with an unpleasant voice.

My mother snorted. My father blushed, shrinking in his seat like a boiled shrimp. Tony joked about a missile crisis caused by a bad connection over an international call. I cast an appreciative glance at my suave husband. Growing up as the youngest boy in a gregarious Italian family, he had accumulated a vast arsenal of jokes to diffuse any tense situation.

The next dinner, my father cleared his throat and announced, "I've moved my return flight to this Sunday."

"What? But the kids look forward to visiting the Glass Flowers Gallery at the Harvard Museum with you this Sunday! Nothing serious, right?" I said, wondering if his earlier departure was precipitated by our cramped house or the medium-rare steak Tony had grilled the other night.

"True. But my boss is pushy, I think," he said, wiping his sweat-beaded forehead. "Could I take them to the museum next time?"

A creaking sound erupted from my mother's plate. Vehemently sawing her well-done swordfish with a serrated knife, she said, "If he doesn't rush back to Shanghai, the Earth will stop rotating."

"You're welcome to return with me—if you like," my father said, pushing up his glasses. Color flushed from his hairline to his neckline.

Mother said with a smirk, "Why waste money on rescheduling *me*? I wasn't needed!"

"What's going on?" Tony was alarmed by her bitter tone. After I translated the gist of their conversation, he combed his fingers through his wavy hair in mock bewilderment. The twins giggled at their father's pantomime. I only shrugged. *A typical conversation between my parents.*

That summer, as planned, my mother taught my children Chinese. But she was often home alone when the twins were in day camp. Tony joked one day, "Gee, after your husband left, your chicken dish tastes even more delicious."

Without missing a beat, she said, "I sleep much better without his snoring."

So, the demanding "boss" was Aunty Tian, the secretary!

Pacing to and fro on the balcony, I cursed under my breath. *Ludicrous. Pathetic. Cruel. Liar. Cheater. Traitor...* Each step fanned the blazes of my rage.

How efficient my engineer father was! *Oh, Aunty Tian and I got married, hmm, five months ago.* By swinging this wrecking ball—this sentence of thirteen Chinese characters—at the cornerstone of my faith, he had shattered the sacred temple into crumbling ruins.

The bottom of the shower curtain rustled in the breeze as if Mother's spirit were trying to crawl into the mahogany chest, her last domain. My hand shook, spilling water from my glass. Now, Mother's enigmatic deathbed talk started to make sense.

"Remember, Mei, men are . . . ," Mother had said, gasping for air, the gurgling sounds frightening. Under the fluorescent light, her sunken eyes appeared huge on her gaunt, sallow face. "Like babies," she finally uttered with a sour breath. "They need . . . *lots* of love, unlike us . . ."

She emphasized the *lots* in the way a gardener might caution his apprentice about a peculiar habit of a rare orchid; while the word *us* was tossed away as if it were an irksome dandelion. Her parched mouth gaped once more, then closed like a drawstring purse, leaving her unspoken words floating oppressively in the muggy night.

Fighting back tears, I focused on wiping away a sheet of cold sweat glazing her waxy forehead. She was losing it. For two days and nights, she'd been slipping in and out of delirium—induced by ever-increasing doses of morphine. I wished that she would just give up her futile fight. Yet she held on, waiting in vain for my father's return from his conference in Beijing.

What an odd piece of deathbed advice from Mother, I had thought at the time. Years before, she had warned me the opposite: *Too much affection ruins a relationship, just like too much sugar spoils a dish.*

Like a Spartan, Mother had practiced that maxim all her life. As a result, she never indulged me—knowing too well what fate awaited a spoiled child. (Eons earlier, my grandpa had been one.)

Once, I saw a woman in a TV commercial burying her lovely face in a fluffy towel and crooning softly. Out of the blue, I blurted out, "As far as I can recall, my mother has never kissed or hugged me."

Tony squirted a mouthful of his beer. With a violent roar of laughter, his shoulders seemed to have popped out of their sockets. As a child, he'd almost drowned in geysers of maternal XOXOs. Then, eyebrows dancing, he elbowed Jeff—his buddy brooding on our couch—and said, "Hey, did you catch that? Mei was raised by a she-wolf!"

But Jeff didn't laugh. His wary eyes were glued to the TV, where LeBron James resumed his beating on our hometown Celtics during an NBA playoff game.

Nevertheless, I got my revenge a few months later. When we picked up my parents from Logan Airport for the first time, I initiated a hesitant, Westernized embrace. My mother's stoic body recoiled; I could feel her buzzing message: *Mei, only the weak and insecure need to demonstrate their love in public!*

Tony's camcorder captured that moment in high fidelity: Mother's stiffened spine and my awkward arms hovering in midair; I took a step back and bowed slightly.

When I turned to a wide-eyed Tony for an introduction, how I wished I had his camcorder in hand!

Naturally, biased by Mother's lifelong austerity, I had discarded the pharmaceutical-altered wisdom at her deathbed. Finally, I was able to crack the riddle: her contradictory teaching was the veiled sorrow of a prideful woman.

Was it her bruised ego that prohibited her revealing my father's betrayal and her suffering? Or, did she deem me a weakling, unable to handle the truth?

Instead of answers, more questions bubbled up: When did she find out about that Tian woman? When did my father begin his affair? How long ago had he stopped loving her? I sighed. With her gone, was there any point speculating?

I gazed at the moonless sky. In four days, the moon would reach her celestial zenith to receive the worship of billions of Chinese worldwide. Tracing the Moon Goddess on the jade pendant dangling on my chest, I sensed an irony. This round disc—a gift from Mother and a symbol of domestic harmony—now posed a geometrical dilemma: Eliminating a ninety-degree angle, what would be the remainder of a right triangle? A thin, unstable line? Or two separate dots?

The most depressing question was: How could I have been so oblivious?

In retrospect, my parents (and people of their generation) had stuck together till the end because divorce was unthinkable. Yet their marriage was supposed to be "a match made in heaven"! At least, that was the prediction of a *feng shui* master consulted by my grandma.

Like everyone else, I took my parents for granted. Actually, I knew far less about them than I knew about my grandparents. Nevertheless, one statistic was verifiable: out of their fifty conjugal years, Mother had been dying during the last one.

Men need lots of love. Testing her words on my lips, I felt a prick from the smooth jade pendant. So, she had been confessing to being an indifferent wife and blaming herself for her marital failure!

As if by osmosis, her guilt seeped out of the pendant and permeated my skin. A pang of remorse bloomed inside me, like a sponge soaking up a bloody puddle.

I had to admit that I'd been a negligent wife, too, settling into marital complacency. After fourteen shared years, Tony and I had smoothed our edges like two well-circulated coins, yet we couldn't weld ourselves into a homogeneous alloy. Instead, we argued, then made peace—a disturbing pattern of increasing frequency. Our most brutal fight was on the touchy subject of parenting. Afterward, Tony seemed to enjoy licking his festering, primarily self-inflicted wounds, and I dressed up mine with padded bandages. Nowadays, entrenched in a drawn-out cold war, we only politely discuss the twins' carpool schedules for hockey games, or the out-of-control crabgrass in the yard ...

I shuddered with a realization: That fight was almost four months ago, and so was our last maintenance sex.

In the past, I'd attributed our waning libidos to garden-variety stress: work, aging, and ailing parents. Having twins late in life didn't help, either. Granted, we never had a massive appetite in that department, even from Day One. I remembered my secret relief when I discovered that Tony was an anomaly too in a hypersexualized society—well, at least that was my impression of America. What if my assumption had been altogether wrong?

The dense clouds over Shanghai were thinning. The faint neon glow from the Oriental Pearl Tower turned the western sky into slices of mealy orange wedged in concrete canyons. The only visible constellation was made up of windows illuminated by many flickering TV screens. A movement drew my eyes to an apartment across the street: a girl was lifting a bowl toward her companion. He gave it a sniff, nodding. One hand cupped under her chopsticks, she transferred a morsel into his anticipating mouth. Cheek bulging, he chewed methodically, then spit into the kitchen sink. She whacked his bent back with chopsticks. His body flinched. Then he lifted his head, a playful smile crinkled his face. Her pouty mouth cracked, too.

The couple's inaudible intimacy brought back an image of the young Tony, a spoiled child at heart: his sun-burned face and wind-chapped lips, his teasing eyebrows, and his hips, always gliding with enviable grace. Recently, I'd spotted the same effortless motion in my adolescent twins—the slightly swaggering gait that could only be mustered by carefree kids growing up in North America.

The young Tony sometimes woke up with a broad smile, draping his lazy arm over my shoulder while singing a sonorous "*Buongiorno, Principessa!*" His bad imitation of Pavarotti never failed to brighten my day. But it had been ages since I last saw that act. The joys of life had been shrinking fast in midlife, like a glacier under the summer sun.

Staring at the couple longingly, I rooted for their long-lasting happiness. With a repentant heart, I made a promise to Tony thousands of miles away. Upon our reunion, I would swallow my stubborn pride and plead, "Let's start all over again." I would kiss him tenderly, hug him, and shower him with *lots* of lavish love. And he would break out his sunny smile and say, "Of course, *Principessa*."

Another sneezing fit interrupted my fantasy. Dampened by extra-fine mist, my pajamas now clung like a wet towel. I always hated this type of sneaky precipitation in East China—without a proper name, flying about like a dense swarm of endemic gnats. Chilled to the bone, I went inside, my mind made up.

First thing the next morning, I'd hop on a train to Nanjing. Once there, I would message my father, regretting my inability to brunch with him and his five-month-new bride.

5

THE TIN BOX

The extravagant, red poppies on the curtain induced many vivid dreams. In one, a doctor tapped my skull with a reflex hammer. I jolted awake. A dim green light blinked from the clock on the nightstand. 4:05 a.m. 09.27.2012. After a few minutes, I dragged myself up.

With a throbbing headache. I reheated the crab soup dumplings and ate half of the plate. The lackluster treat was as restorative as my fitful sleep. I gargled vigorously with mouthwash, trying to rid of a fishy aftertaste. After a farewell glance of the suffocating apartment, I balanced the keychain atop the fake rose and walked out. Behind me, the heavy door latch grated and then clicked into its strike plate.

How would my father interpret my silent departure? I didn't care, even if the mooncakes this year burned a hole in his stomach if not his cruel heart. Yet, a second later, this childish thought sickened me. What price would I pay to punish him?

A salmon-pink hue streaked the sky between silhouetted high-rises. Under the diffused light reflected from the Huangpu River, the drizzle-licked street shimmered in the distance. The city stirred softly like a dreaming fairy in a rosy, gauzy gown. A plucked string vibrated inside me. So, this must be it: by closing that metal door, I had also sealed my portal to Shanghai—the place of my birth, the place of my first love.

A lonely taxi cruised along the six-lane boulevard. A yogurt delivery man talked on his mobile phone while peddling his tricycle stacked mountain-high; his north-of-the-river accent carried near and far. The glass bottles rattled inside his cargo cab, harmonizing with the low rumbles of my rolling carry-on. This commonplace melody of a typical Shanghai morning lifted my mood. Strangely, I felt like I was strolling in the autumn woods of New England.

Nevertheless, my brisk rhythm was short-lived. Ten meters ahead, yellow tapes guarded a pile of jagged debris in the middle of the sidewalk. A posted sign announced a fiber-optic update project. Yet the nearby earth mound stirred up another image: my grandpa's grave on a hill outside Nanjing.

Staring at the fresh dirt, I forced myself to face reality: my father had trashed the tin box and started a new chapter in his life.

In my dreams last night, Grandpa's death certificate was floating around like a wayward feather. Trying to catch it, I was always a few inches short. In truth, it was nothing but a flimsy piece of onion paper. Two faded hastily written lines; a smudgy red stamp of the long-gone Revolutionary Committee of Hu-Ning Railway.

The first time I saw it, I was nine years old. Earlier that Sunday morning, Mother had left, as usual, for a small town that didn't exist on the map on my bedroom wall. Then my father was called into his research institution for an emergency. With another bland day threatening to stretch endlessly ahead, I decided to explore Mother's mahogany chest. I'd glimpsed Mother taking something out of it before her departure.

Standing on a chair, I pulled out the heavy top drawer with two hands. There it was, *my* tin, buried under embroidered handkerchiefs and silk scarves. The lid was airtight. I dug my fingernails into the rim to pry it open. Suddenly, the the lid popped and flew to the air, along with the sweet scent of pine-nut candy.

Laying the now-dented lid on the bureau top, I heard hurried footsteps outside. I froze. Did my father come back to fetch something he'd forgotten? I imagined his surprise, catching me high on the chair. To my relief, the footsteps faded along the common corridor shared by a dozen families.

I arranged the contents in neat rows, making a mental note of the order. (Grandma had trained me well.) On the top were two ten-yuan bills and coupons for rice, oil, and fabric. All sorts of official papers occupied the middle. At the sight of Grandpa's death certificate, my heart thumped as if I had seen something obscene.

On the very bottom was a stack of hand-tinted photos with scalloped edges. One photo was of my bejeweled grandma in ruby-red *qipao*. She sat cross-legged with a baby on her lap and a toddler on her side. It was shocking to see my plain, elderly grandma as a sophisticated lady with a stiff perm and high heels, smiling glamorously. While Aunt No. 2 was crying, perhaps irritated by the flash, my serious mother gazed straight ahead with her big, unflinching eyes.

Another sepia-toned photo was a studio portrait of my newlywed parents in matching Lenin uniforms. Their mouths curved up in mirroring symmetry on their innocent faces.

In that treasure trove, I found a batch of black-and-white pictures: the toddler me peeking from behind a winter plum tree in Grandpa's courtyard; me kissing Cousin Isha, pretending the sleeping infant was my doll; me crawling on the ground, playing marbles with Rei, a spindly boy from next door. Seeing it, I felt a twinge of guilt—I'd left Nanjing without saying goodbye to him.

These borderless photos—all soft-focused—must have been my uncle's practice shots after he bought a used camera. My favorite was the photo of me straddling Grandpa's shoulders, my chubby hand holding a stick of *tanghulu* berries, my dimpled cheeks glossy with dripping glaze. Grandpa steadied me with one hand, his other reaching overhead to steal my bounty. Our mouths were stretched so ridiculously broad that the picture might as well illustrate ecstasy in paradise.

❧

Everybody knew I was the apple of Grandpa's eye, even though I was a girl. Perhaps my mother was his favorite until I, his first grandchild, replaced her. Once, he had smoothed my unruly hair and said ruefully, "If your mother were a man, she should have been a general by now."

Yet my competent, steely-eyed mother couldn't raise me in Shanghai. Constantly on the road, she had to wean me off her milk after the three-month maternity leave and send me to live with my grandparents in Nanjing. Eventually, Grandpa became my best buddy instead of a surrogate father. After Cousin Isha joined us four years later, Grandpa was overjoyed to hear baby voices filling his house again.

Grandpa's house was Hui-style, typical of traditional brick houses in Nanjing's old town. A gray, terracotta tile roof; horsehead walls—that is, white stucco walls with curved ends arching like the ears of a galloping horse. Four wings framed a bluestone courtyard brightened by flower beds, a manicured winter plum tree, a pomegranate tree, and osmanthus shrubs.

For decades, a lichened fence stood rakishly at the center of the north wing, smirking at the tidy complex. Grandma had forbidden children to play near this eyesore. And an adjacent shed. Still, from time to time, we peeked through rotting holes, watching sparrows chasing butterflies among trembling wild roses. *Why couldn't we go there?* We pestered Grandma. *A perfect hide-and-seek place!*

Shui, it's haunted! Each time Grandma wagged a stern finger at us, Isha would cry.

But why?

Eventually, she revealed the secret during her summer morning ritual. Bending over an enamel basin and methodically scrubbing a watermelon, she said, "There used to be three courtyards; one led into another." Then she sighed, pointing at the fence with her dripping hand, "Over there, the Japanese killed two servants during the Nanjing Massacre. Then they burned everything to the ground."

"Everything?" I looked around, confused.

"Everything except this," she patted the stone wall of our well. "What you see now is the first courtyard, rebuilt by your grandpa."

"Why not the other two?" I felt a chill ascending from the ancient well. Year-round, the water was ice-cold.

"He ran out of money."

After giving the matter some serious thought, I said, "When I grow up, I'll make tons of money. Then Grandpa can rebuild the rest."

"Good girl, Meimei." Grandma straightened from her squatting to smile at me. Then she loaded the rinsed watermelon into a bamboo basket, lowered the basket into the well by its attached rope, and tied the end to a green copper ring clenched between the teeth of a lion-like animal carved on the wellhead. After drying her hands on her apron, she prodded me, "Now go play with Isha."

No matter where we played in the courtyard, the mythical animals on the well seemed to watch us—and no doubt, generations of children before us—with their curious eyes.

Every evening, Grandma would retrieve the chilled melon from the well. After devouring the melon slices, we licked our fingers, lay down on a gigantic bamboo bed in the yard, and listened to Grandpa's stories under the stars. It never crossed my mind that treasures other than watermelons could have been hidden in the well.

During that period, Isha and I were two princesses in paradise. Every Lunar New Year and Mid-Autumn Festival, my mother would show up at our door with an armful of boxes: White Rabbit–brand toffees, a doll with fluttering eyelashes when we rocked her, and patent-leather shoes of the latest Shanghai fashion that would inevitably blister my feet. One step behind her, my father, like Santa's helper, would carry even more bundles… Other times, Mother would stay for a few hours during her trip layovers and bring treats, such as in-season peaches from Suzhou.

It's a pity that Isha was a lousy playmate. She was three years younger, and our personalities couldn't gel. I was the happy-go-lucky tomboy; she was the dreamy girly-girl. Being my mother's daughter, I probably marshaled her around and ruffled her oversensitive feathers.

So, when Grandpa wasn't available, I preferred playing with Rei, the boy in our west wing.

A minor complication: sometimes it was impossible to get rid of Rei, who liked to tag along like a puppy nipping at my heels. Many days he hung out in our house until Grandma hinted, "Time for supper with your poor mother."

During summer nights, he would reappear half an hour later, announcing unnecessarily, "I'm back!" He would jump on our bamboo bed without invitation and sprawl his thin limbs. Waiting for Grandma's watermelon and Grandpa's storytelling, he would impatiently drum his extended belly with the flat part of his wooden sword, giggling with a silly, crooked smile.

While the adults were taking their siesta, Rei and I often played marbles under the shade of the forbidden shed—the coolest area in the afternoon. One day, from the corner of my eye, I saw our kitten slink away with a marble in its teeth. We ran after it, but it vanished behind the fence. Rei poked his sword around a pomelo-sized rot hole. *Boom*, the bottom panel collapsed. And a new world opened: a tantalizing wasteland with overgrown tall reeds and tangled vines I couldn't name.

Rei squinted his eyes into two dark slits. Then he dropped to the ground and started crawling through the gap.

"Wait, wait!" I cautioned. "Shouldn't we ask for my grandma's permission?" I bent down, trying to grab his lagging ankle.

But Rei disappeared too, just like the cat. A moment later, his muddied face reappeared. With a huge grin, he whispered, "Lots of treasures here."

I was torn for about two seconds before giving in to the temptation.

Ten meters ahead, Rei was digging up a half-submerged pot with his sword, his sailor crewneck already ripped by some thorny vines.

Trudging through the bramble, I spotted broken terra-cotta shingles and mossy flagstones here and there. A charred wooden column crunched under my plastic sandal, shattering into brittle shards. Inhaling the acrid dust, I remembered a sad story that Grandpa had told me six months earlier. *Aha, I was standing on top of the torched second or third courtyard.*

Between the rubble and weeds, I tried to make out the rough layout of the individual chambers where my ancestors once lived. Something else clicked inside me. Eyes closed, I whispered. *Koi pond, dahlia garden, two more courtyards*, I repeated twice in earnest, urging them to materialize under my magic power. The blazing sun scorched my upturned face; sweat beaded down my tingling spine; my heart soared as I imagined Grandpa's happy face and his belly laugh.... Holding my breath, I counted to ten, and slowly opened my eyes. But nothing happened.

Then, right in front of me, a red dragonfly unfurled its delicate wings and took off from a reed blade, leaving behind a quivering spikelet head.

Even though I couldn't articulate the desolate beauty of our ruined ancestral house that day, something languid was instilled into me, like a condensed mist trickle into a rain cistern.

A year later, the authorities began an urban-population-thinning campaign. "All idle adults in the city," they claimed, "must earn their living in rural communes."

As can be expected, my grandpa—an unemployed and unemployable antique dealer of six years by then—was dead in the crosshairs of a revolutionary viewfinder.

That was 1972, the year I lost my paradise.

6

THE TRAIN FROM NANJING TO SHANGHAI

In no time, the Metro whisked me from Pudong's glittering glass towers to a familiar landmark of the last century—the Shanghai Railway Station.

Inside the worn hall, a dull, dusty LCD screen scrolled the schedules indifferently. The stench of cheap tobacco seeped out of plastic chairs marred by burn marks and the yellowed walls stenciled with *No Smoking* signs.

Luckily, the Online Reservation line was short. I slid my American passport through a window slit. Seconds later, without making any eye contact, the ticket agent shoved it back along with my ticket.

On the dim platform, my fellow passengers had lined up to board Concord—the silver bullet train. These unsmiling, business-attired men with still-damp hair appeared to be silently reciting quotations from motivational books by Dale Carnegie or Jack Ma. At this ungodly hour, I craved a hot cup of green tea. Caffeine would certainly help me to fend off the train-induced sentimentality, which was bearing down upon me like a prodrome.

Over the last century, many crucial events in my family occurred on the railway connecting Shanghai and Nanjing. The Hu-Ning line. No other three Chinese characters could summarize my early existence more succinctly. Even my genesis could be traced to it. I'd lost count of my own trips on it. Yet, without fail, the directions of the track evoked polar emotions. The Nanjing-bound journey always meant homecoming.

As usual, I stepped onto the Nanjing-bound train with bouncy steps. The compartment was awash with shades of calming gray and velvety maroon; the roomy leather recliners were redolent of the new-car smell.

On my way to the dining car, two shabbily dressed young men blocked the passageway in front of the hot water dispenser. One man stirred his instant noodle with chopsticks and said, "This fancy train. . . I'd rather use the dough to hire a fiancée to cheer her up."

The other paused his noodle slurping and said gloomily, "Look, Ma is very sick. We might not make it in time by bus." Noticing me, he pushed his brother aside to clear the path.

By the time I returned to my seat with tea, people had settled into their smartphones or laptops. Nobody paid attention to the scrolling messages overhead: "*Current speed: 356 kilometers per hour. The Concord crew wishes our passengers a pleasant journey!*"

The flying train was disconcertingly quiet. With curtains drawn, my back ergonomically supported, and my feet elevated, I marveled at the progress made during my long absence: the three-hundred-kilometer journey between Shanghai and Nanjing had been shortened to just over one hour. A night-and-day contrast to my first train ride, the bumpy, six-hour ordeal.

I closed my eyes. However, meditation in such luxurious solitude proved impossible. My thoughts, freed from my daily, mundane concerns in Boston, bent on traveling at bullet speed backwards.

In our time, could anyone outrun his restless mind?

Globally, the year 2012 started with the headline of a cruise liner sinking off a picturesque Italian coast. Kodak filed for bankruptcy. *The Scream* fetched a record price at a Sotheby auction. Then the inescapable sound bites of an American election year. Two weeks earlier, the US embassy in Benghazi had been attacked while the signature ink was still drying on the agreement for the 9/11 memorial at the World Trade Center site.

September. My heart ached. There were some personal anniversaries that I would rather forget. By pure coincidence, the last time I saw Grandpa was almost exactly forty years earlier to the day.

It was an ordinary autumn afternoon in 1972, shortly after I started third grade. After school, I walked home along the sycamore-shaded sidewalk. Then, a tug on my canvas bag.

Panting from running, Rei said, "Guess what I got last night."

"Give me a clue."

"A brand-new marble set!" He blurted it out, his obsidian eyes glistening. "My daddy sent it for my birthday."

Rei's boasting was annoying. His mysterious father visited him only twice a year. Rei could never explain why his old man lived in a desert in Gansu, one of China's poorest and most remote provinces. Either his job was top-secret, or Rei simply didn't know. Feeling pity for Rei, I said, "Oh yeah? Show it to me."

We went straight to Rei's room through a side door in the west wing instead of our main gate. Rei crawled underneath his army cot and fished out a hexagon-shaped box, still wrapped in the cowhide packaging plastered with two long strips of exotic stamps.

Examining the contents inside, I became jealous. Unlike my dulled and chipped, black-and-white marble set—a hand-me-down from my uncle to Little Aunt, then to me—the glass spheres in my hand dazzled with swirls of contrasting color bands. Under the slanting afternoon light, each piece sparked like a crown jewel in a fairy tale, or the most delectable candy.

We immediately took the box to the courtyard and started rolling the marbles.

As an eight-and-a-half-year-old girl, I was better coordinated than Rei. I beat him round after round, but he refused to concede to my supremacy. Soon, daylight was fading, and it became hard to find stray marbles in the flower bed. With glee, I said, "Let's call it a day."

"No!" Rei shouted. "Three official rounds, starting now."

We dilly-dallied until my stomach rumbled. Dinner time. Strangely enough, my grandparents had forgotten about me. I grabbed my canvas bag from the ground and said, "See you tomorrow."

"Come on," Rei whined in the near darkness, flicking a marble at me in frustration. "One final round to decide the true winner!"

At the threshold of our backdoor, I painstakingly patted my pants and sleeves. The last thing I wanted was Grandma's childing: *Ah-ya, look at you! Now go wash up.*

The back room was pure madness. Random items were strewn all over the floor: Pots and pans, wooden crates, clothing, spools of hemp ropes.... My first thought was: *Oh, no, our house was ransacked again!*

On the hallway floor, Cousin Isha was hugging her doll and her raised knees; her face was marked with dried tear tracks.

"Why are you sitting here?"

She started to sniffle.

Here we go again! She's probably been expelled from dinner for her tiresome crying! I squeezed past her.

To my surprise, no food was on the dining table. Even more alarming, my jovial grandpa was slumping at the head of the table; his usually sparkling eyes were red and glossy, like the eyes of a dead fish. I frowned. Seeing me, he finished a shot, slammed down his small porcelain cup, refilled it, and called out cheerfully, "Meimei, come, come. Hang out with your *gong-gong* for the last time."

Confused, I took my seat next to him.

"Tomorrow, you're going to Shanghai to live with your parents." He announced, then poured a few drops of liquor into my rice bowl. After clinking his cup on my bowl, he raised it with a shaky hand. "Ganbei!"

Panic-stricken, I quickly reviewed my recent conduct. Finding no fault, I bawled, "Why are you sending me away? I want to stay."

"I wish I could stay here too." Tears spilled out of his bloodshot eyes.

Just then, Grandma plunked down the stir-fry dishes. She said, "They've ordered us to leave within the week. We'll bring Isha to live with your Aunt No. 2." Dusting off a speck of dirt that had escaped my inspection, she sighed, "Even migrating birds won't stop over that poor village to poop. Shanghai is nice, you'll see."

"*Gonggong*, bring me to the village too! You can't leave without me! You won't, you won't . . ." I howled, latching on Grandpa's sleeve and swiveling with the dead weight of my fifty pounds. But he just slouched in his chair, his gaze downcast on his chipped cup.

"Stop shrieking like a feral cat!" Grandma demanded. "What would our neighbors think of you, hmm? Don't you miss your mama?" She choked up, then wiped the tears off her cheek with the back of her hand. "Be a good girl."

A decade later, Grandma told me what had happened while I was at school that day. Around noon, two cadets in olive uniforms pounded on our door.

"Effective immediately!" the meaner of the two men shouted, shoving a piece of paper in Grandpa's face. "Anyone disobeying the Xiafang order will be arrested as anti-revolutionary!"

"Immediately?" Grandpa turned pale.

"Our party is always magnanimous," the other man said with a smile, "You have seven days to prepare for your transfer. Of course, we'll compensate you for your property."

Shivering, Grandpa lost his silver tongue.

After the men left, he pushed away his unfinished meal and ran a block to the convenience store. Using their communal phone, he summoned my uncle and Aunt No. 3 home for the emergency.

Upon hearing that part, I interrupted Grandma, "Wait a second, why didn't he call my mother? Or Aunt No. 2?" I knew Grandpa would never call Little Aunt.

"As the proverb says, a distant river couldn't quench one's imminent thirst," Grandma sighed. "They lived too far away."

Aunt No. 3 got home first, puffing and huffing after a long bike ride. Upon seeing Grandma, she cried out in joy, "Thank heaven! *Bobo* was so vague on the phone. So I thought something must have happened to you."

Before Grandma could explain, my uncle arrived in his greasy overalls, his face red and sweaty, too.

"This way." Grandpa motioned his children toward the rosewood chairs in the hall room. When Grandma served them the pre-Qingming rainflower tea—customarily reserved for VIP guests—my uncle and aunt exchanged anxious looks.

Grandpa said gravely, "We just received an eviction notice from the district housing office."

Arching her eyebrows, Aunt No. 3 said, "Don't we own this house?"

"Yes. But, according to a new directive, all *xianshan renkou* must earn their living in the people's communes." Grandpa laughed bitterly. "Imagine me farming? I could hardly tell the weeds apart from the crops."

My uncle cleared his throat. "I'm aware of this directive. Some retirees and disabled workers have returned to our factory, begging for jobs. But," he set down his teacup and lowered his voice, "nothing could be done about it."

Grandpa pounded his fist on the armrest of his high-back chair and the chair groaned. "Don't you understand? They will confiscate our house after booting us out! Something should be done! And must be done!"

Aunt No. 3 asked timidly, "*Bobo*, what do you want us to do?"

Grandpa turned to my uncle. "Son, buy this house from me for one yuan," he pleaded. "You and your sister continue to stay in your factory dorms but live here on weekends. This way, we'll have a bird's nest to return to—when they allow us to leave the commune in our old age."

Studying the stains on his work boots, my uncle said, "Too late. My boss already talked to me. The district housing authority wants to move its overcrowded headquarters here."

Grandpa glowered at him. "You should refuse! You're an essential machinist. They won't waste a good proletarian in jail."

"I . . . I can't do that." My uncle hesitated, then spilled the beans. "They said they would consider endorsing my application to join the Party soon."

"You! You! You!" Grandpa pointed his trembling finger at his son's nose. Then, abruptly, he turned to Aunt No. 3. "What about you, my smartest daughter? Do you have the backbone to save our house?"

Unable to meet his piercing eyes, Aunt No. 3 mumbled, "*Bobo*, I'm only twenty-two, hardly ready to be the head of our household." Her face turned crimson. "Any bad review in my dossier would ruin my chances for life. They might even stall my application for a marriage license."

All the color drained from Grandpa's face. In slow motion, he crumbled and slid off his chair. Before anyone could reach him, he had hit the floorboards like a log. Grandma shouted to my aunt to get some towels; my uncle knelt in front of him. Seeing the motionless Grandpa, Isha started to whimper.

Finally, Grandpa stiffened his neck and struggled to get up. Staring at the altar table, he let out an anguished cry. "Revered ancestors, after the Japs burnt down our house, I rebuilt it, one plank at a time. But I can't save it now. Shame on me! Shame on me, shame . . ." Repeating these words, he pounded his fist on his chest; tears streamed down his cheeks.

The next morning, I bid goodbye to a puffy-eyed Isha at our front gate. Grandma walked me to the bus stop, taking a break from sorting stuff accumulated over her entire married life. When the bus to the train station arrived, she handed me the overstuffed canvas bag, squeezed my hand wordlessly, and then scissored away on her short legs.

"*Popo!*" I called after her, but Grandpa nudged my elbow. As I hefted myself onto the bus, the shoulder strap dug into my skin.

Disregarding others' stares, I sniffled until Grandpa said severely, "Stop it, Mei. You're a big girl now, big enough to live with your parents."

He didn't call me *Meimei*! Perhaps, overnight, I had outgrown that endearment reserved for children.

Seeing my face, he tried to tickle me. "Shanghai isn't the end of the world! Grandpa will visit you on Lunar New Year, and your birthday. With lots of treats."

"Will you bring me *tanghulu*?"

"Of course."

"Duck-fat *shaobing*?"

"Yes. Everything you like."

"Promise?"

"Yes, I promise."

While Grandpa was wedging my trunk into the overhead track of the crowded train, my seatmate lit up a cigarette and puffed away. I coughed. Sternly, Grandpa asked the man to distinguish his cigarette. From his frowning, I gathered that he disliked the nonsmokers opposite me, too—two fierce-looking men in military uniforms. His eyes darted around and rested on a middle-aged pair across the aisle. After striking up an easy conversation with them, the couple (a doctor and a lab tech from a local hospital) vowed to safeguard and deliver me by hand to my waiting mother at the Shanghai Railway Station. Grandpa thanked them profusely after leaving them with detailed instructions.

Soon, the train conductor announced his final warning. Grandpa leaned over and handed me the last few pine-nut candies from his pocket. He said, "Remember, Mei, you are my brave, big girl." Then he patted my hair with a wink and walked swiftly toward the exit.

Smoldering words choked my throat. Hopelessly, I stared at his retreating back, waterfalls cascading down my face.

A tap on the window. It was Grandpa tiptoeing on the platform. He scrunched up his upturned face and pantomimed, mocking my tears with the wild gesticulating of a clown. I cracked up. Just then, the train whistled and heaved away from the platform. Grandpa chased after us, leisurely at first, then faster and faster to a frantic dash. Wheezing and waving with exaggerated gaiety, he maintained our locked gazes. The tail of his silk jacket fluttered about, like a bird struggling with clipped wings.

Then, all of a sudden, he was gone.

Desperately, I jumped on top of my seat and glued my face to the far corner of the window. Yet, the train had picked up more speed and rounded a curve, leaving the rooftop sign of the Nanjing Railway Station behind. Endless rice fields flew at me then flung themselves away, smearing the post-harvest stubble into a dizzying, yellow foam above a brown sea. A foreign sensation churned in my stomach. Somehow, I knew that this would be my last glimpse of Grandpa—him running on the platform.

Slumping in my seat, I squeezed my eyes to bank another tidal surge.

Then I remembered the unfinished marble match. In the morning rush, I'd forgotten to say goodbye to Rei.

But it's all his fault, and his bad luck marbles. Had I gone straight home yesterday, things might have turned out differently, with a happy ending like so many of Grandpa's stories.

"Meimei," the woman across the aisle called, rubbing my shoulder. Leaning her elbows on the grimy tray table and leveling her gentle eyes with mine, she asked, "Is this your first train trip?"

"No, I took a train before, from Shanghai to Nanjing." Then I added proudly, "When I was three months old."

She laughed, revealing her uneven teeth. "Well, that one hardly counts since you wouldn't remember a thing."

Just then, the train made a jerky stop. Regaining her balance, she said, "Why don't you switch seats with my husband? Sit with me."

I obeyed.

Unlike Grandpa, the woman had no story to tell. Instead, she offered me one snack after another from her bottomless purse: sunflower seeds, pumpkin seeds, watermelon seeds, and sesame candy. She must have been a bird in her past life: with one crack of her front teeth, no lips involved, she produced an intact watermelon seed and two perfect half-shells.

Trying to imitate her, I made a mess. Eventually, I mastered the deshelling technique. I kept cracking, steadily contributing to the growing mound on the table, even though I was still bloated from a hearty breakfast.

With fitful stops and starts, the train lurched on for hours. Outside, power poles leaned severely as if against a headwind. In an empty field, tracks of darker earth rippled behind a water buffalo, trudging wearily under lethargic whippings from an old man; women in straw hats cast fish feed into ponds rimmed with russet trees. Soon, the scenery grew monotonous. I dozed off and on, crushing tea eggs in my canvas bag into a brown goo. Every time I woke up, the woman offered me more seeds she had bought from vendors at stops. I offered her duck-fat *shaobing* in my tin box, but she declined.

Grandpa couldn't have picked a kinder travel companion for me. In the filthy restroom at the end of our compartment, I squatted on the slippery floor, but my full bladder wouldn't cooperate. I was horrified of soiling my patent leather shoes, or, worse, falling into the scary pit over the blurry railway tracks. Nose covered with an embroidered handkerchief, the bird lady grasped my arm and whispered, "Don't worry, Meimei."

At the Shanghai Railway Station, I spotted a tall woman from afar. It's impossible to miss her, who stood like a larger-than-life general. I flung my arms over my head and jumped. "Mother!"

Recognizing me, she waved a military salute, then strolled toward me with brisk strides; the dwarfs around her parted like receding tides.

At first glance, Mother's sparkling eyes were the same as my grandpa's. Yet her steely gaze whipped like a hurricane—enough to make weak men tremble and capitulate. As this familiar yet intimidating figure drew closer, my legs slowed down.

She appraised me expertly, nodding. "You've grown another three centimeters since summer." After thanking my strangers-turned-chaperones, she picked up my trunk and extended her other hand. Under the watch of the kind bird lady, I anxiously latched my hand onto her firm, enveloping palm.

7

MY BOOT CAMP

From two rows in front of me, a heavy-set man in the aisle seat was screaming into his phone. "*Wei, wei,* can you hear me now? Okay, ship me twenty kilos of carrots, fifteen kilos of onions, and forty boxes of eggs from the Suzhou warehouse. No, no, no damn potatoes. I still have thirty kilos left, rotting. . ."

Sipping my cooled green tea, I listened in with curiosity. Judging from the man's grocery list, he wasn't shopping for a Mid-Autumn Festival banquet. More likely, he was restocking pantry staples for a survival boot camp.

My own boot camp started as soon as I set foot in my parents' home in Shanghai. Their apartment was embedded in a *longtang*, a traditional brick alley with a stone-arched gate. The claustrophobic *longtang* was filled to the brim with bicycles, washbasins, and dusty herb pots. Everything in sight had a different shade of gray, including the complexions of the lane dwellers. A droplet from some freshly hung laundry landed on my forehead. I looked up and was greeted by a cobweb of haphazard clotheslines.

Early every morning, neighbors hurried home from the market, carrying in bamboo baskets steamed soy milk in enamel mugs, Shanghai bok choy, and the local's favorite: puny, yellow croakers wrapped in newspaper. I lingered in my narrow bed, studying the watermark maps on the ceiling, deciphering greetings in unfamiliar Shanghainese, and sniffling for imagined duck-fat *shaobing*.

Unlike in Grandpa's house, here, Mother had many unspoken rules. It seemed that every day I would discover one by breaking it, such as *No snacking between meals*. On good days I felt like a guest, other times, a prisoner. When Mother's penetrating eyes fell on me, my limbs went stiff. Lucky for me, she traveled often. So did my father. (Years later, after Rei and I reconnected, he once flipped through our family album and commented: "Hmm, there is only one picture with all three of you smiling at the camera.")

Sadly enough, back then, Mother—a bona fide tiger mom long before the worldwide spotting of such creatures—hadn't figured out a painful truth: I was cut out to be a foot soldier, at most a platoon leader, but never a general.

Being an ultra-early bloomer is a curse. According to Grandma, the expert who raised five children and six grandchildren in her lifetime, I had walked tall and articulated impressive demands while my cohorts were still crawling on floors and struggling with their first *mama* and *baba*. Unfortunately, this developmental anomaly kindled false hopes among my family and subjected me to unreasonable expectations.

The first essential skill Mother taught me was cooking. I learned to sustain myself for a full week by poaching eggs, boiling rice, sautéing carrots or turnips or any slow-to-perish vegetables in the pantry. The first time I made rice, I charred the pot bottom.

"Everybody makes mistakes," Mother said. "An average person makes *the same mistake* twice. An idiot, three times." Then she paused for a fractional second. "Now, remember this, a wise one never repeats his mistake."

So, after my second batch of rice, soggy this time, I rubbed the blister on my burnt hand with relief. *At least I made a different mistake!*

Often, I daydreamed about Grandpa's house. I missed the cacophony of noises: our scampering footsteps and echoing laughter in the bluestone courtyard, Rei animating his swordplay with sound effects, Isha's hour-long whimpering when her skirt was snagged by a splinter on the wooden wall, Little Aunt's soft, placating voice, Carpenter Luo's wood-sawing in the shed, Grandma's scolding when we ran too fast and our cat knocked down a flower pot or two in its flight path. Above all, I missed Grandpa's belly laughs.

Almost every night, I had a recurrent dream in which Grandpa ran on the platform, then suddenly disappeared.

The girls in my new school, decked out with beaded hair bands or silk bows, were adorable as kittens. Even their mundane chitchats in that singsong voice rang with an angelic quality. They mocked my lousy Shanghainese laced with harsh Nanjing dialect. "You sound like 'the folks north of the river,'" the prettiest girl smirked, alluding to the wartime refugees in the slums of the Zhabei district.

"No, I'm from Nanjing," I said, pointing to a map of China in our classroom. "See, south of the Yangtze River." But geography hardly mattered. Indeed, I was a refugee with a despicable accent.

That girl—the star in the Little Red Flowers singing and dancing troupe of our school—lived in the next *longtang*. On our shared route every morning, the princess held her elegant head high, saying nothing to the pauper in her peripheral vision.

The basketball coach in our school liked me because of my height. This delighted Mother: she had been a power forward in a regional championship team during her college years.

In between her trips, Mother would pore over my quizzes, probing endlessly into the root cause of my misplacement of a decimal point, or trying to detect the pattern of my grammar mistakes. So, while other kids were goofing around after school,

I bent over my homework. By necessity, I became a good student—the alternative would have been far more unbearable.

My decade-long training began in 1972, four years before the end of the Cultural Revolution. That same year, Nixon visited China and signed the Shanghai Communique—the first step toward thawing the frozen relations between China and the USA. Coincidence? No. Clearly, Mother had foreseen a future where knowledge and skills would be in demand again.

Mother wasn't impressed by my good grades, drawings, and compositions—those were her minimal expectations. Yet her occasional praise was unpredictable. One day, when I was practicing Chinese calligraphy—one of my daily assignments—she sneaked up from behind and tried to snatch the brush from my hand. But she failed.

"Excellent concentration!" she said with a rare ecstatic smile. "And this is the correct way to grip your brush: like your life depends on these five fingers." Then, she briskly stroked my hair—the only way she allowed herself to display affection.

My face burned with embarrassment. Even a three-year-old child could tell the difference between the master's style of "flying clouds and flowing stream" and my laughable imitation. But Mother seemed to be oblivious. Nodding, she said to confuse me further, "I don't expect you to become a calligrapher. Still, do carry on with your exercises."

After I turned ten, Mother handed me a dog-eared book with a missing title page. "Don't mention it to anyone," she said. "It's a biography of Madame Marie Curie."

"Who?"

"She was the first woman to win the Nobel Prize, and one of only a few two-time Nobel Laureates." Mother flipped to the portrait page of Madame Curie, admiring a foreigner with a similar severe expression.

"What's the Nobel Prize?"

"It's the most prestigious prize for those who have made tremendous contributions to mankind," she said, her eyes sparkling. "If you try hard enough, you could win it, too."

The book reeked of mothballs and was printed in the outdated *fantizi*—Chinese characters before the Communist regime switched to a simplified writing system in 1956. I struggled for two weeks to plow through it. To my relief, Mother didn't quiz me when I returned it to her. Afterward, the book disappeared.

Not to be outdone, my father gave me biographies of Thomas Edison and quantum physicist Richard Feynman two years later. (By then, Western books had made a slow reappearance in a bookstore near the Bund.) He also subscribed to the relaunched *Picture Journal of Sciences*. Soon, I was hooked on the translated sci-fi series.

Gradually, I bought into my parents' grandiose vision for me: a brilliant scientist or an inventor. I wanted to make them proud. But most of the time, I was petrified about making any mistake twice.

Had Mother hoped to hasten my maturation with the hidden contraband, her cherished fantasy? To inspire me to dream big?

Looking back, I realized that Mother had a humble goal from Day One: hardening me into the ultimate survivor, like the clichéd cockroach that could endure a nuclear winter. A loftier analogy would be to groom me into an astronaut who could pass the most rigorous selection process and succeed in a moon-bound mission.

My father, on the other hand, complimented me often. Nevertheless, compared with the few I earned from Mother, his praises sounded cheap, like the souvenirs he regifted me: key chains, notebooks, and pens embossed with the names and dates of his conferences. Perhaps he felt guilty for being absent most of the time. Or maybe he took pity on me—a new subject under Mother's iron-fisted reign.

While Mother was away, my father sometimes took me to his institute after school. The cafeteria food there tasted only slightly better than the scrambled eggs I could manage, yet I cherished the moments when he introduced me as his daughter to his colleagues. People often interrupted our dinner to consult with my father on projects from optic lenses for satellite probes to telescopes for an astrophysical observatory. I listened to their conversation with pride. No wonder my father always had a deadline to meet.

One such evening, my father took a book off the dusty shelf in his reference library. It was an encyclopedia of Chinese medicinal plants. After spreading the book on a drafting table and turning over a stack of papers from his rejected projects, he handed me a fistful of colored pencils and said, "Here, sketch whatever you like."

I browsed the watercolor plates and picked plants with the prettiest flowers to draw. After I was bored, I read. Honeysuckle, plantain, marigold, ginger, dandelion... Page after page, I flipped through herbs for common colds, congestion, and inflammation. *Is there a plant to cure homesickness?*

Eventually, I gave up, yawning, "Baba, can we go home now?"

"Sorry, give me fifteen minutes to wrap things up," he said pushing up his glasses to glance over my sketch. Then he whacked his forehead and said, "Follow me."

The lab goggles were so huge that I had to press them on my face with one hand. Over the workbench, my father rotated the valve of a Bunsen burner. *Whoomph*, a blue flame roared to life. Back and forth, he heated sections of red, green and brown glass tube until they became as pliable as molasses. With metal straws he blew the melting glass this way and that way. His long fingers danced with forceps and tweezers, stretching, tweaking, and pinching. Five minutes later, *voilà*, glistening red berries and vibrant green leaves emerged from a brown sprig.

He presented the cooled branch to me with a shy smile, "Does it resemble the hawthorn you drew?"

"Wow, it looks just like the delicious *tanghulu* Grandpa bought me!" I was overjoyed.

"Indeed. The red fruits in *tanghulu* are hawthorn berries."

It was also in the lab that my father once dissected a kaleidoscope for my benefit. Seeing the fantastic world, symmetrical yet ever-changing, reduced to a few scraps of plastic tubing and glass beads, my heart broke into shards. Must he destroy such a beautiful thing, even if it was just an optical illusion?

On our way to his lab one afternoon, a spectacular rainbow appeared after a thunderstorm. Pointing at the eastern sky, I cried out, "Look, a perfect half-circle!"

"Do you know how the rainbow is formed?"

"Hmm. . ." I recalled one of Grandpa's stories. "There are seven fairies in heaven, dancing and waving their long, silk scarfs. . ."

He laughed, ruffled my hair, then gestured with his beautiful hands. "This so-called white light is a mixture of different wavelengths that human eyes can't discern. When the sun strikes the rain droplets in the air at a critical angle of 42 degrees or less, such as now, the water prism refracts the light back into a color spectrum. That's the phenomenon of the rainbow."

My jaw slackened. Even though I could hardly grasp the scientific jargon, I had intuited a cruel truth: no matter how hard my father tried, we could never be as close as Grandpa and me.

In fact, I only consciously compared Grandpa and Father in my adulthood. Both men, although fundamentally different, were obsessed with inanimate objects. Grandpa was passionate about beauty that transcends the physical law of peaking, decaying, and eventually dying. With the magic of time, certain articles—often intimate, personal, and laced with imperfections—could become sublime.

On the other hand, my father admired materials that were inert, sparkling, and everlasting. Since diamonds were out of his reach, he devoted his life to glass.

Once my father asked me, "Take a guess, what has caused China to lag behind Western civilization in modern history?"

I blinked helplessly. I didn't know that we were behind.

"Our national obsession with porcelain!"

My cheeks flamed. Was he referring to Grandpa?

According to my father, once the ancient Chinese mastered the technology of fine bone china, they stopped experimenting with other mediums. Glass—discovered in Mesopotamia, traded throughout the Roman Empire, and later refined by the western Europeans—requires a higher kiln temperature to produce and, therefore, is more expensive to manufacture. Nevertheless, it was glass—a material with unique optical characteristics—that had ushered in the modern era.

"Without microscopes, telescopes, binoculars, cameras, light bulbs, and even windows, we might as well step back to the Iron Age." He rambled on with a long list of scientific discoveries only made possible with glass. Arms flung wide open and eyes blazing behind his thick glasses, he declared, "Glass is the unsung hero!"

I nodded at my father with admiration. Meanwhile, I was ashamed of myself. By then, I'd inherited Grandpa's preferences for antique porcelain. Giving it a million years, glass could never acquire any warm patina and hidden allure.

One evening, after Mother had finished her letter to Grandpa, I insisted on adding a few lines.

"*Gonggong*, I'm doing well in school. My classmates are snobs, but I'm a big, brave girl now. I miss you so, so much." Then the punchline: "Please don't forget your promise—visit me and bring my favorite snacks."

For the next few weeks, I dashed home after school to check our mailbox. Heart thumping from running, I rummaged through the stacks. *Guangming Daily*, notice for the mandatory neighborhood meetings, water bill . . . nothing, nothing, nothing.

"Could his letter get lost in the mail?" I grumbled.

Mother chortled. "A letter from your *gonggong*? Fat chance! He hasn't written a single letter in his whole life."

"Never? I just want to be sure that he'll visit us soon."

"If he promised you, he will."

Another month passed. Then, one day, a letter—ripped and retaped poorly—appeared in the mailbox. But it was from Grandma.

I brought the tampered letter to Mother in the kitchen. While she was scanning it, I looked on, as eager as a dog panting for the hot bun in its master's hand.

"Your *gonggong* wasn't allowed to come," she said, her forehead creased like the envelope on the counter.

"But why?"

She read out the pertinent part in Grandma's letter.

"*. . . The neighborhood committee has repeatedly cautioned us, 'Receive your re-education with sincerity and humility!' We really can't afford to rock the boat and make enemies here. But your Bobo is stubborn as a mule! You must persuade him not to travel to Shanghai on the upcoming holidays.*"

"But I miss him!" I said, choking up. Tears brimmed in my eyes as I ironed the wrinkly envelope with my palm.

"I can't stop him anyway." She said wistfully, resuming her cucumber slicing. "All right, let's host him for only three days."

Every night, I crossed out a date on the lunar calendar. With the holidays approaching fast, the daylight shortened, and my unease grew.

On the eve of the Chinese New Year, the busiest travel day of the year, Mother returned from the train station without Grandpa. One button was missing from her coat, and her hair was uncharacteristically disheveled.

"The phone in their commune gave me a busy signal the entire time," she said, collapsing into her chair. "The mob at the train station almost ripped me apart for hogging the phone."

After our silent dinner, Mother hurried to the nearest communal phone at the gate of our *longtang*. Around midnight, firecrackers exploded everywhere; my father urged me to go to bed.

The following day, I woke up and found a note next to my pillow. It read: "*Mei, reheat the dishes when you're hungry. Don't wait for us. We'll be back as soon as we can. Your parents.*"

Sporadic explosions continued in the *longtang*. Kids were scavenging last night's misfired crackers from the spent confetti and fighting guerrilla wars against their personal demons. Absent-mindedly, I ate the cold dumplings and the leftover carp from the previous year. A fish bone stuck in my throat. I swallowed vinegar and sticky rice—a trick learned from Grandma—and blinked back tears.

New Year's Day came and went, and as I feared, Grandpa had abandoned me. Waiting for my parents' return, I practiced calligraphy and dozed off. When I woke up, I found myself in my bed at night, my fingers still stained with black ink. It was a relief to hear my parents' muffled voices in their bedroom.

The next day, my ninth birthday, I woke up to a cold, empty apartment again. I curled up in bed, studying the watermarks on the ceiling.

Eventually, my parents returned—with several boxes and an urn.

My mother placed the urn on my desk and laid her hand on my shoulder. She said scratchily, "Mei, your *gonggong* has passed away."

"No! It can't be!"

My father rubbed my other shoulder gently and awkwardly, saying, "He died on the train, on his way to see you."

I wailed , and buried myself in my comforter.

"I wrote a letter to your mama—after your *gonggong* quarreled with our commune's party secretary." Grandma told me a few summers later, "What's the use? He walked ten miles to the nearest town and bought a one-way bus ticket to Nanjing anyway."

On the morning of his departure, Grandpa had another row with the peasant woman with a red armband. He shouted, "Am I a criminal under house arrest? I have the full right to travel."

The woman barked. "Watch your attitude, you parasite! How dare you disobey Chairman Mao's order!"

"Which of Chairman Mao's orders prohibits me from visiting my granddaughter on the holiday? Name one!"

A crowd had gathered, enjoying this rare bit of entertainment in the village.

Enraged, the woman jumped up and slapped Grandpa. Grandpa pushed her back. Aunt No. 2 caught the woman just in time, but even her humblest prostration failed. In the filthiest tongue, the woman cursed eight generations' worth of Hong ancestors.

Noticing Grandpa's pepper-red face, Grandma grabbed his arm in desperation. "Old man, come home with me."

Her grip happened to land on his painful scar. Smacking her hand and wincing, he said, "Stop!"

Defeated, Grandma dropped her hand.

The next day, on that most chaotic day of the year, Grandpa arrived at Nanjing after an overnight bus ride. From the bus terminal, he trudged into the overcrowded train station. After standing in line for hours, he scored a ticket for a cargo train and called Mother. However, he never made it into Shanghai.

On his death certificate, issued by the long-disbanded Revolutionary Committee of Hu-Ning Railways, the cause of death was listed as *Hemorrhagic stroke.*

One of the wooden boxes contained a small porcelain bowl wrapped with Grandpa's silk handkerchief. Inside the dragon bowl was a folded note scribbled in his childish handwriting: *"Happy birthday, Mei! Your gonggong."*

Tears tapped the bowl as I ran my fingers around its thin, smooth rim. Days earlier, its previous owner had undertaken the same journey I had taken less than five months before—the miserable, bumpy train ride from Nanjing to Shanghai. But this time he failed to pick himself a kind companion, a smiling bird lady who could console him with all kinds of seeds.

That night, Grandpa visited my dream for the last time. However, instead of running then vanishing, he planted his feet on the platform and spoke with a raised hand. I read his lips and deciphered his words: "Don't cry, my brave, big girl. *Gonggong* will always be with you."

I woke up, drenched in sweat. A shaft of moonlight caressed my wet cheeks, as cool and soft as Grandpa's silk handkerchief.

"I won't cry," I promised the moon.

8

MY GRANDPA'S HOUSE

Outside the train window, the concrete forest of the Yangtze River Delta swirled into a gray screensaver. No more stubbled rice fields, nor plowing buffalo and leathery men. No straw-hatted women, nor fishponds. Even the russet hills seemed to have evaporated... Nothing remained the same, yet forty years later, the thought of that dragon bowl still stung like a fresh stab.

Once the bleeding edge had scabbed over, my childhood in Shanghai cleared up like the sky after the monsoon season.

The transformation was catalyzed by an in-class fifth-grade assignment: Write a composition about a family member. Instantly the image of Grandpa popped into my head. But I knew better: he wouldn't be appreciated by anyone else in the world. So, I wrote about Grandma instead. Once I started, words flooded out page after page. Forty-five minutes later, I turned in the paper, which bore many holes punctured by the tip of my fierce pen.

Two days later, the teacher read my essay in class. Somehow, her inflected voice made my snobby classmates bow their heads. Then, on our way to school the following day, the ice princess crossed the street to tell me, "I like your writing."

I nodded, my tongue suddenly heavy and numb. *Did she need a secretary to reply to all the love letters from her secret admirers?*

Three months later, the same teacher summoned me during recess. Pointing to my printed name on the latest issue of a local children's magazine, she said, "Look, your essay is published!"

Stunned, I burst out, "How come?"

"Ah, I made minor corrections and sent it to a competition." Beaming a self-congratulatory smile, she said, "Your grandma should be very proud of you."

Why didn't she ask me first! When she was reading my hasty writing in class, I realized, much to my dismay, that I'd revealed a guarded family secret: my grandpa—the legendary antique dealer in Nanjing, the discoverer of a national treasure—could only read, but not write. *Now, everyone would know.*

In hindsight, I had made an intelligent choice of not writing an essay about Grandpa—he was a complicated man. Years later, when I began to write Grandpa's stories for my children, I even attempted to sketch a crude portrait of the storyteller. Somehow, with the fate of the Hong tribe hinging on my signature on a waiver, I also felt a renewed urgency of documenting all I knew about our late patriarch.

And I would be the first to admit that my childhood memory was as watertight as an old, fraying fishing net. Nevertheless, between my research, family lore, and anecdotes spilled directly out of Grandpa's mouth, I had managed to tie up some loosened knots and mended the torn mesh. And, I believe that I had har-vested harvested all the big catches among the bounties of his eventful life.

In 1911, Dr. Sun Yat-Sen and his fellow revolutionaries over-threw the last emperor of the Qing Dynasty. Nine months later, my grandpa was born in the capital of the new Republic of China, the ancient city of Nanjing.

Hao-Ran, the father of my semiliterate grandpa, was a learned scholar and former judge. He was among the first batch of lawyers who graduated from Fudan University—one of the oldest universities in China. (Sixty years after his graduation, I also attended the same university.)

Hao-Ran named his newborn son Ping-An. These two Chinese characters mean peace and security, respectively. Soon, the wishful name became a blaring irony. After the sudden demise of two millennia of imperial rule, China had plunged into mayhem, with ruthless warlords fighting incessantly to fill the power vacuum.

A mild case of smallpox spared the toddler Ping-An's life but left a few faint pockmarks on his forehead. Ever since then, Judge Hao-Ran's precious heir could get away with murder.

When Ping-An turned five, he went to a private school. Unfortunately, the spoiled boy was a terrible pupil. He muddled through the first three years by memorizing everything on the blackboard. But he dodged the mind-numbing homework of practicing Chinese characters stroke by stroke.

(I suspected that Ping-An might have had an undiagnosed learning disorder, some condition akin to an art aficionado who can instantly recognize works by Van Gogh or Monet, but is unable to draw in the artist's distinctive styles. My hypothesis was based on the pictographic origin of the Chinese characters. Incidentally, I'd lost my own ability to write in Chinese after decades of living in the States. Even a blank holiday card would bring on a bout of frustration. Yet, just like Grandpa, I had no difficulty reading Chinese newspapers or books.)

Often, young Ping-An feigned headaches in order to skip school. But, once coaxed into the classroom, he would kill hours of boredom by playing pranks on his unsuspecting fellow students. One day, Ping-An's elderly teacher was writing a poem on the blackboard when he smelt something burning. Turning around, he saw boys jumping in a circle; at the center, Ping-An was fanning his flaming practice booklet with a flourish, ready to perform a fire-eating act.

After stamping out the fire, the ashen teacher shook his blackened finger at the grinning Ping-An and yelled, "You! You are nothing but trouble!" Between fits of coughing and violent quivering, he barked, "Get out! Never ever show your smug face here again!"

"Yes, sir." Ping-An bowed with glee. But, instead of going home, he went straight to a movie theater and watched a matinee of Mickey Mouse—the sensational novelty that was all the rage in town.

Of course, my great-grandma scolded the troublemaker when he wandered home after dusk. "Tomorrow, you must apologize to your teacher with all your heart. If he refuses to accept our gifts," she sighed, "you'll have to attend a less prestigious school."

"Apologize? No way! See, he hit me with his brass ruler first." Ping-An demonstrated his swollen knuckles.

Hao-Ran was a soft-hearted enabler. While his angry wife massaged his son's delicate hand with tiger balm, he clasped his hands behind his back and paced the room. Finally, he declared, "For my son, a lofty hobby is a must. A career? Not necessary. As long as he can read and write his own name, why bother him with the tedious character practice? Pointless," he concluded.

The learned scholar's anti-schooling stance made perfect sense. For years, the weary judge had been sitting on his tired bench, frowning at the unyielding stacks of paper filled with meaningless words, festering in his resentment toward the rampant corruption within the Nationalist government. He had been yearning for a serene monastery atop a mist-veiled mountain, where he could study ancient Buddhist scriptures, chant, meditate, and seek enlightenment. Instead, his life had been an utter joke—to implement Western-inspired laws in a society stuck waist-deep in the foul dregs of feudalism. *All individuals are equal before the law? Ha, dream on! The balance of justice always tilts toward the mighty overlords.*

Originally, the Hong clans were tea merchants from Anhui province. After the Ming Dynasty was founded in Nanjing, Emperor Zhu exiled the ex-noblemen and gifted the confiscated properties to his generals and relatives. Following the influx to the new capital city, the aspiring Hongs flourished. Within six hundred years, they diversified into trading grains and the

by-products: rice wine, tofu, and soy sauce. For future generations, they sank their accumulating wealth into real estate in the
city and fertile land in the country. When colleges sprang up in
China, they decided to send their brightest boy to Shanghai—
to become a judge. They picked Hao-Ran, the book-smart boy
who was reluctant to get his hands dirty in their Qian Zhuang
(the precursor of a regional bank), where paper bills reeked of
fermented grains. Alas, they placed a wrong bet and thus halted
their ascension.

One day, Hao-Ran was daydreaming when Mr. Liang, a
college student charged with sedition, presented his defen-
dant's statement. The young man's passionate speech aroused
Hao-Ran out of his stupor. Hao-Ran lectured Mr. Liang on his
dangerous illusions about communism, then released him on a
token bail. The next day, Hao-Ran resigned from his post.

However, solitary withdrawal from the chaotic world wasn't
an option for a middle-aged family man. Hence, Hao-Ran chose
the next best thing: *Nao Shi Yin Ju*—a scholarly retreat from
society yet living within the confines of a hustling and bustling city.

Naturally, when Hao-Ran sided with his son against his
formal education, he'd assumed that a substantial family fortune would sustain Ping-An for life. Unfortunately, that turned
out to be the first in a series of grave misjudgments.

Nevertheless, Ping-An's carefree adolescence coincided with
the Nanjing Decade of the Republic era. This was a relatively
stable period—after Generalissimo Chiang Kai-Shek wiped out
the Northern warlords and moved into the Presidential Palace
in Nanjing in 1927.

The ambitious Capital Plan that had been languishing on
blueprints gradually materialized: a new Academia Sinica, a new
National Museum, new colleges, new theaters and libraries, and
a botanic garden boasting the best collections in the Far East.
New trolleys clanged and clunked along wide boulevards graced
with arching sycamore trees, and imported German Holsteins
grazed happily in a new dairy farm on the rolling meadows east

of Nanjing.... Prosperity looked within reach, even for ordinary Nanjinese.

Life was fantastic for a well-heeled boy in a booming town. After his tai chi practice in the courtyard every morning, Ping-An trailed Hao-Ran to the largest teahouse near the Confucius Temple. With Chinese operas squeaking and squawking in the background, nimble waiters wove between tables, pouring piping-hot tea from gigantic kettles into teacups several feet away. All the customers were male—merchants, local politicians, retirees, scholars, musicians, or anyone who enjoyed nursing a cup of tea over hours of cheap talk. Topics of the day ranged from the new factories in the Pukou district, property transactions after a high-profile marriage, rumors of Stalin's purges in the new country to the north, the first-ever Chinese Olympic team heading to Los Angeles, feuding words between Lu Xun and Liang Shiqiu over styles of literature translation, the latest movies of Charlie Chaplin . . .

"Did you see the latest art exhibition in Shanghai?" a man in a chic beret asked his bespectacled friend.

"Oh, *that* one!" Mr. Xu, a bald man with protruding ears, butted in from the adjacent table. "I heard someone had the nerve to chop up a woman's head and torso, reassemble the grotesque pieces and call it 'cubist art'!"

His remarks evoked a vigorous round of tongue-clicking and headshaking among the stirred crowd. One obtuse man gasped, "Wait, did he kill her first?"

Behind the table where Hao-Ran held court among the distinguished elders, a precocious boy always occupied his usual corner, sipping tea, scanning newspapers, eavesdropping on multiple threads of conversations, and taking everything in with his sparkling eyes and eager ears. Cordial banters and heated debates were all part of his education.

After the teahouse ritual, Ping-An roamed the town at large. The new Xinjiekou district always tempted him with its ever-expanding selections of shops: department stores, sporting goods stores, bookstores... Alternatively, he happily parted with his easy money in the old town, which teemed with antique shops, gambling parlors, jewelry stores, and flower and song-bird markets.

Noon. Time to choose between a Western-style café and a traditional *guanzi*. After treating his buddies to a sumptuous lunch, fiery liquor, and tall tales, Ping-An heeded his body's call for a siesta. The modern veneer of downtown was merely window dressing; life still flowed at the pace of the Qinghuai River that meandered through the ancient capital of ten dynasties.

Late afternoon. Ping-An and his friends explored the billiard halls, fun houses, and movie theaters that had mushroomed in midtown. When an older lad suggested checking out a popular girl in a dance hall, Ping-An's heart galloped in his chest. (Hao-Ran had forbidden him to visit opium dens, courtesans' quarters, and pleasure boats docked along the river.) Boys laughed at the sight of his pallid face. "Ha! You think she would sting like a wasp? Her stage name is Hua Hudie—a butterfly among flowers!"

When the daylight faded, the spent boys headed to a bathhouse to finish their exhausting day with deep massages. The masseur/barber/chiropodist who had known the Hong family teased Ping-An, "Junior, do you need a shaving yet?"

Ping-An lifted his head off a terry cloth towel and ran his fingers over his smooth chin. "You'll have my business soon. Maybe next month."

His older friends chuckled, "Next year, you mean."

Sufficiently pampered, the pink-cheeked teenager headed home for another feast. Sauntering in his mirror-shined, two-tone Oxfords, humming *The Evening Primrose*—a popular tune of the Shanghai Jazz bands—Ping-An looked like a million bucks.

When he turned eighteen, Ping-An decided to parlay one of his hobbies into a career. After securing a prime spot on the bustling antique street behind the Confucius Temple, he pestered Hao-Ran to fund his antique shop.

As usual, Hao-Ran, a man of gentle heart and persuadable purse, paced the courtyard with hands folded behind his back.

Before humoring his son's whim, he mused, "How long will this last? Three months?"

To everyone's surprise, Ping-An thrived in the antique trade. Of course, charisma, photographic memory, and exquisite taste—honed by growing up with antiques—helped. However, what really distinguished him from his colleagues was that his heart was never in it for profit in the first place.

Ten Bamboo Studio—Ping-An's spacious shop—looked like a scholar's retreat. A pair of Huangyang *bogu* shelves showcased scholar's rocks and antique porcelain; a Hui inkstone, a jade brush holder, and a stack of *Xuan* paper adorned a *zitan* desk; rolls of paintings and calligraphy were stowed in drawers, waiting for the most discerning eyes. Beneath a spotless window, an ivory inlaid *guzheng* (the Chinese horizontal harp) beckoned its master's touch.

Whenever a customer—usually a friend—stopped by, Ping-An always greeted him with genuine delight. "Long time no see, Mr. Wu! Come, come, you must have a cup of tea with me."

As Mr. Wu's eyes lingered on a libation cup made of rhinoceros horn, Ping-An beamed. "You're in for a treat: I just scored this treasure from Baoji."

"Wow, look at this thin lip, almost translucent," said Mr. Wu, a wealthy collector from Shanghai, raising the cup against the light. After marveling at its naturalistic carving, he speculated on its provenance. "I might have seen it in Prince Gong's residence many years ago. Did you get this from his descendants?"

Ping-An chuckled. "The similar piece you saw is locked up in the Forbidden City now. You'll never guess where I found this one . . ." He paused for effect, then launched into a convoluted story about his recent shopping trip for Tang *shancai*, polychrome glazed terracotta from the Tang Dynasty. He could never resist the urge to embellish for any appreciative audience.

". . . So, after tucking in the Tang *shancai* camel into my trunk, I followed this odorous man out of the market. On that dog day in July, I was sweating buckets, but he kept walking. Miles of dirt road later, we reached a thatched hut—a far cry from a princely palace!" Ping-An hollered out another hearty laugh. "When he dug this cup out of his sorghum bin—by the way, you'll be amazed by the places people hide their valuables—the dingy room brightened . . .

"Like you, I was so taken by the cup. . . I was counting out money when a white light flashed in the corner of my eye, and the cold tip of a dagger rested on my neck! Oh, my, I was stunned," Ping-An said, fanning his nose, "by his garlicky stench! So, without a word, I handed him the thick wad in my hand— more than five times the agreed-upon amount. My damn fault. Should never have tempted him with the sight."

"So, he just let you go?"

"Well, only after we finished his dreadful sorghum moonshine! The wasted bastard had such a good time that he even sent me off to Xi'an in his friend's night soil cart, with this cup! And I thanked him from the bottom of my heart. In that part of the arid land, being robbed and stinky surely beats becoming a rich mummy lying in a ditch. Oh, I had another cache stashed in my shoes."

"What can I say? You're a lucky boy—ha, ha, ha . . ."

During his early career, Ping-An only hunted for things he relished. All his rare findings were pricey though never exorbitantly so. If a piece couldn't sell itself, the better for his own enjoyment. Scholars and college professors frequented his shop. Even though he could hardly write anything beyond his name, he held lively conversations with intelligentsias like any gracious host.

On rainy days without customers, he plucked his *guzheng* and sang, gazing at his collections with pure content.

> *Idle at home*
> *I listen to the rain*
> *The raindrops*
> *Tapping on the canna lilies.*

Or, one by one, he cradled his beloved pieces in his palms, his eyes tender as that of a doting father.

Nevertheless, Ping-An wouldn't hesitate to marry off one of his daughters if he believed that he had found her a loving home. Repeat customers became his friends, and referrals rolled in like snowballs. Soon he hired more and more people: a book-keeper, a clerk, and helpers in the warehouse. In a short span, his expensive hobby had turned into a flourishing business.

During my boarding years in his house, Grandpa had told me many stories: fairy tales, tall tales, and actual events of his treasure-hunting adventures—the best part of his inci-dental business.

"I've been to almost all historical sites in China." He once boasted after flushing down a shot of his favorite *wuliangye*; the faint pockmarks on his forehead shinning conspicuously. "Meimei, have you heard this motto? *Travel a thousand miles; read ten thousand books*. Of course, the second goal is impossible for me—that's for you to achieve," he laughed. "But your *gonggong* has certainly more than quadrupled the first!"

After a few drinks, he would sometimes let slip stories inap-propriate for a child. For instance, the story of his house. Still, all his descendants had heard it: my mother when she was nine and my uncle, fifteen. And, by a gross overestimation of my maturity or, perhaps sensing his encroaching demise, he told it to me on my seventh birthday.

That night, after teasing me with a pine-nut candy from the tin, Grandpa motioned at me to sit down, and then demanded, "Have a nightcap with me!"

Finishing a shot with gusto, he rolled up his sleeve and revealed a purplish, three-inch-long, gruesomely bumpy scar on his right forearm. Stunned, I asked, "Does it hurt, *gonggong*?"

Rubbing his angry scar, he tipped his emptied cup toward one of the windows. "See that windowpane? The one with a putty-filled hole on the frame? Guess why it is darker than the rest."

I barely noticed the subtleties in color then. And I struggled to follow his story that night, let alone digest its meaning.

Years later, our school took a field trip to the Memorial Hall of the Nanjing Massacre. Once there, we saw wall-to-wall, black-and-white photos and enlarged old newspaper clippings. All nightmare-inducing images. One particular picture—of grinning Japanese soldiers aiming their bayonets at a row of bare chests for target practice—made my brain click, finally. I was fourteen, about the same age as the kneeling Chinese boys in the foreground.

In the summer of 1937, a fierce battle erupted outside Shanghai between the invading Imperial Japanese Army and the defending Nationalist Army. Within three months, half of the Chinese's elite divisions and all of its three tank battalions were wiped out. After Shanghai fell, the remaining troops retreated three hundred kilometers upstream along the Yangtze River, regrouping at Nanjing, the capital.

In the fall of 1937, the Japanese breached the Xicheng line, the Chinese Hindenburg, the final fortified defense of Nanjing.

In late November, Ping-An attended a morale-boosting rally near the Presidential Palace. Above the anxious populace and the exhausted soldiers in tattered uniforms, General Tang—the newly promoted commander—straddled a magnificent white horse, every pore of his body emanating ultimate resolve. "Citizens of Nanjing, rest assured. I, and my army, will defend our capital." The general then raised his sword skyward and bellowed out, "Till the last man and the last bullet!"

The crowds cheered. But their lukewarm applause died out in the winter chill.

"One to two," one teeth-chattering attendee whispered to another, referring to the ratio of their defenders—the remnant of Division 88, plus a hastily assembled local garrison—to the Japanese invaders.

"The new conscripts were trained to fire rifles only a few days ago," echoed his friend, rubbing his hands for warmth.

"The Cheng-Guang factory has geared up to a three-shift schedule. But they still couldn't catch up with the ammunition shortage." The first man sighed. "Time to skip town, buddy. The sooner, the better."

Dispirited, Ping-An walked home and reported what he'd heard to his father.

"Rumors! Son, I've just heard a BBC interview of Chairman Chiang over the radio," assured Hao-Ran. "He would never abandon us."

Though it would have been unfathomable to Hao-Ran and Ping-An, at this very moment panic-stricken clerks were already burning classified documents; only two days later, Generalissimo Chiang Kai-Shek would fly out of the besieged capital in his private plane.

When a massive exodus had paralyzed the roads, Hao-Ran finally said to Ping-An, "Take your mother and sisters to our village. I'll stay to safeguard our home. Lots of looting when Shanghai fell."

"*Bobo*, it's not safe here," Pin-An protested. "Let's all leave at once. We could hunker down in the abandoned quarters behind the village temple. Our supplies should last for weeks."

"Don't worry," Hao-Ran dismissed his son with a feeble wave and said gravely. "I speak a little Japanese. And, Alei—" Before he could mention that their gardener of thirty years and Alei's wife will also stay, a loud thunderclap boomed nearby.

They rushed to the vibrating windows at once. A Japanese bomber was nosing up, leaving a trail of black fumes in the sky. Smoke and fireballs jumped out of the collapsed roof of a house down the street.

Ping-An, an articulate young lad, gave up his argument. *No time left*, he thought, rubbing his ringing ears. *Better obey your elders.*

The rest of the day, every household member was in a mad rush, preparing for the *paofan*—fleeing their hometown for an unforeseeable future.

Hao-Ran and Ping-An wrapped their heirlooms with cotton quilts: two Chenghua-period vases, an ivory Guanyin statue, a bronze *ding* from the Shang Dynasty, a silver teapot inlaid with rubies, sapphires, and pearls, and a painting by Tang Yin, the master painter from the Ming Dynasty. After loading the heirlooms and some gold bullion into a giant earthenware jug, they sealed the lid with wax. With the help of Alei, they buried it in a flowerbed in the third courtyard. Then they camouflaged the disturbed topsoil with wilted dahlia flowers and decomposing leaves.

They packed their property deeds and jade seals into a waterproof lacquer box, stuffed the box and a set of heirloom jewelry into an antique ginger jar, wrapped the jar with oilcloth, and secured it to a sturdy bamboo basket. Carefully, they lowered the basket into the ancient well and dropped the rope, too.

Most items inside Ping-An's Ten Bamboo Studio were too bulky for burial or transportation. Helplessly, they surveyed the large-scale paintings by Bada Shanren, entry-hall-sized porcelains, the *guzheng*, and *huanghuali* satinwood furniture. *BOOM-BOOM-KA-BOOM*—the shelling in the outskirts intensified. With aching hearts, they barred the front door and padlocked the back door.

When they got home, Hao-Ran's wife was painstakingly sewing wads of money into her belt under the dying winter light. Headshaking, Hao-Ran spoke bitterly, "Forget it."

"Why?" She looked up, jabbing her finger with the needle.

"Mother, it's too dangerous to sit near the window," said Ping-An. "Besides these banknotes probably would be as good as toilet paper in a few days."

"No! These are *sifangqian* from my late parents." She clutched the stack with her bleeding hand and bit her trembling lips. "I've kept them all these years for a rainy day."

"You should have spent it on gold rings to pass down to my sisters." Seeing her stricken face, Ping-An softened. "Take off your jewelry and sew those instead. You don't want to draw attention on the road."

She let out a cry. But immediately Hao-Ran's frowning extinguished her sobbing.

The following dawn, Ping-An and his charge loaded sacks of their provisions and a trunk containing the remainder of their gold bullion, silver coins, and portable items—rock-crystal snuff boxes, silver lighters, jade jewelry, and ivory fans—onto an oxcart, one of the last available vehicles in town. At the front gate, Hao-Ran bid a hurried farewell. "Son, take good care of your mother and sisters. I'll send you a message as soon as it's safe to return."

Ping-An ushered the weeping Hong women into the oxcart and directed the driver toward the Zhonghua Gate, the southern gate on the five-century-old city wall.

The outflow moved at a snail's pace. All lanes of all the roads were clogged. Horses, mules, buggies, rickshaws, and bicycles all jostled for openings. Some refugees were Shanghainese who had arrived only a few months before. A man pushed a three-wheeled wagon with children balancing precariously on top of a rattan lounge. Less fortunate families slogged along the curbsides on foot, with crying babies and odd-shaped bundles on their backs. An elderly woman with bound feet swayed her arms frantically, trying to keep pace. Then something slipped out of her parcel and smashed. As she was crouching down to gather the fragments of crockery, people squeezed by her, cursing. A man fought his way against the current to reach the woman. "Move, move!" He yanked her up. The woman almost toppled over.

No cars on the road. The wealthiest families with modern means of transportation had left town long before. A military jeep honked, trying to maneuver its way out. In its dusty wake, people spat and glared at the backs of the uniformed passengers—those were the same generals who had sworn to hold their positions at all costs during the rally only days before.

When the oxcart was approaching the Cheng-Guang Heavy Machinery Factory, a Mitsubishi G3M bomber hummed by, and the red dots on its wings glinted like two evil eyes of a taunting fly. It squeezed out one black egg from its bloated belly, then another, before buzzing off into the gray clouds. Seconds later, two deafening explosions were followed by millions of fire-crackers. A spectacular fireball blasted out, blindingly white. Open-mouthed, the crowds watched a mushroom cloud rise and expand obscenely. Someone muttered, "Shit, they hit the ammunition warehouse."

As if in confirmation, a heat wave roared toward them, blasting off Ping-An's hat. Hot, yellow, sulfurous dust pelted their faces and stung their eyes and noses. Women covered their faces with handkerchiefs, coughing. Ping-An nudged the driver out of his stupor. "Jah! Jah!" The man stood up from his seat, whipping a limp willow branch to cajole his ox. The jittery bovine swung his thick tail, dropped an impressive dung, then stared at the shrapnel-littered road with his gentle, teary eyes, refusing to budge.

Ping-An jumped out. He blindfolded the ox with his scarf and shouted to the driver, "Quick, throw me the reins."

Portions of the road had been torn up by the intensified bombing; the oxcart detoured through the frosty fields. Time and again they looked back, until the imposing Zhonghua Gate on the twenty-meter-tall city wall was no longer visible. Ahead, the gray path unspooled like a thin ribbon, chasing the gloomy horizon bend after bend.

By afternoon, the overcast sky had darkened to slate. Northwestern gusts whipped snow flurries onto exposed skin horizontally. No one spoke anymore; even children's cries about their blistered feet or hungry tummies had petered out. The miserable crowd trudged on and on, heads down, eyes squinted, brows white.

By the time Ping-An and his entourage reached their village the following evening, Nanjing was under complete siege.

After settling their exhausted mother in the house of their land agent, a distant relative, Ping-An and his sisters climbed a nearby hill. Their eyes fixed on the north, where bolts of inverted lightning slashed the night sky like bright orange machetes;

each round of thunderous rumbles from their hometown sank their hearts lower.

The following day, from the same vantage point, Ping-An observed a fleet of Japanese bombers zigzagging above the city like a swarm of flies circling a dead fish. But he didn't hear any familiar blasting sounds nor see any ascending dust columns. Straining his eyes, he thought he caught reflections of something white, spiraling down like giant snowflakes.

In the village, he turned on his battery-operated Zenith farm radio. Nothing but crackling noises came through. He carried the bulky tube onto the roof with a borrowed ladder, switched the dial back and forth, and rotated the antenna at every angle, in vain.

While Ping-An was fidgeting with his useless radio, the Japanese warplanes had scattered thousands of propaganda leaflets over Nanjing. On one, General Matsui demanded General Tang's envoy meet him at the Zhongshan Gate by noon— "to discuss terms for the peaceful occupation of Nanjing."

At noon, December 10, 1937, the Japanese craned their necks and trained their eyes on the rampart above the Zhongshan Gate. Alas, not a single person appeared on the parapet, and the brass-studded gate remained stubbornly shut. Mustache twitching with seething rage, General Matsui blew his whistle and declared, "Full-scale attack!" Unknown to him, at dawn that morning General Tang had issued an evacuation order to his troops and escaped among the chaos.

At one o'clock, the Japanese cannons fired from all sides. The Chinese soldiers who had never received the last-minute order, some still chained to their trenches, continued their counterattacks.

Nevertheless, once the high points on the Purple Gold Mountain to the east and the Rainflower Plateau to the south were overtaken, Nanjing became undefendable. Heavy artillery pounded the topographical basin relentlessly. Within hours, gaping holes appeared in the five-meter-thick city wall. The "suicide squadron" crossed the city moat on makeshift floats and infiltrated the city. Soon, a convoy of tanks rumbled in.

Three days and a casualty list of 7,000 soldiers later, the Japanese conquered the capital of China. To their dismay though, the bloody war wasn't over. Instead of surrendering, the Nationalist government had retreated to Wuhan, a hastily promoted wartime capital five hundred kilometers farther inland.

Before the confetti hit the ground, General Matsui realized the prematurity of his victors' parade. He had created his own Trojan horse by trapping Chinese soldiers inside the besieged city. Snipers, camouflaged as civilians in street clothes, now ambushed his army from the windows of abandoned houses.

Thus, a "pacification operation" began. Street by street, house by house, the Japanese searched for those Chinese men who "bear marks on their shoulders from carrying weapons" or who had "foot blisters, calluses, extremely good posture, and/ or sharp-looking eyes."

Day and night, men between the ages of fifteen and sixty who fit the criteria were tied up ten in a row, herded onto the riverbank, and slaughtered with bayonets. Within a week, the Qinghuai River was clogged.

By day five, the battery light on Ping-An's radio had died out. Still, no news had reached the village. From the hilltop, Ping-An listened to the sporadic gunfire. The heavy shelling had ceased, but ominous black clouds still hovered above the city, with flickering orange edges visible at night. Wafts from the inferno drifted downwind, carrying the unmistakable odor of acrid gunpowder, burning wood, burning plasters, burning fabrics, and— he sniffed again—hints of burning leather and fat.

With each passing day, Ping-An grew increasingly restless. Pacing in the muddy yard, he sidestepped chicken droppings and ducked under crowded clotheslines. By day twelve, the dogs' barking and hens' boasting of their newly laid eggs drowned out his mother's pleadings. At daybreak the next morning, he took off, leaving his remaining gold with the host. Unable to find a willing driver, he resolved to walk the twenty miles home.

The deserted road was littered with bullet casings and explosion pits. Here and there, Ping-An mentally blocked out a blood-stained shoe or a stiffened child's mitten. He walked on the edge, almost hugging tree trunks. Once, he spotted the Japanese patrol in the distance. He hid in a roadside thicket, holding his breath until the soldiers marched past.

Halfway home, Ping-An saw a man in rags hobbling from the opposite direction. He rushed forth. "Sir, did you come from Nanjing?"

The haggard man tensed up, regarding Ping-An's dusty oxfords with narrowed, bloodshot eyes. Then, without a word, he scurried away with a limp, ignoring Ping-An's pleadings.

Puzzled, Ping-An continued his journey.

The closer to town, the more frequently he encountered Japanese patrols. Ping-An slowed his pace, constantly scanning all directions.

Before dusk, the Rainflower Terrace loomed ahead.

Rainflower. Ping-An's heart swelled. Years earlier, Hao-Ran had told him a legend about the origin of the poetic name: Sixteen centuries before, a pious monk delivered a three-day sermon on the terrace. Even the gods were touched. They showered thousands of flowers on him, calling for an encore. Once the celestial flowers splashed to the ground, they became colorful agate pebbles.

As a child, Ping-An had treasure-hunted the scattered rainflower pebbles countless times. As an adult, he frequented a teahouse on the hillside. Merely two months before, he had entertained a visiting friend there. That day, they played chess on a stone ledge while the fine-needled tea leaves danced in the boiling spring water. Nearby, a boulder was carved with praise for the "No. 2 Spring of the World." Pointing it out to his friend, he had joked, "Of course, the No. 1 title went to the hometown of Mr. Lu, the famous tea connoisseur." Their laughter startled a bird chirping among the blooming osmanthus.

Inching closer to the Rainflower Terrace, Ping-An cringed: the lush hill had become a honeycombed wasteland. He hiked up the almost obliterated trail and observed his hometown from behind a fresh mud mound. Under the sinking sun, the city within the wall was as still as a sarcophagus. A massive flock of vultures circled above, their silent silhouettes blocking the blood-orange sky. A pink garment billowed near the riverbank like a sluggish hand. Then a faint odor of rancid meat made him retch.

In front of the Zhonghua Gate, a Japanese soldier manned a checkpoint on the Changgan bridge. A man flashed some sort of paper and passed through without incident. Five minutes later, an old man teetered toward the guard, waving a cane. The soldier buried his bayonet into the man's chest. The man hollered, then collapsed against the bridge railing. After wiping his bayonet on the man's coat, the soldier kicked the body with his boot. A splash later, it disappeared into the water.

"*Yamero!*" The sudden shout was followed by a *POP*. Three hundred meters east of the gate, a Japanese soldier aimed his rifle at a man crawling through a gap in the city wall. *POP*, another echo. The reaching arm slumped down, dropping like an anchor into the gaping hole.

When darkness obscured the bridge, the soldier at the checkpoint lifted up his rifle and marched into the gate. Three minutes later, a much taller and bulkier soldier returned with a lit kerosene lamp.

At midnight, the giant soldier started to march back. On the other side of the bridge, Ping-An ripped off his oxfords and stuffed them into his pockets. After a deep breath, he pulled down his felt hat and sprinted soundlessly; his black wool coat melted into the moonless night.

Before the shift change was over, he'd dashed across the bridge and reached the gap. Still breathing heavily, he saw the pile of corpses against the wall, with blood dripping from the newest victim on top. The wind howled. Something creaked, swooped down, hit the bottom, and ricocheted toward his head. He ducked reflectively. A chunk of chipped brick kissed his ear. Rubbing his earlobe, he looked up. Fifteen meters above, the remaining masonry hung menacingly, each brick weighing twenty-plus kilos. With damp palms, he climbed onto the slippery heap.

A dog barked insistently from a near distance, and heavy boots struck the pavement at a steady clip, closing in. In a panic, Ping-An buried himself under a corpse. Hairs on his back shot up when an icy, sticky finger poked his cheek.

The sound of boots stopped merely steps away. The dog now growled excitedly to fever pitch. A few syllables of Japanese were exchanged. A light shone through gaps between the corpses. Ping-An shut his eyes. A shove, then a pointed object piercing through the body above, resting on his coat button. He tucked in his abdomen and held his breath, bracing for the advancement of the bayonet tip. His heart pounded so loudly that he was certain that the soldiers could hear it, too. Suddenly, the pressure was withdrawn and reapplied to the adjacent corpses. Moments later, he heard yelling in Japanese and the clanking of a metal chain. Then, the dog whining and the sounds of boots clicking petered out.

Emerging from the dead, Ping-An jumped off to the other side of the city wall and ran. But his calf seized up. Cursing under his breath, he slapped his cramped leg, massaging roughly. It loosened up.

In the old town's labyrinth, whenever possible, he walked stealthily in alleys too narrow for two soldiers to stroll abreast. He cut through skeletons of burnt houses, a few of them familiar to him.

At Zhanyuan Road, the street of his home, he froze. Not a single intact house in sight. The connector between the Confucius Temple and the main city axis was eerily dark and silent. Instead of streetlights filtering through sycamore trees, a few dying cinders flickered here and there. The air reeked of smoke and despair.

A movement in the knee-deep debris rattled him. Two greenish-yellow spots—the glowing eyes of a scavenging dog. Detecting no threat, the dog went back to gnawing at something like a log. He shushed the dog repeatedly until it whimpered and scrambled away.

Step by step, Ping-An dragged his numb feet. In front of what was left of his former home—three charred columns and a few clinging terracotta shingles—his leg gave out. Clutching the lame limb, he sobbed uncontrollably.

Then he heard someone coughing.

In disbelief, Ping-An trudged through the rubble. Deep in the former third courtyard, a lowly structure miraculously stood: three charred brick walls and a warped door frame braced with an upturned wheelbarrow. The garden shed! He pushed the door a crack. Two shadows screamed. It took him a minute in pitch-darkness to recognize the figures huddling on the floor.

"*Bobo*! Alei!" Ping-An cried out with joy.

"I thought I just saw a ghost," Hao-Ran whispered between coughing and adjusting his smashed glasses. "Is your injury serious, son?"

"What? I don't have a scratch." Raising his arms to show them, Ping-An saw the smeared blood and soot on his hands; it was probably on his face, too.

Hao-Ran wept feebly. Ping-An saw a plum-sized bulge on his forehead, and his singed eyebrows. Then he noticed that Hao-Ran couldn't move his left side.

Alei sat silent, his eyes feverish, his emaciated body trembling. The right shoulder of his winter coat was torn open, with a dark stain underneath. With his left arm, Alei pointed to a lump next to the door— a burlap sack with two charred claws sticking out. "My wife," he said flatly.

A week prior, after the shelling had stopped and the tanks had clanked away, Hao-Ran, Alei, and Alei's wife gingerly emerged outside. The house remained structurally sound, with only a few windowpanes shattered. Nevertheless, the devastation around the neighborhood was heartbreaking.

The last few remaining neighbors had also ventured out, dazed.

"Did you hear about the victory parade tomorrow? Peking, Shanghai, now Nanking—half of China is gone. Finished." Mr. Xu, the frequent social commentator from the teahouse, shook his bald head. "We are *wangguolu* now."

"No, we aren't slaves without a homeland," Hao-Ran corrected Mr. Xu, "because our government hasn't surrendered."

Another neighbor joined them. "That's right, not yet."

"Ha!" Mr. Xu countered. "Do you think General Tang will ride his white horse back to town to rescue us? My friends, better stick some Japanese flags on your doors—that way, maybe they would harass us less."

"Not me," Hao-Ran said stubbornly.

"Be practical, Hong Lao," Mr. Xu said. With a twitch of his protruding ears, he insisted, "One has to protect one's own family first."

"Good luck!"

On the third day after Nanjing fell, two Japanese soldiers banged on the door with rifle butts. In broken Japanese, Hao-Ran said, "Officers, no soldiers inside. Only me and a servant couple."

The soldiers shouldered him aside and strode in. Room by room, they explored every nook and cranny. Along the way, they pocketed a pair of gilded candleholders, a silver thimble from a sewing basket, ivory chopsticks, and hot buns from the bamboo steamer. They turned the wardrobes upside down, slashing the brocaded quilts for "hidden soldiers."

After an exhaustive search, the soldiers grunted with incredulity. *Such paltry loot from such a large and elaborate house!* Raising his bayonet at Hao-Ran, one soldier demanded gold and silver. The other grabbed Alei's wife, dragging her toward the adjacent room.

Alei tried to disentangle his woman from the beast's paws. The soldier stabbed him with his bayonet. It pierced Ali's shoulder, and he rolled to the ground.

"Let them go!" Hao-Ran pleaded. "I'll give you my hidden treasures."

With rifles trained at his back, Hao-Ran led the soldiers to the third courtyard. After he indicated the area under dead dahlias, the soldiers poked the flowerbed with bayonets until they hit something solid. Soon, they unearthed the buried terracotta jar and pocketed the gold bullion bars.

When the sunlight hit the precious stones inlaid on the silver teapot, the soldiers gasped, then wrestled for it. The more brutish one forced his buddy to relinquish his share of the spoil. The loser spat on the scroll by Tang Yin, then threw it into the flowerbed.

When the disgruntled soldier tossed a Ming vase into the air, Hao-Ran lunged forward to catch it. But a rifle butt sent him flying. The last sound he heard before hitting a stone curb was the cackling of the Japanese.

When Hao-Ran came to, choking smoke had engulfed the courtyard. Through his shattered glasses, he saw Alei crouching below a buckling column, sobbing. He shouted, "Get out, Alei!"

Still clutching his dead wife, Alei didn't heed. Hao-Ran staggered forward and pushed him away—right before the column smashed into the patio with a roar, stirring up a cloud of terracotta dust.

Faces covered with wet handkerchiefs, the two injured men hauled water from the well. Yet as soon as they splashed the water onto the fire, it hissed into scalding steam, and the flames raged higher. A blustery wind fanned tangerine tongues, licking clean the third courtyard, then second and the first. They were forced onto the street. When the last wooden panel of the front gate blazed, *whoosh*, a fireball gushed from Hao-Ran's heart to his temple. Thousands of wasps buzzed in his ear, as he dropped to the shifting ground.

For the next seven days, the two weakened men subsisted on the dead koi and charred lotus roots from the bottom of the dried fishpond.

One morning, Mr. Xu's familiar voice drifted from the street. "Residents of Nanjing, report to the Confucius Temple to register. . . A.S.A.P. . . ."

They called out for help, but their thin voices didn't carry far enough. Back-to-back, the two moribund men lay among a pile of burlap sacks in the garden shed, coughing, sneezing, shivering, listening to the howling wind, and praying for quick deaths.

At night, Hao-Ran coughed repeatedly, yet he couldn't dislodge the choking phlegm. Through his blurry eyes, he saw his forebears rolling in their graves.

A life is lost. Our ancestral house is gone, and so are the buried treasures. I'm a disgrace. Tears stung Hao-Ran's burnt face. *Why didn't I listen to my son and leave town with him?*

At the gate of the Confucius Temple, chest-high sandbags buried the claws of the familiar stone lions. Japanese soldiers glared from behind barricades, their fingers poised on machine-gun triggers. Cartridge bandoliers coiled around, glinting like metal cobras. At the head of a long line, Mr. Xu and another order-maintenance officer were busy at work behind an altar table.

Handing the Good Citizen Card to Ping-An, Mr. Xu said wryly, "Carry this *liangmingzhen* with you at all times. Don't blame me, son. We all have mouths to feed. Be extra cautious at night—poor people have started to loot, too."

"Not a problem for us. We have nothing left." Ping-An laughed bitterly. "Could you issue safe passes for my father and Alei also? They're too sick to walk here."

"Are they still . . . ?" Mr. Xu's face turned as red as the circle on the Japanese flag behind him. In a hurry he wrote out two more cards, then fake-coughed. "Your family will recover, no doubt. Your fertile land is still out there, and your Ten Bamboo

Studio still stands—well, last time I checked. Tell your father to get well soon. We really need people like him who can speak some Japanese."

With a curt nod, Ping-An left. On the way home, he paused in front of the wreckage of the former bathhouse. Rubbing his stubbled chin, he itched for his jolly barber and the soothing touch of a warm terry towel. Looking down at his stained coat and smeared oxfords, he couldn't help laughing at the irony of fate. Three years prior, Hao-Ran had bailed Mr. Xu out when the river flooded his warehouse and ruined all his silk goods. Soon afterward, matchmakers started to barrage the Hong family, lobbying for Mr. Xu's daughter Gui-Zhi. Ping-An wiggled out each time, claiming he was too young to settle. He couldn't stomach the servile smile of Gui-Zhi, a pretty girl a few doors down.

Their fortunes were reversed thanks to a homemade Japanese flag above Mr. Xu's door knocker. That irregular flag—two pieces of disproportionate fabric hastily sewn together by Gui-Zhi—had kept paying dividends: not only was their house spared from citywide arson, but also Mr. Xu now drew weekly salaries from the Japanese.

Spitting on the ground, Ping-An decided to take a longer route home to avoid any chance encounter with Gui-Zhi.

After tying the warped shed door onto the wheelbarrow, Ping-An took two trips to transport Hao-Ran and Alei to the hospital a few blocks away.

In the hospital, the stench of festering wounds and human excrement overpowered that of the antiseptics. The frizzy-haired triage nurse motioned to Ping-An to deposit the new arrivals on soiled reed mats on the floor. Gesturing toward the moaning and dying people in the sardine-packed corridors, she said hoarsely, "This is the best we can do now."

Nodding, Ping-An turned away from the exhausted nurse. But miseries were inescapable no matter where he laid his eyes.

A few days later, Hao-Ran's coughing from inhalation bronchitis subsided; Alei succumbed to sepsis stemming from his shoulder wound.

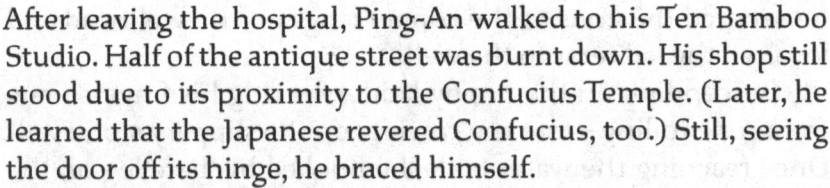

After leaving the hospital, Ping-An walked to his Ten Bamboo Studio. Half of the antique street was burnt down. His shop still stood due to its proximity to the Confucius Temple. (Later, he learned that the Japanese revered Confucius, too.) Still, seeing the door off its hinge, he braced himself.

The shop floor was covered with a carpet of gray ash embedded with porcelain fragments and ripped scrolls. He sifted through every inch of debris. Nothing, nothing, nothing.

The International Red Cross had set up a soup kitchen uptown. After walking three miles and standing for hours in queue, Ping-An received two ladles of thin porridge. Even though he was hungry again once he returned to his ruined house, he kept digging, finding an intact windowpane here, a terracotta shingle there. . . .

Two days later, in the former flower bed of the third courtyard, he saw something like an abacus bead poking out of a coat of dirty snow. He knelt to inspect. A blackened end of a scroll rod. With trembling hands, he pried the scroll out inch by inch and unfolded it with stiff fingers. *A Court Lady with a Fan*, the masterpiece by Tang Yin, had suffered only a smudge and a burn mark near the scroll edge. His eyes smarted with tears of gratitude.

Before curfew, Ping-An wheelbarrowed the burlap sacks with the hidden scroll to his gutted shop. Sleeping on the floorboard and staring at the intact roof, he thanked Confucius. Then he prayed for his recuperating father, and for his mother and sisters who were still at the mercy of their village relatives. He had to act fast to rebuild the ancestral house. After the hospital and burial expenses of Alei and his wife, he had only one gold bullion bar left, plus a few silver coins in his belt pocket. Where to get more money? Sell the salvaged masterpiece? The sacrilegious thought sickened him. Aha, the heirloom jewelry at the bottom of the well! But the long bamboo pole for retrieving the basket was burnt to nothing but a hook at its end. *Asking for help from people like Mr. Xu?*

The following day, Ping-An rolled some burlap and used it to fashion a crude rope ladder. After yanking it with satisfaction, he secured the ends to the copper rings on the wellhead and lowered the ladder into the well.

Descending on the floppy ladder, he dug his fingers—raw from rope rolling—into the crevices on the slippery stone wall. Once reaching the water table, he hooked his bare leg on the ladder, tied a quick-release knot to his waist, pinched his nose, and ducked his head below. He almost gagged on the icy water. But nothing was visible in the darkness. He resurfaced, teeth chattering.

Fishing blindly with the hook tied to a rope, he fought the urge to give up.

At last, the hook caught the handle. Holding his breath, he lifted the heavy basket out of the water. As soon as he gripped the handle, *plop*, the hook slipped out and disappeared into the dark water. He cursed. *Damn it, no more mistakes!* Firing up every nerve ending he possessed, he clawed his toes into a mossy crevice, balanced the basket on his wet thigh, and tied the handle to a ladder rung.

Trying not to tip the hanging basket, he ascended at a snail's pace, taking one deliberate step, then another. Once he reached the top, he lifted the ladder up one rung at a time. Heart thumping in his throat, he unwrapped the layers of oilcloth.

The lacquer box was nested cozily inside the antique porcelain jar. All was safe inside: the deeds, and the heirloom jewelry set. Gold and jade—in the crown, hairpins, earrings, necklace, wrist bangles, and rings—gleamed too brilliantly in the sun. Dizzy and hungry, he collapsed. White breath condensing on the icy stone well, he patted the mythical animals on the panel to thank them for guarding the treasures, "Good job!"

Early the next morning, Ping-An walked eight rubble-strewn miles to the train station. Limited rail service had been restored, yet tickets to Shanghai were sold out. Flashing his most charming smile, Ping-An smooth-talked the ticket girl into selling him a standing-only ticket on a slow train.

The platforms were swarming with luggage-laden refugees. With a small rucksack, Ping-An stood out. A Japanese soldier approached him, demanding, "What're you doing here?"

"Sir, my father is ill, and I'm going to the hospital." Ping-An presented his *liangminzhen*. Technically, he wasn't telling a lie, although he'd muddled the sequence of his agenda and failed to disclose the location of the hospital. The real purpose of his trip—the heirloom jewelry set—was hidden in the inner pockets of his coat.

A woman shrieked. "My purse! Stop him, the little thief!" In the direction of her pointing, a street urchin in dusty rags was elbowing the crowds left and right, scurrying away like a rat. The Japanese soldier blew his whistle and gave chase through the thick throngs of onlookers. Ping-An slipped onto the train amidst the commotion.

After four months of Japanese occupation, Shanghai had returned to some semblance of normalcy. There, Ping-An lucked out again. He located Mr. Wu, his old client/friend, through an antique shop. Under the circumstances, Mr. Wu offered a very reasonable price for the complete set of premium-quality Feichui jade-and-gold jewelry.

Another obstacle arose once Ping-An returned to Nanjing. Half the city needed rebuilding, and the few surviving lumber-yards charged exorbitant prices. After searching in Zhenjiang—a relatively unmolested city, Ping-An scored the necessary lumber and hired a horse-drawn wagon to transport the goods.

At the Zhongshan Gate, a Japanese soldier stopped the wagon: the driver lacked the pass to enter Nanjing.

"One-time exception, please," Ping-An pleaded. "Sir, I must rebuild my house. My sick father won't survive the winter without shelter."

"Wartime speculation!" The Japanese spat out one harshly sounded Chinese word after another, like firing a machine gun.

Swallowing his anger, Ping-An presented his Good Citizenship card; his once-soft palm was covered with fresh blisters from recent bouts of labor: pushing wheelbarrows, rolling burlap ropes, and loading lumber.

Blisters! One of the telltale signs of the Chinese plain-clothes soldiers. The Japanese squinted his eyes to scrutinize Ping-An. The agitated young Chinese man wasn't of great posture, but his eyes were extremely sharp. *Aha!* He blew his whistle. Two more soldiers rushed out.

Losing his cool, Ping-An reached for the horse's reins.

"*Bakayaro!*" The Japanese cursed, sinking a bayonet into Ping-An's forearm.

Ping-An tumbled to the ground.

The interpreter on duty was unmoved by Ping-An's lumber ordeal or his dripping wound.

Out of desperation, Ping-An screamed, "Contact the damn Mr. Xu! He knows about our burnt house."

"Ah, you know our Mr. Xu," a quick smile flickered across the interpreter's blank face. "Let's summon him."

Upon arrival, the sweaty Mr. Xu bowed ninety degrees to present his full-moon baldness to the Japanese. After his vouching for the Hong family's good standing in the community and a thorough search, the soldiers reluctantly released the confiscated cargo to Ping-An.

Upon leaving, Mr. Xu said smugly, "Son, today is your lucky day. Gui-Zhi is now engaged to Mr. Ha, the interpreter over there."

"Congratulations!" Ping-An muttered as chills crept up his spine.

In the end, the hard-won lumber, plus the salvaged and locally sourced bricks and terracotta tiles, was barely enough to rebuild the first courtyard. For the remainder of his life, Ping-An dreamed about finishing his project.

9

AN UNFULFILLED PROMISE

Even though the tin box had been trashed by my father, I could still smell it even now, that sweet, buttery, nutty aroma of pine-nut candy.

That night of my seventh birthday, after Grandpa unsealed the box, he scooped up a fistful of the hard candies and dangled them under my nose teasingly. "Smell it first," he instructed. Then he peeled off a cellophane wrapper, revealing an amber-colored crystal embedded with ivory-white, torpedo-shaped nuts. Easing it into my wide-open mouth, he said, "Don't crush it. Don't rush it. Let it melt slowly at the tip of your tongue."

The memory of that night, infused with the unique smell and taste, had become indelible.

At the end of that long night, after the convoluted tale of his first ugly scar, Grandpa's gaze pierced my half-closed eyes. "If your *gonggong* can't restore our ancestral house, your mother or your uncle and aunts must try. If they all fail, then it will be your turn someday. Promise me, Meimei."

"Okay, I promise." I stuck out my pinky for a solemn seal, then staggered off to bed.

Sadly, nothing had gone according to Grandpa's blueprint.

While Grandpa was impatiently waiting for me to grow up, tall weeds continued their relentless reclamation of our ruined courtyards. Two years after that night, he died on the train; the local government cleaned out the brambles and crammed a cluster of concrete buildings on the wasteland.

In Shanghai, I sometimes fantasized about Grandpa asking Mother to buy his house instead. Eventually, I grew out of my naiveté. Under the Party's thumb, even Mother's steel spine would be crushed.

Still, I couldn't help feeling guilty from time to time, for I had failed Grandpa, too.

10

THE LEANEST YEARS

As our bullet train flew silently toward my hometown, that familiar guilt crept up, chewing my viscera. *Your guilt is unfounded*, my rational brain assured me. If Grandpa were watching over me somewhere in heaven right now, he would certainly concur. So would any scholar on contemporary Chinese history. As a matter of fact, the Hong family could be a good case study: what drove a once prosperous family to the brink of extinction?

I held no academic interest, but this question had plagued me since I started writing about Grandpa. Our family wasn't a random victim of fate. Reluctantly, I drew the conclusion: Our decline was inevitable, as illuminated by pivotal events that occurred between the times Ping-An acquired his two dreadful scars.

There is no Chinese word for this type of angry, raised scars. Its Greek and Latin name is Keloid. But I preferred the English words of "proud flesh," as if one could brandish the excessive scar-forming wound as a badge of honor.

During the Sino-Japanese war some families retreated to the mountainous hinterland with the Nationalist government. Yet the majority, like my family, stayed and endured the eight harsh years of Japanese occupation of Eastern China.

Recovering from his stroke, Hao-Ran improved steadily. In good weather, he limped around the restored first courtyard with a cane. However, whenever Mr. Xu's voice boomed through the gate, he immediately deposited himself into one of the strategically placed rattan chairs, regressing into helpless hemiplegia.

Mr. Xu, a pragmatic man with a limited repertoire, preached ad nauseam upon each visit. "Hong Lao, you've been a pillar of our society. Now, your house is partially restored; but our beloved city is still struggling to rise from its ashes like a phoenix. We need your support!" Leaning in closer, he said confidentially, "Just showing your face for five minutes at our next meeting will suffice."

Hao-Ran remained seated like a Buddha. His large eyes, further magnified by his new glasses, seemed to gaze at the mythical animals on the well in the distance.

Discouraged by Hao-Ran's faraway look, Mr. Xu shook his shiny head and lamented, "But why? A wise man never fights the undercurrent of time."

Then one day Mr. Xu burst into the courtyard, shouting, "Have you heard the news? Wuhan has fallen! The Nationalist government has retreated further inland—to Chongqing, yet another wartime capital!"

Hao-Ran nodded imperceptibly. Then, focusing his enormous eyes on the thick skull of his visitor, he silently dictated a long telegraph: *Have you heard the news? The guerrilla warriors are sabotaging the Japanese supply chain on a regular basis. The railways through treacherous terrains would be challenging to maintain even in peaceful time. Mr. Xu, brace yourself for a protracted war. At this rate, it would take the Japanese ten years before reaching the Tibet plateau. Meanwhile, we have plenty of candidates for wartime capital.*

"Sorry, but I have to answer nature's call right away," Mr. Xu shuddered and left in a hurry. That marked the end of his friendly visits.

After spitting into a spittoon, Hao-Ran hauled himself up with his good arm and resumed his interrupted exercise. Nevertheless, his prediction proved slightly off. The Sino-Japanese war dragged on for eight years, not ten.

Due to mounting international outcry, the wanton killing, raping, and looting in Nanjing stopped. Ping-An halted his restoration project and diverted his remaining funds to restock his Ten Bamboo Studio.

Ping-An's reopening couldn't have been timed better. A fresh wave of *nouveau riche* had just arrived. Hiding his disdain, he doubled, even tripled, the prices for these collaborators beyond what he would charge his old customers. When they balked at his price, he would sigh, "Mr. So-and-So, I'd love to sell you at the prewar price, but I have to recoup my costs. During the siege, my shop was looted and my house burnt down." He enjoyed rolling up his sleeve to show off his nasty scar. "You see, I almost got killed."

One day, Ping-An was examining the Japanese military notes in his shop when his forearm tingled. Scratching his scar, he wondered irritably, *How many of these paper notes without serial numbers have they printed? What's the fastest way to convert these junks into gold?*

Just then, a bespectacled Japanese walked in, followed by Mr. Ha, the interpreter. Judging from Mr. Ha's utmost deference, the Japanese with a refined manner must be a high-ranking noncombatant.

While Mr. Ha was initiating some awkward small talk, the Japanese paused in front of a painting by Qi Baishi, of shrimp foraging under lotus blossoms.

"Good eyes, sir," said Ping-An. "You can almost smell the flowers and taste the lively shrimp. If you like Master Qi's style, allow me." He fetched another scroll from a drawer and spread it on the desk.

As the Japanese was admiring the painting, depicting a plate of bright red crabs against two blue drinking cups and a golden chrysanthemum in a Meiping vase, Ping-An suppressed a wicked smile and said, "In my humble opinion, this piece showcases Master Qi's brilliance in color and spatial composition."

The Japanese bent his neck lower.

Ping-An continued, "You see, this is an implied scene of the Mid-Autumn Festival. In celebration, we Chinese eat crabs and mooncakes, and drink liquor. Crabs are the most succulent in the fall—their mating season. Am I right, Mr. Ha?"

As Mr. Ha dutifully translated, his face blushed as red as the boiled crab, then turned white, then red again.

"Aha, the Harvest Moon Festival," the Japanese said eagerly, his eyes fixated on the painting. "We call it Tsukimi in Japan. On this special day, my ancestors would have admired the moon's reflection from a boat, offered sake to the Moon Goddess, and read tanka—just like you Chinese reciting Li Bai's poems."

"Ahh, the bygone years before the Meiji period," Ping-An agreed.

Eyes shut, the Japanese savored the evoked festive memory. Eventually, he wanted the painting of dead crabs instead of the painting of lively shrimp.

Counting the military notes, Ping-An could hardly contain his belly laugh. Lucky for him, Mr. Ha didn't translate the painting's mocking inscription of the ruffian crab now dead on the plate: "*How much longer could you crawl sideways?*"

Once the transaction was completed, the Japanese asked the still-grinning Ping-An if he had any archaic bronze. Ping-An went to the backroom and carried out a heavy *zun* with both hands.

The Japanese craned his neck to peek into the ajar door. Pointing to a rolled-up scroll on top of an altar table, he said, "What's that over there?"

"Oh, that's not for sale. A friend asked me to evaluate it."

The Japanese's interest was piqued. He insisted on viewing it too. At the sight of the unraveled *A Court Lady with a Fan*—the rescued and repaired masterpiece by Tang Yin—he sucked in his teeth and said greedily, "Tell your friend, I can pay a good price for it."

"Sorry, I can't do that. My reputation would be ruined: it's a fake."

"What? Who painted it, if not Tang Yin?" The Japanese picked up the painting, then brushed the barely noticeable burn mark at the end of the scroll rod with his bony index finger.

A singeing sensation pulsated on Ping-An's own fingertip. Suppressing his rage, he commented mildly, "Have you heard of Mr. Zhang Dachan? Before he became a famous painter in his own right, he made his living by counterfeiting old masters."

The Japanese shook his head.

Ping-An continued, "Mr. Zhang was a master forger. He used only aged ink on the correct type of paper, and his brushstrokes were scrupulous." Turning the painting over, he pointed out a faint smudge. "See his clever tricks? Besides burning the edge of the scroll rod, he even soiled the backing of the painting. I wouldn't be surprised if he'd brushed it ever-so-slightly with diluted vinegar and salt to achieve the alleged patina."

The man's face fell.

Seeing it, Ping-An added, "Well, I have a landscape painted under Mr. Zhang's own name and stamps, 100 percent authenticated."

The Japanese sighed, then took his leave. Mr. Ha followed a step behind, carrying the dead-crab scroll with both hands.

The following afternoon, Ping-An's heart stopped when the bespectacled Japanese returned with Mr. Ha. But, to Ping-An's relief, all the Japanese wanted was *the fake*. He had learned that Zhang's forgeries had been collected by museums in New York and Boston.

Behind the desk, Ping-An scratched his scar and cursed himself under his breath. He had heard the rumors, too. Why hadn't he made up a story of a not-so-famous counterfeiter? Then, he opened the door to reveal the emptied altar table: on a premonition, he had transferred the restored painting back home after the close call. Grinning from ear to ear, he said, "Very sorry, sir! After you left, I arranged for a carrier to take the fake back to its rightful owner. It should have arrived in Shanghai by now, I believe."

After the duo left empty-handed, Ping-An took out a handkerchief and wiped off sweat beading on his pockmarked forehead. *Phew.*

A side note. Soon afterward, Mr. Ha was promoted and held a high rank in the puppet government propped up by the Japanese. Mr. Xu roamed around the neighborhood, holding his bald head high and displaying his nostril hair.

In 1945, Japan surrendered unconditionally after the atomic bombing of Hiroshima and Nagasaki. While serving a life sentence for treason, Mr. Ha hung himself in his cell; Gui-Zhi had managed to divorce Mr. Ha right before his suicide; Mr. Xu was released from prison three years later. Often, he could be seen sweeping the Zhanyuan road, ear-twitching, and bowing sincerely to passersby.

Yet Mr. Xu's second full-moon phase didn't last long. After the People's Liberation Army entered Nanjing, Gui-Zhi remarried well—to Comrade Liang, a widower, and a district official. Soon, she proudly bore a precious son.

After the Sino-Japanese War ended in 1945, almost overnight the decades-long civil war between the Nationalists and the Communists flared up again. Yet Ping-An had three banner years. Nanjing had been reinstated as the capital. Flocks of prominent families returned one by one. Flush with wealth confiscated from the puppet government, the victors' wives waged white-hot competitions in home decoration: they needed to stage their dated homes in order to marry off their debutante daughters; they wanted to host talk-of-the-town parties in houses newly refurbished in a sophisticated style; and they yearned to fulfill their eight years' worth of pent-up desires for the finer things in life.

By 1949, the wind had shifted its direction again. The Communists were winning. Preparing to flee at a moment's notice, the well-heeled stopped buying. Even those rarest antiques, which would have ensured a bidding war earlier, didn't sell. Instead, they came to unload. And Ping-An scooped up their hoarded treasures. He simply couldn't resist the temptation to hold beautiful things in his palm, even just for a few seconds.

One day, Mr. Wu returned with the set of Feichui jade-and-gold jewelry that he had bought from Ping-An a decade earlier. He said, "Old friend, could you buy your heirlooms back? Gold yuan is fine, but dollars or pounds would be even better."

Ping-An happily obliged.

After squirreling away the gold yuans, Mr. Wu scanned the Ten Bamboo Study, alarmed. "Are you prepared to leave town soon?"

"What for? The Communists couldn't be any worse than the Japanese. Besides, I have a bedridden father at home."

Bedridden was an exaggeration. Yet the former judge made another error of judgment—perhaps due to equal parts of his declining health and some residual influence of a memorable speech by a certain Mr. Liang years before. (Years of education and meditation could never cure his naiveté.) "Buckle up," the figurehead patriarch told his family in a thin voice. "A more equal, just, and democratic China is coming."

Ping-An, an eternal optimist, had his own reasons to believe that he could weather yet another storm brewing on the horizon. After all, hadn't he and his family survived the Battle of Nanjing, the hellish aftermath that leveled half of the town, and the ensuing eight humiliating years?

For almost a year, Ping-An didn't make a single sale. In the meantime, hyperinflation roared on, and his expenses had more than quadrupled. By then, he was married and had three children—my mother, Aunt No. 2, and Aunt No. 3—and my uncle was on his way. To make ends meet, Ping-An rented out rarely used guest rooms in the west wing to an out-of-town carpenter and a cleaver sharpener. The family's agent still brought in sacks of rice and soy, jugs of sesame oil, ham and salted carp from their village, and, occasionally, cured rabbit and smoked pheasant. Although the cargo size had shrunk each time, Ping-An assured his worried wife, "We'll manage, one way or the other."

Then came Red October 1949. Rich people fled to Taiwan, Hong Kong, or overseas; Ping-An's most loyal customers, mainly college professors and other intelligentsia, migrated en masse to Beijing, seeking opportunities in the new capital.

After new posters were plastered over the former Presidential Palace, Hao-Ran staggered into a provisional office. Leaning on his cane, he handed over the deeds for the family's land with his trembling hands. In the preceding year, he had lost a few college friends to public executions during the sweeping Land Reform Campaign in the North. Their capital crimes: being landowners.

A week later, a middle-aged man knocked on the gate. Presenting a certificate to Hao-Ran, he said, "Hong Lao, we deeply appreciate your land donation. In addition, I'm here to personally thank you for setting me free years ago." He took off his red-starred cap, smoothed his gray-streaked hair, then winked. "Remember me?"

It took Hao-Ran a minute to recall that passionate college student whose eloquent speech in his courtroom had led to his resignation. Meshing the image of that pale, thin youth with this dark, strong man, who probably could march twenty miles a day with a rifle and a forty-pound backpack, he laughed, "Ah, it's you, Mr. Liang! Sorry, Comrade Liang."

After reminiscing over tea, Comrade Liang made the purpose of his visit clear: Hao-Ran should donate his commercial real estate near the Confucius Temple as well. The district government desperately needed office space, he explained, since the new provincial offices and liaison office to Beijing had filled most of the former Nationalist government office space.

Hao-Ran's mouth gaped. Who would have imagined that the demotion of his hometown would increase its administrative complexity?

"If I were you, I would take quick, proactive actions," Comrade Liang said. Then, lowering his voice, he added, "Trust me, real estate holdings will become hot potatoes, too."

"Thank you for enlightening me . . . er . . . about the situation." Hao-Ran took out a silk handkerchief to wipe his glasses. At last, he managed to pronounce his visitor's official title correctly. "Liang Qiuzhang, as soon as I locate the deeds this afternoon, I will send them over to your office."

"I know our party could always trust an old friend like you," Liang Qiuzhang said, pumping Hao-Ran's atrophied hand with his firm, calloused one.

A few weeks later, Hao-Ran suffered another stroke and became truly bedridden. And he lost his speech capacity, too.

More door-knocking followed. First, the cadres reminded Ping-An, now the head of the household, "You can no longer collect rent from Carpenter Luo and old Li." Another day, they ordered Ping-An to "stop exploiting your employee." *Phew.* Ping-An let go of his last clerk with relief. His business had completely dried up anyway.

In the first year after Nanjing's liberation, Ping-An invented a new business. He and his partner, Carpenter Luo, disassembled and recycled his antique furniture. The backs of rosewood chairs became storage boxes for cosmetics, stamps and seals, incense, and any mundane, utilitarian objects conceivable. The cherrywood bed-poles were converted into bows for musical instruments; spindly legs from game table became abacus beads and Buddhist chanting necklaces; carved ivory inlays were reincarnated as the spines of folding fans. These fancy, affordable novelties were as popular as hot buns on a wintry morning. Ping-An even toyed with the idea of expanding to neighboring cities, perhaps even Shanghai. But soon the market was saturated, as every other antique dealer and their cousins started to imitate Ping-An.

In the early fifties, the Hong family starved in the Land of Fish and Rice—the richest soil in the Yangtze Delta. Unlike in the miserable winter after the Nanjing Massacre, no one had come to town to set up soup kitchens.

As a teenager, I questioned Mother when she lamented these leanest years. "How did you survive?"

"Barely. We fed furniture scraps to the kitchen stove. The broken legs, the drawers, the useless carcasses," She said with disgust. "Guess what's the best firewood? Mahogany! One small peg could last long enough to make a big pot of porridge and veggie soup."

After a reflective pause, she continued. "We were as skinny as the pegs. Every weekend, we hit the black market on Mochou Road or the crowded square in front of the rail station. Rain or shine, we spread portable antiques on bedsheets. Around the corner, your *gonggong* watched for patrolling police or any troublemakers."

When a passerby cast a casual glance at the young girls sitting cross-legged on the pavement, my mother perked up, locking her bright eyes with his. The man squatted down, picking up a porcelain bowl. "Hey, kids, how much is this knickknack?" Then he put it down. "Never mind, too small."

"Uncle, look how pretty it is!" My mother tilted the bowl and the goldfish swimming among aquatic plants came alive under the sunshine. Then, tapping its rim, she produced a crisp, ringing sound. "See, perfect condition. How about buying it for your child? Your cat? Your collection of rainflower pebbles?" She rambled on to engage him. "Anything you fancy!"

While the man was contemplating, she whispered, "Why not make an offer?"

"Well, I can only give you two maos," the man said, red with his lowball offer.

Simultaneously, my mother and Aunt No. 2 turned their heads toward Ping-An, who was leaning against the wall.

Ping-An's nostrils flared. *Two maos? You idiot, this is from the Qianlong period!* Then he caught the hopeful looks of his daughters, who had been languishing under the scorching sun with nothing but water. He tightened his jaw and nodded, lowering his hat rim over his eyes.

Seeing Ping-An's struggle, my mother beamed her most beguiling smile. "Uncle, three maos, please."

"Okay, okay," the man laughed, knowing a thing or two about the sound of porcelain and its quality.

"All yours." My mother wrapped the bowl in an old newspaper and presented it with two hands and a bow. After checking the three wrinkled bills for counterfeit, Aunt No. 2 smoothed them over Ping-An's silk handkerchief and tied the corners with two careful knots.

"Uncle, what about this white rabbit?" My mother proffered an intricately carved jade rabbit with her thin hand, murmuring, "Cheaper than the tin soldier toys you would buy for your boys, and it won't dent. The Mid-Autumn Festival is just around the corner."

"Cutie, how old are you?" The man pinched my mother's apple cheek.

"Nine."

"Well, if I had a son, I would certainly take you home to be a *tongyangxi*. Then, in just a few years, you could be his wife, ha ha, ha . . ."

From his corner, Ping-An shot the man a dirty look.

II

MY BIRDCAGE AND
THE COURT LADY WITH A FAN

My seatmate shut down his laptop with a heavy sigh. Ever since our train left Shanghai, he had been working on what appeared to be a monthly sales report. In profile, he resembled Cousin Binbin. Yet, ambition was written all over his baby face. Head shaking, he took a green apple out of his briefcase. After tossing it back and forth between his hands, he brought it to his nose and inhaled thoughtfully, then put the apple back.

Apple sniffing might help the young man to decompress. Nevertheless, this peculiar act reminded me of Mother.

Two decades before, when I took Mother to Stop & Shop in South Boston for the first time, she approached the fruit stand suspiciously. After picking out a wax-polished green apple from the top of a pyramid, she rotated and inspected the shiny sphere 360 degrees. She sniffed the blemish-free object for a long second, then chuckled, "I thought these were for display."

Wandering wide-eyed along the aisles—the first supermarket she had ever set foot in—she gestured at the seemingly endless selections of chips, cookies, cakes, and glazed donuts and exclaimed, "Look at these! Look at these! How could anyone stay thin in this country?"

No doubt, constant hunger had branded Mother's young brain. After comparing the unit price of three types of Raman noodles, she chose a jumbo pack of the on-sale brand. Then she bounced a large tub of *I Can't Believe It's Not Butter!* on her palm and marveled at its package. "Looked at these beautiful colors, gold and jade—just like our heirloom jewelry." Against my objection, she hefted the margarine into our cart and said, "What a pity, we sold the set piece by piece in the black market, all for a few lousy *fens*."

"The entire set? What about this ring?" I showed her a gold ring on my right hand. "Grandma gave it to me."

It was an August afternoon right before I left China when Grandma handed me a small velvet case with the ring. Seeing its intricate dragon motif, I had stammered, "*Popo*, that's too much."

Grandma had said, "Well, I hope you'll never need to pawn it. But, just in case."

At the time, we burst out laughing.

Mother glanced at my ring and said, "Ah, that ring. Grandma bought it for you in the eighties."

"With what?" I was alarmed, recalling Grandma's minuscule pension.

"Savings squeezed through her tooth gaps."

Pressing the gold ring into my palm, I saw Grandma's face, radiating like her dahlia blooming under the summer sun. My eyes misted. I turned away from Mother, then, discreetly shoved the margarine back onto the shelf.

At the checkout line, Mother frowned at the firewood pile near the entrance. Then she said darkly, "Those miserable years. After we ran out of furniture scraps, we fed the stove with wooden rods inside scrolls. Then the paintings. But your *gonggong* always guarded one particular painting—*A Court Lady with a Fan*."

"Oh, that painting," I felt a micro-tear of a vestigial tissue inside me. Unlike her, I had witnessed it burning up in smoke. In hindsight, its tragic end was what did Grandpa in.

After we returned home and stuffed the refrigerator to the brim, Mother was still brooding. Beating eggs with two violent chopsticks, she said, "Once, after a long day, your *gong-gong* decided to squander our few meager coins on a useless snuff box! Aunt No. 2 and I had to drag him away, one sleeve each. He couldn't resist any temptation!" Picking up a runaway onion ring from the floor to rinse, she concluded, "A spoiled child never grows up."

In silence, I kept chopping onions, trying to eradicate an image in my blurred vision: a tween girl hustling in the black-market day after day, just to stay alive.

In the past, I had always resented Mother's harsh judgment. I had thought she never loved Grandpa, at least not as much as I did. Now, the cutting edge of her remarks had dulled, and I started to taste her bitter truth. When Mulan fought on the battlefield, her gallantry only magnified her father's fragility.

Just before the whole clan would wither away, Ping-An's lucky star shone once again. As the Korean War dragged on, the Chinese People's Volunteers quickly depleted the treasury's reserve in the new, isolated country. To fulfill its quotas, the local government combined the last few antique shops into a co-op to extract precious foreign currency from the scarce international visitors. They appointed Ping-An to manage the Nanjing Antique Store.

Ironically, Ping-An, a middle-aged man with few valuable skills, had to pick up a pencil to practice writing again. Yet, despite his best efforts, his penmanship remained embarrassing, worse than the handwriting of Aunt No. 3, who had just started her second grade.

That was where my grandma stepped in. With Ping-An dictating, she wrote business correspondence; she filled out required forms—weekly, monthly, quarterly, and yearly. She did all those on the dining table after the dishes were done and the children were put to bed.

In that fifth-grade essay to praise Grandma's virtues, I'd sugar-coated the reason for Grandpa's semi-illiteracy. Naturally, I also omitted his other faults that had infuriated Grandma.

One payday, Grandpa came home earlier while Grandma was in a neighborhood anti-Confucius rally. Seeing me shaking my finger like Grandma and lecturing our cat in the courtyard, he laughed. Tossing his fat wallet in the air and catching it with itchy fingers, he announced, "Let's go treasure-hunting."

In the black market near a defunct Catholic church, a bright, chirping canary mesmerized me. So, Grandpa bought the bird and its bamboo birdcage for me.

Once we were out of the alley, he pointed to a seed cup in the cage and whispered, "Meimei, take a close look. Could this be a *jigangbei* from the Chenghua period? One of these priceless few?"

The small, porcelain cup was half full of sunflower seeds. All I could see was a crude drawing: an odd-looking rooster strutting among flowers and rocks; a bony hen and three tiny chicks pecking at a worm on the ground. I nodded with hesitation.

"Good guess. But no. Still, it's a rare Qing Dynasty imitation." His eyebrows danced, "Let's celebrate your first lucky find!"

Grandpa's exuberance was contagious. I jumped up and shouted, "Yeah, let's celebrate!"

We entered a century-old Muslim restaurant along the river. Seeing Grandpa, a weary waiter flew over from the far corner of a near-empty hall, his bored eyes suddenly fired up. "Hong Laobang, long time no see!"

Grandpa cleared his throat. "Comrade Hong nowadays."

"Whoops, bad habit." The waiter smacked his whitish hat. After seating us, he roughened my hair and teased, "Well, look at this cutie! Her big eyes are like carbon copies of yours . . ."

Soon the restaurant's signature dishes piled up on our table: Nanjing duck, vegetarian goose, kosher dumplings, and sweet lotus rice. I attacked them greedily.

"Slow down, slow down," Grandpa chuckled. "In the good old days . . ." He abruptly halted his hearty laughter. Just then, the waiter brought a small cup of yogurt for me, and placing a shot glass on the table, he winked at Grandpa. "Digestives on the house."

"Thanks, my old friend." Grandpa saluted him with his raised glass.

While I was digging at the green pistachios floating in the yogurt, Grandpa concentrated his gaze on his glass as if it were a rescue boat in a foggy sea. Then, he dipped a chopstick into his drink and passed it to me, saying, "Lick it."

The sharp, fiery droplet burned my tongue. "Yuck." I spat the liquor out and gobbled down more yogurt. How could Grandpa enjoy this vile liquid?

"A little sting harms no one." As if reading my mind, he said, "You build up your endurance this way."

We staggered home, Grandpa's wage mostly gone. When Grandma saw our flushed faces and our treasure, she gasped. Immediately, she yanked the birdcage out of Grandpa's hand and stormed out. It was hours later when she returned with our "good buy" still hanging on her short arm and my canary pecking nervously at the last few sunflower seeds in the cup.

After "the darn birdcage" incident, Grandma insisted on visiting Grandpa's co-op on paydays. Nevertheless, her iron-fisted fiscal control was short-lived. Only a few months later, Grandpa returned home early again. Handing over his wallet, he said, "The government shut us down this morning."

"You should've seen this coming!" Grandma grumbled, stuffing Grandpa's last wage into her inner pocket. "I have to attend another struggle session now."

To my delight, Grandpa began spending more time with me. In the mornings, he scanned the headlines before throwing the newspapers into the wastebasket. Once, Grandma asked him to save the paper for her. "It's unfit even to wipe my ass!" he thundered. Then he grasped my hand and said, "Meimei, let's go for a walk."

At all costs, we avoided the square. There, Confucius Temple was dwarfed by a newly erected platform for frequent public denunciations. Instead, we sought refuge at White Egret Park, where weeping willows swayed along the curvy lake, nodding at reflections of the painted pavilions. Slowly, Grandpa's eyes would shed forty-years-worth of weariness. His steps became bouncy at the sight of a high-arched moon bridge. Long ago, he'd once jumped off it on a dare, splashing water onto a boat of screaming girls on their spring outing.

Entering the third, and then the fourth year of his unemployment, Grandpa often preferred solo outings. Despite my pleading to tag along, he would say in a tired voice, "Meimei, go play with Rei." When I came back, I sometimes found him slouching in his high yoke-back chair, his unsteady hand clutching his *jigangbei*—the liquor cup rescued from the birdcage—and his pockmarks glaring from his reddened face.

Grandpa's drinking spiraled out of control after the afternoon when a swarm of teenagers banged on our door, feverishly waving their little red books. In theory, I couldn't possibly remember all the details. But, reinforced by Grandma's version years later, my memory was as vivid as a technicolor movie.

The ringleader was a tall, pimply boy dressed in the highest fashion of the time—a faded military uniform with a brass-buckled belt cinching his thin waist. "We're Red Guards from Zhonghua High School," he announced hotly. "Today, we come to smash *the old fours!*"

Grandpa's face blanched. Weeks before, an inflammatory editorial in *People's Daily* had called for "destroying the old ideas, old culture, old customs, and old habits of the exploiting classes." Immediately afterward, saber-rattling youth defaced Buddhist statues and murals throughout the country. They torched ancient paintings and books and toppled all the cultural icons they could think of. Even a century-old restaurant, Peking Roast Duck, was shattered to pieces "to make room for a new era!"

The pack tightened their circle around Grandpa. Fists pumping, they shouted, "Destroy all ox-ghosts and snake-demons!" "Down with the stinky leeches!" "Down with the class enemies!" They worked themselves into a mouth-foaming frenzy. "Down with the Japanese collaborators!" "Down with the Nationalist spies!"

Chuckling, Grandpa asked, "How could anyone possibly be all of the above?"

"How?" The leader barked, jabbing his slender finger at Grandpa's chest. "Let me show you!"

Grandpa stumbled backward three steps; the jeering crowd behind him parted aside as if he were contagious.

Room by room, the gang searched for anything smashable. Helplessly, Grandpa followed them, pleading, "I'm merely a temporary custodian here. We're all going to die someday. I beg you, young comrades, save these treasures for future generations . . ."

"You and your moldy relics belong in the dustbin of history!" The leader shoved Grandpa with his sharp elbow. "Back off!"

Grandpa careened sideways and pitched toward a marble console table. Crouching on the floor, he pressed his hand on his bleeding cheek, then spat a bloody tooth onto his handkerchief. Slowly, he stood up, and said coldly to the crowd, "Mark my words: someday, you'll be ashamed of what you've done today."

A girl's trembling voice broke the silence. "Report to Liang Duizhang: we've missed a chest in the master bedroom."

All heads turned to the petite girl, who had been hiding behind tall boys all this time. My fifteen-year-old Little Aunt! Grandma gasped. Grandpa slumped into a side chair, white as the candles on the console table.

The Red Guards unearthed a camphor dowry chest under the draped bed. Beneath Grandma's silk *qipao* were masterpieces by Bada Shanren, Zheng Banqiao, and Qi Baishi. Then, at the very bottom, *A Court Lady with a Fan*, the scroll by Tang Yin.

"How decadent!" a girl cried out, picking up a pair of dusty high heels from under the bed, dangling and twirling the thin ankle strap looped on her pinky; her nose wrinkled with horror and fascination in equal measure. I was bewildered, too. How could Grandma walk in such impractical shoes?

Liang Duizhang—the leader—turned to Little Aunt. With a curt smile, he said, "Good job, comrade Little Hong! I applaud you for severing ties with your feudal and capitalist family." Then he frowned. "Family is a bourgeois concept. As Chairman Mao has instructed us, '*A revolution is not a banquet.*'"

Little Aunt blushed as the boy's approving gaze lingered on her pretty face. Then she lifted her head to smile back at him, her eyes sparkling with yearning. Everyone in the room looked away.

After contraband was dumped in the courtyard, a clumsy boy fumbled with a matchbox they took from our kitchen. After several strikes, he threw the lit match onto the pile. *Whoomph*, the silk wedding *qipao* on the top was aflame. In seconds, it shivered into a thin film of ash. The teenagers hooted, laughing and clapping their hands. Even though the pungent smoke made me cough, I couldn't take my eyes off the roaring bonfire.

From the edge of the pile, our cat dragged out a high-heeled shoe. Liang Duizhang stooped down, seized the reactionary cat by its neck, and flung it into the fire, along with the incriminating evidence still in its jaw. Grandma shut her eyes. The cat flipped and landed with a nightmare-inducing howl. As it limped into the wasteland behind the fence, a toe tuft blackened, Little Aunt ran after it.

When the tongue of flame licked inch by inch at *A Court Lady with a Fan*—the masterpiece that had survived the Japanese arson in 1937—tears washed out a bloody track on Grandpa's contorted face. When they threw in my birdcage and my canary fluttered its wings against the bars, I bawled. "No!" But the adults stood numbly around me. An autumn chill knifed my spine.

After the mob left, Grandma tended to Grandpa's wound. Wringing a towel soaked with cold water from the well, she asked, "Do you know who this Liang Duizhang is?"

Grandpa shook his head.

Gingerly, Grandma cleaned his swollen cheek. "Son of Gui-Zhi and Liang Quizhang—oops, I mean the former Liang Quizhang. *Zhuonieya!* Last week, the boy beat up his counterrevolutionary father in the square—with that same belt on his waist."

Grandpa winced, pushing the towel away from his cut. A moment later he burst out with a bitter laugh. "What a stroke of misfortune! You tell her—she'll no longer be my daughter if she utters another word to that boy."

❧

Like the rest of the graduates from the Classes of '66, '67, and '68, Little Aunt went to "the countryside" as soon as she turned sixteen. She volunteered for the Beidahuang—the harsh northern wilderness that bordered the Soviet Union. Comrade Little Liang had been sent there the prior year, we heard.

The morning when Little Aunt was leaving, Grandpa spoke to her for the first time since the raid. "Remember what I said? You'll be ashamed of what you've done for the rest of your life."

Tears gushed out of Little Aunt's eyes. She bolted out of the house, her shiny, pigtail braids lashing her backpack. At the gate, she hesitated briefly before she mounted a waiting military truck heading to the train station. From there, she and her classmates would embark on a three-day journey by train and bus to reach a vast virgin wasteland.

At the time, we wept as her lithe, petite figure was sucked into the vortex of the sent-down youth. We couldn't imagine that four years later she would marry Liang Duizhang without telling us. Neither could we imagine that her idol-turned-husband would habitually grab her hair, beat her with his belt, and call her a whore after he'd had a few shots of potato moonshine in the long winter nights, nor that she would never see my grandpa again.

❧

In the following years, as Grandpa remained unemployable, Mother and Aunt No. 2 sent the lion's share of their salaries home. Even Aunt No. 3, an accounting apprentice in a factory, chipped in here and there. When my uncle visited us on week-ends, he patched leaky roofs and fixed crumbling walls.

Grandma still managed our household budget. But she could never control Grandpa's mouth, increasingly careless since he lost a tooth and gained another nasty scar—on his cheek this time. One evening, after gulping down a shot, he slammed the chipped *jigangbei*—rescued for the second time from the bon-fire ash—and started bawling, "Damn it! Should have sold the painting to that four-eyed Jap! At least he appreciated it . . ."

Grandma scurried over. Covering Grandpa's outrageous mouth with her hands and stomping her feet, she shouted, "Old drunkard, do you really want to ruin us all with your stinky farts?" Swiftly, she thrust out her chin, motioning Isha and me to close the windows.

That's how I knew that her scolding was meant for the eaves-dropping neighbors who might misinterpret Grandpa's alcohol-induced ravings.

A year after Little Aunt left, I overheard whispers in Grandma's kitchen during the New Year's gathering.

Mother told Aunt No. 2 about her visit to Little Aunt's vil-lage behind Grandpa's back. Upon her arrival, the villagers sent Mother to the site of a river-dredging project.

"At first, I couldn't find her. Then I saw a peasant woman staggering up the steep riverbank, a bamboo stick with two buckets balanced on her thin shoulder, black slurry sloshing all over her rolled-up trousers, her bare feet caked with muck and slime . . ." Mother's voice started to break. "Don't tell Ma. The men around her wore nothing but loincloths."

The sisters' eyes moistened every time they whispered about Little Aunt. On the rare occasions when sardine cans or lunch-meat tins appeared on the perennially empty store shelves, they stood in long lines to use their own quotas to buy these luxury goods, then they wrapped them in used clothing and mailed them to their baby sister.

Six years after Little Aunt left, she returned home for Grandpa's memorial service. Her wrinkled face was framed by dusty hair, cropped short as if with a chaotic sickle. Inside the bamboo basket fastened to her back, a snotty baby cackled at the sight of white, silk garlands draping Grandpa's photo.

Five more years after the memorial service, I'd grown into a full-fledged teenager.

One summer night, I lay next to Grandma in her bamboo bed. The mosquito net emitted the scent of white narcissus—the essential oil she rubbed on her arthritic hands. The bamboo sheet below us was lukewarm, yet the soft flesh under her sagging arm was as cool as a chilled watermelon. Our slowing breathing became synchronized, and then I heard Little Aunt's name and a sigh as faint as an exhalation. When her roughened hand touched mine, I stiffened. Was it a slip of the tongue? Was she dreaming of Little Aunt? And of her granddaughters a thousand miles away—my cousins growing wild like Siberian tundra grass under the Northern Lights? A sliver of moonlight sliced past the curtain, just above the dark frame of Grandpa's photo.

In the distance, a train whistled—two short, melancholy notes followed by a long and haunting sound. A familiar tune of changing pitches of a French horn. Crescendo or decrescendo? I listened resolutely, trying to decipher the direction of the train, and its destination.

12

THE MOON GODDESS
AND OTHER TALES

A nudge on my arm. I opened my eyes and found myself nestling on the shoulder of my seatmate. Blood rushing to my cheeks, I jerked away. "Sorry, sorry."

"No problem," the baby-faced young man chuckled good-naturedly. "Glad someone got a good snooze."

But, before I could blabber about my jetlag, he had turned diligently to his spreadsheet again. Still blushing, I furtively checked for any wet spot on his crisp button-down shirt. Finding none, I sighed and quietly wished the Binbin-look-alike a successful day ahead. *May you blast away a gigantic boulder between you and your own apartment in town!*

Then, I thought of our modest saltbox house in South Boston, and the slowly dwindling mortgage which had made my weekends in the lab and Tony's long drives crisscrossing New England worthwhile. Motivated, I punched the keyboard of my own laptop.

The screensaver remained frozen. Staring at it—a closeup of an antique vase—I felt a twinge of shame: despite my father's corrective attempts, I still favored porcelain.

The blue-and-white vase on the screen depicted the transformation of an earthly beauty into the Moon Goddess. Here, amid her celestial flight, Chang'e turned her head over her shoulder to steal a sad, last glance at the Earth, her lithe arms stretched in a stylish pose, her yard-long sleeves and decorative belts trailing in the clouds, above which the Moon Palace peeked through a magically verdant moonscape.

I managed to retrieve my draft about the Moon Goddess. Minutes into my editing, a lingering headache forced me to quit. Then it dawned on me: *What jetlag?* It was merely my problematic jaw joint acting up. I'd forgotten to pack my mouthguard for this trip. It always reminded me of Cousin Isha, now a dentist in Portland, Maine. Did my omission reveal some kind of repression? Maybe.

During a holiday gathering a decade before, Tony imitated the sound of my teeth grinding at night.

"Obviously, Cousin Mei has a TMJ problem!" Isha breezily handed out my diagnosis like a New Year's red envelope. A woman with no sense of humor, she tried to crack a tactless joke anyway. "With such a loving husband, aren't you supposed to just dream sweet dreams and blissfully gain weight?"

I grimaced. The number on my scale had trended north; a stubborn roll in my midsection was starting to resemble a three-month pregnancy. Aesthetics aside, at my last physical, my PCP frowned upon my steadily creeping-up cholesterol level. Fantasizing a good, hard spank on Isha's bony butt, I hissed through my teeth, "Watch out, Miss Size Zero! If you shrink any further, you'll end up in negative territory. Custom-made clothing costs a fortune!"

Suppose a correlation between a woman's weight gain and her spouse's indulgence does exist. Since Isha's husband always treated her like a queen, she should be the one to balloon with impunity. Yet she preserved her willowy figure.

Clearly, something had been eating Isha from inside and out. I had attempted heart-to-heart talks with her, but my only cousin in the States remained aloof. I had to cut her some slack: she had turned bitter during her college years—after a brush with the Party.

Nevertheless, her often-barbed remarks convinced me that she still held a grudge against me after all those years.

The summer when Isha turned ten years old, she visited us in Shanghai. One evening, while helping Mother set up the dinner table, she dropped my dragon bowl—the last gift from Grandpa.

I froze. Everything was in slow motion: Isha's awkward hands trying to catch the white light. A wobbling aerial dance of the bowl. A kiss of its thin, delicate lip on the concrete floor. A crisp, heart splintering sound. Her stepping towards the broken bowl. Her cry of "*Ow!*" Her removing the thin sandal, penetrated by a jagged white shard. A red dot weeping out of her sole.

My stomach thrust toward my squeezed throat. Waves of nausea and cold sweat. I breathed rapidly and hard. Then a switch turned in my head. "You . . . you . . . you . . ." Fighting my spasmatic tongue, I yelled, "You idiot! You dropped it on purpose!"

She gaped at me, stunned. Then she looked down at her bleeding foot, sobbing. "No, it just slipped from my fingers!"

"Stop, both of you!" Mother dashed out of the kitchen with dishes in each hand. Swiftly, she ushered Isha to the bathroom while ordering me, "Mei, clean up the mess."

Staring at the red-dotted trail on the floor, and the white fragments of my precious link to Grandpa, I quivered with a searing sense of injustice. *What about my invisible wound?*

That night, I lay still on a military cot, pretending not to hear Isha tossing, turning, and sniffling in my bed two meters away. The following morning, she packed in silence, then hobbled to Mother with her bandaged foot, demanding to be sent home.

In Shanghai station, Mother made me to apologize to Isha, but for over a year afterwards, we didn't talk.

Truth be told, half the time Isha possessed clumsy hands. Still, I couldn't rule out her envy about the bond between Grandpa and me being the reason for my monumental loss. Either way, I found it impossible to forgive her.

Three decades had passed since that incident. Nowadays, Isha busied herself with her dental practice in Maine, and I immersed myself in my lab in Cambridge. Between work and kids, we met at most once or twice a year.

A few years back, while Isha was helping me in our kitchen, I caught a reflection on the cabinet glass: three kids were engrossed in a Harry Potter movie. A flicker ignited in my mind. I asked her urgently, "Hey, have you told Grandpa's stories to your son?"

"Grandpa's stories?" She hesitated. "I recall only bits and pieces. I do remember lying on the bamboo bed though. And waking up in Grandma's arms."

Her words smashed into me like a tsunami. A disorienting moment later, I tumbled ashore to where she dropped my bowl. My tongue seized up again.

I'd hoped that we could recount these stories with laughter, perhaps after an honorary round of *wuliangye*. But did we really share any childhood memories at all? I might be the last custodian of the riches of Grandpa's tales.

Still, I doubted Isha. Surely, she would remember Chang'e. How could any Chinese forget the unusual tale of a beautiful yet desperate housewife levitating herself into the moon—by stealing her hero husband's ambrosia?

Growing up, I'd discovered many versions of this myth. In some, Ho Yi, the husband, was portrayed as a benevolent ruler, other times, a tyrant. This hero had a complicated persona: a superman in the public arena and a terrible man who frequently abandoned his wife to seek his glory. Still, his inaction toward her betrayal was perplexing. Upon his triumphant return, when he spotted the emptied vial on the floor of his empty house, shouldn't he have burst into a rage? He must have harbored some residual love for her, enough to restrain his arms from reaching for his mighty bow. Or was it guilt or grief that prevented him from shooting down the moon?

Yet, despite the wild variations of the tale, Chinese families reunite every Mid-Autumn Festival to feast. Seated around

round tables, we sample mooncakes, toast to another bountiful harvest, celebrate Chang'e's fantastic ascension from a mortal to a goddess, and seek blessings from this goddess who is nevertheless powerless to bestow her own happiness.

If Chang'e was frivolous and vain, as told in some versions, who would worship such a creature year after year? If curiosity of the mysterious liquid was her motive, why not stop after her first sip? Did she consider the ambrosia her due—for all her unacknowledged sacrifices behind the scenes? Did she steal to spite him, suffering from his habitual neglect? Or was she like Little Aunt, falling for an illusionary hero in her impressionable youth, only later trying to escape from an abusive, power-hungry man? Why cry every night? Remorse for her action, or its unintended, fate-changing consequences? For the whim of a foolish youth? The dime intuition of a clueless young wife? Was she yearning for Yi or a secret lover? Maybe the goddess was homesick for a big, warm house populated with grandparents, parents, aunts, uncles, siblings, and cousins.

In college, I read *Timon of Athens*. To my surprise, Shakespeare had also accused the poor moon of being "an errant thief who steals her pale fire" from the sun. *Stealing!* I was furious. *Too bad, if only my father could have explained to the Bard the concept of reflection.*

I thought of the Moon Goddess often, especially during the holidays when I gazed at the full moon alone—on the Atlantic shore instead of the farther shore of the Pacific. Rei would call me, but instead of bringing solace, his echoing voice only intensified my holiday blues. Pressing the cool jade pendant to my chest, misty eyed, I imagined my parents gazing at the same moon, each other, and my empty chair. Then they would raise their tumblers and finished their shots. If I listened harder, I could almost hear their faint blessings bouncing off the pitted lunar surface, reaching me twelve hours later.

I blinked back my tears. Unlike Chang'e, I'd volunteered for my own moon landing, though my coming to America was probably under the influence of a college professor and

President Reagan—the greatest salesman who ever lived. But I wouldn't cry because my clan had prepared me well for my exile.

I shouldn't cry, especially after Tony, and later my twins entered my life. Even in the coldest New England nights, I could feel a ray of sunshine, or, at least lukewarm moonlight, beaming down on me.

"Dear travelers, if you wish to purchase holiday gifts for your relatives and friends, please contact us. For your convenience, we've selected a limited edition of premium mooncakess," a female voice boomed from the overhead speaker. On cue, a woman in uniform pushed a well-stocked cart into our compartment.

Without batting an eyelash, my seatmate bought three expensive-looking boxes with Alipay. The attendant said with a professional enthusiasm, "You'll make your family very happy!"

"I wish!" he groaned. "These are for my clients."

When the woman beamed at me expectantly, I shook my head. The printed image on the gift package had always irked me. It was pilfered from an ancient painting by, surprise, surprise, Tang Yin—the old master, Grandpa's idol.

I must have seen thousands of renditions of Chang'e. As ubiquitous in China as the Virgin Mary in Catholic nations, the tragic, ethereal beauty was often portrayed like a tumbleweed in her moon-bound flight, her sorrowful hands outreached, desperate to latch onto any cosmic jetsam in ether.

Here, of course, Master Tang Yin painted his Chang'e with impeccable details: her cloud-like hair, the branch of osmanthus blossoms trembling in her exquisite hand, and her gaze cast downward to the invisible earthlings in the far distance. But what irritated me was her incredible smile. Looking more closely, I could even detect a hint of amusement hovering on the corners of her curved lips. She appeared to be congratulating herself, "*Well, I've got it all figured out.*"

An all-knowing, almost smug smile of a damsel in distress? What a bizarre point of view, from a cultured man nevertheless!

I felt compelled to challenge Tang Yin: Comb through all photos of me and my fellow expatriates. I dare you to find a single serene smile since our landings in the United States.

Straddling precariously between two worlds, one could never achieve tranquility, period. Of course, quantum physicists might insist that electrons could reside in two places simultaneously. But for the rest of us, we could only visualize a tiny particle oscillating miserably between allegiance to one realm or the other, perpetually second-guessing its decisions.

Despite its opaque meaning, jotting the myth down provided me with inexplicable relief, nevertheless. So, I soldiered on with Grandpa's other tales, including the story of Mr. Sai.

On the sultry summer nights of my childhood, the Milky Way shimmered above; darting fireflies and the burning tips of mosquito-repellent coils dimly illuminated our courtyard; crickets serenaded tirelessly among the shadows of dahlias; the evening air was perfumed with the soapy scent of moonflowers in nocturnal bloom. Night after night, three bathed-and-powdered children sank their teeth into melon slices, cold, sweet juice trickling down their cheeks and staining their whitened necks.

"A long, long time ago," Grandpa started, rocking in his bamboo chaise lounge and flicking his fan in a matching rhythm. Whiffs of dried ink and sandalwood tickled our noses as he unhurriedly narrated the story.

At a cliffhanger, he would pause, folding his fan with a snap; as if on cue, we would cry in synchrony, "Then what happened?"

"For the rest of the story," Grandpa yawned, "you three little monkeys will have to wait till tomorrow."

"No, tell us now!" We begged and begged.

He closed his eyes and pretended to snore. At this point, our adolescent Little Aunt would burst out laughing—she had been through the same drill. Grandma clicked her tongue to goad him on: "Old man, stop teasing the kids."

"Only after I tickle the stickiest monkey first!"

Squealing, we shrank into balls to protect our armpits and rounded bellies.

Hovering above us with his clawed hands, Grandpa became indecisive in choosing which sticky monkey to tickle. A hearty laugh later, he unfolded his fan with another loud snap, ending the intermission.

Thus, in this usual fashion, Grandpa told us the story of Mr. Sai. "A long, long time ago, there was a wise old man named Mr. Sai. He loved horses, and he could talk to them.

"One day, he went to a market and saw a huge gathering around a horse. A loser was auctioning his prized stallion to pay off a gambling debt."

Grandpa imitated people's shouting in different voices: "'Two hundred silver coins!' 'Three hundred!' 'Four here!'

"What a majestic thoroughbred! Its smooth coat shone like the indigo night sky, and its intelligent eyes twinkled like diamonds. Oh, and its powerful legs, its well-proportioned torso, and its huge flaring nostrils . . ." Grandpa gestured with his expressive hands the physical beauty of the horse—all good indicators for its endurance. On and on, as if in a trance, he relished the minutest detail of the horse, its sterling record in competitions, and the frenzy of the bidding war.

"Suddenly, the stallion stopped its restless prancing and trotted toward the crowd. Raising its forelegs high with a neigh, it pointed its hoof at Mr. Sai. At once, all eyes turned to the lovestricken Mr. Sai.

"As Mr. Sai combed its bristling mane with his fingers, the horse lowered his velvety nostrils to muzzle Mr. Sai's elbow, nickering like a docile foal reunited with its mother . . .

"In the end, Mr. Sai paid a fortune to bring the horse home. When his neighbors came over to congratulate him, he only nodded and said sagely, 'Is it good fortune or a bad omen? Only heaven knows.'"

At this point, Grandpa folded his fan with a loud *pa*.

"Then what happened?" We barked like Pavlovian dogs at the sound of the meal bell. Grandpa laughed, performing his usual antics.

Soon, the entire Sai household was under the spell of the stallion. They fed him the best hay and fresh spring water. They dressed him in a jeweled saddle. They hired the best trainers to groom him, massage him, play harp for him, and exercise him in an expansive pasture. Their love for him grew boundless.

Then, on a moonless night, the stallion just vanished. Nobody knew how it had escaped—the stable doors were still barred.

Upon hearing the sad news, friends and neighbors offered their condolences. Shaking his full head of white hair, Mr. Sai said again, "Is it good fortune or a bad omen? Only heaven knows."

As the night deepened, Grandpa unfolded the twists and turns of the story with his busy fan: As mysteriously as he had disappeared, the stallion returned one day, bringing along a herd of mustangs. Mr. Sai built another stable to accommodate his sudden gain. Then the stallion sired a beautiful pony, and Mr. Sai's youngest child rode the pony daily, until he fell and broke his leg while jumping a fence. Years later a war broke out, and every able-bodied young man was drafted except the crippled son. . . Following each event in this rollercoaster of a tale, Mr. Sai would utter the same ambiguous statement to his bewildered neighbors: "Is it good fortune or a bad omen? Only heaven knows."

I couldn't remember how Grandpa ended this story. Perhaps I, too, had fallen asleep on the bamboo bed, just like Isha.

Then, in fourth grade, I stumbled upon the origin of Grandpa's heavily embellished story in a dictionary: Sai Wong Shi Ma, Yan Zhi Fu Hou, an eight-character idiom! I was in awe of Grandpa once again.

Even into adulthood, this tale without a neat and tidy ending continued to fascinate me. Who knows? Maybe we all descended from Mr. Sai's crippled son who was spared from the war; maybe we continued to play our small parts unwittingly in this perpetual fable.

Many times, I wanted to comfort my children with this tale, for instance, when Aurora sprained her ankle during a basketball game; or when Leonardo lost his favorite stegosaurus among the Fourth of July crowds at the Esplanade. The phrase "*A long, long time ago*" was curled under my tongue, poised to spring out. Each time I swallowed it back. I'd lost confidence after I butchered the fable of the Moon Goddess.

Occasionally, I even felt the urge to tell this cautionary tale to my colleagues. Right before this trip, a typical lunchtime banter in our cafeteria had degraded into a pointed debate on Romneycare vs. Obamacare. Then, *Racists! Tone-deaf! Hypocrites!* The crossfire of toxic rants was animated with finger-stabbing in the air.

I wanted to say, "Guys, guys, guys, why do you think this election is a choice between life and death, good and evil, or black and white? The difference between these two Ivy League–educated men is skin-deep. It doesn't matter one bit which candidate enters the White House; good fortune and bad omen are bound to happen during his term."

Still, I held my tongue and watched my red-faced co-workers with detached amusement. When the microwave oven dinged, I took out my reheated egg rolls and joined the two technicians watching reruns of *Days of Our Lives* at the far corner. I knew better. My colleagues, friends, and even my husband—anyone who grew up with a horizon span of four- to eight-year cycles—would never understand the perspective of Mr. Sai. In a society that believed in the mantra of *You Are the Master of Your Own Destiny*, Mr. Sai's Eastern agnosticism—devoid of intellectual rigor and elegance of reasoning—sounded like philosophical flippancy.

I guarded this tale not solely because of our worldview differences or my ineloquent rhetoric. Being a scientist, I distrust language per se due to its inherent imprecision and fallible nature. Meanings and nuances tend to be lost in translation, sometimes even among people sharing a common native tongue. Evidence is aplenty.

Perhaps, I could only tell the story after we all manage to grow antennae as seen in ants—the greatest communicators that have spread super-colonies across continents, or more likely, when we would be fitted with some synchronizing headsets or chips in our brains.

On the other hand, such a future would render tales obsolete: Chang'e would never have attempted to fly to the moon, Shakespearean tragicomedies would be moot, and all human behaviors could be decoded into a narrow repertoire of programmable rituals.

In that bleak world, Grandpa's tales would die with me.

No! An inner voice protested. *Sooner or later, the twins will grow mature enough to read the complex tale of the Moon Goddess!*

13

SUZHOU

"Next stop, Suzhou," the voice from the overhead speaker jolted me out of my daydreaming.

Suzhou used to loom large in my imagination due to a Chinese proverb: *If you can't reach heaven, visit Suzhou.*

Of course, emperors in the Forbidden City had a lazy approach: bring Suzhou to Beijing. They had a Grand Canal dug to siphon the city's coveted bounties: "scholar's rocks" from Lake Taihu, luxurious silk garments, gourmet food, and famed Suzhou ladies, all sailed on barges along the canal . . .

This ancient city—nicknamed "the Venice of the Orient" due to its interlacing waterways—also evoked endless tear-drenched dreams. "Rain Alley" was the most celebrated poem written by a hometown poet from the Crescent Moon School:

> *Wandering alone in the long, long, rain alley,*
> *I yearn*
> *for a maiden under an oilcloth umbrella.*
> *She has*
> *the color of lilacs,*
> *the fragrance of lilacs,*
> *and the melancholy of lilacs . . .*

I had translated some poems for my children. Far from perfect, I believed my translation had captured the mood of Suzhou here. Yet, I found this popular poem utterly unrelatable, and my countrymen's fascination with lilac girls peculiar.

Suzhou was also my father's hometown. When I was eight years old, he brought me to visit *nainai*, my paternal grandma. To my great disappointment, the legendary rock gardens were almost identical to the Zhanyuan Garden a few doors down the road from Grandpa's house. All the girls on the streets were plain and nondescript. With one shallow breath, I could probably blow their under-defined facial features away like seeds of dandelions.

I remained unimpressed with this earthly version of heaven—until we went to a tiny restaurant a stone's throw from *nainai's* house. The *sheng jian bao* there had a crispy golden bottom and a ruffled crown sprinkled with toasted sesame and sliced scallions. I took a bite into its thin shell, and fragrant juice from minced ginger and jellied pork belly burst into my mouth. Relishing the dish, I also savored the conversations around me. The Suzhou dialect was so soft—as if every harsh sound had been muffled by cotton candy. Later, even a rare quarrel in the market—between a fishmonger and his fussy customer—sounded like a musical.

A few years later, my family visited my ailing *nainai*. When Mother recommended a specialist in Shanghai, *nainai* dismissed her suggestion with a resigned smile. The contrast between the two women was dramatic: my take-charge mother sounded like metal, the solid and impenetrable element; *nainai*, like water— the misty rain, the murmuring ripples under a canal bridge, the morning dew on magnolia petals. My nodding father sat next to the headboard, holding *nainai's* pale hand, playing the role of an attentive, filial son.

Observing them, I was struck by the oddity of my parents as a couple for the first time. Immediately, I brushed the thought into the black box of yin-yang theory, the enigma of the opposite and complementary matter.

In retrospect, my father's choice of his second wife—a woman of an inferior yet more pliable substance—seemed more sensible.

During my college years, I brought Rei to Suzhou once. After the obligatory tour of the leaning pagoda on Tiger Hill, we strolled toward another thousand-year-old landmark, the Hanshan Temple.

The temple, obscured by crimson foliage, was famous due to another poem: *A Night-Mooring by the Maple Bridge.*

A crow caws from the frosted maple over the bridge,
Waking me from a troubled sleep.
The moon falls into the river.
A fisherman's torch flickers on the bank.
Beyond Suzhou, a bell rings from the Hanshan Temple,
Welcoming the midnight arrival of my boat.

"Ahh, the midnight bell." I said, hands theatrically pressed to my heart. "It totally resonates with me."

Rei laughed nervously. "You aren't planning to join the nuns in their quarters, I hope."

"Nah," I assured him. "What for? My great-grandpa had devoted his whole life to Buddhism. Still, enlightenment was beyond his reach."

After the temple, we walked toward the house of my late *nainai*. Soon we entered a deep and narrow alley. Green, velvety moss filled the gaps between the shiny bluestones. Sounds of an amateur's *erhu* practice drifted out of a wooden door with layers of peeling paint. A sunbathing cat perked up from a short wall, his back arching. A moment later, he broke off his intense scrutiny with a yawn and slunk away. Rei fidgeted with his camera to follow the cat. Then he looked up from the viewfinder and gasped, "Man, this *is* the *Rain Alley!*"

"Yep. And believe it or not, in her days, *nainai* looked and smelled just like that *Lilac Girl.*"

A glimmer skidded across Rei's black eyes. "You know, your father does have Mr. Dai's temperament."

I burst out laughing. "The melodramatic poet who killed himself? Come on! My dad is a nerdy engineer, not a narcissist. Remember, he married my mother!" As I was ridiculing Rei's inappropriate remark, I saw his point: my father's mild, dreamy smile.

By then, the midday sun had lifted the blue haze and burned off half of the city's charm. A sweet and rotten odor permeated the air. (Those were the days when vendors on boats dumped unsold vegetables and rubbish into the canals at will.) We walked wordlessly, my low heels clicking the polished stones underfoot. Then we reached a dead end.

"Forget about that second-rate poet," I said. "I know the best place for *sheng jian bao*. After just one bite, you will crave it for the rest of your life."

We wandered in the maze, but the restaurant was nowhere to be found. Just then, hordes of camera-wielding tourists swarmed in, choking the alley. Like a broken record, that moldy poem about the Lilac Girl stuck in my head. My mood soured. *So, we are part of the cliché.*

A woman in pajamas appeared; a basket of lotus pods bounced with her lazy hip-switching. I asked her for directions to the restaurant.

"It's gone," she said in a singsong voice. "Demolished long ago."

"But why?"

"To put a public restroom in that corner lot." She smiled sardonically. "One-mao entrance fee, five fens for tissue, busloads of tourists, you do the math."

Defeated, we ended up in a random diner. Once our young and hungry stomachs were satisfied, I started to pity that erstwhile restaurant from my childhood. Its ghost must be sighing at its forced incarnation to serve the opposite human needs. Little did I know at the time that we ourselves were at the end of one era and the beginning of another.

The bullet train had transformed Suzhou into a bedroom community of the sprawling metropolis of Shanghai. On the opposite platform, long lines of suited and groomed people were bending over their PDAs while waiting for their morning commuter train.

More passengers exited than entered during our stop. My heart fluttered with a glimpse of a young man with a full head of jet-black hair—Rei used to have hair just like that.

An odor of over-ripe fruit lingered in our compartment. Instantaneously, my olfactory memory—a strange, illogical library—retrieved the image of the green, murky canal. I looked around. A new arrival across the aisle fumbled in his backpack, tossed a blackened banana into a trash bag. I couldn't help noticing the Foxconn logo on his backpack. Registering my gaze, he swiped the screen of his Xiaomi phone peevishly.

Soundlessly, the train glided out of the station. I craned my neck, hoping for the sight of the leaning pagoda on Tiger Hill. Had the maple foliage peaked yet? But I failed to spot the hill altogether. I wasn't even sure of the boundary between the old town and the new high-tech zone. Instead, as in any self-respecting city of twenty-first-century China, endless, monotonous concrete boxes jutted toward the sky.

14

OUR SYCAMORE TREE

The brand-new Nanjing South railway station contrasted sharply with the grimy Shanghai Station that I'd left behind only a little over an hour earlier. The granite-clad mammoth gleamed from floor to ceiling. *High-Rise, Platform, Surface, Underground Level 1, Level 2*... my eyes scanned the busy signage on five levels.

Finally, I found my target sandwiched between *Lost and Found* and *Home Original Chicken*—the *Taxi* in the north plaza.

A familiar figure waved fanatically among the placard-holding greeters and the flag-toting tour guides. "Over here, Mei! Here!"

Seeing her, my heart trembled. Aunt No. 2 didn't resemble Mother in her youth. Although both had inherited Grandpa's eyes, she had a soft, oval face, while Mother's finished with a boxer's jaw. And Mother appeared much taller in the way she held her athletic carriage. Nevertheless, the two sisters grew more alike once gravity played its tricks and time carved wrinkles on their faces. A short while before, a similar pair of twin creases, the nasolabial folds, had also crept up on my own face.

"Mei, long time no see!" Aunt No. 2 exclaimed, enveloping her warm, pillowy hands around mine.

Remembering her red, blotchy face during Mother's funeral six months earlier, I said, "Aunty, you look well."

"You've lost some weight!" she replied.

Before I could object to her implied plans to fatten me up, she squeezed my hand and croaked, "You look just like your mother."

My eyes misted at the thought of the different versions of Mother in our memories.

"That's all you have for luggage?" She raised her eyebrows at my carry-on. She'd always traveled with jumbo suitcases bulging with extra underwear, saltines, sardine cans, medicine for common ailments, and a week's worth of toilet paper in case she found herself stranded on an island during the worst cholera outbreak. Should she live in the States, I could bank on a well-stocked, nuclear-proof bunker in her woody backyard. No one dared to laugh at her, though. In the early sixties, she had lost a newborn to malnutrition on the heels of the so-called three-year natural disasters. Ever since then, she'd been padding her midriff with extra doomsday fuel for any looming catastrophe, natural or man-made.

In the taxi to Grandma's apartment, Aunt No. 2 patted my knee and asked, "Have you seen Isha lately?"

"Not since last Christmas. You know how crazy our lives are. We'd be lucky to get a half -hour lunch break."

"You make time to meet." She fixed me with a stern look. "Family is most important. You'll understand when you get older." Then she sighed, perhaps realizing our conceptual difference of "family."

Aunt No. 2's cuddly, Michelin Man appearance was deceptive. She had always been the kind of woman who could lift a car to free her trapped kid with a primordial force. When city-bound migration was still prohibited in the early eighties, by sheer Hong doggedness, she managed to lift her children out of an impoverished swampland—for the sake of their education. So, I nodded to her, making a mental note to reach out to Isha.

Her mood brightened after we exited the taxi. Pointing at a construction site a hundred meters away, she said, "That's going to be a stop on the subway Line 3. So, when you visit next time, you can get off right there!"

But the future convenience would be pointless for me—Grandma's chicken coop would soon become Binbin's love nest.

Despite the nearby construction, the apartment windows were spotless. After showing me four kinds of snacks, shampoo, toothpaste, and the switch for the bedside reading light, Aunt No. 2 tipped her double chin toward a piece of paper taped to a router: "The password."

"Wait, did Grandma surf the Internet?"

"Ha!" She laughed at my cluelessness. "She could barely see figures on TV in the last couple of years! That's for the hired *ayi*. Besides, your other two aunts and I took turns spending nights here, too. Now, are you hungry? We should eat before going about our business."

As usual, she lavished a feast on me. The double-cooked pork brought out my inner smile. Years before, Isha and I used to exchange our rationed food under the table—my crisp tofu for her pork. When Grandma caught us, she declared, "No picky eater in my household! You have no idea how lucky you are!" Then, with an inscrutable face, she watched Isha swallow her pork cubes in tears. From that day on, she always inserted herself between us to blockade our fair trade.

"So delicious," I praised the beef sautéed with longhorn pepper; my tongue tingled from the heat.

She proudly balanced a beef strip on the tip of her chopsticks, "See how thin the slice is? This way, it soaks up the spiciness of the pepper." Effortlessly, she pivoted to her favorite topic—comparative cuisine. "A lazy American cook would just plunk down a slab of meat, barely seared on the surface and bloody in the center, and ask you to saw it up on your own!"

We burst out laughing. Many summers earlier, Tony served her a medium-rare steak during her visit. Struggling to swallow it, Aunt No. 2 muttered under her breath, "*Ru mao ying xue.*" That expression describes the lifestyle of prehistoric cavemen: "Gnaw on unplucked birds and drink the blood dripping from the carcasses."

I said, "Just so you know, I've tamed the barbarians at home. Nowadays, Tony seldom eats raw food."

"Good. Here, your favorite," she said, pushing a plate piled with eel chunks toward me.

Even though she'd confused me with Isha, the fish lover, I took a hearty bite of a fat belly piece. The intense flavors of star anise, garlic, and cloves bombarded my palate. This was Grandma's signature dish. My brain sputtered with happy memories. Encouraged by my aunt's indulging smile, I chomped on one more big chunk, then another, until I choked on an embedded fishbone.

After that sumptuous brunch, we went to visit the designated notary near the old town. To my surprise, Aunt No. 3 was waiting in the building lobby. Handing me a typed-up waiver and a receipt for the prepaid fee, she explained, "It's very convenient for me. Our accounting office is nearby."

Under the watchful eyes of the notary public, I wrote my John Hancock on the dotted line with exaggerated solemnity. The man scrutinized my signatures, then disappeared into the back office. Two minutes later, he returned with the form, now bearing both the red and the embossed stamps.

Aunt No. 2 sealed the notarized waiver in a clear document pouch, then a padded envelope, then zipped it inside the inner compartment of her tote. Finally, her tense face softened.

Thus, my obligation was unceremoniously discharged. I felt ridiculous for being dragged halfway around the globe for such an anticlimactic performance. I had imagined a herculean fight with some official busybody, a man in a dark den who would surely sniff and balk at my US passport and stall the process. Anticipating the *Come-back-tomorrow* game routinely played by my unseen nemesis, I had budgeted two extra days. Now I had nothing to do but relax in my hometown before the arrival of Tony and the twins. *Two extra days, it's like winning a lottery!* Then I worried about the taxes that the universe was bound to extract.

On our way out, my aunts thanked me profusely. Embarrassed, I said, "What for? Didn't everyone else sign the waiver for Binbin?"

"But you've gone the extra ten thousand kilometers." Aunt No. 2 exhaled. "Now Grandpa, Grandma, and your mother can all rest in peace."

Really? How could Mother rest in peace? My heavy stomach churned. During her call, Aunt No. 2's voice had turned chilly when mentioning my father. She must have known about his presumed infidelity. Yet, she only shared information on an as-needed basis—to protect me, no doubt. I felt the urge to ask her point-blank. But, with the presence of reticent Aunt No. 3, charged words got stuck in my throat, like the fishbone from lunch.

My aunts insisted on accompanying me to the nearby market-places around the Confucius Temple. They noted that it had undergone a major facelift since my last visit.

As we ambled leisurely toward my childhood stomping ground, Aunt No. 2 sighed, "Hopefully, Binbin won't have to postpone his wedding again."

"Relax. The wedding is still two months away." Aunt No. 3 then turned to me and explained, "Your uncle's best buddy is a reputable contractor. We all chipped in toward the renovation."

"I see. It takes a village to get married in Nanjing."

"Or anywhere else in China," Aunt No. 2 said, and then frowned. "Mei, why didn't you invite us to your wedding?"

"Well, I didn't have a wedding in the traditional sense."

Aunt No. 3 said to her sister with a chuckle, "You didn't get an invitation to your own daughter's wedding, either."

"That's different. Isha and Ed were poor students then. Never mind," Aunt No. 2 said, conceding defeat. "Only we Chinese fuss over weddings like it's one's ultimate goal in life. Americans are pragmatic."

I let the complex topic pass. I'd had a glimpse into the multi-billion-dollar wedding industry in America—after accidentally walking into a bridal show at the Hynes Convention Center in

Boston. But, I liked Aunt No. 2's general notion of my adopted country: at least some of us were pragmatic.

Then I saw the majestic sycamore tree. Its brown leaves and their lighter undersides undulated in the autumn breeze with a subdued grace, as if welcoming my return. I beelined toward it.

"Ah, you remembered our sycamore!" Aunt No. 2 exclaimed, then pointed to a concrete building with no visible sign or logo. "Yes, our house used to be right over there."

I bent down to touch the smooth, variegated tree bark. There it was, my name carved into the lower trunk, growing fatter and fainter but not taller. Rei's name, or rather, the first five strokes, paralleled mine. When Rei was carving his name four decades before, a buck-toothed woman from the neighborhood committee charged toward us, her plastic sandals slapping the pavement. "You brat!" she yelled, raising her flour-dusted rolling pin, "Drop your knife or you'll have a taste of this!" Rei was spared from her revolutionary wrath that day. Yet, I felt queasy now. Was that incident a harbinger of his eventual downfall?

In silence, I paid homage to the surviving tree. Behind it, one of the upper windows on the boxy building opened a crack. Something feathery pricked my skin. I sensed that behind the facade of this faceless monstrosity, our stone well still existed in the bluestone courtyard, perhaps guarded by the mythical animals on its panels. Instantly, my mind whirred with Grandpa's stories, and that seventy-year-old secret once hiding below the water. I could visualize a suspended watermelon, still waiting for Grandma's age-spotted hands to free it from the bamboo basket. A cold, sweet sensation serenaded my tongue. Impulsively, I said, "I have to take a look."

After a second of hesitation, my aunts followed me in lockstep toward the building's entrance.

A stone-faced security guard tapped a sign behind his desk with a gloved hand: *No Visitors*.

"Sir, we used to live here," I said. "Could we just take a quick peek at the courtyard, please?"

He stood up and puffed out his giant chest. Before I could plead again, he had reached for his pistol holster with his ill-humored fingers while stretching out his left arm. With this unmistakable gesture, he corralled us out, the pesky wannabe visitors.

At the curbside, a rattled Aunt No. 2 swept her marshmallow arms to gesture and said, "Mei, think about it: your great-grandfather donated that half of the block to the government. Then they took this part from your *gonggong*. Nowadays, we must beg and beg just to keep a piece of shingle over Binbin's head."

Aunt No. 3 stared at the dark-tinted glass door of the ugly building, then called me, strangely, by my childhood pet name. "Meimei, do you know, Grandpa had once asked your uncle and me to buy his house for one yuan?" Her voice cracked. "Our refusal broke his heart."

"Certainly not your fault, Aunt No. 3," I said, alarmed by my usually reserved aunt's sniffling.

"Don't cry over spilled milk," Aunt No. 2 chided, handing her sister a wad of tissue from her tote. But, instead of grabbing it, Aunt No. 3 sank into her sister's shoulder and sobbed loudly, oblivious to people's gawking.

Linking arms around my trembling, gray-haired aunts for a group huddle, I couldn't help thinking of Grandpa's angry scars, and his lifelong quest to restore the courtyard—mission Impossible in the People's Republic of China. Patting Aunt No. 2's bouncy back, I proposed, "Let's take a picture with *our* sycamore tree."

After we smiled at three sets of cell phones, tourists pooled around us. They ogled the stately but otherwise ordinary tree, the nondescript building behind it, and then the three red-faced women. A rubber-necking girl across the street snapped a shot with a flash. Detecting a commotion, the security guard rushed out and planted his combat boots on the concrete stoop. Hand on his pistol, he shouted, "No photos!"

We had put away our phones, but we stood our ground, glaring at the guard without giving in one inch. *You can rob us of our ancestral house, you can deny our entry to pay homage to our guardian angels on the well, but you can never annihilate our memories!*

After the standoff, I asked my aunts, "What's inside this mysterious building anyway?"

Aunt No. 3 said after a hesitation, "Bank after bank of screens. A state-of-the-art surveillance system for the entire market area." Then she whispered. "Someone I know has a son who works there—has something to do with facial recognition software."

"Oops, did I just get you two in trouble?"

"Ha!" Aunt No. 2 scoffed."We dead pigs aren't afraid of boiling cauldrons," then, she joked, "but you might have a hard time leaving Nanjing."

I couldn't laugh. Unlikely as it was, a scenario of this kind could—and did—happen from time to time. As we walked on, I noticed the presence of cameras above almost every traffic light. Sinister rain clouds swirled above the green river. Perspiration began to streak down my armpits.

Trudging toward the bustling marketplace, we were utterly drained. Then, Aunt No. 2 said to me, "Why don't you go and rest at Grandma's place? I'd better bring the waiver to Binbin right away." She fished out the key from her tote and pointed it at the Temple gate. "Meet me over there tomorrow at noon. Let's stroll along the gourmet snack street. Save some appetite, though, for your welcome-home banquet tomorrow night."

15

MY GRANDMA'S CHICKEN COOP

The afternoon traffic thickened like congealing aspic. In the taxi, I observed in real time the vertical growth of my hometown behind numerous scaffoldings.

In contrast to all the beehive activities around it, one block looked abandoned, with a battlefield of bare rebar piercing through unfinished concrete shells. In Nanjing dialect, I asked my driver, "What happened there?"

"You don't know?" The driver said, checking me through the rearview mirror as if I had just been released from an asylum.

"Well, I've been out of town for a while," I admitted meekly.

"Aha! Well, a big-time developer grabbed that prime lot dirt cheap, but he got caught bribing the district officials on a hidden camera." For my education, he pointed into the distance and snorted, "See those finished buildings? Before he went to jail, the crook had already offloaded that *xiaoqui* and fattened his secret account in the Cayman Islands."

Then it occurred to me that Grandma's shabby apartment had ceased to be at the margin of this booming city.

How Grandma acquired her "chicken coop" was another story.

In 1978, six years after the local government "purchased" Grandpa's house from my uncle, the Party revoked their directives of wiping out "idle" city dwellers. Millions exiled in communes trickled back to Nanjing. My grandma was among them, with a photo of her late husband in a suitcase. Homeless then, she lodged in my uncle's cramped apartment for a while. After Binbin was born, the living conditions became unbearable for two strong, opinionated women. So, she moved in with my parents and me.

But the heavily chlorinated water in Shanghai didn't agree with my delicate grandma. From head to toe, her body protested with massive, blotchy rashes. One day, she threw three ointment jars in the trash bin and announced, "I'm heading back to Nanjing. Even a golden palace in heaven couldn't match one's own chicken coop."

"Ma, you don't have a chicken coop anymore."

Grandma broke down in sobs.

Eventually, Mother obtained the "sales agreement" from my uncle. After poring over all the documents for hours, she found a discrepancy: the affixed lot map in the exhibit was an outdated copy of a building permit dated 1938. So naturally, it excluded the much bigger shed built in 1948—when Grandpa tore down the dilapidated garden shed to make room for a storage place for his restoration project.

Mother told Grandma, "According to this contract in 1972, the Housing Authority bought our house and the adjacent buildable lots for a laughable 300 renminbi. So, your chicken coop has to come from this," she said, pointing to the forty-eight-square-meter storage shed on Grandpa's later blueprint. "Ma, ask them to compensate you for this shed they didn't buy."

"Aha!" Grandma perked up.

"It's going to be a very long and hard battle," Mother warned her. "None of us has the time except you."

"Do tell."

"First, I'll draft a petition. Bring it to our house, excuse me, the headquarters of the District Housing Authority. Don't mention a word about the unfairness of the forced sale. Just plead for an apartment of forty-eight square meters. If they refuse, tell them you'll have to move back into the storage shed."

"That's impossible," Grandma laughed bitterly. "They'll just ask me to leave."

"Exactly. Just say you trust that our government will help a desperate widow in a dire situation. Hand them the letter, smile, then leave."

"Then what?"

"Next day, politely ask if they've come up with any solution to your pressing issue."

"They'll say no."

"Of course. Tell them you have all the time in the world to wait. Bring with you the *Little Red Book* and a folding stool. Put your stool in a far corner that doesn't interfere with their workflow."

"What if they just ignore me?"

"Pretend to read your *Little Red Book*. From time to time, make eye contact with the clerks and smile. Some of them might still have a conscience."

"What if they grab my arms and drag me out?"

"If anyone tries to lay his hands on you, shout as loudly as you can, 'Back off! This old lady has brittle bones.' Then pick up your stool and leave. Return the next morning just the same." Suddenly, Mother's face aged twenty years. "You know what, forget it. This tactic isn't for people like you."

"Don't you underestimate my will!" Grandma defiantly bit her lip.

"Will is irrelevant here," Mother said, and folded the ancient documents and stuffed them back into the yellowed envelope. "A thick hide is needed—when you wage wars against rogues, thugs, and robbers."

Gritting her last few remaining molars, Grandma said, "You just wait and see."

From springtime through fall, Grandma executed Mother's plan flawlessly. Every morning, rain or shine, she reported to duty at the housing office; she sipped tea from her thermos cup, read newspapers, or knitted while daydreaming; from time to time, she wandered into the courtyard, inspecting the shed (sagging under stacked cardboard boxes), the neglected flowerbeds, and the mythical animals on the well. For lunch, she went to the same street vendor around the corner. While waiting in line for her steamed vegetable bun, she chatted with the office girls. Once or twice, she even volunteered to fetch a broom and duster from the shed for the friendliest girl.

Gradually, she started collecting newspapers and mail from the postman at the gate. She deadheaded the spent dahlias, and irrigated the parched shrubs with well water. For old times' sake, she hung up a birdcage with a canary on the same branch of the plum tree—planted by Grandpa four decades earlier—and practiced Tai-Chi under its shade.

The head clerk kept telling her, "You don't have any permit for the shed. We'll never compensate for any illegal construction."

"We filed a permit, but you lost it." Biting her lip, she decided against mentioning the chaotic years of civil war or the Cultural Revolution. "Anyway, you've been using my shed for all these years. You should start paying rent, plus past balance and interest."

"Nonsense," he said, putting on his reading glass to scrutinize his newspaper.

Then, the shed vanished into thin air over a weekend.

"My goodness, I was only joking about charging rent! Good thing is that I still have proof. Do you want to see it? Here," Grandma dug a bookmark out of her Little Red Book—a time-stamped photo of the contested shed—and handed it to the head clerk with a smile.

Red-faced, the man fled from his office.

Since the verbal stalemate about the shed ended, the staff began complimenting her on *her* dahlias, which had rebloomed magnificently. Even the top brass nodded curtly at the harmless, unpaid gardener when they passed by. Yet, month after month, Mother's strategy produced no results.

On a November day, a clerk bumped into Grandma in the courtyard. Brushing her elbow, the woman scolded loudly,

"Watch out, old lady! Hang out here any longer, and you'll get pneumonia before you get your shed back." Then, she whispered, "Bring your case to the court. They've just started to hear property disputes like yours."

Grandma gaped at her. True, every paralyzed government branch, including the window-dressing judicial system, was undergoing a slow rehabilitation. Still, a toothless, little old lady suing the *Ya Men*—the almighty government? She shuddered.

The next day, she quit her volunteer job and took a Shanghai-bound train to visit my mother.

On their court day, Grandma, Mother, Aunt No. 2, and Aunt No. 3 were dressed in their finest. In a dusty, rumpled jacket, Little Aunt arrived just in time. But my uncle couldn't be persuaded to be a plaintiff. "Not a fat chance," he laughed. "Ma, you're wasting your time. For what? A stomach ulcer!"

When the District Housing Authority representative failed to show up, the judge asked the weathered woman trembling under his gaze, "Where is your husband, Comrade Hong?"

"Dead." Emboldened by the restored title of *Comrade*, Grandma added, "Four months after we were kicked out of our house."

The judge grimaced, "Where's your son? Isn't he the one who signed the sales agreement?"

"Too ashamed to come here. You see, he had put me on the street with his pen." Then, remembering her late father-in-law, the kind Hao-Ran, she pleaded, "I'm at your mercy now, judge."

The judge, newly released from a reform camp for cadres, shifted his eyes away from a disturbing sight: the quivering plaintiff was grasping her lectern. Her gnawed hands were covered with liver spots and earthworm-like veins burrowing under her leathery skin; her white hair shook over her large head propped on a petite frame, like a top-heavy bonsai in an undersized pot struggling in a gust; her beseeching eyes and parched lips pleaded for so little, just a drop of justice.

The judge stared at a handwritten statement on his desk. A red, boldface heading declared: **The Highest Command from**

Chairman Mao: Down with Bourgeoisie. He cleared his throat and read aloud, *"I, Hong Jianguo, a representative for the estate of Hong Ping-An, voluntarily sell our property at No.5 Zhanyuan Road to our government for a sum of 300 RMB..."*

Repeating the word *voluntarily*—twice underlined with a ballpoint pen—a wry smile emerged upon the judge's face. People in the courtroom murmured and sneered, "Yeah, right, 'voluntarily.'"

In the end, the Hong family lost the war but won the battle. The judge ordered the absentee Housing Authority to compensate Grandma with an apartment equivalent to forty-eight square meters of floor area in the same neighborhood. Teary-eyed, Grandma thanked the judge who had restored her faith.

A month later, the head clerk from the Housing Authority presented Grandma with a set of keys. "Old lady," he said, "we've found you a place of forty-five square meters. It comes with a six-square-meter courtyard. So, lucky you, the total is fifty-one square meters."

With two hands and a deep bow, Grandma accepted the keys, thanked him repeatedly, and invited him for tea.

Soon, Grandma moved into her chicken coop—the servants' quarters of a perished family she used to know. During her first winter there, an uninsulated pipe burst. In summer downpours, she rotated three buckets for roof leaks and recycled the rainwater for her dahlias in the postage-stamp-sized courtyard. Year-round, the place smelled damp and musty, yet Grandma couldn't have been happier. During the day, she babysat the new crop of my young cousins and enjoyed her solitude at night. Every summer, I shared her bamboo bed. Whenever Isha and, later, her little brother Ixin visited, we laid planks over chairs at night for makeshift beds.

"We'll demolish the entire block—to make room for commercial high-rises." A decade later, another man from the Housing Authority knocked on Grandma's door and announced the news. "Old lady, considering your age, we've assigned you a unit on the second floor of a brand-new building," he said magnanimously, omitting its location. "Lucky you, including the balcony, the one-bedroom apartment is fifty-two square meters in total."

Once again, Grandma thanked the Party and served the men her best rainflower tea.

Grandma's chicken coop version 2, on the southern fringe of Nanjing, was hard to reach due to a sporadic bus schedule. Yet it had remained the nerve center of our clan for almost a quarter of a century, until Grandma's passing five weeks before.

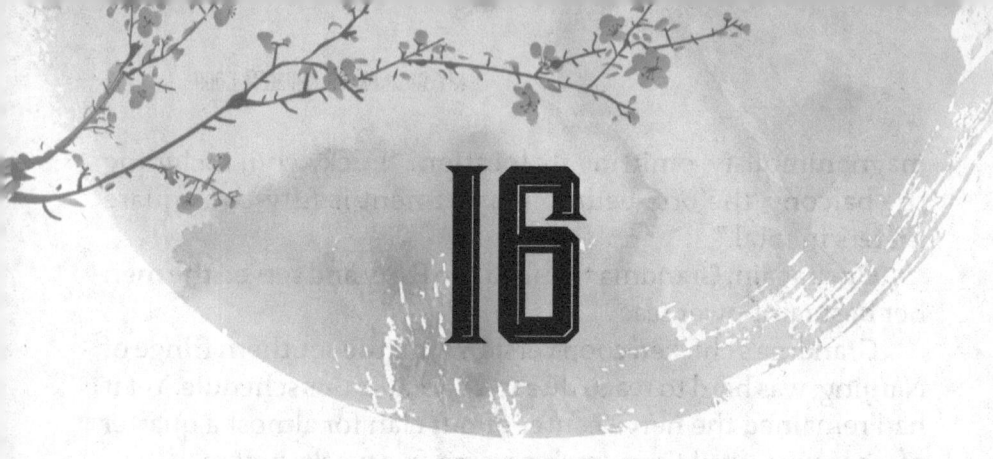

16

MY GRANDMA'S DIARY

Struggling with the worn-out key to Grandma's apartment, my hand was suddenly drained of its strength. In a few days, I would relinquish this communal key and pass it to Binbin. But, with the prospective subway station and the city's relentless radial growth, how soon before someone else would knock on this door? And how long could Binbin, the weakest link of my generation and possibly the last man of our clan, hole up inside?

Before settling in, I called my own family in Boston. To my great disappointment, no one picked up the house phone. The call to Tony's cell phone went unanswered as well. Being a pharmaceutical rep responsible for a large region, he was probably driving on a rural road somewhere in New England.

I brooded in the chicken coop. Upon close inspection, the mismatched furniture consisted entirely of hand-me-downs acquired from my uncle and aunts over the years. On the peeling wall, a thirty-two-inch flat-screen TV appeared out of place. Apparently, "Old Panda"—the bulky black-and-white tube—had finally expired. Under its flickering glow, we used to watch the evening news or laugh at the imperial melodrama while Grandma rubbed essential oils all over her aching joints. Later, we'd all pledged to pay for an upgrade at one point or the other. "Nah, it isn't broken yet." To demonstrate, Grandma would stagger out of her armchair to give a whack on Panda's side. Sure enough, the blurry-eyed beast would jolt out of hibernation for a few minutes. "My buddy and I doze off after meals. That's all."

With the same stubbornness, Grandma repeatedly brushed off the cataract surgeries that her doctors recommended. "I can see," she insisted. "Why do I need perfect vision? I no longer cook or sew."

Once, I painstakingly explained the ten-minute procedure over the phone. Then, I cajoled, "Be brave, *popo*. Only a few days of inconvenience."

"I know. Your aunts have told me the same."

"Is it the cost then? I can help with the medical bills."

"No need," she boasted. "I haven't had a single operation in my whole life. So let me enter my grave with an unmolested body."

Ultimately, in a willpower wrestling match, nobody was her equal.

A faint floral scent wafted through the air, phantomlike. I inhaled deeply. Of course—the white daffodil essential oil emitted from the disintegrating armchair. Then I detected an undertone of a stale, greasy odor—from decades-worth of cooking in the poorly ventilated kitchen.

Entering the galley kitchen, the size of my walk-in closet in South Boston, I remembered our past holiday gatherings: Days before, Grandma would stock up on *nianhuo*, the special goods for the lunar New Year. On *the* big day, one of my aunts scaled carp over the sink; another wielded a formidable cleaver over a thick section of tree-trunk (Grandma's cutting board), mincing pork with *shanyao* for meatballs; someone in charge of the ten-vegetable medley might dash to the market at the last minute for a missing leek or golden-lily petals; Grandma banged the wok and various pots with gusto, mopping the sweat streaming down her forehead with a towel. With choreographed precision, the Hong women maneuvered around each other in this claustrophobic space, churning out dish after delicious dish. Now the chef was gone, and the kitchen was quiet. Nevertheless, her recipes had been passed down to her daughters, granddaughters, and perhaps someday her great-granddaughters, too.

Once, Grandma taught me to make sweet lotus cake. First, she scraped off the rough skin of a lotus root with the grooved edge of a coin, then sectioned off the ends, and cleaned each air shaft with a quill. After filling the cavities with sticky rice and osmanthus blossom preserved in honey, she capped the ends with toothpicks and loaded the stuffed roots onto a bamboo steamer. Twenty minutes later, a sweet, heavenly fragrance suffused the entire kitchen. When the tip of her probing chopstick sank in effortlessly, she wiped it on her apron and announced, "Done!"

Watching her slicing the lotus root for plating, I brushed the quill on my finger and swallowed loudly. A thought came to me. "*Popo*, did you learn all these tricks from your mama?"

"No, from trial and error," she admitted with embarrassment. "You see, I never entered any kitchen until almost ten years after marrying your *gonggong*."

"Why didn't you cook for him from the beginning?"

"Well, we used to have an excellent cook."

Staring at her with an open mouth, I thought that she could convincingly play the role of a cook instead of the lady of the house in a movie. Unlike Grandpa, Grandma always brushed away my inquiries about her past.

Then, during the reforming eighties, I happened upon an article about the resurrection of the antique market in *Shanghai Daily*. It dawned on me that almost everything in Grandpa's house was antique. At the time, I was annoyed by those odd-shaped and overly decorated pieces of fine bone china. I even envied my classmates for their indestructible plastic cups. Through everyday use, Isha and I had chipped many of these fussy bowls and plates. Once, I broke a ginger jar on New Year's Eve. To my surprise, Grandma announced cheerfully, "*Shui shui ping an!*"—a broken porcelain rings in a peaceful and safe year.

After reading that newspaper article, I remembered the bonfire in our courtyard. Then, I recalled that a few heavy pieces of furniture had survived—the Red Guards gave them up after some struggles. So, I called Grandma, "I'm just curious, what happened to your camphor chest—the carved one with mother-of-pearl inlay?"

"Ah," she laughed. "Remember the time when Isha hid in the chest? Good thing your *gonggong* heard her tapping. I gave her a good chiding, didn't I?" Then she said dismissively, "Carpenter Luo probably took it when we left for the commune. Who knows?"

I was speechless. If not for Isha's mishap, that piece from her dowry set would not have even any sentimental value to her.

A bigger surprise surfaced when I brought Tony to Nanjing to meet my clan for the first time. "How do you do?" Grandma gracefully arched her old maid's hand and greeted Tony in English—with a Southern drawl. Aunt No. 3 spilled her tea.

I exclaimed, "I didn't know you could speak English!"

"Only a little." She blushed. The truth turned out that she had once attended a missionary school; her English teacher was a lady from Macon, Georgia. During the years when nothing good could ever come out of even the loosest association with the imperialist USA, naturally she'd hidden her secrets well.

A worn desk was tucked in the corner of Grandma's bedroom. Underneath its glass top, photos were arranged in spirals. In the center was me in my doctoral regalia, beaming from an ocean of purple and white—the jubilant crowds in front of the Washington Square Arch.

Below my photo was a smiling Grandma among blooming dahlias on her balcony, dwarfed by Tony, our twins, and me. This photo was taken during our visit six summers before my present visit. Soon afterward, her cognitive decline accelerated excruciatingly. Starting the previous autumn, she would abruptly interrupt our shortened phone conversations with hesitation, "Now, child, tell me who you are again?"

A water-stained group photo caught my attention: my grandparents stood in our courtyard, flanked by Little Aunt and a grinning Rei on the left, and me and sulking Isha on the right. Half of our faces were black. I felt a sharp sting in my eyes as if I was still squinting against the noon sun: three of my loved ones in the photo were gone.

I lifted up the glass top to pilfer the unflattering photo. Grandma's reading glasses, which were still perched on the desk's upper-right corner, skidded forward. Seeing them, a compliment she once paid me rushed to my mind.

On my first day at school, the blackboard was a whitish blur from my assigned seat in the last row. Unknown to us, I had inherited my father's myopia. Grandpa took me to an optical shop in midtown. Once home, I stared at the mirror with horror—I'd disappeared behind the big, black frame. The two deep dents on the shallow bridge of my nose smarted, and I felt blue for the first time.

"Mei, you look like a learned scholar now!" Grandma exclaimed. "One day, you'll go to college, maybe even earn a PhD!"

Through my new glasses, I saw that she was regarding me with glistening eyes. Then, dabbing away tears with the back of her knuckles, she murmured, "How Grandma envies you! The five-and-a-half years of my schooling were the happiest time of my life . . ."

Fast forward to New Year's Eve, 1990. After I reported to Grandma from New York about my successful defense on the oral exam, the line went quiet. "Hello, are you still there?" I pressed the receiver more tightly to my ear. Then I heard a muffled sobbing from the opposite side of the globe.

A moment later, she collected herself. "Congratulations to the first PhD of the Hong family! This is the happiest news I've ever heard."

Another two decades had passed since that day. Closing my eyes, I wished she had been born in a different country or a different time. Then I saw her in her doctoral gown, hood, and that pair of burnt high heels, climbing solemnly onto a stage. Everyone in the packed auditorium applauded, cheering her on. I whistled the loudest from the front seat. She turned to beam at me, waving my diploma—a piece of gilded cardboard that she'd always cherished.

Retractable ballpoint pens were comingled with sewing kits in the desk's top drawer. Among those touched by Grandma's arthritic hands, I recognized the two I had given her, one with the logo of Fudan University and the other with that of NYU.

The lower drawers contained stacks of Grandma's diaries. In the past, I'd peeked at some of the entries after she jotted them down. In truth, these diaries were mundane social calendars of the Hong clan over the years. Birthdays of her five children, six grandchildren, and four great-grandchildren; anniversaries; visits from her offspring; overseas phone calls from Isha and me; and the occasional delight of encountering an old neighbor in the Confucius Temple.

In the booklet from the very top of the stack, her hand-writing had deteriorated rapidly towards the end. The last entry, recorded on her wedding anniversary three years before, had only one shaky line: *August 1st, 2009. Overcast. Thirty-two degrees Celsius.* Then, an ink blot bloomed from a hesitant pen, like a black dahlia.

I opened my laptop. The file labeled "Grandma" contained mere snippets, like a collage of scattered thoughts about her. Now, with the aid of her diary, I tried to stitch together a more coherent story.

When my grandma was still a toddler, her father passed away. Her affluent yet backward uncles took charge of the finances for the widow and two fatherless children. They often commented, "Why bother sending the girl to school? Once we marry her off, she is as valuable as discarded dishwater. To improve her prospects, better to set aside the money for her dowry."

One winter morning, her older brother saw Grandma blow on the window to melt the frost. Noticing how desperately she gazed at two girls in starched uniforms and fancy boots— her former playmates on their way to school—he said, "Don't be so sad, sister. I promise, as soon as I get the money, I'll send you there, too."

During Nanjing's booming decade, her brother apprenticed in the first photography studio in town. Afterwards, the young entrepreneur opened his own studio in the nascent factory district. Soon, as every new hire needed a picture ID, and a trend of announcing weddings with the newlyweds' pictures in the newspaper caught on, his business exploded.

When she turned ten, Grandma's dream finally came true.

Alas, only five and a half years later, the missionary school was disbanded at the eve of the Japanese invasion. And Grandma's family fled town.

For the first month after the siege of Nanking, no one dared to leave their isolated village. Then, one morning, Grandma's brother insisted on a reconnaissance trip to the closest town. Mounting his bike, he promised his beloved sister, "Be back by noon."

But he failed to return as promised. Another two hours passed. Tired of pacing and reheating her son's lunch, my great-grandma decided to consult a relative in a village a mile away.

At the gate, Grandma glued her gaze on the hillside village. Soon the tepid winter sun slanted behind the knoll, the valley wind picked up, and her padded cotton coat felt porous. In the distance the cluster of thatched roofs turned dark, and she couldn't make out any white smoke from the chimneys. A dog barked incessantly, yet the entire village seemed to hold its breath. Gritting her teeth, Grandma finally mustered her courage to venture out. Before leaving home, she scooped out a handful of ashes from the oven. As a precaution, she smeared the ash over her face, neck, and hands, methodically applying the wartime reverse cosmetics.

Arriving at the relative's house, Grandma paused at the woven-twig gate, then shrieked. Three corpses were haphazardly strewn in the courtyard: her mother, a man, and a dog. Under the twilight, their pink intestines glistened above a dark reflective pool. The wife kneeled in front of the slashed body of her man, pounding her forehead on the soiled ground; her disheveled hair was matted with splattered red gel; her breasts, half-exposed through her torn winter coat, bounced with each silent bout of wailing. Behind her, the kitchen door swung back and forth in the piercing wind, squeaking like exclamation marks.

Tears flooded down Grandma's smudged face. Wrapping her arms around the woman, she begged, "Aunty Qiujiu, stop, please, stop."

Grandma never found out what had happened to her brother. Months later, an acquaintance spotted a rusty bicycle in a roadside ditch a few miles outside Nanjing. Its top tube—engraved with her brother's name—was twisted like a pretzel, and its tires and saddle were missing.

During the hushed funeral, the villagers speculated on the increasingly frequent Japanese excursions into remote villages; Nanjing had been more or less "secured."

After a fruitless search for Grandma's uncles, the villagers hid Grandma among tall baskets in a cabbage cart and smuggled her into a refugee camp inside the Nanking Safety Zone.

Two months later, Grandma's remaining uncles came to claim her. Those men, who had declared it an unnecessary luxury to educate a fatherless girl in peacetime, fretted about the burden of keeping a fifteen-year-old orphan safe during the war. So, they instructed their wives to thoroughly delouse her in preparation for a quick marriage.

The matchmaker showed Grandma's picture around town to a severely shrunken stock of eligible bachelors. She ceremoniously curled her pinky around her teacup to draw attention to a sizable jade ring. Clearing her throat, she said, "In our troubled times, a girl as pure as jade is a rarity." She had banked on the effect of the jade—a euphemism for unmolested girls—to counter her client's severe shortcoming of having an insufficient dowry. The patriarchs of the (often-truncated) families winced, nodding with downcast eyes. But, war or peace, life must go on.

Somehow, Ping-An immediately recognized the girl in the photo as the younger sister of a friend who was still missing. He had seen the preteen Grandma once in passing. Hao-Ran, recovering from his first stroke, approved the union. The future daughter-in-law had more formal education than his son. Hence, as soon as Ping-An rebuilt the first courtyard of the torched ancestral house, he married Grandma.

Grandma kept a skeletal recording of milestone events in her decades-long diary. The only exception was her cousin Yin's wedding. She had described the minutest details of that prewar fanfare: A deafening marching band and firecrackers heralded a mile-long procession from her uncle's house to the groom's. Yin, properly concealed in a red silk veil, a traditional gown, and embroidered platform shoes, rode the wedding sedan on four strong men's shoulders, followed by a caravan of her dowry on display. The bride's entourage brought up the rear, tossing wedding candies to the cheering neighbors and clamoring children. In the ancestral hall, after Yin and the groom bowed to heaven, the earth, and the forebears' nameplates on an altar table, then to each other, the groom unveiled the bride. He sighed with relief—this was the first time he had laid his eyes upon her. After the traditional ceremony, Yin squeezed into a white gown for a Western-style photo session, and Grandma helped her to button up. For the all-night banquet, Yin donned yet another red *qipao*, which had taken two seamstresses several months to embroider. Hundreds of rowdy guests, children in tow, shouted and cackled, demanding that the newlyweds perform the tricky task of emptying their liquor cups while keeping their drinking arms locked. The guests refused to leave until being thoroughly entertained.

As for her own wedding a year later, Grandma wrote only a few bitter lines. Her humble outfit consisted of a poor-fitting, hand-me-down bridal *qipao* and jewelry from her late mother. Her uncles didn't buy enough liquor to inebriate the scant number of attendees. Everyone rushed home before the curfew, and "Cousin Yin could hardly conceal her glee."

I could speculate as to why Grandma left so much unsaid in her diary about her most important day. As a curious teenager, I once grilled her about her wedding.

"Well, I was an orphan, barely sixteen," she confessed. "Of course I was nervous. The matchmaker said, 'The family is solid; the boy is tall and handsome.' But what if he was also a maniac? An opium addict? A gambler? I couldn't sleep the night before. Then, when your *gonggong* removed my headcover, I saw a pair of kind eyes on an open, smiling face. My heart burst with joy. But his smile froze, then disappeared altogether. Oh, how I wanted to drop dead right there!"

"I felt cheated," Ping-An told her later. His friend's excellent portrait had captured the femininity and resilient spirit of the young girl, but not her height. And the floor-length wedding gown, high-heels, and a six-inch, elaborate headpiece had camouflaged her short stature—until the moment of unveiling.

Grandma's bitterness boiled to the surface again in the diary entry about Aunt No. 2's birth. Supposedly, Ping-An frowned at the crying newborn and said, "When are you going to give me a son?" Then, to rub salt in her wound, Cousin Yin visited, showing off her chubby boy. Grandma forced back tears and complimented Yin's good luck. Fortunately, the patriarch had never given her a hard time. During each of his granddaughters' hundred-day celebrations, Hao-Ran propped the baby up on his lap and proudly announced, "A healthy girl, as precious as any boy!"

In her 1998 diary, Grandma wrote a one-line entry about the banquet she hosted to welcome Tony to the family. Reading it, I started to laugh. Half-drunk on Chinese liquor, Tony—the clueless *laowai*—had the audacity to ask Grandma about her arranged marriage. Grandma admitted that occasionally some old grudges against Grandpa would percolate in her mind. Then she said with a smile, "So what? I'd lived happily with him for thirty-five years."

I teased her, "Is Grandpa your soulmate?"

"Soulmate?" She slapped my wrist lightly with her chopsticks, "Don't *ever* let that silly notion enter your head. You work hard to make your marriage work. If I didn't marry your *gong-gong*, I bet I would have had an equally happy life with a different man."

Everyone except Tony burst out laughing. After I translated the funniest thing Grandma had ever said, to my surprise he raised his tumbler gravely and said, "Thanks for imparting your wisdom. A toast!"

"Thanks, Grandma." I raised my glass, laughing even harder at Tony's feigned maturity.

Continuing to flip through Grandma's diaries, my finger caught something in the notebook from 1952. A rusty paperclip fastened a yellowed photo of a tall vase on a pedestal, surrounded by a dozen giddy men. Near the center was Grandpa, holding a certificate of some sort.

Recognizing the magnificent vase, my heart leaped with joy. Even though I had no inkling of its existence, this photo verified a family legend.

About five years earlier, I'd gotten a phone call from Mother, uncharacteristically happy. She reported her sighting of this vase, now a national treasure, in the newly renovated City Museum of Nanjing. After telling me the story of Grandpa's discovery of the vase, she said, "I'll send you some pictures I took." Then she demanded, "Next time you come to China, you must see it yourself. And bring the twins, too."

The twins. I muttered to myself. Why bother taking them to Shanghai to celebrate the Mid-Autumn Festival with my traitorous father? Scratching this pointless reunion off our crazy itinerary, we could easily squeeze in half a day to see this storied vase, which meant so much to the Hong family.

No one picked up our house phone. I checked my watch—7:28 a.m. Boston time already. I could see my children dumping their cereal bowls into the sink, grabbing their backpacks, and bolting toward the door. Yet again, Tony didn't answer his cell.

The night before, similarly unable to reach Tony, I had only left him a brief message by voicemail. Now everything had become crystal clear. So, I left him another message. "Hey, Tony, a last-minute change. Let's meet in Nanjing instead. The situation in Shanghai is—" I hesitated. "Too delicate—"

A beep cut me off, so I redialed and spelled out the updated logistical details.

Would we be better off if I booked a hotel room near Pudong Airport instead? I resisted the urge to leave yet another convoluted and contradictory message. No matter. Plenty of time to catch Tony before their outbound flight.

Depositing myself in the armchair, a plate of reheated leftovers on my lap, I dove back into Grandma's diary.

17

THE TANGHULU

A strong tremor disrupted my deep sleep. Bleary-eyed, I saw Grandpa's photo vibrating on the opposite wall. *Earthquake!* I jumped out of bed. Before I could grab my laptop, the ground had ceased pulsating. By then, my brain had registered the epicenter of the subterranean rumbling—the subway construction site nearby. Outside the window, a milky mist was thinning. A white-bearded man was perfecting his already fluid tai chi movements in the park diagonally across the street.

It was dinner time in South Boston. Oddly, my phone calls to my family remained unanswered. Had they gone out for pizza or maybe Chinese? My stomach growled. Brushing away a growing unease, I decided to hunt for my own breakfast.

From the street, familiar aromas greeted me: boiling soy milk, yeasty steamed buns, scallion pancakes, and slightly burnt *youtiao*—fried dough shaped like two conjoined cigars. I inhaled deeply. My sinuses were clear and the lingering headaches gone. Then I realized that my headache was from a seasonal allergy flareup while I was still in Boston.

Technically, I shouldn't call Nanjing my hometown because I'd spent more years in Shanghai and then the States. Even so, my immune system still assigned Nanjing as my True North while overzealously rebelling against the purer New England air—laced with abundant pollens from fall meadows and forested hills.

Soon, my unclogged nose tracked down a cluster of mom-and-pop eateries near a bus stop. With each eager step, my craving grew for a puffy, crunchy *shaobing*. This breakfast staple of my childhood was as ubiquitous in China as donuts in the States. Rei and I used to peek into a bakery on our way to school. Ogling the golden-brown crust of sesame on the trays and inhaling deeply the buttery fragrances, we swallowed mouthfuls of saliva. "Don't be late for school," the humming baker said, waving us off, then went back to kneading flour doused with melted duck fat, or slapping the soft dough onto the hot clay oven wall.

No luck in the first two bakeries. In the third, a man was busy loading a tray of uniform dough into a stainless-steel oven. Sticking my head beyond the counter, I called out, "Excuse me, Shifu, where can I get the duck-fat variety?"

The man looked up. "A picky eater!" Mopping his sweaty brow with a washcloth draped over his neck, he said grudgingly, "Try Qifangge near the temple. They might still do it the old-fashioned way."

The plain and generic *shaobing* turned out to be serviceable. But the local yogurt, made with milk from the descendants of the happy German Holsteins in the oldest dairy farm, was a pure and simple joy in a glass bottle. I sucked out the last heavenly molecule with a straw, desiring more. Then I remembered my exciting day ahead: strolling the gourmet street in a few hours, then the evening banquet.

To kill time before meeting Aunt No. 2, I decided to take a bus to the old town.

Under the canopy of the bus stop, three elderly women with false teeth were enthusiastically comparing notes on this year's mooncake selections. Out of the projectile range of their straying spittle, a girl in a school uniform cupped her hands over her friend's ear to whisper. When they snickered, the high color flushing their young cheeks brightened the autumn sky.

With hometown pride swelling in my tender heart, I boarded Bus No. 414—the one with the most meandering route.

After everyone tapped their commuter cards or phones at the entrance, I tendered a ten-yuan bill to the driver with a smile. He groaned and returned to me a pile of small, wrinkly bills and soiled coins—probably from migrants working in the construction sites.

From the empty last row, I spotted new streets with names like Software Boulevard, all lined with thin-limbed ginkgo trees struggling from square grills on sidewalks. Soon the girls got off in front of a trade school for HVAC and iPhone repairs. After the bus crawled into the old town, the widened streets got clogged with double-decker tour buses. I disembarked a few stops ahead of the temple gate.

The old willows were still weeping along the Qinghuai River, but the promenade was packed cheek-by-jowl with tourists. Brightly colored boats bobbed on the green water. The black-and-white houses with the horsehead walls of yesteryear—haphazardly stacked together yet harmonious, like a pastiche of cubist painting—had been replaced by indistinguishable buildings of uniform height, decked out with festive lanterns and banners. A colossal LCD marquee in front of the temple gate was scrolling advertisements for Audi, Diet Coke, and deluxe condos in a skyscraper near the Drum Tower. "Package tours to the Presidential Palace, the Ming Tomb, and Dr. Sun Yat-Sen's mausoleum!" A girl in a duck costume yelled, waving her fliers at me.

I threaded my way through the crowds, feeling like an exhausted extra on a set for a soap opera loosely based in my hometown. Just then, a tap on my shoulder. I turned to find a beaming Aunt No. 2.

"Ready to snack?"

Over the past few decades, snacking has morphed into a competitive sport in a rising country obsessed with food. Along the mile-long gourmet row, vendors shouted from stall after stall, "Come, come, take a look, fabulous Xinjiang lamb skewer!" Or, "Sample our delicious Sichuan *mala* kidney!" Or, "Crunchy

spicy fava beans! Once you start, you can't stop!" The cornu-
copia of smells whetted my appetite.

After the flavorless "flavorful duck-blood pudding", I tried
the "stinky tofu on a stick." The tofu, fried and dipped in a black
hot sauce, lived up to its offensive name, but its soft interior still
lacked the umami I craved. "The Famous Nanjing Snack" had
become globally inclusive. Curry squid, chicken hearts, or pine-
apple cubes—anything grilled on a stick paired surprisingly well
with Tsingtao beer. An obese boy was licking his Häagen-Dazs
cone while his mother wiped his dripping cheeks, whispering,
"Slow down, Baobei."

Sticks of *tanghulu* fanned out of a styrofoam column like
porcupine's quills; red glazed berries glinted under the sun.
I stopped. Aunt No. 2 bought one with her Huawei phone.
"Enjoy," she said, handing me the stick and shaking her head. "I
have sensitive teeth."

I took a careful bite and winced. The coating screamed
of oversaturated high-fructose corn syrup and stinging vinegar. The tiny square of nonabsorbent napkin from the vendor
was a joke, and my sticky fingers itched for Grandpa's sleeve.
Reading my mind, Aunt No. 2 fished out a wad of tissue from
her handy tote.

We found a teahouse on a quieter side street. Huddling over
a pot of pricy, pre-Qingming rainflower tea, I said, "Aunt No. 2,
do you know that my father has remarried?"

"Yes, almost as soon as your mother passed away!" she said,
glaring at the unfurling tea leaves in her cup. The wrinkles
around her tightened mouth deepened.

"How could he?" I muttered, feeling the old, hot prickling
sensation in my eye sockets. Forcing the brimming tide back, I
tilted my head to admire the elegant Zisha teapots on the top
shelves. *Don't sob like an orphan shivering in the cold.*

"I'll never forgive him, but ... he's still your father," said Aunt
No. 2. Then she sighed, handing me another wad of tissue, "Your
mama wasn't an easy woman to live with, you know that."

I gulped down the hot, green liquid, trying to rinse away the
sour taste of *tanghulu* from my tongue.

18

THE HONG
FAMILY BANQUET

Half a block from the Riverside Restaurant, I started to hear the familiar sounds of Hongs' greetings.

My loud family loved feasts, and my homecoming provided a perfect excuse. In the years after the decline of Grandma's vision, the expansion of my relatives' wallets, and the emerging of a new crop of cousins, the Riverside restaurant had become our default gathering place. "This banquet hall has an excellent quality-to-price ratio," Aunt No. 2 explained unnecessarily.

Over the years, the Hong siblings had returned to their hometown like salmon swimming upstream to their birth river. Little Aunt was the last arrival. After fighting Little Liang like a lioness for a divorce, she took her two girls out of the wolf-howling northern wilderness. Being among the "wasted generation" robbed by the Cultural Revolution, she'd raised children on her hairdresser's wage. They used to live in a shack with a corrugated metal roof at the urban–rural frontier, where at night, women in heavy rouge and plastic heels canvassed cracked sidewalks littered with rusty auto parts while ogling the least desirable passing truck drivers. To our relief, my cousins had turned out fine.

Little Aunt arrived at the same time as we did. Next to her plump sister, she looked as lively as a week-old, squeezed lemon. Releasing our embrace, Little Aunt turned to a docile girl one step behind her. She said proudly, "My Shu-Xiang is now a PhD candidate in Economics at Nanjing University."

"Awesome, Shu-Xiang!" I congratulated her enthusiastically. Then, remembering the time when she and her feisty sister dressed in my decade-old, castoff clothing like two "mini-mes," I asked, "Where is Shu-Zhen?"

"Ah, the busy journalist in Beijing. I see my troublemaker on TV occasionally. Can you believe it, she is approaching forty!" Little Aunt sighed, "My girls are only interested in pursuing careers, not husbands. At this rate, I'll never get any grandchildren."

"Ma!" Shu-Xiang said, knotting her shapely brows. "Don't mind her, Cousin Mei. My mother is so old-school."

Seeing her young, blushing face, I had a *déjà vu* moment.

Every Hong except Little Aunt was blessed with solid bones and soprano lungs. In the past, winning a shouting contest had been the only way to get one's point across. Yet the banquet in my honor was subdued—due to the recent passing of Grandma and my father's conspicuous absence, and our raucous cousins turning into dull adults.

Binbin's sadness broke my heart. So, I asked, "Why didn't you bring your fiancé tonight?"

"Don't get me started. Her folks forbid her to come!" He said, his eyes shrinking to dim beads in his puffy panda face. "Yesterday afternoon, I went to the Register of Deeds with all the waivers. Oh, by the way, thank you so much, Cousin Mei. Guess what? The city denied my application, again."

"What?!" Everyone around us cried out.

"A new clerk is in charge. She said our waivers were insufficient. We also need three affidavits to attest to Grandpa's death. Must be from individuals unrelated to us."

"Will this saga never end?!" My uncle said in disgust.

Winking with a businessman's shrewdness, Cousin Ixin said, "Was she angling for some special mooncakes? You know, the festival is right around the corner." Noticing my puzzlement, he assured me, "It's a common practice to stuff things into hallowed mooncakes and hand-deliver them, you know, to grease some palms."

"You mean cash?" I was appalled.

"Cash, jewelry, gold watches, gift cards, membership cards to exclusive clubs . . . use your wildest imagination," Ixin said smugly. "This is China, the second largest economy in the world since 2010."

"Enough, Ixin! She'll never get a cent from us!" Aunt No. 2 exploded. "This isn't how I brought you up."

Everyone looked down at their plates.

Aunt No. 3, the level-headed accountant, said, "This isn't as difficult as it sounds. Let's think of our potential witnesses for the affidavits."

The entire clan brainstormed. Only two people at Grandpa's memorial service four decades earlier had managed to attend Grandma's funeral.

Aunt No. 2 said, "Oh, I ran into Gui-Zhi at the temple a month ago. She's still sharp as a tack."

Little Aunt snorted with contempt. She and her ex-mother-in-law hadn't been on speaking terms in years.

Immediately, Aunt No. 2 waved her dimpled hand and said, "Never mind her. I know two old-timers in a nursing home, still alive and kicking."

"My wedding is only two months away," Binbin muttered warily. "Cousin Mei, you're invited, of course."

"I wish I could attend, but I have *zero* vacation days left." Disheartened by his gloomy face, I said, "Do you have a picture of your fiancée?"

Binbin passed his Huawei phone to me.

So, Aunt No. 2 had been spot-on: the girl was bamboo-stick thin, her ribs countable through a pale-green dress. Even with her auspicious family trait (of producing mostly male offspring,) as the misguided Aunt No. 2 had hoped, the Hong clan's continuity seemed doubtful. Yet, I envied her. With the blessing from our entire tribe, sooner or later she and Binbin would build their nest in Grandma's chicken coop.

We toasted Binbin's imminent conjugal happiness, my safe travels, and everyone's health and wealth.

"Speaking of wealth, Mei, what's your opinion on the ripple effect of the upcoming American election on the Chinese economy?" asked Aunt No. 3's husband. For the entire evening, he had been conversing in the corner with Aunt No. 2's husband about the recent rout of the Shanghai Stock Exchange, which had wiped out the past five years' gains.

"I wish I had a crystal ball," I laughed at this sweeping question. Then I pointed to Shu-Xiang. "Why don't we consult our in-house economist?"

Shu-Xiang spoke softly. "As a matter of fact, there is an excellent analysis in the latest issue of *Chai-Jing*. The gist of the article is: It doesn't matter who will win." She lowered her gaze to the errant napkin on the floor, "Both parties have vested interests in staying the course, and continuing the trajectory of the Sino-American relationship blueprinted by Nixon four decades ago."

"Cheers to Nixon!" Ixin raised his glass.

"Cheers!" Everyone followed.

I joked, "Wow, Nixon's ghost would be relieved to find a fan club here."

Then, the topic shifted to my American kids. I showed them the screensaver of my Samsung Galaxy. It was my twins in front of Castle Island. I snapped that shot on our ice cream stroll to Sullivan's the previous summer, before emerging acne marred their sweet faces.

Predictably, compliments flooded in. Like everywhere else, fair-skinned people enjoyed an unfair advantage in China, where magazine covers were plastered with faces of bean-sprout complexions. Ixin's wife Chun, an ex-model who used to appear in kitchen gadget commercials, still possessed that fluorescent whiteness idolized by the Chinese. When our eyes met, the waning beauty flashed her signature TV smile and asked, "Cousin Mei, do you own a dog?"

"No. Why?"

"Oh," she said, her lips somehow pouted more dramatically than she sounded. "I thought every American household owned dogs. It's getting popular here, too. We just got our Tibetan mastiff."

"Cousin Mei, do you know that's the newest status symbol of wealth?" Binbin smirked. "Well, I'm still working on getting a maximum-security steel door for the middle class."

Mercifully, Ixin intervened, steering us to the safe topic of my research.

"My company is a front-runner on drugs for Alzheimer's," I explained. "Before conducting clinical trials, we must develop models for lab testing. That's my area."

The banquet hall became quiet, with Grandma on everyone's mind.

"Aunty Mei, you work with models?" chirped Yuanyuan, Ixin's preteen daughter, inclining her tiara-adorned head.

While Chun smiled at her daughter, Ixin said, "Yuanyuan, don't butt into adults' conversation."

"That's quite all right," I said. "My models aren't pretty like your mom. They are transgenic mice with APP mutation—altogether different kinds of poor creatures." Seeing the twinkles diminishing in Yuanyuan's sparkling eyes, I added in a hurry, "However, they're allowed to eat to their heart's content."

Everyone laughed, but Yuanyuan coquettishly pouted her lips and said in English, "Yuck, mice! That's not hot!"

Her tone and expression were an unmistakable imitation of Paris Hilton. I was amused to hear that trademarked American phrase "That's hot" amended by her. Technically, western TV, YouTube, and Google were all banned in China. So, Ixin must have installed a VPN at home. I chuckled, "It's a disappointment to me, too. Sadly, my mice refuse to behave."

Ixin, an inquisitive man who had built up his own gaming software company after college, took my bait. He asked, "How so?"

"Well, they failed to demonstrate the predicted symptoms of cognitive decline. Cute as they are in Disney, mice are lousy animal models for primates—I mean, for us humans."

Aunt No. 3 commented with sympathy, "Bummer. I hope you didn't waste too much time on this project."

"Even a negative result isn't a waste of time in research. Besides," I boasted, "we just started a novel approach in this field: creating a human brain organoid by building a 3D model of neural networks from stem cells."

"Wow, sounds like science fiction!" Ixin's eyes lit up.

"Hey, maybe I should consult you on computer-generated 3D modeling." As soon as the words left my lips, though, I froze. I was in no position to propose this kind of collaboration. Simultaneously, I thought of Rei. How could I forget the hefty price he'd paid for a similar, well-intentioned mistake?

"Sure thing."

"For heaven's sake, spare us your technical talk, would you?" Aunt No. 2 goaded Ixin with maternal pride. Her timely interruption rescued me and saved the rest from drowning in boredom. "Now, listen to this: Mei showed me a picture she found in Grandma's diary."

Dutifully, I whipped out my trusty Samsung again and brought up a picture I had taken the night before—of the old vase photo.

"Ahh, the Yuan vase discovered by *bobo*!" Aunt No. 3 said, pointing to the paper in Grandpa's hand. "And that certificate was for his donation of this national treasure to the city museum." Immediately, her husband craned his neck to peer over her shoulder.

Ixin zoomed in on the certificate. "Don't bother," I told him, "You can't read it even in the original photo."

My uncle teased Little Aunt, "You were still in diapers when the photo was taken. But we all touched the vase with our own hands for good luck."

"That's right," Aunt No. 2 chuckled. "*Bobo* made you wash your dirty hands first."

Binbin groaned, "Why didn't he keep the treasure for us?"

"The vase was unearthed by a clueless tomb raider," Aunt No. 3 explained. "By law, no individual was supposed to trade or keep it."

Everyone took turns admiring the vase in the photo. While Aunt No. 2 told us the story of how Grandpa orchestrated a rescue operation to prevent the desperado from smuggling it overseas, I had another *déjà vu*. Mother had told me the same story, albeit in a more imperia tone.

Seeing the great interest among my cousins, I retrieved an archived article from my phone. I found it the night before in the "Treasure Trove" section of *China Daily*, USA version.

After fumbling in her oversized tote for reading glasses, Aunt No. 2 read it aloud.

At the beginning of the article, the author reported "a record-breaking $34 million auction price at the Christie, London in 2005" for a blue-and-white Yuan Dynasty vase titled *Gui Gu Xia Shan Tu*. Then, he compared it to the vase that Grandpa discovered, and quoted Mr. Ma Weidu, a renowned porcelain connoisseur and founder of the Guanfu Museum. According to Mr. Ma, "The decoration on this superior vase in Nanjing is multi-layered and unique, emanating brilliant artistry..."

Aunt No. 3's husband whistled upon hearing the city museum's insurance price for its Yuan vase.

At the end of the article, the author claimed that a certain Mr. Chui, a local collector, had bought the vase with ten gold bars when it appeared at an antique market in Nanjing. Supposedly, Mr. Chui hid the vase in his home until he donated it to the city museum in 1953.

Aunt No. 2 snorted, "What laughable bullshit! If that's true, then Chui should have ended up in jail for hiding the vase. Yes, he did contribute to the rescue fund, but so did almost every antique dealer in Nanjing at the time. The donation list was quite long—Grandpa, Li Shoutong, Chen Cibei, Wang Nejie, and our friend 'Chui Dafa' . . ." Thrusting the phone back to me, she continued venting, "For an entire evening, your mother recorded every donor's name and amount, and I sorted and tallied all the loose bills!"

She talked faster and louder with simmering agitation. "A few years after the donation, the director of the city museum told Grandpa about an opening for a curator's position. Guess what—Grandpa recommended Chui!"

"Why?" Ixin asked.

"He considered that ambitious young lad his protégé."

My uncle scoffed, "So typical! A good deed never goes unpunished in China. Two years ago, I saw an even more malicious article in the *Yangtze Evening News*. It claimed that a few lawless, crooked merchants had bought the vase from a tomb raider. The tomb raider was sentenced to death, and the crooks went to jail."

Aunt No. 2 exploded. "A lawless crook! Who could defend *Bobo*'s name now? Everyone involved is dead—his colleagues, the officials from the municipal office." She paused to catch her breath and palmed her contorted face which had turned ambulance-red. I panicked. At any moment, she might pop an engorged vessel and suffer the same fate as Grandpa and Great-Grandpa.

"Let's sue the son of a bitch for defamation!" Binbin declared, pounding his fist on the table. Hot tea spilled out, racing dangerously toward his crotch. At the same time, his mother and Little Aunt dove forward from his flanks, rescuing his family jewels with napkins.

Aunt No. 3 turned to my uncle and asked, "Did the author specifically point the finger at *Bobo*?"

"No. *Bobo* wasn't even mentioned anywhere in the article."

"There you go," she continued calmly. "I read that article, too. In fact, I called the museum and managed to reach a sympathetic director. According to him, the original documents on the vase acquisition were lost during the Cultural Revolution. The only thing in their files is a handwritten statement by Mr. Chui—their employee of many years. Nevertheless, a correction could be made if we provide the original donor list and the city's Certificate of Appreciation."

Aunt No. 2 cried out, "Who would have kept that sixty-year-old junk? We've thrown away far more important papers. Just look at the mess with Ma's chicken coop!"

"Let bygones be bygones," My uncle said, rubbing his gray beard. "Remember, Binbin, we little potatoes don't need glory and recognition."

But it's about Grandpa, not us! I strongly disagreed with my uncle on principle. Complacency toward one humiliation would only invite more. But how could we dispute the authors' false claims? Grandma had jotted down a line about the vase donation in the diary—circumstantial evidence at best. And the certificate in the old photo was too small and blurry. I bit my tongue. My turn to impart wisdom in a tribal meeting would probably be years to come.

"To peace and tranquility," Aunt No. 3 said rationally, raising her glass. "That's all we could wish for."

"We should go see the vase," Su-Xiang ventured shyly from her corner. "That would make Grandpa happy."

"Great idea, a toast!" I raised my glass, now determined to bring my twins along.

❧

Sumptuous meals would always perversely trigger the Hong clan's memories of their bleakest years. As the night mellowed, we shifted to this inexhaustible topic. For the umpteenth time, my kin relished a story:

On a New Year's Eve, Grandma divided a precious sardine seven ways—head for Grandpa, tail for herself, and each child got a fifth of the belly. Before anyone could devour his or her portion, the mean cat leaped to the table and snatched the juiciest part from my uncle's bowl, leaving him whimpering all evening.

"Nowadays, I won't touch sardines even if they're free." My uncle made a face, then chuckled heartily. "We eat well. Just last month, we spent a fortune at that new Italian restaurant—what's its name, Binbin?" Seeing raised eyebrows around the table, he added, "We went there for Binbin's thirty-fifth birthday."

Red to the neck, Binbin said, "My fiancée's idea."

"How was the food?" Aunt No. 2 perked up.

"Ha! A rip-off!" My uncle snorted. "They charge an arm and leg for dishes made of flour, tomato, and garlic. Linguini, spaghetti, tagliatelle... Call it by a hundred different fancy names, but everything tastes the same to me!"

"They did give us lots of freebies, like, bread, extra-virgin olive oil, and shaved cheese and fresh ground peppercorns," my uncle's wife said, trying to justify their splurge.

"Don't forget, you also pay for the ambiance. I heard their Murano chandeliers alone cost tens of thousands," Chun chimed in, winking at me knowingly. Twice tonight, I noticed, she had taken out a cosmetic mirror from her Chanel tote to apply a quick dab as if preening for a curtain call.

"Ambiance my ass," my uncle groaned. Then, pointing his chopsticks at a chunk of braised meat in a bowl, glistening like amber, he said, "Look at this gorgeous *dong-po* pork. Now that's honesty."

Everyone laughed. I wondered, *what would Tony say to defend his beloved Italian food if he were here?*

My uncle's satiated face triggered my memory of another feast at Grandma's apartment years earlier.

"Had I been properly fed, I would have been as tall as *bobo*," my uncle said after a burp, massaging his belly.

"You certainly don't look the part of the malnourished," Aunt No. 2 sneered.

All the children at the crammed kiddie table giggled.

Then Mother threw us a stern look. My face burned. How could we forget about Aunt No. 2's baby girl who was starved to death?

"What a shame!" Grandma wept, dabbing the corners of her eyes. "Even with a big courtyard like ours, none of us ever thought of raising chickens for eggs, or growing bok choy in the flower garden. We were indeed social parasites . . ." By then, she'd acquired a pair of knobby hands and some agriculture skills through her reeducation in the commune, and she genuinely believed in that labeled stigma.

Outside, firecrackers were in full blast. From the decade-old Panda TV above our heads, a cheerful duo announced at a state gala, "Happy New Year!"

Mother killed the conversational lull. "Well, Hong Mei is as tall as me now. Soon, Binbin will be taller than his *bobo.*" She raised her glass. "Cheers to our next generation!"

"*Gang-Bei!*" we echoed.

The same crowd at tonight's banquet had all expanded in size. Aunt No. 2 deftly rotated the jumbo lazy Susan and positioned the famous Nanjing salted duck right in front of me, the guest of honor to her right. Picking out a choice piece of breast meat and depositing it on my plate, she said, "Eat, eat. You won't find anything like this in Boston."

Indeed, the duck was tender, juicy, and flavorful.

For the entire evening, Little Aunt had been the quietest one. When our gazes met across the table, she said, "Mei, have you talked to Rei recently?"

"I . . . I haven't." The half-eaten duck meat slipped out of my chopsticks and landed on my plate.

"Mei doesn't even have time to talk to Isha, let alone Rei," said Aunt No. 2, sounding annoyed. But she didn't know that I was closer to Rei than her daughter.

When the toddler Rei and I started terrorizing the butterflies in our courtyard, Isha was still a sleeping baby; Aunt No. 2 was teaching in a remote village then; and Little Aunt, a budding adolescent, was attending the middle school nearby.

Above us, the chandelier suddenly flickered as if trying to send me a message in Morse code. Unable to correct Aunt No. 2, nor tell Little Aunt the truth, I pressed my back against my chair.

"What's wrong, Mei?" said Aunt No. 2, alarmed.

I could only mutter, "I'm not used to eating so much rich food."

"I see." She snapped her fingers at the waitress, asking her to fetch me a fresh cup of oolong tea.

The hot tea scalded my lips, but I deserved the punishment. I'd just told my aunts a white lie.

19

REI AND MEI

Little Aunt would be crushed by Rei's tragedy, I was certain. Since day one, she had been particularly fond of that rambunctious boy.

Whenever her school had a free-movie day, Little Aunt would fetch Rei and me first. Then, hand in hand, the three of us would walk three blocks to the Red Star Cinema.

Back then, only eight "exemplary" Peking operas and a handful of war movies were approved by Madame Mao for the eight hundred million Chinese. As a result, we had seen each of these mandatory movies at least half a dozen times. Little Aunt could sing all the tunes from start to end. Even at the fervent zenith of the Cultural Revolution, gun-toting factions would occasionally declare a cease-fire for two hours of peaceful coexistence in the dark. Anytime Japanese soldiers were blown up by a landmine or a hand grenade—usually in a hilarious, cartoonish style—we clapped our hands thunderously. The best part of the movie was always the treats that Little Aunt bought with pocket money she had squirreled away: candied kumquats, cured olives, and neon-bright popsicles.

Often, short documentaries heralded those familiar features. Yet even those clips were predictable: a smiling Chairman Mao shook hands with visiting foreign leaders while surrounding children waved flowers and sang, "Welcome, welcome, Regent

Prince Sihanouk!" or the names and titles of some other third-world dignitaries. At the time, I'd envied those lucky kids basking under Chairman Mao's ruddy radiance.

Only one film of my childhood was memorable—in fact, haunting. It was a documentary on the excavation of a Shang Dynasty royal tomb. After the camera surveyed the marvelously carved bronze sarcophagus in the somber chamber, it panned into the surrounding burial pits. Blinding whiteness flooded the screen—piles and piles of stacked skeletons! We screamed. Clutching Little Aunt's clammy palm with one hand, I covered my eyes with the other and peeked through the finger gaps.

The sacrificial slaves were bound in various torturous poses. When the lens zoomed sadistically into a fractured skull with dark eye sockets and a menacing, toothy smile, everyone gasped again, and I shut my eyes. No use. The gruesome image lingered behind my clamped eyelids, sending chills down my spine.

On a sweltering August afternoon, I sneaked out of my bed. The adults and Isha were taking their siestas. A chorus of snores fanned out of the open windows in our courtyard.

As a spirited five-year-old, I stalked our cat, which was in turn stalking a dragonfly with droopy wings. Then, a shadow flashed in the corner of my vision.

A topless boy was teetering toward me. Thrusting a wooden toy sword, he shouted, "Surrender!"

Chasing after the boy, a pale woman waved a white shirt in hysteria. "Stop, Rei! Don't hurt the little sister . . ."

I giggled. Hurting me? This kid could barely run! He was a foot shorter; his sweaty ribs dripped like Grandma's washboard. Under the blistering sun, his dense, jet-black hair glinted a metallic blue.

Hearing my laughter, he halted his momentum. Then, he broke out a lopsided smile, showing a big gap among an untidy row of milk teeth.

Since that day Rei and his mother had lodged in our west wing. With their arrival, the roster of our permanent guests was bloated to nine people. Everyone was transplanted from the North except Carpenter Luo and old Li, the original renters.

In the following three years, Rei's mother, a quiet nurse in the nearby hospital, spoke fewer than two dozen sentences to me.

Once, Rei showed me a photo of a handsome young officer in a starched uniform. "My dad," he announced proudly. However, in person his father was a wrinkly man with salt-and-pepper hair, more ancient than Grandpa. Whenever the old man visited, which was rare, Rei's mother would send Rei to us in the evening. Grandma always tucked him in my twin bed, head to toe. "Why my bed? I hate to smell Rei's stinky feet!" I protested. Grandma hushed me. "He won't be here long." Sure enough, Rei's father had never stayed more than three nights.

One winter night, I woke up with a cold back. Our shared quilt had migrated to the soundly asleep Rei. Furiously, I wrenched the quilt from under him and wrapped it tightly around me. The following day, unfortunately, he came down with a sore throat and I had to face Grandma's wrath.

After his nose stopped running, Rei returned as usual, the way our cat clung to its default sunbathing spot in front of our shed. He probably couldn't have helped it, but with his silly grin, Rei had a way of ingratiating himself with my grandparents and charming Little Aunt.

"Before you go to bed, brush your teeth, and wash your face, hands, and feet. And don't forget your butt." While scrubbing us every night, Grandma always repeated her claim that "every Chinese does this."

One night during one of Rei's involuntary intrusions, I noticed something strange when Grandma hovered over a basin of warm water, with buck-naked Rei on one arm, a washcloth on the other.

Between his splayed legs was a hidden object: a pinky-sized protrusion dangling like a broken teapot spout. Somehow, this offended me. Pointing, I said, "What's that yucky thing?"

Grandma chuckled, then straightened her face. "Mei, look away. Don't be rude. Boys have them; girls don't."

"Yeah! Do you have a *jiji*? Show me if you've got one," Rei egged me on, relishing a rare triumph.

After hanging out with me for a year by now, Rei ought to have known better than to challenge me! Narrowing my eyes and wrinkling my nose, I racked my brain for something nasty to say. Finally, I shouted, "I didn't want it! Only an idiot would want to own such an ugly thing!" While trying to maintain my facade of supremacy over him, I was panic- stricken. Grandma's words had whipped me: I had a deficiency. Would this strange thing sprout out if I wished for it?

"Stop bickering, children. It's bedtime." Grandma patted Rei dry and sprinkled a fresh coat of baby powder on him. Instantly, that anatomical oddity turned into a whitish, monstrous lump.

The entire courtyard was our playground, except the forbidden area near the fence. The storage shed was off-limits, too. We often peeked into it anyway: dusty lumber, bags of hardened mortar, and crate after crate of unsold knickknacks from Grandpa's antique shop. The rest belonged to Carpenter Luo and spiders.

In warm weather, Carpenter Luo kept the shed door open. His rhythmic sawing, the scent of fresh sawdust, and fine particles dancing in the sunlight lured us like catnip for cats. We inched closer. Coils of wood shavings spewed out of his planer and scattered around his bench like honey-hued confetti; planks were cut into interlocking pieces; after he joined them together, *voilà!* Dressers for brides, cradles for babies, and occasional coffins.

Carpenter Luo spent more time smoking than working. *Pong! Pong! Pong!* After hitting his wooden pipe against the fence post, he refilled the emptied bowl with tobacco filaments from a waist pouch. Puffing out a cloud, he gazed at our wasteland like a melancholy philosopher.

That telltale whacking sounded like an open invitation for us. We sneaked in to inspect his giant jigsaw puzzles. We admired his tools. The most fascinating one was the diamond-tipped glass cutter. Whenever he caught us, he would raise his shiny pipe to threaten us, cursing in a dialect too thick to understand.

Infrequently, he would pat Rei's velvety hair with his calloused hand, murmuring nonsensically, his furrowed forehead ironing out a bit.

One day, he even showed us how to mark his cuts—with a magical flick of his ink line. Taking advantage of his uncommon good humor, Rei left many black smudges on the scrap. But when I reached for this new toy, Carpenter Luo barked, "Don't dirty your hands! Here." He handed me a consolation prize—his boring level.

From time to time, Carpenter Luo would disappear for a few days. The shed would be locked, with pieces of torn paper money pasted on the windowpanes from inside. When I asked Grandma about this peculiar phenomenon, she shook her head and muttered, "Poor Hua Hudie. Full moon again."

"Hua Hudie?" What did the beautiful image of a butterfly flitting among flowers have to do with Carpenter Luo?

"Never mind." Grandma said, dismissing me with two pieces of plum candy. "Now go, share one with Isha."

It was Rei who told me a horrible story. Supposedly, a mad woman had been living in Carpenter Luo's room adjacent to the shed. She slept during the day and emerged at night, wandering barefoot among the brambles behind the fence. On full-moon nights, she would rip up Carpenter Luo's meager paper bills, and stuff the pieces into a chamber pot full of her feces. Laughing at the moon, she would try to yank out her messy hair with her six-inch-long, filthy fingernails. Poor Carpenter Luo, awakened by her howling, had to slap her left and right till she collapsed. Then he had to wash and dry the pieces and tape them back together into circulatable currency. He had dragged that loony to a hospital many times "No, not the one where my mother works." Nothing helped. Eventually, he just locked her up in a village hut during these episodes.

"You made this up," I laughed. "I've never seen such a mad woman."

"Why should I do such a thing?!" Rei said indignantly.

"To scare me."

"Come, see it for yourself."

As we walked past the guest kitchen, I saw Carpenter Luo squatting in front of the stove, smoking and stirring a simmering clay pot. The bitter, pungent odors from his herbal medicines overpowered the sharp stench of his cheap tobacco.

Thick curtains blocked out the window of Carpenter Luo's room. Rei rattled the doorknob. Then he tapped the locked door. No response.

Standing on tiptoe, I peeked through the keyhole. The room was dark, and I couldn't make out anything. Straining my ears, I heard nothing either. Relieved, I said to Rei, "Liar!"

"Like I told you, she's sleeping right now," Rei cried out. "Come back tonight!"

"Ha! You know Grandma would never let me wander at night."

Just then, Carpenter Luo rushed back with his pot and chased us away with his harsh curses.

Still, after hearing Rei's tall tale, I always cringed whenever intriguing patterns of torn bills appeared on the shed window.

It was also on such a money-laundering day that we discovered that new world. After crawling through the gap created by the collapsed fence bottom, Rei started digging up a half-buried terracotta jug with his wooden sword; I stood by, touched by the beauty of our wasteland.

In my peripheral vision a shadow slithered on the ground. I turned, screaming: a five-foot-long snake, black with yellow bands.

"What's the matter?" Rei dashed toward me, abandoning his excavation.

I couldn't utter a word.

The snake raised its triangular head and hissed with a forked tongue, training its sinister eyes on me.

Rei charged forward with his trusty sword. "Kill!"

"No!" I cautioned him, flinching. "Back off!"

Before the snake could retreat into the jungle, Rei tripped over a loose brick, flopped to the ground in the fashion of a Japanese soldier in war movies, and landed on the tip of his sword. Blood gushed out of his chin.

I pressed my handkerchief on the gash, the way our heroes did for their dying comrades. Rei was turning pale in front of my eyes. I began to cry. *He would die soon, just like in movies.*

By the time Grandpa kicked down the fence, the handkerchief had been soaked through with blood. Carrying Rei on his back, Grandpa ran to the nearby hospital where Rei's mother worked. Grandma and I ran after them.

After a few stitches and a tetanus shot in the ER, Rei's mother took him to the Hemorrhoid Clinic, where she still had two hours left on her shift. She blew out a latex glove and drew a funny face on the balloon. Soon Rei was bouncing the five-spiked head in the waiting area while the miserable onlookers smiled, shifting on their benches. Having such a wonderful time, Rei refused to leave with us.

On our way home, Grandpa said, "I'll have Carpenter Luo fix the fence right away."

"Meimei," Grandma said, raising her voice, "how many times have I told you to stay clear of the fence, hmm?" Then she softened, "Thank heavens, it's only the boy's chin. You could have blinded him."

My first impulse was to correct her—Rei was the one who had led me astray, not the other way around. Then I remembered Rei's gallantry, trying to protect me from the snake. I smiled.

"This isn't funny!" Grandma was furious. "We'll have to send you back to Shanghai if you become too naughty!"

I was petrified. "No, *Popo!*"

"Let her be, old woman," Grandpa said, squeezing my hand. I smiled again at Grandma's toothless threat.

The next day, Rei returned. Framed by bulky bandages, his grin grew even more crooked. Brandishing his new toy gun, he said, "Look at what I got!"

"Wow!" I examined it with exaggerated interest. That was the only way I knew to express my gratitude. Then, for the first time I envied him—instead of threatening him, his mother just substituted a gun for his sword.

Three months later, the scar on Rei's chin was barely visible, and Rei and I had become conjoined twins.

After Grandpa enrolled me in first grade, Rei threw a tantrum: his birthday was a week after the cutoff date. After that, Rei and our cat would station themselves near our front gate every afternoon. As soon as he spotted me, he would dash out to greet me, his onyx eyes sparkling.

During the first semester of my schooling, I learned nothing new except a revolutionary song, which was blasted out of the loudspeakers five times a day.

Wuchanjieji wenhuadageming, hey!
Jiushihao lei jiushihao ao, jiu–shihao!

That is, *The Proletarian Cultural Revolution, hey! It's great, it's great, it's just great!* The song kept repeating these two lines like an angry man trying to win an intractable quarrel.

I tried to teach Rei the song as a tongue-twister, but he couldn't get the cadence right. Flustered, he refused to repeat after me. At once, I was annoyed by my younger brother.

After the housing authority took over our old house, we lost touch with Rei and his mother. Yet I thought of him from time to time.

One evening, Grandma turned on the Panda TV in her chicken coop. A rerun of a modern ballet, about a mad girl with long white hair, appeared on the screen. Recalling Rei's absurd story, I paraphrased it with laughter.

Grandma said, "Ah, Carpenter Luo's wife."

"What? For real? How come I knew nothing about her?"

"I warned you to stay away from that area many times, didn't I?"

"Why didn't you just tell me?"

"What a shame," she sighed. "She's twenty years his junior. Hua Hudie—that's her stage name—was once very popular in a grand dance hall, you know, before the liberation."

"What happened?"

"*Shu-uii . . .*" Lifting a finger to her lips, Grandma glued her eyes to the familiar drama unfolding on the screen.

So, I owed Rei another apology—for calling him a liar.

Entering Fudan University in 1981, I observed that the nightly cleaning ritual preached by Grandma wasn't a universal practice. Unlike us—Southerners spoiled by abundant water—my roommates from the North were far less fussy. In fact, one girl informed me that villagers in some northwestern regions took a bath thrice in their lifetime: at birth, at death, and on their wedding day.

My enlightenment happened to coincide with the groundbreaking of the Nan Shui Bei Diao—a colossal conservation project. Unfortunately, this still-ongoing folly—of diverting southern water four thousand kilometers north by three gigantic canals—was dreamed up by Chairman Mao in 1958. As a freshman ignorant of macroeconomics, ecology, and climate science, I only had a knee-jerk reaction upon hearing the news. *Had anyone tried to convince Chairman Mao to move the millions of his stinky-butt followers to the South instead?*

Then I remembered Rei, the Northern transplant to Grandpa's courtyard, the scrawny boy with his intrepid sword, my severed, conjoined twin brother. Was he still in Nanjing, or did he join his old man in the parched North? Would he grin from time to time, remembering me and our lost paradise?

On an autumn evening of my sophomore year, my roommate dangled a letter in front of me when I returned from basketball practice. She teased, "From a mysterious admirer."

"Yeah, right." I snatched the letter from a stranger with my sweaty hands. I'd just returned from basketball practice.

The letter was filled with neat, unfamiliar handwriting:

> *Remember me? A skinny boy next door when you lived with your grandparents? All these years, I have been wondering about you.*
>
> *Last week, my mother and I shopped at Xingjiekou for my college-bound trip, and we ran into your Little Aunt. Even now, I still can't believe my luck—the odds of bumping into her that day were less than one in two million . . .*
>
> *You have no idea how happy I am, finally track you down. Don't forget, you still owe me a marble match!*
>
> *Qian Jia-Rei*

All of a sudden, the tissue-thin paper under my damp fingertips felt like a cool glass sphere, gleaming under a slanted autumn sun. *Oh, Rei!* I burst out laughing. A warm, tender sensation oozed out of my chest, something I hadn't experienced for a long time.

Rei had just started his freshman year at a university across town. In the postscript of the letter, he invited me to visit his beautiful campus, with the word *soon* underlined.

I savored the letter for a second time. Forgetting to turn on the desk lamp, I promptly replied in the failing light: *Sure, I officially accept your challenge of a marble rematch!*

Early the next Sunday, with jittery nerves I knocked on a dorm door. The door opened. A young man with a sinewy build emerged, bearing a passing resemblance to the scruffy kid in my memory. His hair was dense and dark, shining like overfertilized grass blades after spring showers. On his chin, an almost-invisible indentation winked conspiratorially at me.

He blinked, seemingly startled by the abrupt sight of a stranger.

True, I had shot up like a poplar tree, towering over my girl-friends. Still, he shouldn't have had too much difficulty recognizing me.

Awkwardly, we stared at each other across the threshold. Then he broke out a broad, off-center smile, exclaiming, "Can you believe it? A decade has passed!"

We laughed stiffly, as if our changed facades were somehow embarrassing. When he clumsily sandwiched my hands in his own, a current reverberated through us, calibrating and recalibrating.

Rei decluttered a notebook-sized area on his desk and laid down the teacups. Cradling my cup with clammy hands, I suddenly grew self-conscious. We shifted on wobbly chairs, inquiring about each other's lives in the intervening years. But we were constantly interrupted by his roommates' comings and goings. Each door opening blast in fragments of ABBA's *The Day Before You Came*.

Rei cocked his head toward the source across the hall. "For two weeks now, our show-off friend hasn't stopped playing that tape. His father bought it for him after a conference in Munich."

"Oh, I don't mind. Actually, I kind of like it."

"Not me," he laughed. "After listening to it three hundred times, it starts to grate like that revolutionary song you once taught me."

"*Tried* to teach you," I corrected him.

His asymmetrical smile widened, fully displaying his uneven teeth. I started laughing, too.

At once he paused, gazing at me. My heart skipped a beat. *What did he see?*

A second later, he said, crinkling his onyx eyes, "Have you been to the Jinjiang Amusement Park?"

From miles away, we could spot a flashy roller coaster and a gigantic Ferris wheel. Looming against the empty farmland, they were as eerie as spaceships plucked out of a sci-fi movie. The new asphalt road toward the entrance was rimmed with cabbage patches on either side; a faint odor of night soil still lingered in the air.

The grand opening of the amusement park, the first in mainland China, had been headline news only a few months back. To my surprise, the line at the ticket booth was short: two women in identical, oversized sunglasses and polyester blouses, a smug man clutching a Polaroid camera, and a trio of kids practicing moonwalks. Another boy enthusiastically kicked everything in sight. Was he testing the new railings or his Puma sneakers? Then the posted ticket price gave me pause—way too expensive for college students.

"My treat," Rei insisted, grinning. "I've been twisting people's arms to come here for weeks. Finally, you come along."

Alas, the loudspeakers in the park suddenly roared with Jackie Chan's *The Great Wall Will Never Fall*, making our conversation impossible. Worse, when my first and last roller-coaster ride was over, I careened toward the nearest trash bin and bent over to retch. But nothing came out.

Rei tapped my back. "Are you all right?"

"I'm . . . dizzy. I just want to close my eyes and lie down," I shouted into his ear over the shrieks of the next round of riders. "Sorry, but I must go home."

Rei looked mightily disappointed. *With me or the unused portions of the combo tickets?* I felt guilty. Barely able to stagger in a straight line, I took Rei's extended hand. His hand was warm and surprisingly substantial. I didn't let it go even after the ground stopped spinning.

At the bus stop, Rei said, "Let me escort you home. I really look forward to seeing your parents again."

"Ah, my mother is on a business trip."

"That's okay. By the way, you're the spitting image of her—when we were kids."

"Is this supposed to be a compliment?" I said warily.

He raised his eyebrows. "Of course! Honestly, though, I don't remember what your father looks like."

"He's still the same bookworm with thick glasses." I pushed up my own sliding glasses. "Hasn't been promoted by the general yet."

Rei laughed. Immediately, I regretted my poor joke, which now sounded like a cruel betrayal.

There was a note on the dining table of my parent's apartment: "*Mei, Urgent matter at work. Sorry, unable to have supper with you. See you next week, Your father.*"

"My father has no concept of weekdays and weekends, only deadlines," I sighed, then gestured to the sofa with a secret relief. "Please, have a seat."

Returning from the kitchen with tea and snacks, I saw a handsome young man in front of the bookshelf, browsing my father's manuals. "Look here," he said, pointing out the caption under a mechanical drawing. "See this optic lens your father designed for this satellite? My father helped to launch the satellite from Gansu a few years back."

The coincidence struck me speechless: Rei and I might never have crossed paths if it hadn't been for our parents' demanding work. I probably wouldn't have lived with my grandparents, and Rei might never have lived in Nanjing at all. Now our fates had converged again, maneuvered by an invisible hand.

Fortified by the strong tea, my mind drifted back to my earlier fiasco. "Sorry for wasting your ticket and ruining your adventure," I said sheepishly. "I hope at least you enjoyed the ride?"

"Absolutely!" he chuckled. "Remember the endless equations from high school physics classes? Finally, a chance to test some theories in the field."

"Oh yeah? Was Newton correct in the real world?"

"Hmm, hard to tell. I was distracted by you during the experiment."

"Wait a minute, I didn't utter a sound!"

"See, that's the problem. I kept watching you from the corner of my eye and wondering, *when is she going to scream?*"

"Oh, give me a break! I saw those white knuckles." I jabbed his hand, my finger tingling with delight.

"Ouch!" He rubbed his hand, feigning pain. We laughed and laughed, turning five years old again.

When the laughter died down, we locked our gaze for the longest time. Slowly, our pupils dilated, reflecting each other's image; our thoughts traveled back and forth, linking like the roots and branches of two adjacent trees. No, more like limbs of tango dancers, intertwining and separating, yet always in contact.

Lifting the glasses off my face, he closed the blurry distance between us. Suddenly, I felt a feathery hurricane—soft, warm, and sudden—land on my lips. I closed my eyes. But I was startled by the flavors of peppermint toothpaste, jasmine tea, and a tinge of sour tartness. Before I had time to think, his impatient tongue had pried my lips apart and slipped through sloppily. Smooth and rough, it raked and probed like a wet, velvety rasp. Then, his breath quickened, and his kisses grew urgent, with the desperation of a dying man in the desert trying to quench his thirst. A primordial fear arose in me, and I tried to break free. But his mouth pursed mine, smothering, devouring, and bombarding me with astonishing dimensions of pleasures I could never have dreamed of.

Every fiber of me was in excruciating agony, yearning and resisting at the same time. *Yes, yes, yes, surrender and yes!* A defiant chorus sang louder and louder in my ears, until a wave surged and crested over, obliterating me. Lightheaded and dazed, I cupped his face with my jittery hands, searching in the bottomless pools of his pupils. Measure for measure, my mouth reciprocated his moves, wandering ravenously, longing to know him, every millimeter of him.

The heat of our bodies expanded into a giant cocoon, insulating us from the outside world. In a feverish trance, we plunged into my bed. Buttons, belts, and bumbling limbs...Our fumbling hands peeled off layer by layer of clothing and discarded them recklessly onto the floor until nothing was left. He took in my naked, grown form, gasped, then dove into the pale hollow between my breasts. Sinking in his nose and mouth, he moaned softly and unabashedly, rolling his cheek left and right as if unable to pick a side. His short, dense hair and wet licks prickled my skin. With goose bumps crawling on my skin, I whimpered, "Stop, Stop." But that elicited even harder pressure from his relentless tongue. I trailed off with shudders.

In the aftermath, I caught Rei wordlessly glancing down at my rumpled yet unbloodied bed sheet.

Waves of chills paralyzed me. Clenching my fists against my sides, I stared at the watermark map on the ceiling, counting the seconds, and dreading the calamities that were bound to strike. This was the early eighties, only a few years after the Cultural Revolution—when romance was a bourgeois taboo, love was unspeakable, and premarital sex could land one in jail.

"A lot of personal firsts for me today," Rei reflected in a shy voice.

"Me too." My face burned.

Wrapping his lean, muscled arm around me, he murmured, "How fortunate, we are together again."

Earlier that spring, Rei had declined an early admission offer from the prestigious University of Science and Technology of China, much to his father's chagrin. Instead, he opted to take the three-day college entrance exams. He told me that his intuition had driven him to Shanghai, to find me.

"Curious, how did you persuade your father?"

"Well, my old man was furious to hear 'no' from anyone, let alone his own son. It was scary trying to stare him down." Rei laughed. "But it's worth it. You can't imagine my thrill when I bumped into your Little Aunt."

Then, his face turned thoughtful, and he spoke with solemnity, "Mei, you've always been on my mind."

"Oh, Rei—" Unable to complete my sentence, I stroked his hair and traced the indentation on his chin. He closed his eyes and parted his lips, drinking in every ounce of our ebbing tenderness.

Everything had happened faster than a roller coaster ride. Yet, at some dim level, I understood that it was destiny. We had to muddle through this necessary rite of passage to achieve a new level of intimacy. Pagan or sacred, this ancient ritual of lovemaking bonded us as securely as a blood seal.

Nevertheless, I'd just broken a rule. To be specific, clause 4 of the *Rules of Conduct of College Students*: "DO NOT engage in love affairs while in college!" These prominent, block-printed characters were impossible to ignore every time I walked past the bulletin boards near the campus gates.

Then, exhilaration coursed through my veins. *So what?* My inner voice soared as I clasped Rei's hand, tight enough to count his resting pulse.

When our stomachs growled, I made scrambled eggs with tomatoes. Wordlessly we ate, shy smiles between bites.

After dinner, like an old couple, I washed dishes, and Rei dried them, whistling.

The tune sounded familiar. Then I recognized it. It was from one of Madame Mao's exemplary operas decades before, and the lyrics were about an open secret. Suddenly, I felt like I had just bitten into a moldy peanut after a delicious mouthful.

On the rare weekends when my parents were home, we were more than proper. My father enjoyed conversing with Rei; Mother kept replenishing the peanut tray on the end table in silence—as if hoarded words could be redeemed into rationed coupons in a famine. Yet, she used to like "the boy."

Then, as soon as Rei left one afternoon, she lifted her gaze from her piles of travel-related invoices and darted me a stern warning. Clearing her throat, she said, "Mei, don't do anything stupid to ruin your future."

"No, Mother." I blushed, instantly understanding her opaque hostility toward Rei.

"You're too young. Focus on your studies."

Nodding, I retired to my room. Too young? We were eighteen, old enough to vote, to drink, to smoke, and even to kill in wars. The minimum age to get a marriage license was twenty. But was there a legal age for love?

During this enlightened era in China, Shanghai was one of the most liberal cities, and Fudan University had its own liberal bent. In fact, our president, Dr. Xie Xide, was a woman physicist educated at Smith College and MIT. As a result, we interpreted the threatening "DO NOT" in clause 4 as "Recommend Against," and, literally, only while we were standing on campus ground.

Nevertheless, the price for misinterpretation could be costly. A month later, a tear-streaked girl withdrew from our department—after our supervisor somehow found out about her abortion at Huashan Hospital under a fake name.

After that wake-up call, we visited one of the state-owned medical supply stores, the only condom vendors in the eighties. While I was feigning interest in adult diapers and colostomy bags at the far corner, Rei whispered to the haughty saleswoman. She gave him a crass once-over, then shouted for all to hear, "Do you have a marriage certificate?" An old man hunched over the counter snorted. Red-faced, Rei bolted for the door faster than a thief caught with a purse. I ran after him, bombarded by even more raucous laughter.

I went home and dug out my parents' marriage certificate from the tin box in the mahogany chest. But it was useless. The date would give us away. Hoping to steal a few condoms, I combed every inch of their bedroom. No luck. Fully licensed or not—it only occurred to me then—I'd never seen or heard any hints of amorous activities between my parents.

Careful as we were, the threat of a disaster hovered over me like a rain-impregnated cloud. My menstrual cycle became irregular, and my anxiety grew exponentially. Infinite feedback loop.

What could we do? The fruit always tastes sweeter when forbidden.

In the first few weeks after Rei and I reunited, I could hardly recognize the luminous girl in the mirror, blossoming with love. But my father, of course, noticed nothing. Mother, however, was on heightened alert, and she adjusted her travel schedule to spend more weekends at home.

Sadly, her maternal apprehension became a false alarm in merely a few more months. Of all people, she should have known better—euphoria never lasts.

Undoubtedly, part of the thrill was due to the rebellious nature of our love. But once the novelty wore off, instead of liberating, lovemaking felt like another predictable drudgery, a tedious chore to put off until the last second on Sunday if I could.

Soon, Rei and I charted a new territory. My love for him somehow transcended the merely physical sphere and entered the metaphysical realm. Devoid of desire, I often thought about him, carrying out long conversations with him in my head. I longed to be with him, yet regarded him more as my estranged younger brother of many years—my surgically separated Siamese twin. We were two peas in a pod. Even our names rhymed: Rei and Mei.

Increasingly, I found his passion incestuous and unnatural. When I fretted about our great love being tarnished by his corporeal lust, he grinned, pressing my hips tighter. "What's wrong with that? Tarnished or not, our love is great. You said so yourself."

Under his unabated *amour*, I was suffocating, drowning in dark thoughts. Thoughts I couldn't share with him. No matter how hard I tried to banish those nagging thoughts, they would surface from time to time, like the eyes of a Yangtze alligator lurking in a murky swamp.

I observed that in Rei's presence, my reasoning capacity would deteriorate under his corrosive persuasion. To preserve my sanity, I came up with plenty of excuses to distance us: my course load, my part-time lab work for a professor in my department, and basketball practice for our intramural team.

Alas, my retreat ignited a fresh cycle of unabridged ardor in
Rei. He would show up unannounced. One Saturday night, he
called to me from the darkness as my roommates and I were
exiting the auditorium after a grainy Western movie, *Duel in
the Sun*. My friends teased, "Oo-oo-ooh, *someone* is oversched-
uled tonight."

Embarrassed and upset, I pulled him away from the crowd.
Then, pointing at the ivy-clad wall of a nearby building, I
exploded. "Stop stalking me! You're like this choking vine,
leaving me no room to breathe."

He bit his lip; his eyes dimmed. Under the moonlight, his
transparent face was as unbearable to watch as that of an abandoned puppy. Immediately, I hated myself. To repent my cruelty,
I grabbed his hand wordlessly and led him into the building.

In an empty classroom, physics equations scrawled all
over the blackboard. As soon as we switched off the lights and
blocked the doors with benches, Rei grasped my face and kissed
me like a man in his last fight, a fight to assert his ownership
of a lost-and-found treasure. Heat rushed to my head. I pushed
him onto the bench savagely. I wanted to avenge the torments
he inflicted upon me . . .

Suddenly, a light flashed through the hall window. We froze.

"Open it!" A man yelled, pounding the door.

I jumped off Rei and straightened my skirt.

After ramming the door open with his shoulder, the security
guard—built like a hydrant—flipped on the light and demanded,
"What's going on?"

"We were discussing quantum physics," Rei said with a
straight face, "before you barged in."

"Yeah, right. In the dark? With the doors blocked?" The
man yanked a spiral notebook out of his breast pocket and bit
off the cap of an attached pen, then demanded, "Names and
Departments!"

"We did nothing wrong," I objected.

He leered at me, digging his meaty paw into my shoulder
where my pocketbook hung. "Your name first."

I jerked back. The thin strap snapped into two.

"Let go of her!" Rei hissed.

"Fine." With a lewd smile, he released his sausage fingers from me and grasped Rei's arm instead. "Come with me, lovebirds."

Once outside, I realized he was corralling us toward the security office for interrogation. Rage flamed in my heart.

I turned to run, shouting, "Chang-Le Road. Sunday." My parents' apartment was in the longtang off Chang-Le Road.

From my back, I heard Rei's "Got it."

Then, a furious "Son of a bitch! Stop! I'm warning you!"

I glanced back. Rei was dashing in the opposite direction toward the gate. The man ran after him, huffing and puffing. Then, he came to his senses and turned to chase me. But he had wasted two precious seconds and could hardly gain on me with his shorter legs. Seeing the people congregating for the late-night movie, I ducked into the auditorium.

"Just quit!" Someone called out to the guard. "You're too old to chase girls!" While people were booing and laughing, I exited from a side door.

Before the purple marks on my shoulder had even faded, I became agitated again. Yet anytime I entertained the idea of breaking up with Rei—as if the universe frowned its disapproval on me—minor mishaps would ensue. Test tubes got mixed up; a misplaced paper cost me an entire evening to locate . . .

I yearned for Rei's warmth, yet his insatiable desire—a devouring black hole for my body and soul—repulsed me. In this tug of war, I wavered to and fro. A tormented mess.

I never ceased to love Rei. But in the deepest chamber of my heart, I grew convinced that Rei belonged to my past, my lost paradise, my innocent childhood among the summer dahlias and firefly-lit nights.

At the junction of our reconverged fates, The only future that I could envision for us was like a bleak landscape unfolding on a scroll: fulfilling the quota of the one allowable child after our marriage, childcare, housing, money issues, and all those inescapable trials and tribulations of adulthood in this controlled society. Eventually, the wheels of time would flatten any emotion into its cheap, mocking shadow. We wouldn't be able to handle it, the coarsening of our pure love. Bloated with resentment toward each other and ourselves, we would bicker nonstop until, in the end, old age reclaimed our frail bodies and feeble minds. I shuddered. A predictable tale: the decay of a perishable love.

No, not us! I would rather preserve our precious love in a brown bottle, wax-seal it against oxygenation, and lock it up in a sacred altar.

Shortly after our Suzhou trip, perhaps, infected by the city's melancholy, I couldn't stop obsessing about our breakup. Dreading Rei making a scene, I picked People's Park, the mid-point between our two campuses, as our final meeting place. On Sundays, it was packed with sun-bathing elders, young families with strollers, kite-running children, and lovers whispering in the shade. A perfect neutral ground for a clean break.

"Rei, let's move on." After dropping the bomb, I gestured toward a group of fashionable girls parading in their Sunday best. What could be a better illustration of the benefit of meeting fascinating newcomers in our separate lives? "Look, we should see other people."

"Other people? Who cares about other people?"

"Listen, I'll always be your friend, I promise. Just not your girlfriend."

"No!" He pounded the bench with his knuckles. "But you're my future wife!"

How could I make him understand? I grew desperate. Then, in the deafening silence, a gut feeling, a self-preservation instinct, propelled me to speak. "Have you ever heard of the imprinting of ducklings? Instead of Mother Duck, you, unfortunately, have imprinted upon the girl next door."

He stared at me with parted lips.

Zhi-zzhi-i—a shrill, metallic sound vibrated from above. I looked up. The autumn sky was absurdly bright. Somewhere among the yellowing willow branches, a cicada was screeching his unbearable song, another hopeless love.

Tightening my jaws, I patted his elbow and got up. "Sorry," I said.

The color drained from his incredulous face. He grasped my wrist with his bruised hand; his grip almost crushed my bones.

"Let me go, Rei!" I said, raising my voice. From adjacent benches, curious couples now openly stared at us. I tore myself free and sprinted away, forbidding myself to look back. With even one glance, I would be crushed by his raw anguish. But I must be strong, for both of us. *I must, I must, I must....* Repeating it again and again, like a mantra, I ran blindly, tears streaming down my cheeks.

"No! But he is such a great guy!" My baffled roommates refused to believe in our breakup.

I couldn't articulate a convincing reason that would satisfy them, or even myself. Only, a feeling, amorphous and unpleasant like a miasma, haunted me. I was too ashamed to acknowledge it, let alone analyze it.

A few years would pass before I could finally come to terms with that feeling.

To make any explanation plausible, I must first provide a broader context. In a nutshell, sex was a highly regulated industry in China at the time. For the central planners in Beijing, the sole purpose of sex was its byproducts—batch after batch of chaste, productive worker bees. To replenish the aging and dying human resources, the Party would mercifully switch on the green light to breed. With proper timing, the subjects only needed to perform their duty once in their lifetime to fulfill their quotas. What sex education? No finesse was necessary.

In retrospect, it was a small miracle that upon our reunion in Shanghai, we had intuitively figured the process out on our first lovemaking. In the heat of the moment, our ignorant bodies were like an unhesitating key seeking its matching lock.

But afterward, I was stunned by the unstained bed sheet. For many traditional Chinese families, the lack of proof of the bride's virginity would be a sufficient ground for a marriage annulment.

The following day, I ducked into the Medical Reference section of our library. An hour of clandestine scanning later, I found a poorly illustrated diagram of a partially obscured anatomy in *The Country Doctor's Handbook*. A buried line confirmed what I'd overheard years before—from two gossiping and squealing fifth graders in a water closet. The problem was, I hadn't felt the dreaded pain, nor had I experienced "minor bleeding associated with a laceration of the hymen."

I was dumbfounded, like a thief who got away with snatching a fat purse, only later to open it in a dark alley and find the money missing. To whom could I complain about this touchy matter, the unreportable theft? Definitely not Rei. Torturous thoughts whirled in my head. Was he equally clueless? Or did he regard me as a loose woman? Most troubling was my own self-doubt. *What's wrong with me?* Just then, our white-haired librarian pushed a squeaky cart in my direction. I shoved the book back onto a shelf and fled.

Then, a month later, on a Sunday afternoon, Rei kissed the nape of my neck while I was latching the door in my room. Out of the blue, a blurry, remote event—seemingly inconsequential—came into focus. Waves of nausea rippled through me.

🌺

It is another Sunday afternoon a decade before, shortly after your first train ride to Shanghai. You mill around in your longtang, a ping-pong paddle dangling in hand. The crisp sounds of ping-pong volleys behind the wall make your palms itch. You want to join the laughing kids in the adjacent housing complex, but the ice princess who mocked your accent reigns there.

Heavy footsteps approach from behind. A stocky man with a bloated, florid face appears. Dragging on his cigarette and blowing out a puff, he smiles at you. "Why don't you play with your friends, Meimei?"

So he knows your name. Encouraged, you say, "They aren't here. I have lots of friends in Nanjing. My grandparents, my aunts, uncle..."

He interrupts you. "Got an extra paddle? I can play with you."

You dash home and retrieve another paddle.

The first five minutes of your game are merely you chasing after the ball as it bounces on the ground. Then, finally, you manage a rally of ten rounds: you hit the ball with all your concentration, and he returns lazily, the lit cigarette perched on his plump lips. Then he tosses his cigarette butt, grinds it with his heel, and declares, "That's all for today. Uncle is tired."

You take back his paddle and spin it on its mate. You don't want to return to your parents' empty apartment yet.

"Anytime you want to play, just knock there," he points at the third door down the hall, telling you. "I'm home every day."

You walk toward home reluctantly. Just then, he calls you, "Do you like picture books? I have plenty."

Your eyes light up. "Oh, I love to read."

"Come." He beckons with his fat index finger.

"No, my mother forbids me to go to a stranger's house."

He snorts. "Silly girl, we are not strangers. We're neighbors."

And your new ping-pong buddy! You follow him.

His room looks just like your own: a single bed, a desk, and a chair. Yet the room reeks of stale cigarettes and damp, dirty laundry. Therefore, you couldn't believe your luck when he opens a drawer to reveal a treasure trove of picture books and says, "Pick one."

You point to the one with two pretty girls on the cover. The Little Sisters from the Prairie.

He sinks into his chair and slaps his lap, motioning you to sit. You hesitate for a second. You used to ride your grandpa's lap when you were a baby. So, cautiously, you perch on the sloping edge of his chubby knee. The warm cushion dampens the sirens in your ears.

"Read it aloud for me," he instructs you, then lifts you to sit closer and sticks out his thumb. "Now hold this."

Obediently you read on, turning the pages with your free hand; he rests your joined hands on his thick thigh and begins to sway. Yet, despite his strange behavior, you become engrossed in the story.

Two sisters were tending sheep for their sick father when a sudden blizzard blanketed the prairie. The disoriented sheep started to scatter. The poor girls were stranded in the wintry wilderness. Oh, no, would someone rescue them? You flip the pages faster and faster, pausing only to ask about an occasional unknown character or two.

When he stops responding, you turn to look. His red face is crunched, his eyes squeezed shut, and his lips trembling in pain.

"Aww!" You cry out. What is in your palm is no longer his thumb but a warm penis. You jump up. He yanks you back, twisting his sweaty face into a smirk, and hissing, inches from your ear, "Naughty girl, you ain't going nowhere. Go on, finish the book."

Tears drip down your cheeks, onto his muffling hand over your mouth...

When he collapses against the chair with an agonizing moan, you bolt for the door. It won't budge. You unlatch it with your shaky, sticky hand. You flee the room. His husky voice echoes from behind. "Don't be stupid! If you dare to tell anyone..."

You hurtle into your apartment, slam the door shut, and double bolt it, your heart thumping in your rib cage like the wings of a panicky canary.

When your father returns home, you are already in bed, feverish. He pokes his head through the door to check on you. You tell him that you've eaten the leftovers and washed the dishes. Yes, and brushed your teeth, too.

"Good girl. Sweet dreams," he says with a smile, then switches off the light.

With his phantom silhouette still lingering in the darkness, you pray for his return, for a light touch on your forehead, and a gentle "What's wrong?" You promise to tell him about your rigorous lathering and scrubbing hours earlier, and your failure to get rid of the smell on your hand. But your throat dries up like a concrete hose—what if he would tell your mother that you've gone to a stranger's house against her warning?

The next day, you get home from school, and the apartment smells strongly of disinfectants. In the kitchen, your mother is vigorously stirring her clothes in a bubbling enamel basin over the stove. This is her standard procedure to kill the unlucky fleas and bedbugs who would have otherwise hitchhiked their way into the apartment from remote villages. When she sees you, she waves her long-handled spatula and says gravely, "Mei, a bad guy has moved into our longtang, three doors down. Remember, don't ever let him get near you."

Stomach fluttering, you stare at her. You try to work up the courage to tell her, to come clean. But what if that man has already contaminated you with his wickedness? Will she stick your hands in that boiling basin, too?

"No need to worry," assures your sharp-eyed mother, the astute mind-reader. "The neighborhood committee only approved his stay for a month. Oh, I left a box of pine-nut candies on your desk."

A month! You walk to your room in a daze, your heart heavy with shame for your duplicity.

Every morning, you run in the common corridor, the skin on your skull tingling. Any second now, the third door down might fling open, and a fat hand with smoke-tainted fingers will seize you.

One evening, your mother announces over dinner, "Thank heaven, the jailbird has left earlier."

"What?" Your father asks, lifting his head from his journal.

"Aling's brother! I told you two weeks ago, remember?"

"Ah, right." Your father relaxes his wrinkled forehead. He picks up a pickled turnip and chews thoughtfully before returning to his pages.

Secretly you let out a deep breath that you didn't know that you had been holding.

Soon, you forget about the whole event.

A decade after that bizarre encounter, when Rei nuzzled the nape of my neck, the memory of a similar latch on a similar door jolted back with vengeance. I sharp-elbowed him away, then flattened myself against the wall, breathing fast and hard.

"What's wrong?" He took two steps back, his eyes widened.

Still hyperventilating, I reminded myself that I'd escaped from that apartment three doors down, shaky but otherwise unharmed. Then a terrible thought: could my mind have played some tricks—interpreting an uglier truth with alternative narratives? Cold sweat snaked down my armpits.

Claiming an upset stomach, I got rid of Rei and rushed back to the library. My surreptitious browsing proved far more productive the second time. *Phew!* I signed. A hymen could rupture during sports. Then, I combed every recess of my brain, trying to recall any event traumatic enough. Nothing surfaced.

The puzzle with missing pieces remained unsolvable. In the end, all I could ascertain was the unreliable nature of childhood memories. Nevertheless, I couldn't stop torturing myself with faulty, imaginary recollections.

Since the day that buried memory resurfaced, a simple act of door-latching became foreboding and illicit. My fingertips turned icy at the touch of the metal; even the slightest scratching sound sent blood thumping in my ears. By inserting the saggy zinc hook into its worn-out eye, I transformed my room into a dark den, permeated with the foul stench of a caged animal.

"What's wrong?" Rei had asked me again and again. I couldn't bring myself to tell him. I wouldn't know where to begin even if I wanted to. What could I say? *I think—I'm not sure—I might have lost my virginity somewhere, somehow.* So, I chose silence instead of broaching this taboo topic.

Why didn't he say something about my ivory bed sheet? Anything, even a hint of accusation. His silence had deprived me of an opportunity to exonerate myself, no matter how ridiculous my defense might sound. Frustrated and furious, My resentment for him grew.

My grown-up self was ashamed to admit this: my resentment toward Rei had been unreasonable. Yet this epiphany would arrive years too late.

After our breakup, Rei continued to write to me, pouring his heart out in beseeching lines of neat handwriting, often quotations from sad poems. It was impossible not to shed tears. So, I made a point of not replying. Eventually, the letters trickled to a stop.

Meanwhile, I buried myself in my study and Dr. Zhang's lab.

Before Rei reentered my world, I had had a crush on Dr. Zhang, the youngest associate professor in our department. Fresh out of Cold Spring Harbor Laboratory in New York, he established a brand-new course in molecular biology. His lectures, and even his everyday speech, were peppered with hard-to-translate English words.

I imitated Dr. Zhang's Westernized gestures, laughed at his self-deprecating jokes, and regurgitated his novel expressions. And I couldn't help admiring a photo on his office wall: him conversing with the white-haired James Watson, the co-discoverer of the DNA double helix structure.

At the time, the entire university shared a DNA sequencer that Dr. Zhang had brought back from the States. This expensive workhorse must be kept running around the clock. So, when he needed an assistant for the undesirable evening shift, I jumped on the opportunity.

Since childhood, I'd excelled in hyper-concentration. Once, Dr. Zhang commented that my temperament boded well for research. Blushing at his praise, I glided out of the office, suddenly two feet taller. I imagined that I was inching closer toward the Holy Grail—the Nobel prize—by being a groupie of a groupie to one of the godfathers of modern biosciences. Hand in hand, Dr. Zhang and I would embark on our lifelong journey of discoveries as significant as the DNA structure.

The repetitive lab work turned out to be heaven-sent when I broke up with Rei. After adding sequential chemical agents into row after row of tiny test tubes, my eyes strained, and my thumb sore from pipetting, but my mind was in a blissful state of numbness.

One evening, a young girl on the phone demanded to speak to Dr. Zhang. I said, "Sorry, but he can't talk at the moment."

"Tell him to rush home NOW!" she snapped, "I want him to cut my birthday cake."

Hearing my relayed message, Dr. Zhang stripped off his latex gloves and chuckled, "I'm in deep trouble. My princess is nine today."

I turned green with envy.

Even though Dr. Zhang had never fallen in love with me as I daydreamed, he encouraged me in other fields. "We're at least thirty years behind in life sciences," he told me. "Go west, Hong Mei. If you decide to studies abroad, I'll happily write you a recommendation letter."

The stars were aligned in the spring of 1984. During his historic visit to China, President Reagan gave a speech in our auditorium.

Unlike any speaker we were accustomed to, Reagan began with a personal greeting from a Fudan alumnus studying at Harvard. With his signature charisma, he added, "You'd be proud to know that he received straight A's last term." We roared. Poor lad, could he afford a single B? Then Reagan forged another connection by declaring that his wife Nancy had graduated from Smith College, just like our own Madame Xie.

Straining our ears and eyes, we tried to catch every word and even the slightest gesture from Reagan. When he paused, I heard our party secretary slurping tea in the row behind the podium.

(A few years back, I read the speech transcript posted on the website of the Reagan Presidential Library. Even though the monumental advancements envisioned by Reagan, such as a cure for diabetes, had yet to come, I got emotional again recalling the fantastic speech delivered by the world's most powerful man; the warming trend between our two countries; our progress in promoting peace and curtailing nuclear weapons; the potential cooperation in international space programs . . .)

I was spellbound by the country that Reagan showcased, "a nation of immigrants that values the diversity of race, religion, and culture; a nation that tolerates different viewpoints; a nation that believes in individuals' dignity and their unalienable rights; a nation of fair-minded, hard-working, idealistic, optimistic, and compassionate people . . ." Before the thunderous applause was over, I'd made up my mind: I must see such a wonderful country across the pond.

At once, I tackled this mission: TOEFL and GRE; lectures at the new Center for American Studies; mingling with like-minded fellow students and conversing with visiting foreign teachers in Chinglish; maintaining decent grades and the confidence of Dr. Zhang.

During my senior year, I finally received two offers from American graduate schools. Because of its location, I chose New York University.

"Congratulations!" Rei wrote, "I also plan to study in the States. When can I talk to you in person?"

After deliberating for days, I mailed him an encouraging letter and all my test preparation material in lieu of seeing him.

"The wind is up, the current is swift, and opportunity for a long and fruitful journey awaits. . . ." With President Reagan's speech still ringing in my ears, I weather-proofed my heart, now as watertight as a sea-worthy vessel before my Pacific crossing.

20

SAILING TO THE USA

"Cousin Mei," Chun interrupted my deep thought. With her radiant smile, she said, "Ixin and I are considering sending Yuanyuan to a private boarding school in Maine. But Isha thinks the kid is too young. What's your opinion?"

"How much is the tuition?" Binbin pried, then retracted immediately, "Never mind!"

I knew the ballpark expenses and efforts required for such schools because I'd investigated a few. Saddled with another parent's dilemma, I replied warily, "You know your daughter better than anyone else. Does she have the maturity to live in the states—without much supervision?"

The smile receded from Chun's impeccably made-up face.

While Chun and Ixin were exchanging their undecipherable glances, a thought struck me. Among millions of new arrivals at the American ports, young and old, how many truly possessed the maturity to navigate the New World?

Summer, 1985. As soon as I landed at JFK airport, a cacophony of alien sounds assaulted my ears. After the confusing Immigration lines, people—of a whole spectrum of size, shape, and color—were funneled into the Luggage Claim Hall. Harried groups shouted, hefted gigantic luggage off the carousel then back on. Colliding carts added to the chaos. Not to mention the astonishing array of body odors, and the pungent perfumes! Born and bred in a homogenous society, I was exhausted from the sensory overload. And, to my dismay, I could no longer peer over other women's heads.

The scenery along the Long Island expressway was tinted with a familiar and drab urban gray. Misinformed (at least by the few Western movies that had passed the Chinese censorship), I had half-expected a vast blue sky and an expansive landscape dotted with broad-shouldered men swaggering in dusty cowboy boots, blonde damsels waving from their ranch house porches, and a few taciturn Indians huddling behind thorny cacti.

The olive-skinned driver spoke some kind of fluent English that I couldn't understand. Despite his obsession with weaving his dented yellow cab into any two-meter gap that appeared in an adjacent lane, he managed to drop me off in one piece at NYU housing near the medical center. He dumped my luggage on the street and gave me a stink eye. *Oh, the tip!* I dug out the dog-eared *Handbook on American Customs*. But before I could flip to the page on tipping, the taxi had taken off with a growl, ejecting a puff of hot exhaust against my legs.

My roommate—a second-year medical student—welcomed me briskly before whirling out. Alone, I turned on her small TV in the common area. A beautiful brunette in a bikini reclined on a beach, caressing a beer bottle. After raising it to her scarlet lips for a long gulp, she moaned, ecstatically shaking her hair. Embarrassed, I rotated the dial to another channel. By coincidence, another woman in nothing but an apron and five-inch heels turned her head over her bare shoulder; the shaft of a vacuum cleaner positioned suggestively between her shapely legs. . . . *Aha!* Now I understood the meaning of a puzzling expression I encountered in an old, well-thumbed *Reader's Digest*: "Sex sells."

After my jittery nerves were sufficiently calmed, I reported to the Office of International Students. When I asked for directions to the lab of Dr. M, my graduate advisor, the front desk consulted a thick spiral notebook. "Excellent!" She said with a practiced smile, "Dr. M has open-office hours this afternoon."

"Welcome to our program, Mei Hong!" Dr. M extended his tepid hand.

Hearing my first and family names in reverse order, I reminded myself that I was now standing on the opposite side of the globe.

After the cursory handshake, Dr. M rummaged through a messy pile on his desk. Tossing a piece of coffee-stained paper across toward me, he said, "I'm afraid I have some unfortunate news to share. In this letter that I received last week, NIH informed me that they won't renew my grant. You might not know, but there's been a budget cut mandated by Congress."

While trying to comprehend his words, I studied him, the first American professor I had ever met. A graceful forehead and dignified nose led to an undefined chin, as if a thirsty Michelangelo decided to call it a day at happy hour, then abandoned his task due to a hangover.

"As a result," Dr. M continued, "I'll run out of funding in nine months." Then he shrugged, gesturing with upturned palms. "So, you see, I can no longer offer you the research assistant position."

My heart plunged.

Immediately he straightened his slumping posture. "Now, the silver lining: your timing is perfect. Unlike the other two graduate students in my lab, you haven't wasted a single day. So, I suggest you call on two of my better-funded colleagues and start afresh." He wrote their info on a pink Post-it note and cheerfully handed me the entire pad. "Here. Best of luck finding another position!"

Thus, my thirty-minute meeting ended in three. Out of Dr. M's office, I walked unsteadily as if strapped in a lead lab apron. Without a stipend RA position, how could I afford graduate school?

The two professors' offices were on opposite wings. I hesitated in a glass corridor. Outside, a flashing ambulance blared along the hazy First Avenue. Nearby, two students exchanged their summer news and high-fived. People purposefully walked to their destinations, veering away from me, the eye of a swirling storm. An arctic gale blasted from an overhead air-conditioning vent. I sneezed. Then I understood an old joke that I'd read somewhere: August is the coldest month in North America.

"Bless you," a passerby said without slowing down. The image on his tie-dye T-shirt was a smiling man with unkempt hair and a guitar, and huge sunglasses perched on his nose.

I was dumbfounded. Could this stranger bestow upon me such a welcoming benediction? I'd heard this expression three years before—from a robed priest in Shanghai—after the Party reopened a few showcase churches and reappointed their own cardinals and bishops. On a whim Rei and I had decided to check out a Catholic church. Throughout the mass, white-haired believers struggled to kneel and get back up on their arthritic limbs; Rei and I kept exchanging grimaces . . .

Was it a mistake to come to New York? Shivering in my thin summer dress, I scolded myself. *Now, focus on your problem at hand.*

I decided to visit the first name listed on the pink pad.

Dr. B. was a fortyish man in a three-piece pinstripe suit. Tall and lanky, aquiline nose, and a neat mustache! I tensed up. As a rule, men hiding behind their bushy beards were untrustworthy. But trimmed, waxed mustaches were far scarier: think Hitler, Stalin, or Tojo Hideki.

Stretching his mouth broadly, Dr. B revealed two formidable incisors. Yet his penetrating eyes were without a smile, like that of a stalking cat. Shaking his manicured hand as firmly as I could, I detected whiffs of odor emanating from his attention-grabbing mustache. Chives? Cheese-gone-bad? (Not much later, I figured it out: it was the scent of an alpha male on a beta-blocker.)

To my surprise, Dr. B barely asked about my academic credentials or research interests. Instead, the questions he threw out seemed random.

"What's your favorite music?"

At the time, I could sing only two American songs: "Take Me Home, Country Roads" and "Coal Miner's Daughter." (A visiting Australian, a retired English teacher, had lent me her home-dubbed cassette.) But those couldn't be Dr. B's type. In a pinch, I spit out a name that popped into my mind, "ABBA."

Dr. B's mustache twitched with a disguised sneer.

Oh, no, I must have ruined the interview.

Nevertheless, fifteen minutes later Dr. B flashed his intimidating smile and declared, "I look forward to having you in my lab!" His eyes winked in sync with his expressive mustache. "I'm a huge fan of all things Oriental ... One of these days, I'll show you my favorite Chinese restaurant nearby."

At once, a vibe unnerved me: he was more interested in what was under my skirt than in my skull.

The next day I visited Dr. K, the second professor. A newly appointed assistant professor, she had impeccable credentials: undergraduate from Harvard, PhD from Yale, and postdoc at Columbia. Even more impressive, she had just secured a decent-sized grant.

In the flesh, Dr. K was a disturbingly young-looking woman with intelligent, ice-gray eyes. She scrutinized my transcripts and my application package, then grilled me over my lab experience. She appeared unimpressed by Dr. Zhang's enthusiastic endorsement and my declared devotion to the sciences.

Before dismissing me, Dr. K fetched a thick volume from her bookshelf. "My current research stemmed from this book on yeast," she said. "Read it first. See if you can come up with your own proposal. Remember, basic science is fun, but NIH is always more generous toward research with clinical potentials."

The six-hundred-page book wouldn't fit into my purse. Carrying the brick out of Dr. K's office, my legs trembled. A research proposal on my second day in New York! I had yet to write anything remotely like that in Chinese, much less in English.

In the lobby, I ran into the stranger who had blessed me the day before. Stupidly, I grinned at him.

He introduced himself as Sammy. Seeing the tome in my hand, he said, "Early bird, looks like you got your worm already!"

In sputtering English, I explained my situation.

"Ah, we're in the same boat. I'm one of the two unlucky graduate students in Dr. M's lab." He laughed bitterly. Before departing, he dispensed a piece of unsolicited advice: "Don't kill yourself over this assignment!"

"Agreed. There are still so many things I have yet to do, like visiting the Empire State Building."

"Good Luck!" Unamused, Sammy walked away with the same slouchy posture as that of his former boss.

In less than forty-eight hours since my arrival, I'd already gleaned some wisdom: You must prove your value in this country. Therefore, I glued myself to my desk. Crawling on the brick at a snail's pace, I stopped at almost every sentence to consult four dictionaries I had brought: English–Chinese biology, English–Chinese microbiology, English–Chinese biochemistry, and the English–Chinese Oxford.

A solid week later, somehow, I emerged into the bright summer day with an idea: to study the surface antigen of *Candida albicans*. The fruit of the research could be easily translated into test kits for yeast infections.

In our library, I searched in vain for a typewriter. The three IBM PCs were occupied. The first user scratched his scalp between popping handfuls of M&M's into his mouth; the second, eyes glazed, tapped his sandal to music from his Walkman; and the third—I couldn't believe my eyes—was manically pommeling the beige keyboard with the greasy fingers of a mechanic. At Fudan University, I'd touched an IBM once, but only after changing into an anti-static gown and shoe protectors to enter the high-security lab in the new Department of Computer Sciences.

The next day, after turning in my handwritten, error-laden proposal with a red face, I took a seat across from Dr. K. The polyurethane chair was pre-warmed. *By Sammy or the other unlucky graduate student?* As I imagined this plausible scenario, the slim page in Dr. K's hand looked even more pathetic.

Miserably, I reconsidered Dr. B. Could I have overreacted? Perhaps, my instinct honed in China was groundless here. I tried to persuade myself: *Stop eyeing your new surroundings like a shipwrecked sailor entering a rumored cannibals' island.* Yet the thought of Dr. B made me queasy.

But going home was never an option. Perhaps my jumping off the Empire State Building might be a more acceptable failure for Mother.

Dr. K's austere face was pensive but otherwise unreadable. Waiting for her verdict, my seat grew hot and damp. As the wall clock ticked away, I shifted furtively. The loud friction noise was startling.

After what felt like an eternity she looked up, and her stern gaze softened. "Not bad for your first proposal." Opening a file cabinet, she gathered a few reprints of journal articles and said, "Read these before you report here tomorrow morning."

"So . . . does this mean I'm going to be your research assistant?"

"Well, the first month is your try-out, and mine, too." She smiled curtly. "See you at eight tomorrow."

"Sure thing!" Once outside, I jumped in the air, screaming silently. The blessing from Sammy had worked! As for the try-out period, well, no big deal. I could work harder than anyone else.

My assumption soon proved wrong: my boss worked the hardest. Being young and hungry, Dr. K relentlessly pushed herself and everyone around her. So, I wasn't exactly shocked to see her show up in our lab on the afternoon of my first Thanksgiving.

"Dr. K! I was told that all Americans would be at home today, eating turkey with their families."

"We've done that," she said, checking off an imaginary list in air. "Just so you know, watching football games is another boring American tradition. I left my husband and in-laws home, and walked ten blocks," she patted her stomach and broke out a rare laugh. "To digest the bird."

Encouraged by her first attempted joke in three months, I asked, "Have you been to the Macy's Thanksgiving Day parade?" Earlier that morning, a classmate had tempted me to watch the parade across town with her. I declined. I had to babysit an ongoing experiment and study for the upcoming final exams.

"Never. Believe me, you haven't missed anything important," she assured me, then closed her office door.

That was the extent of our social interaction in the first semester. Dr. K, shy and reticent by nature, didn't mingle with her colleagues, our lab technicians, or postdocs either. Yet we got along fine. I was used to Mother's no-nonsense style and my father's concept of work–life balance.

A year later, Dr. K got pregnant. One afternoon, when I returned to the lab after a *Biostatistics* class, I froze at the door. Atop a ladder, Dr. K was reaching for a cardboard box on the top shelf. As she stepped down, her enormous belly almost tipped her over. After she landed on the floor, visibly shaken, I let out my breath and rushed in. "Dr. K! If you need anything from above, please, wait until I get here, or fetch the technician from next door."

"Thank you. But I'm not an invalid yet." One hand resting on her belly, the other massaging her back, she said ruefully. "This *is* the best place to be. If anything happens, the hospital is right across the street."

On her due date, Dr. K reluctantly left the lab on the order of Dr. S, our department chair. Later, when we visited the maternity ward, she stroked the newborn sleeping against her chest and sighed, "This slacker took his sweet time. I could have worked at least three more days."

A year into my graduate program, a postcard arrived. It was a vintage picture of a crowded San Francisco cable car. People spilled over onto the running board, grasping the trolley poles with white-knuckled hands. Below the steep hill, scales of roofs cascaded into the blue bay.

Joy ride.
P.S. I've just started graduate school at Stanford.

Seeing it, tenderness bloomed inside me; a moonflower unfurling its petals in the darkness.

Soon, Rei and I spent a small fortune on long-distance calls. The dreaded Mid-Autumn Festival would pass quickly while we ate our separate mooncakes over the phone. Rei occasionally tempted me to visit his beautiful San Francisco or hinted about visiting New York. Each time, I agreed in principle and was evasive about the execution.

I was plagued by the blues. By then, I had woken up from my juvenile dreams. Scientific research was far beyond bench work. One must constantly publish, apply for grants based on publications, use the funds to crank out more publications, then grab more grants—an endless feedback loop.

Even tenured professors couldn't rest on their laurels. A case in point: poor Dr. M had started working in the well-funded lab of Dr. B, taking orders from his former protégé. In essence, academia is a game of climbing a broad-based pyramid with a spire-like apex, and contestants risk disastrous falls on each precipitous step. Of course, the winner at the top won't necessarily take all, but at least will get the lion's share of a pie controlled by Congress, NIH, and a few wizened theologians and untouchables.

I started to doubt Dr. K's ability to guide me in crucial battles, namely, the PhD qualification exam and the oral defense of my dissertation. The admirable Dr. K had never been a graduate advisor before. A true believer of the *sink-or-swim* mantra, she had never bothered to rescue me during the humiliating journal club rounds.

Ever since I snubbed Dr. B—by daring to decline the RA position he offered—he'd gone out of his way to punish me. And he hid his hostility under the cloak of intellectual integrity.

Whenever it was my turn at the journal club rounds, I would buy a box of fresh kosher bagels from Ess-a-Bagel in the early morning—hoping to stuff my tormentor's mouth. The bagel was Dr. B's most noticeable weakness.

While I was presenting the article, Dr. B methodically spread the cream cheese on his "everything" bagel and savored every bite. Seeing an opening to pounce, he fired away one leading question after another. He was not only on the cutting edge of his field but also quick and witty. After setting up his bait, he crossed his long legs at his ankles, hooking his hands in the pockets of his three-piece suit, and smiled disingenuously. He reminded me of a gentleman I once saw in Central Park, whistling the tune of *London Bridge Is Falling Down* as a newbie juggler struggled to catch his balls.

The audience (including Dr. S, our chairman) chuckled at his elegant yet lethal way of trapping me. Fending off Dr. B's volleys with my increasingly flustered English, I clutched the damn article—which now looked more like a sieve than a pierced shield.

After his last crunchy bites, Dr. B bared his fang-like incisors and faked a sound of orgasm. (Dr. K would only frown at this disgusting sight.) Then, he brushed the poppy seeds off his mustache and tossed the balled-up napkin into the recycling bin in the far corner. This feat had always elicited a "good shot!" from Dr. M, tilting his nonexistent chin toward the talented sportsman.

Soon my intuition was vindicated when Xiao Lin, (that is, "Little Lin") joined Dr. B's lab. The girl, with a round face framed by valance-like bangs and a buttoned-up shirt, had grown up in a conservative city in inland China.

Entering the restroom one afternoon, I heard muffled sobs. The sound stopped when I took the adjacent stall. Still, I recognized Xiao Lin's size-5 Converse sneaker through the partition gap at the bottom.

After I turned off the faucet and simulated the opening and closing of the restroom door, the smoldered sob immediately erupted.

"What's wrong, Xiao Lin?" I tapped the stall door, "Please, talk to me."

Finally, she emerged, dabbing her puffy eyes. "Every afternoon I've endured all these filthy Howard Stern talks. And his snickering. Today, he asked me to reseed a fresh batch of our cell line. I was in the walk-in freezer when his paws suddenly grabbed me from behind . . ." She broke down again.

"You must report him to Dr. S."

She battered her lush lashes frantically, and her reddened face turned a translucent white. "No! I can't."

"Okay, switch your thesis advisor."

"Then I would never graduate. Look at the way he attacked you during the journal club rounds."

I took a deep breath. "Listen, whenever you go to the freezer, lock the door behind you. Same with the darkroom or storage room. When you must enter his office, leave the door open. Yell if you have to. Talk to me anytime, okay?" Patting her quivering shoulder, I wished that I had warned her before. Yet, before that day I had only a hunch, not proof.

I dragged myself into Dr. B's lab. To my relief, only Sammy was there, hunching over his bench. Sure enough, Howard Stern, his minion, and a guest sex worker were cackling over the radio.

"Sammy, can't you listen to something else?"

"Why? That's Dr. B's favorite program."

"Xiao Lin just complained to me."

"Well, not much I can do about that," he said, shrinking a little under my glare. "I can switch my bench with hers if that helps—ten feet farther away from the speakers."

Deflated, I left.

Before I could muster enough courage to talk to Dr. S, Xiao Lin just vanished.

Then I found a key wrapped in a note in my mailbox. The message read:

Thank you for everything. Sorry to leave in this fashion. Feel free to help yourself to my stuff in my dorm room. I hope we will meet again in the future, Xiao Lin.

A semester later, I heard via the grapevine that Xiao Lin had transferred to a graduate school in Boston.

In an underheated conference room, three professors—Dr. S, Dr. B, and Dr. K—sat in a row, their faces hanging as solemnly as foot-long icicles. The only person smiling was our department secretary in a wool Aran sweater, her ballpoint pen poised over a yellow legal pad.

Cold sweat drenched my armpits. This tough crowd would soon determine the outcome of my PhD qualification exam.

Earlier that day, I'd run into Dr. B at the entrance. "Morning," I said, and broke out the brightest smile I could manufacture. He nodded with his catlike smile, baring incisors that seemed sharp enough to slice through the insulated coffee mug in my gloved hand.

For the comprehensive part of the examination, Dr. K grilled me first. Her questions were similar to those in the mock drill that she and I had practiced beforehand. I relaxed, answering each with clarity and confidence.

Then Dr. S spoke. Decades had passed since the last time our chairman had donned a latex glove. Nevertheless, he had mastered the art of seeking support from the institutional trustees, the review board, and the demigods at the pantheon of NIH. He was instrumental to our success: proofreading every manuscript coming out of our labs, diligently adding his sterling name to the tail end of the author list, and above all, steering the articles toward peer-reviewed journals with editors-in-chief who were lifetime members (if not the founding fathers) of an elite league where Dr. S also belonged.

The first question from Dr. S was about the molecular transport mechanism. Satisfied with my answer, he shifted the topic to a rare, autosomal recessive disorder of lysosomal storage—a field he had pioneered a quarter of a century before. This genetic condition, without an effective therapy then, affected a few clusters of the Ashkenazi Jewish population. According to office rumors, its scarcity always prompted Dr. S to open a bottle of champagne whenever blood samples from a new case arrived.

I smiled appreciatively at Dr. K. Upon her suggestion, I had surveyed Dr. S's lengthy publications. As a result, I answered his tricky questions and came out alive after treading the land-mine field.

Finally, it was Dr. B's turn. His first question related to a passing sentence in our textbook. Regrettably, I had failed to deepen my vague comprehension of an obscure footnote. Just as I had dreaded, I found myself in a mental fencing game. I managed to block his first lunge, but my footwork faltered. Under his continued attack, I lost my balance and fell. From the ground, I hopelessly watched his nimble sword approaching my throat.

After the PowerPoint presentation on my thesis work, Dr. B declared with his twitching mustache, "Without adequate control, your experiment is fundamentally flawed."

Fumbling with my laser pointer, I explained my practical rationale for designing my research method.

Nevertheless, he nailed my coffin with: "Garbage-in, garbage-out!"

In desperation, I turned in the direction of Dr. K.

"Dr. B, keep in mind that Ms. Hong's thesis at this stage is—as its title indicates—a preliminary study. Her work is . . . it's, it's, it's not completely meritless . . ." Suddenly stuttering, the red-faced Dr. K could only mount a meager counterattack to defend the "hogwash" under her mentorship.

After a closed-door conference, the panel handed me an unfavorable verdict. Mercifully, I was given another chance to pass.

Back to our library. Back to the lab. Gritting my teeth, I swore I must redesign a bulletproof experiment.

Like the legendary Mr. Sai once said, "Is it good fortune or a bad omen? Only heaven knows." The false start wasn't a deal-breaker in the grand scheme. One year later, I sailed through my second attempt. Ultimately, I got my doctorate degree within five and a half years.

21

ISLAND HOPPING

A burst of Hong laughter brought me back to the banquet table. Having lost the conversational thread, I smiled vaguely to my merry kin, unable to cut in. When the proud Aunt No. 2 bragged that Isha's talented son would be attending a robotic competition in New York next week, my mind drifted again.

In the spring of 1989, the fourth year of my graduate study at NYU, Rei showed up at my door one Sunday morning. "My advisor is a keynote speaker for a conference in town," he said with a grin, handing me a daffodil bouquet from the Korean corner store. "I just tagged along—so I could pay you an overdue visit."

Seeing that off-centered smile, a dormant synapse sparked joyfully in my brain. A pang of pain followed: strands of gray had sprouted around his temples since I saw him five years earlier. I quickly stole a peek at myself in the doorway mirror. Boy, I looked awfully pale and tired after being cooped up in the lab over a long winter. Wordlessly, we embraced.

"I found you again," he murmured, folding me tighter in his arms. His cold breath tickled my ear.

As we were blowing on hot cups of *biluochun*—the closest to rainflower tea I could find in Chinatown—a sudden gust from the East River rattled the windowpane. "It might be too windy for a stroll in Central Park," I said. "Would you like to visit some museums? The Metropolitan has an excellent collection of Asian art."

"Art?" He arched his eyebrows and chuckled. "Have you forgotten? I'm your stereotypical scientist."

"How about the Empire State Building? The Twin Towers? Or the Statue of Liberty?" I laughed, playing "the local guide." In truth, I hadn't visited most of the New York landmarks. "Oh, the UN headquarters is just a short walk away."

"Definitely not the UN," Rei said. "Politics isn't my cup of tea either. I'd vote for the Statue of Liberty. Nothing sounds better than spending a day with you on an island."

"But Manhattan is an island, too."

"Doesn't count if you can reach it without a boat."

"As you wish. You'll get more than you bargained for: the ferry ticket covers two islands."

Under the morning sun, the Twin Towers gleamed from the smoothly receding skyline of Lower Manhattan. As Liberty Island grew in distance, camera-clicking tourists rushed from the stern to the bow. "Oh, no!" A few cries of dismay erupted in the commotion. The Lady of Liberty was unphotogenic that day, with an orange construction mesh draped from her green crown.

A cranky boy prodded his sister away. Teary-eyed, the girl tugged the sleeve of a French-accented woman who was conversing with an aloof man. Rei and I exchanged knowing glances from a deserted middle row. Smiles crept up our faces. Then Rei reached for my hand. Our fingers caught and locked, all too naturally. Seagulls glided in the updraft above; a frisky mob of Atlantic herring jumped in the white wake of our boat.

Disembarked, we were greeted by a sign: "*Pardon my appearance while under maintenance.*" We were told that the line to the scaffolded observation deck would be at least three hours long. Our climbing ambition thwarted, we circled the island and admired from all angles the lady in an orange veil.

Rei raved about his thesis advisor, a superb quantum physicist, and his role model. Unlike me, Rei had passed his qualification exam at record speed. Barring some freak event, he should get his PhD before me.

By late morning, the sun had hurtled into thick clouds, and the wind had picked up. When I interrogated Rei about his love life, he confessed to dating a fellow Chinese student in the mathematics program.

"What's she like?"

"Mimi is brilliant." Then he added, "And pretty."

A sour taste rushed to my throat.

"But not as beautiful as you." Casting an amused glance at me, Rei said, "By the way, contacts suit you. You look too serious in those black eyeglass frames."

"For heaven's sake! Since when have you paid any attention to this kind of thing?" I said, suppressing a smile.

"Trust the scientists," he said, brazenly fixing his gaze on my face. "We might lack art cells, but we're objective observers."

Compelled by a desire to win any contest, I said, "Well, I have been busy dating, too. Chinese graduate students from NYU and Columbia, MBA candidates from Baruch, day trips to Princeton and Yale . . ."

He interrupted, grinning. "Are you a recruiter for a Fortune 500 company?"

I slapped his wrist in annoyance. He laughed harder.

The wind blasted the exposed rocks. Licking my chapped lips, I regretted not applying some lipsticks earlier. But, camouflaging myself in Rei's presence felt wrong.

I continued. "Funny thing is, I've never succeeded in getting a second date."

"Are these men blind or stupid?" Rei's incredulity looked genuine.

"I wish. Somehow, my strong vibes turn them off."

"Their loss." His onyx eyes glistened, and he said in earnest, "Remember, there is a man who appreciates you, always."

Waves crashed on the rocky embankment with loud claps. Sensing pressure building up dangerously behind my sinuses, I switched topics. I was in the middle of retelling my epic clashes with Dr. B when Rei interrupted again. "Your friend transferred, so why couldn't you?" He demanded. "Come to California. Plenty of good schools in our area."

I laughed at his naivety. "Are you kidding me? Or do you think Dr. B doesn't exist on the West Coast? Besides, I'm almost done here." The metal rings of the lanyard above our heads banged the flagpole ferociously. So, I shouted over the hollering wind, "I'm not going to flush my four years' worth of hard work down the toilet."

Rei froze for a split second. Then, just as quickly, he picked up his camera and aimed it at me in close range, saying, "Don't move. Your face comes alive when you're upset."

We bought hotdogs and pretzels, and then "I ♥ the Big Apple" baseball caps from a vendor. Fifteen minutes later, my hat was lost to the sea, and my mustard-smeared hair flew wildly again. Rei took off his denim jacket and wrapped it around me. A familiar scent from the collar punched me in the gut: the green watermelon rinds withering under a hot summer sun, and the pewter coating of his toy gun. Staring at his purpled lips and the faint scar below, I blinked back tears that were starting to pool.

By afternoon, the fierce wind forced us to seek shelter. We huddled in an old brick building on Ellis Island, just like the twelve million immigrants who had passed through here, the pitiful people waiting in mile-long lines for the screening interview and the "six-second physicals."

In the vaulted hall of the museum, people bent over black-and-white photos in display cases. Out of curiosity we typed our surnames on an interactive screen. Rei's search yielded only one match, and mine—surprise, surprise—were more than a thousand hits! How did these Hongs get here after the passing of the Chinese Exclusion Act?

"Oh my god!" Six feet away, two robust redheads gasped. The older woman jabbed her finger at the shatterproof glass as if trying to connect to a spirit locked inside the captioned photo.

The younger one covered her mouth with her hands. Then they hugged, repeating, "Oh my god! Oh my god!"

Watching their teary eyes and flushed faces, I couldn't help contemplating the inception of America. Only the physically and mentally fit pilgrims and the enslaved Africans chained in squalid conditions had survived the months-long voyage in open seas to reach the New World, to pass along their legacies. The horrendous genocides in the forests, prairies, and deserts had preserved only the few Native Americans endowed with natural immunity against germ warfare. Only the most determined latecomers from the developing world could overcome the prejudice of a rigged system. The so-called God-chosen country is a men-chosen, and self-chosen nation, too, inadvertently compounded by natural selection. Constantly infused with fresh blood for four centuries, America had been quietly harvesting the hybrid advantage of a diverse genetic and cultural DNA makeup—without fully acknowledging the reason behind its greatness.

Observing the hugging women, Rei wondered aloud, "Someday in the future, maybe our children could trace their ancestors' first footprints in this country too."

"Hmm, interesting thought." Did he just toss out *our children* in the most literal sense? I deflected. "Do you think our entry records are kept at the customs in airports?"

Rei's eyes burned with a startling intensity. Grabbing my hands, he said urgently, "Mei, just say the word. I can transfer to New York in a heartbeat."

The pressure from his warm palms sent me tumbling in a riptide. Once resurfaced, I said, "Be practical! You know I won't allow it." Had I led him on—with our late-night chats over the phone and our finger-lacing hours earlier? Upset and frustrated, I wanted to scream. *Why can't you see? We aren't meant to be a couple.*

"Wait for me, then," he said, and squeezed my hand. "I can wrap everything up in ten months."

"Oh, Rei . . ." I realized that Rei still clutched to our star-crossed past like a war veteran longing for his amputated leg.

Despite the passing years, despite the fitted prosthetics, in those disorienting moments upon awakening he still tries to roll out of bed and walk with his phantom limb.

But, to me, Rei was a beacon above a rocky headland—yet I couldn't navigate the savage seas to reach the alluring harbor, not without wrecking my ship. I had to escape from his beckoning in order to reach my true destination. Avoiding eye contact, I croaked helplessly, "I love you like my blood brother . . ."

His hands instantly became flaccid.

We were each lost in thought on the walk from Battery Park to Bowling Green. The subway entrance was littered with footprinted fliers promising remedies for hair loss and the Everything-Must-Go liquidation sale of a furniture store on Seventh Avenue. A blind man with a cardboard sign and an empty cup sang "Moon River" out of tune while stabbing the platform with his rhythmless cane. A ripped plastic bag fluttered on the vent like an asthmatic lung. Soon, a No. 4 train squeaked in with blue sparks, stirring up the fetid subterranean air. We boarded the train.

I got off at 33rd Street. As the graffitied train hurried away with Rei, I waved, trying to purge from my mind the chewing gum mosaicked wall, the subway stench, and the butchered song.

A seasoned biologist by then, I'd gained a new insight into my conflicted heart. A woman's dilemma can often be explained at a molecular level—Major Histocompatibility Complex (MHC) plays vital roles in reproduction. Animals, including humans, can detect trace amounts of those telltale molecules in sweat and other body fluids. While women bond naturally with men of similar MHCs—lulling with the soothing promises of kinship and familiarity, they are biologically wired to choose mates with complementary MHCs. This way, mothers can gift their offsprings the maximum genetic diversity for survival. Evolutionarily speaking, the so-called woman's instinct is nothing but a sniff test. Case in point: Mother selected my father, her polar opposite. On the flip side of the same token, I rejected Rei, twice.

While Rei and I were dancing our peculiar tango that spring, paradoxically, the background music was a grand overture—to a tragedy that eventually impacted the fates of 1.4 billion Chinese.

In April 1989, a pro-democracy demonstration erupted in Beijing. Soon, similar events swept across China like an unstoppable forest fire.

Thanks to the extensive coverage from the BBC, CNN, and all major news networks, the overseas Chinese had a clearer view of the historical moment than our countrymen inside China. The irony was not lost on us. During lunchtime, a large crowd would gather in our lounge to watch students' hunger-striking at Tiananmen Square seven thousand miles away.

In the past, Freedom of Speech resided in a framed poster displayed on the white court wall. But, trying to exercise it? A guaranteed walk on the gangway toward the gallows. Now, only thirteen years after the Cultural Revolution, the images on the screen shocked us: a sea of brave, young faces with *Freedom* and *Democracy* handwritten on their headbands. These trailblazers waved banners and shouted: *Political Reform Now! Stop the Corruption!*

Someone clapped his hands, and then we all applauded. Hope swelled in our hearts. With the backing of the entire world, their dream—our generation's too—was within reach.

Then, on June 4, 1989, another set of unbelievable images appeared: the deserted square of abandoned banners and blood-smeared headbands; a young man laid motionless on a tricycle flatbed while people tried to plug a gushing hole in his leg; a thin man confronting a fleet of tanks, trying to block the roving column with nothing but his arms and two plastic bags. . . . A girl started to sob. A lunchbox flew towards the TV and hit the frame, accompanied by a scream, "Butchers!"

A week later, Mother called me with the news: Cousin Isha, who was graduating from college, was rejected by a research institute that had signed her up. "A careless child!" Mother clicked her tongue, vaguely alluded to Isha being "carried away in an unfortunate event."

"Oh, no!" I cried out, catching her euphemism for the unmentionables. Of all people, the dreamy and quiet Isha had become political?! "Is she okay?"

"Every morning, she'll take a shuttle bus to a chemical plant for her re-education. Hopefully, it won't be too long." Mother sighed, lowering her voice. "Everywhere, we all need to take turns to read out the editorials in *People's Daily*, denounce the rioters, and write self-criticism letters." Then, abruptly, she switched to Grandma's failing eyesight.

That was her signal for dropping the subject. Overseas phone calls were routinely monitored in a police state. And we couldn't discuss sensitive topics in letters either. Poor Isha. And these young, earnest faces on TV. And all my ill-fated countrymen. My heart plunged like a lead ballast.

But I must do something. I decided to join the rally in front of the Consulate General of the People's Republic of China.

A notice in both Chinese and English was posted on the shut door: "Our consulate is temporarily closed until further notice. Please excuse the inconvenience."

We waved our own banners and passed denouncement fliers to passersby. We pumped our fists and stomped our feet. "Butchers! Liars! Cowards!" We shouted and shouted; some of us lost our voices. "Come out! Show the world your bloody face!"

The heavy doors remained sealed. Eventually the wind from the Hudson River drowned our hoarsened outcries, along with the whirling of local news helicopters, the sirens of NYPD cruisers, and the rumblings from the Lincoln tunnel.

Exiting our impotent rally, I was indignant and bitter with disillusion. I swore to myself, *Forget about a better China. Become a true American.*

A year later, Rei emailed me, announcing his acceptance of a postdoc position in the Bay Area. "P.S. I've broken up with Mimi."

I congratulated him by email as well. "P.S. Sorry that the 'pretty and brilliant' girl didn't work out. Well, you're one of the most eligible bachelors in the Golden Gate City now."

22

A POPPY FIELD AND A HYDRANGEA BOUQUET

"Mei," Little Aunt said, rubbing my shoulder to get my attention, "Do you or Tony know any good Chinese bachelors in Boston?"

"Hmm, good Chinese bachelors in Boston," I repeated, combing through my brain. Unable to think of any eligible Chinese bachelors at my pharmaceutical startup, I tried to clarify. "Do you want us to help Shu-Zhen to find a husband?"

"No, I've given up on the journalist long time ago," Little Aunt whispered, deepening the wrinkles on her forehead. "For Shu-Xiang! I'm worried that this PhD thing only increases her chance of becoming a *shengnu*."

Shengnu, a leftover lady. The nightmare of every Chinese mother. Nodding my sympathy at Little Aunt, I said, "I'll ask around once I get back home."

I was a *shengnu* myself when I started my own postdoctoral training in Boston in 1991.

Unlike the windowless cubicle deep in the bowels of NYU, my new lab at Tufts Medical Center boasted a live view of cars snaking through a bottlenecked section of the "Big Dig" mess, and a darkened brick wall adjacent to a Chinese restaurant. My fellow postdocs could form a mini-UN, showcasing talents from Australia, South Africa, Germany, Spain, Israel, and the well-represented Asian countries.

I got along with everyone. That is, until I found out that Ken's real name was Kenichi. The poor guy seemed puzzled by my sudden coldness. But how could I explain? Maybe his grandpa was among the beasts who had ravaged Nanjing. Maybe even the very one who had scarred Grandpa. Or the one who had stabbed Alei and burned his wife in our ancestral house. If not Kenichi's grandpa, what about his great-uncles?

Nevertheless, I arbitrarily discounted the probability that Wolfgang, the German postdoc, had Nazi connections. Being six feet tall, the blond walked as if a special sunray followed him around. I hated to be superficial or a hypocrite, but I couldn't help but squint in his direction.

I could only blame Mother for my selective bias.

"Mei, we need to talk." Mother beckoned me on a sweltering afternoon before I left China.

Entering the sauna-like living room, I was alarmed by the sight: my parents sitting side by side on the couch. I braced myself and sat down. Then, Mother gave me a parting gift, the jade pendant of the Moon Goddess. As I was admiring it, she said without preamble, "Mei, you're no longer young."

I almost dropped the pendant. I had turned twenty-one merely six months earlier! And she'd told me the opposite only three years prior—when she warned me to focus on my studies. Had I already squandered my short-lived youth?

Pa, she opened her folding fan and cut to the chase. "Time to discuss an important matter—your future husband." With a side glance at my father, who'd shrunk on the sofa and wisely deferred this topic to her, she pronounced, "You aren't foolish. After all, you're *my* daughter."

While I was savoring her approval, she predicted, "But, you'll be far away, alone in a different environment. And you won't consult us."

Detecting her bitter undertone, I protested. "*Of course* I will."

She paused her rapid fanning for a second, then resumed. Damp patches on her cotton shirt continued to spread. For the first time, I noticed liver spots on her hands, and her unhealthy aura. Then, it dawned on me: what my menopausal mother meant was, "*I'm* no longer young. I can no longer guide you."

Dabbing her forehead with a handkerchief and fixing her gaze on the pendant, she sighed, "Be prudent. Long-lasting marriage is only possible between people from similar backgrounds. We Chinese understand it well, after millennia of matchmaking."

I turned to my father, but he only smiled noncommittally.

It turned out that Mother had already plotted an algorithm for my potential mate. College-educated Chinese from the Mainland (preferably from south of the Yangtze River) ranked higher than those from Hong Kong or Taiwan, followed in turn by ABCs—American Born Chinese. In the worst-case scenario, marry an American, but never a Japanese.

As I nodded away, my mind wandered: Did she expect me to pass down the family hatred to my future children, like the intergenerational grudges of the crows?

Pa—she closed her folding fan with a flourish, in the exact manner of Grandpa. However, her gesture signaled the finality, not a cliffhanger.

Five and a half years after that serious talk, I'd scaled the highest peak in education; Mother's long-distance nagging had also escalated to a higher octave. As a result, the first thing I checked in men was their left hands. Among the male postdocs, Wolfgang was the only one who didn't wear a wedding ring.

As I explained to Rei on Liberty Island, in my precious spare time I had diligently blind-dated my fellow Chinese expatriates. To ameliorate my geekiness and my vanishing youth, I wore contact lenses and lipstick. Nevertheless, my dates collectively rejected me astonishingly fast, usually before the arrival of the fortune cookies. Once, a time-pressed MBA candidate from Stern even faked a sudden-onset gastrointestinal emergency to flee, after only two bites of a jellyfish appetizer.

So, I took the initiative. But everyone I had asked politely declined. Soon, I exhausted my potential husband pool in the metropolis. A serious relationship requires time, financial stability, and a nurturing mind. Sadly, I had none.

In Boston, my love life failed to improve. After two futile matchmakings attempts, a kind lab technician from Taiwan gave up on me, too. She claimed, "You scared your dates away with your indomitable spirit!"

"What?!" I laughed, then categorically denied her assessment, "No. My mother thinks I'm a pushover!"

"You should see yourself in the mirror now!" my friend exclaimed. "Trust me, 99 percent of Chinese men don't desire a debate partner. Now watch." With a gentle dip of her perfect bangs and a dainty smile, she said, "*This* is the way to encourage a man's monologue."

Her demonstration stirred up the image of that Lilac Lady of the Rain Alley, the traditional subtle beauty, the idol for 99 percent of my countrymen. My face burned. During my last dinner date, a haughty businessman from Beijing had slighted us Southerners. I balked, pointing out that Dr. Sun Yat-Sen, Mao Zedong, and Chiang Kai-shek—the movers and shakers of modern China— had all hailed from the South. He stared at me with the horror of seeing a horn sprouting out of my forehead. Predictably, ten minutes later, I bid my overlord a cheerful farewell.

Okay, I got it. My soldierly gait, frank gaze, toothy laughter (often at my own jokes), and, after years of fencing with Dr. B, a sharpened tongue... No wonder I intimidated those men high on Mother's marital totem pole.

Yet, despite my friend's candid feedback and excellent tutoring, I still couldn't play the ill-suited part of the Lilac Girl. As my twenties hurtled to an end, wedding invitations came and went; one by one, my girlfriends vanished behind bottles and diapers. But I had no viable prospects on the horizon. *You are running out of time.*

Nevertheless, whenever my lonely heart ached for Rei, I scolded myself. *Don't take that well-trodden path to a dead end.*

On a sleepless night, I brutally evaluated my dating fiascos with the objective lens of a scientist. Then, a eureka moment: All my miseries stemmed from Mother's ill-charted roadmap! Why limit myself to these elusive Chinese one-percenters? Instead of staring down these flirtatious non-Chinese men, I should have coolly handed out my business card with an added home phone number. At least to these eligible bachelors aged from twenty-five to fifty. *Now, be bold and reckless in your pursuit of a husband!*

In retrospect, Wolfgang's timing was impeccable.

On my third day at Tufts, while I was copying a journal article a golden fleck floated into the edge of my vision. Turning toward it, I was blinded by an oppressive light, the murderous heat of an August sun. Then, a pair of icy eyes, as steel-blue as the North Sea, pierced me. I gripped the heavy-duty copy machine, and my throat seized up. Without even a nod, the tall blond walked into our administrative office.

Minutes later, our secretary appeared, all smiles. "Excuse me, Dr. Hong," she said, "Could I jump ahead of you really quick? Dr. Schneider needs something urgent."

I obliged, stepping aside.

Before the Canon could spit out the last of the copies, the phone rang down the hall. The harried secretary grabbed the stack and ran, forgetting the original in the feeder.

According to Wolfgang's résumé, he was in his second year of a second postdoc position. I tossed it into the recycling bin. *Good luck!*

From that day on, I had observed Wolfgang from afar. To my amusement, the brash German was fair, practicing universal rudeness toward anyone who happened to be in his way. Soon my mild peeve morphed into morbid curiosity.

Shortly after I made my dating resolution, Wolfgang shared an elevator ride with me one morning. When he nonchalantly suggested that we grab a quick bite after work, I said yes, giddy as a teenager.

In a flash I convinced myself that, despite his glacial eyes, I had caught a glimpse in him of a soft and meltable interior, something like a liqueur encased in Lindt white chocolate.

At Dim Sum Garden, Wolfgang ordered curry chicken noodles. *Impressive.* It takes considerable chopstick skills to handle such a messy dish. But his choice of beer proved unwise. Seeing his comically crunched face after a swig of Budweiser, I waved down our waitress and ordered a Tsingtao beer for him.

"Not bad," he said, appraising his new can. "I've never tried any Chinese brand before."

"Some trivia for you: Tsingtao brewery was founded by German settlers in Shandong Province around the turn of the century."

"Really?!"

I continued, "During World War I, the Japanese took over the brewery from the Germans after the siege of Tsingtao. Later, of course, World War II turned two old enemies into cozy bedfellows."

"You know history well," he remarked. After another appreciative gulp, he pointed his square jaw at the ditched can and said, "Do you know what Arnold Schwarzenegger once said about Budweiser?"

"That it should be terminated?"

"It's like making love in a canoe."

"What?!" I choked on my complimentary tea.

"Fucking close to water!"

We were still laughing after we split our bill and left the restaurant. A quartet of potty-mouthed teenagers in Nike Air sneakers swaggered out of the movie theater. Following them, we jaywalked toward the park. Willow branches swayed over the swan boats that had reappeared in the spring pond. Lovers kissed on benches. A Berklee student played violin on the footbridge, and the evening air vibrated with Mendelssohn's sweet melodies. In my mind, the Terminator who precariously rocked a canoe morphed into Wolfgang. Fortunately, he marched on without noticing my flushed face.

During our long walk, we discovered that we both admired Beethoven and dissed Mozart as too delicately balanced. Staying on the German theme, I boasted that I'd read Hegel's *The Science of Logic*—a trendy book during my college days in the early eighties. Yet, digging for some memorable lines, I came up short.

"You must have read Marx's books, too?" he ventured.

"Nope. I was too young when Marx was mandatory; when I was old enough, he was no longer fashionable."

"Interesting." He added, "But I've read *Das Kapital*."

"Ah, 'From each according to his abilities, to each according to his needs'—what a lofty dream of your countryman! Come on, human needs are boundless." I mocked Marx with glee. "No wonder his ideas have failed miserably in reality around the world. What would you do if your repeated experiments yielded no expected results? Ditch the working hypothesis!"

Wolfgang was just about to rebut, but we had arrived at a hip nightclub near Fenway Park.

Thump, thump, thump... Punishing soundwaves threatened to pierce my eardrums and liquefy my brain. A crystal light dome rotated over the dark dance floor, fractionating amorphous forms gyrating like spawning octopus; each face glistened like a bioluminescent jellyfish. Mirroring the spasmodic moves of the undersea creatures, I couldn't help jiggling—I imagined myself an amoebae wiggling under a microscope. But no one cared. One by one, the hard knots that had tightened my back for years were pounded away by the relentless thumping of the tech house music. One cocktail later, I was floating on a bubbly microcosmos.

As the night deepened, the DJ dimmed the lights and amplified the sultry voice of Madonna spelling out her desires in her *Justify My Love*. In the semidarkness, mascara-smeared eyes lingered on Wolfgang's gleaming golden locks; his charm increased by the second in the pressure chamber of lust.

At closing time, Wolfgang cocked his head, licking his thin lips. His steel-blue eyes softened like a glassy bay under dancing moonlight. As if watching a movie preview, I saw myself linking arms with him.

Not to break the spell, I kept our arms locked during the taxi ride. Once inside my apartment, he killed the light and tilted up my chin. I froze. When I remembered to breathe, I was assailed by a tidal surge of odors: alcohol, a musky cologne with a sharp bite around the edge, and the long finish of an unfamiliar yet enticing scent of a healthy male. I closed my eyes, letting my mind follow the roaming pressure evoked by his large hands. "You are beautiful," he murmured, licking my cheek. My knees wobbled under his wet, warm grazing of my earlobe.

That night, we barely rolled beyond the living room carpet. When my timer went off at dawn, I tiptoed out of bed. Once I returned from my rescue mission for some test tubes floating in a water bath, the sleeping beauty was gone. Only a strand of almost-translucent hair remained on my pillow.

Once Monday arrived, Wolfgang and I had become just co-workers again. And so it seemed throughout our liaison.

Hegel once said, "*Nothing great in the world has ever been accomplished without passion.*" I felt compelled to couple this with my own two cents: "*Yet, few things accomplished with passion have ever been great.*" No, Wolfgang's grandfather wasn't a Nazi, as I had feared. However, Wolfgang flew to Germany from time to time to visit his official girlfriend.

In the beginning, I pretended not to notice. Our mutual chemical attraction was undeniable. We were meant to be a couple, I reasoned; it was only a matter of time before Wolfgang would fall for me, this new version of the liberated, fun-loving Mei.

But who was I kidding? Deep in my bones, I was still the same all-or-nothing type of girl. Without commitment, I held back my soul. Lovemaking became as exhausting as scaling

Mount Everest without oxygen, constantly eyeing the elusive summit, so close yet tauntingly unreachable.

Often, I lay awake while Wolfgang snored. In those vulnerable moments, I shamelessly craved another man's embrace. The night was still young on the West Coast. Rei would pick up his phone, I was sure. But how could I? Something stung my eyes. Acting upon my impulse, I would only violate the unbreachable line, the line I'd drawn up myself.

Tapping our bare feet on the Tanglewood lawn to the rhythm of Beethoven's Emperor Concerto, kissing among the blazing foliage of the White Mountains. . . Life was good, as long as we lived in the moment and avoided the future.

Once, Wolfgang and I went to the Museum of Fine Arts for a Georgia O'Keefe exhibition. Up close, the iconic red poppy was terrifying. Like a hapless insect, my gaze spiraled down from the gigantic, velvety petals toward the stippled vortex. I was trapped between the fuzzy stigma and the purple, sticky stamen—as if hypnotized by the lethal chemicals being synthesized in the dark center right in front of my eyes.

Decades earlier, Grandpa had planted a strip of poppies in our courtyard. The day after the flowers bloomed, a man blasted in, whacking the red blossoms with his billy club and ripping the roots out of the bed. Isha cried, Grandma trembled, and Grandpa raised his arm. "Stop! Stop! What's wrong with you?"

"Opium is made from poppy pods!" The man pushed Grandpa back with the tip of his baton, and said with a grin, "Old man, try growing this contraband again, and we'll confiscate your property."

I was stunned. How could misery derive from such a delicate beauty?

When Wolfgang tapped my shoulder with concern, I woke from torpor. After I told him about that remote incident, he said,

"Poor Mei!" Then, he lifted my hand for a kiss, his eyes softening like a moonlit lake.

I was embarrassed by his sudden burst of compassion. Of all the injustice we'd suffered, that one seemed to be the most trivial. Still, I welcomed his comforting hand. *Oh, he loves me, after all!*

❧

If only I could brush away an image in my mind. A blonde with dull, bovine eyes and a pinched mouth. Laid face-down upon my visits, the picture nevertheless guarded Wolfgang's night-stand, as faithful as a petulant floater in my vision.

During a visit, I woke up at night to whirring sounds. Outside the bedroom, a fax machine was hard at work. I picked up the first page that had landed on the floor and made out a loopy line by the nightlight: *Guten Morgen, Mein Liebling . . .*

The warm paper scalded my hand. I dropped it and kicked it under the desk. However, one by one, more loose pages oozed out of the machine, piling up like entrails of a gutted animal.

I studied the sleeping Wolfgang: his peaceful breathing, his damp and clumped blond hair, his sculpted jaw. Then his eye-balls rolled rapidly under his eyelids, and his thin lips curled up. Stilling my propped elbow, I fought an urge to shake him awake and demand, "Who are you dreaming of?"

At that moment, everything became crystalized—an exotic lover I might be, I was still a convenient placeholder, nevertheless.

My waiting strategy would never work. Still, I waited until breakfast. Finally, I asked him point-blank, "Do you plan to break up with your old girlfriend?"

He flinched. After scrutinizing his perfect, sunny-side-up egg for a long minute, he narrowed his eyes and said, "I thought you were a modern woman. Aren't you?"

Brilliant! Deflecting a tough question with a tangential question. By mocking my outdated bourgeois idea of exclusive love and uncool monogamous instinct, he challenged me to accept him as-is. Why not? The status quo suited him fine.

Who was that stupid girl who had held his covetous gaze and slid her arm into his on a warm spring night not so long ago? Ha! *Now* she wanted it all. Blinking back the rising tide, I said with a feigned dignity, "This is a raw deal for me, you know and I know."

He chewed his toast thoughtfully. Staring at his jaw, I ached for our aborted happiness ahead and our strong and intelligent children who would never be born. The crunching sound became unbearable. I shoved my untouched plate toward his and stood up. "You idiot! You're throwing away a beautiful thing."

"Mei, be reasonable," he pleaded.

But his frosted blue eyes failed to captivate me this time. I stormed out.

On the way home, my blood-boiling rage slowly evaporated like the morning dew. I thought of that sour-looking blonde. Poor unhappy thing, did she sense the existence of another woman who tried to steal her *Liebling*? Did she also yell at him, calling him an idiot in harsh German? Somehow, the plausible scene tickled and saddened me equally. Tipping my hat, I bowed to my faraway rival and said, "You win. Good luck!"

At the lab, whenever Wolfgang approached, I grabbed a random X-ray cassette to flee into the darkroom, counting to five hundred before resurfacing. Once, I even ducked into a passing elevator, enduring its "Going Down" reminder as if I needed it. In meetings, I entered a few minutes late, hoping to claim the blind spot of a pair of pursuing blue eyes. But my own treacherous eyes would involuntarily track the flickering of a golden light. Many nights, my index finger was poised on the smudged No. 2 on my speed dial. Then I would force myself to visualize the coiled fax paper on the floor.

I was exhausted by the time he flew to Germany for vacation. Good riddance!

Less than a week into my reprieve, a glossy postcard arrived in my mailbox, a photo of a vast poppy field somewhere in southern France. And on the back, a note:

Dear Mei,

You won't believe how beautiful these poppies are!
No policemen to harass them here. Thinking of you . . .

Wolfgang

First, I couldn't believe the efficiency of the transatlantic postal services. Then I couldn't stop laughing. Did Wolfgang expect me to stick this preposterous postcard on my refrigerator? Surely, every morning, I would thank him for thinking of me while kissing his GF in the poppy field. What arrogance! I ripped the postcard in half, then quarters, and kept going until my hands were too weak for the thickening wad. After throwing it into the trash bin, my fingers were still unsatisfied, so I dropped a lit match. As the burning fragments quivered into ash, a siren screeched from above. "Oh, shut up!" I yelled at the smoke detector, fanning vigorously.

My phone rang almost as soon as the ear-piercing shrills died down. It was Rei. He would attend a conference in Boston the following week—as a speaker this time.

A distinguished scholar in gray tweed peeked out from behind a striking bouquet of blue-and-white hydrangeas. His once-vibrant hair—as if an overflowing life force had finally found some outlets to spring out—was thinning and dusted with frost. Yet his eyes twinkled the same way behind the bifocal lens. A warm current washed over me.

At dinner, Rei praised my cooking. Smacking his lips, he said, "The best tofu dish I've ever had."

He was humoring me. I sighed, "But this duck didn't come out half as good as my grandma's."

"A true statement, too," he said with a grin, brandishing his patented crooked smile. "The Pinot Noir paired it well enough."

We laughed.

When Rei regaled me with his research project on quantum computing my mind wandered to my father and his occasional soliloquy.

"Lucky me," Rei said. "I've stumbled upon an exciting field—the artificial brain." He was still grinning like a kid with his greedy hands in a candy jar. "If the conditions are right, I might consider going back to China to teach a course or two."

"Not me," I said, feeling like I had just swallowed a fly. "I'll never lift a finger for this current regime." To diffuse the tension, I pivoted, "Enough about academia. Now tell me about your new girlfriend."

"Well, she is a shy girl." He said, swirling the wine in his glass. "From Chengdu."

"And?"

"She's a year younger than me."

"And?"

"She is, hmm, about this tall," he said, gesturing to about my shoulder height. Then he flicked his wristwatch. "We met only a few months ago, at a Mid-Autumn Festival party in Palo Alto."

A shy and younger girl. A Lilac Lady? I felt disappointed. Wait, did I detect a dismissive edge in his tone? Then I ordered myself to stop this silly game and feel happy for my younger brother. Nevertheless, acid chewed at my stomach. With alcohol buzzing in my head, I unburdened myself with the story of my humiliating affair.

"Stay away from him!" Rei hissed, clenching his fist. His dark eyes burned savagely; a blue vein jumped out of his temple. "That bastard! You deserve far better."

Even after two glasses, I knew that my own mistake far exceeded the wrongdoings of Wolfgang. Yet my protector had a blind spot. If I handed him a gun now, he would probably pull the trigger without qualm, blasting a hole in that bastard's heart.

Thus, I declared with a feeble smile, "I'm over him now. His loss."

"I couldn't agree more!" Rei drained his wine swiftly and slammed down the empty glass. The stem broke.

After bandaging his cut, I said, "my couch isn't as comfy as your hotel bed. But you had too much to drink."

"Good idea," he said, staggering to his feet. "I'll stay."

That night, I barely slept. In the wee hours, I could hear the pacing in the living room. Then footsteps approached and paused in front of my bedroom. Impulsively, I jumped up and walked toward the door. The cool floor creaked underfoot. Resting my hand on the doorknob, I heard my pounding heart. Only an inch of plywood separated us, damming the turbulence of desire and innocent longing. In the darkness, I envisioned his outstretched arms; I heard his heavy breathing and his silent pleading, *Come here, my love!*

A tight coil sprang up inside me. Every muscle tensed, fighting an urge to fling the door open and run into his embrace, into that warm, comforting, awaiting chest. For what felt like an eternity I was rooted there, burying my hands deep into the pockets of my nightgown, transmitting my thoughts to Rei a foot away. *Forgive me, but I shouldn't selfishly hog your love that I can never return. I mustn't sabotage your chance for happiness, with that shy, petite girl from Chengdu.*

A few hours later, we hugged our last goodbyes. Somehow, I'd known that as I let him go.

The rest of the day, I roamed around at work like a zombie. Then a golden light burst through the lab door—the last straw.

By consuming all my willpower in rejecting Rei in the early morning, I ended up in Wolfgang's bed that night. Nevertheless, desperate lovemaking was followed by a fierce war. I lashed out with my compounded anguish.

Of course, Wolfgang remained the same. Yet I continued wallowing in this torrid affair for much longer than I dared to admit even to myself. Why did I keep repeating the same old, same old missteps and expecting a different outcome? By Mother's definition, I was an incurable fool.

I no longer picked up Rei's calls. Still, I replayed his messages again and again, savoring the bittersweetness of hearing his concerns. I couldn't talk because I couldn't lie to him, and he would be devastated by my despicable truth. I would be, too. Severing our bond and drowning in sorrow was better than losing his respect and love.

Night after sleepless night, my-older-but-not-wiser-self stubbornly challenged my reasons for pushing him away again. But my inner evolutionary biologist was always more persuasive. Life was irreversible anyway—the distance between the two coasts seemed to stretch with each passing day, same with our diverging beliefs.

In the dark, all I could do was clutch the memory of our love, as everlasting as a fossilized insect trapped in amber.

❧

Three months after Rei left, I attended a conference at Hynes Convention Center in town. During the lunch break, a woman with a round face, framed by neat bangs, beamed at me. Joyfully I cried out, "Xiao Lin!"

We caught up where we had left off eight years earlier—in a restroom at NYU.

Only six months after her relocation to California, Xiao Lin was already exuding a sunny vibe. "Great weather, abundant Chinese restaurants, and warmer people," she said. "What's not to like? You should totally move to the Bay Area."

"Oh, I heard this gospel before," I laughed, washing down potato chips with Poland Spring water, all complimentary of a pharmaceutical company. Its ubiquitous logo reminded me of Dr. B, who had been sponsored by that same company in the past. "Do you know, Dr. B has become the new dean?"

A dark cloud raced across Xiao Lin's porcelain face.

I said, "Too bad we didn't reconnect during all these years."

"I meant to reach out to you after I fled, but . . ." She said, batting her long lashes. "Gosh, I still can't believe that you've escaped from his claws unharmed."

"Well, it depends on the definition of *unharmed*. He has certainly killed my passion for science. Nowadays, I have serious doubts about my career path."

"Who doesn't? But as the proverb says, *when a door closes, a window opens*."

I envied her rosy optimism. It probably stemmed from her participation in the fruitful Human Genome Project. Meanwhile, my own research on neuron signal transducers had so far yielded scant positive results. After tilling the field for two years, I probably would have to publish yet another disappointing article: "Compound X *does not* play a significant role in the regulation of Na-K channels . . ."

Dispirited, I changed the subject. "Any luck in your personal life?"

Blushing, she said, "Not much when I was in Boston. But things are looking up now."

"Aha! Now I see the real allure of sunny Palo Alto: swarms of well-educated, eligible Chinese bachelors."

"I think I have found the one." Pink all the way to her ears, she stopped nibbling at her roast beef sandwich.

"Excellent! Do tell."

"He's a postdoc in physics."

My heart skipped a beat. Immediately I reassured myself: *There must be hundreds of Chinese physics postdocs in the Bay Area.* With artful calm, I said, "What's his name?"

"Qian Jia-Rei."

Ohoomph, I went deaf. Somehow, I managed to say, "How long have you been dating?"

"Hmm, almost five months now. We met at a Mid-Autumn Festival party." Then she halted, "Something wrong?"

"I know Rei. We were neighbors when we were kids." Arranging my two-hundred-pound lips into what I hoped was a gallant smile, I said, "You suit each other well, lucky girl."

"Wow, what a small world! Tell me, what was he like as a boy?" Her face glowed like a full moon.

"Back then, he was the skinniest kid on our block. We went to the same grade school in Nanjing, until I moved to Shanghai," I recounted mechanically. "He was very competitive with everything, even with marble games." A sharp pain lacerated my throat as if I had swallowed a chipped marble. Rei could fill her in on if he wanted to.

"He's still competitive. You should see him playing foosball. *Hee, hee, hee!* " Suddenly, she braked her hand-covered giggles and asked gingerly, "Any news about your life?"

I hesitated. From the perspective of a girl in love, perhaps, a bad relationship looked better than nil. So, I said vaguely, "I've been seeing a fellow postdoc, off and on."

"Why is that?"

"He's German." Cornered, I offered this explanation as the root cause of my problem.

"Oh," Xiao Lin's eyes widened. "An interracial romance! You're brave."

"And foolish."

"Have fun!" Then she added, looking straight into my eyes, "As long as you remember what you are seeking by the end of the day."

I was stunned. This was no longer the timid and docile girl that I thought I knew, and she was absolutely right. Wolfgang could never deliver what I wanted. How stupid could I be—hinge my happiness on the hope that someone else would change?

Suddenly, the noise level in the exhibition hall dropped twenty decibels. Every head turned toward TV screens flashing with *"Breaking News: Paula Jones's case against Clinton has been dropped."*

After exchanging uncomfortable glances, Xiao Lin said, "I've been a coward, I admit. Then I realized something when I watched the confirmation hearings of Judge Thomas. It must take years to muster the courage to speak up. I wish I could be brave—like Anita Hill, like you."

My cheeks burned at Xiao Lin's misplaced praise. At the same time, I was relieved: Rei would be all right in life with such a mature woman on his side.

After the conference, Wolfgang's golden sheen suddenly lost its luster. Two miserable months after our final breakup, he moved to Chicago for a faculty position.

In the ensuing years, Rei and I faithfully exchanged our news: me marrying Tony, and him marrying Xiao Lin; the birth of a baby boy for Rei, and our twins a year after; he became an associate professor, and I pivoted into the pharmaceutical field.

23

A SCIENTIST
WITHOUT A BORDER

Earlier at the banquet, when Little Aunt inquired about Rei, she had probably assumed that he and I would always stay in touch. It was unfathomable even to me that our last phone conversation had been three years before.

When Rei had called that spring afternoon, I was weeding in my backyard, readying the ground for a my tomato garden.

"Sorry to return your New Year's greeting so late," Rei said. "I've just returned from a hectic trip to Shanghai. You see, my alma mater has awarded me a full professorship."

"Congratulations!" I said automatically. "Did they roll out the red carpet for you?"

"I guess," he chuckled. "Do you know anything about the Thousand Talents Plan? They enticed me with a state-of-the-art lab."

"What?" I perked up. "I thought you were just teaching. Are you doing similar research over there?"

"You bet. Believe it or not, my Shanghai lab is better funded."

Electricity zapped through my skull. I cried out, "No! they're using you." Hearing no response, I waved my muddy trowel desperately in the air as if that could get his attention across the continent. "Stop playing with fire!"

"Listen, we're racing toward a major breakthrough," he said breezily. "Why not have two independent teams compete and collaborate at the same time? The beauty is: any update can be applied to each team in a few clicks."

"Rei! How could one serve two masters? Have you forgotten that China is still a totalitarian country with an incompatible ideology, atrocious agendas, and—and corrupt bureaucrats all the way to the highest level? You've pledged your allegiance under oath." My eyes moistened, remembering my own citizenship ceremony at Faneuil Hall years before, my hand trembling among a small forest of raised arms—of every shape, texture, and hue. "Our homes are here now."

"But human beings are capable of dual loyalty, just like a man could love both an old flame and—" He dry-coughed, then continued, "Anyway, I'm a scientist without a border. You must understand, we're at the cusp of another industrial revolution, a game-changer for the whole human race, not just a few-percent productivity boost."

I raised my voice, "But advanced technology in the wrong hands is dangerous!"

"Technology has always been a double-edged sword. For example, nuclear energy can be harnessed for destruction or fueling the power grid. Science is always dangerous in any society, at any time. Remember Galileo? That's the price I'm willing to pay."

The bucket dropped from my hand. Fluffy dandelions tumbled out and danced in the wind. Staring at my dirtied fingernails through the ripped latex gloves, I said, deflated, "What did Xiao Lin say about this?"

"Oh, the usual objections." He laughed. "Being overcautious has its own cost, too. Great things can never be achieved without someone taking a risk."

"You're so . . . so naive!"

He laughed ."Maybe. Trust me, I can manage."

Soon the conversation ended on a forced note. *He has made a grave mistake!* Furiously, I chased the denuded dandelion crowns all over the backyard. Yet I was angrier at myself, at my inability to articulate my worries. Like in some paranormal tales of twins, I could sense the perils ahead of him. But how could I convince him? He would simply laugh off my gloomy premonition as a woman's hysteria.

By then, we had lived more years in our adopted country than in China. I had assumed that we were fully assimilated. Just look at me. Married to a *laowai*, raising American kids, and ditched the lofty academia for a career in profit-driven pharma. Could I be any more mainstream American? Even my dreamscape was a petri dish of bubbling anxieties of the American middle class. Now, though, the phone call proved me wrong about the inevitability of our Americanization—Rei still couldn't let go of his severed umbilical cord or phantom limb.

I couldn't let go of him either, yet—I dreaded—I was losing him fast. Perhaps I'd lost him already.

Why did the chasm between us widen? Running three generations deep, my mistrust of the Chinese Communist Party was encoded right down to the cellular level. On the contrary, a few years earlier Rei had shaken hands with prominent Party leaders who attended the funeral of his father, a renowned rocket scientist in China. Even after the Tiananmen massacre, he still gazed at pink China through a rosy rearview mirror. How could we possibly see eye to eye in the most fundamental things in life?

After that frustrating call, our communications were downgraded to short text messages. Holiday greetings, congratulations, and condolences. . . Nevertheless, a ritual continued. Every September, like clockwork, a smiling face would peek from my phone on the anniversary of the roller-coaster misadventure of our youth. To that, I had always replied with apprehension, "*Another year, another ride.*"

Still, the intervals between my worries grew longer. Sometimes I even forgot about Rei's existence on the West Coast, or (heaven helps us) Shanghai. Midlife had hardened me up. Since I couldn't change him, I should invest my finite time on Earth in myself and my own family.

But, whenever my children clamored for Six Flags, Tony would be the one to take them there, along with Uncle Jeff. Citing my queasy stomach, I'd always secretly relished those quiet Sundays when I could put in productive hours in the lab, or just indulge myself by gardening at home.

I could never bring myself to tell Little Aunt about Rei's tragedy. The worst part: I learned it from the FBI.

Five months before, I gulped down a cup of hot tea and dashed out of our house—I was late for work on account of Leonardo's misplaced baseball glove. Halfway down our narrow driveway, a man stepped from behind my Ford Escape and blocked me with his broad shoulders. I jumped.

"Agent James Wright," he flashed his badge, his bulging biceps made his navy suit appear two sizes too tight. His baritone voice was rich and smooth, evoking the memory of Carl Kasell on *Wait Wait... Don't Tell Me!*

The American flag clip on his scarlet tie made my heart flutter like a hummingbird, and my mind raced for a plausible reason for this ambush. I wished that Tony hadn't left home. Even after living in the States for nearly thirty years, I still harbored an incurable phobia of authority, uniformed or plain clothed.

With a curt smile, Agent Wright produced a picture from his briefcase. "Ms. Hong," he demanded, "do you recognize this person?"

It was a professional photo of a middle-aged man smiling in front of a muslin backdrop; the off-center smile could easily be interpreted as a hint of arrogance or derision. The photo appeared to be downloaded from the website of the university where Rei was now a tenured professor, a rising star in the field of artificial intelligence, and a Nobel laureate in the making.

"That's Professor Jia-Rei Qian," I said with equal parts panic and pride.

"Thank you, Ms. Hong. Could you elaborate on your relationship with Mr. Qian?"

"*Dr.* Qian. But why? What's going on?"

"Three days ago, Dr. Qian," he paused, "jumped off a building on the Stanford campus in California. I'm hoping you can help us with the investigation of his death."

A shriek—a foreign, terrifying sound as if a vital organ had just been ripped out of a beast—burst out of my own throat. My knees buckled. I collapsed against my car, oblivious to the arm proffered by Agent Wright.

A few rapid and shallow breaths later, the sharp pain abated. I managed to murmur, "I am—I was—his childhood friend. But we haven't talked for a while, several years, I think."

Under Agent Wright's penetrating gaze, I recalled our last heated debate over the phone.

"We've processed the hard drives of Dr. Qian's computers," he said with a neutral expression. "Your name has come up in his diary on multiple occasions. Are you aware of his political affiliation?"

"As far as I know, he had none. He considered himself 'a scientist without a border.'" A chill swept over me. Rei had kept a diary!

"I see. Do you know anything about his medical history back in China? Did he have a history of depression or any mental illness?"

"Rei? Absolutely not!" I raised my voice, wanting to slap his blank face. "Why is the FBI involved in his suicide?" As I was arguing, cold sweat started to drip down my back. Vaguely, I already knew the answer on some level.

"You must understand, this is an ongoing investigation," he said gravely. "There was an eyewitness at the scene. However, we haven't completely ruled out homicide. I'm sorry, but I'm not at liberty to give you more details regarding your friend's death."

Death. Once that word was repeated, it vibrated with the somber finality of a church bell. The man glanced at my house and gave my elbow an almost imperceptible nudge. Rooted in my driveway, I denied his unspoken offer to escort me to my couch. *You can't force me to participate in a one-way information exchange. Any unwise words uttered now might be twisted into a weapon against Rei—or me in the future.*

Staring at this man's moving lips, I heard no sound. A version of me, a boiled-down version, had drifted above and was now watching the dandelions trembling on my crabgrass lawn.

Eventually, he handed me his business card, shook my hand, then disappeared into a black Buick with tinted windows parked across the street.

As if on a pair of wobbly stilts, I staggered into the house and sank into the couch. I closed my eyes. But I couldn't erase an image from behind my eyelids: Rei swaying on the thin ledge of a flat roof, his face pensive, his silvering hair sparkling under the cheerful California sun. From below, I gestured frantically, shouting, "Step back, please!" But he didn't see me, nor hear my desperate plea. Then, he smiled crookedly into the vacant distance, dragged in a deep breath, leaped forth, and flew into the bright sky. A black speck cut a perfect arc, faithfully observing Newton's law of gravitation. *Boom*, a volcano erupted right in front of me, scalding me with its blinding, molten lava . . .

Had I tried harder, could I have succeeded in persuading him not to entangle himself with his alma mater in China? Perhaps I should have emphasized the enormous difference between the mother *culture* we couldn't wean ourselves from, and the "motherland"—the so-called *People's Republic* of China. Why had I stopped talking to him? Why? Why? Why? Briny liquid brimmed my tightly shut eyes.

I couldn't stop blaming myself. Yet, deep down, I also knew that I was powerless to alter his trajectory, even if I'd won our last argument. He had been a marked man since his fateful Shanghai trip—just like the sacrificial slaves chained in the Shang Dynasty tomb in that gruesome documentary from our childhood.

Then I felt another stab in my chest. Rei hadn't bid me goodbye, hadn't even bothered to send a smiley face. Did he think he could just pop up outside my door with a hydrangea bouquet sometime in the future? A crisp edge of the business card jabbed my palm. A torrent of hot, fat tears gushed down.

I turned on my laptop. Combing through our past email correspondence, I gave up halfway. No doubt Agent Wright had already read them. What else could I tell him? That I'd lost not only my childhood friend but also my brother, my first love, and my soulmate?

Later, I woke up to find Tony rattling my lunch tote above me. "Funny, I found this on the hood of your car."

"Oh! I'm not hungry."

He frowned. "Are you all right?"

"No." I said, tears streaking again. "Rei died."

"What happened?" Tony eased onto the edge of my bed, laying his hand on my forehead to check for a fever.

Between choking sobs, I told him about the surprise visit from Agent Wright. He tucked wayward strands of my hair behind my ears, murmuring, "*Shhh*. Mei, let it out, let it all out. It's okay."

"No! It's not okay!" I clawed away his hand. He'd used the same words and tone when our kids lost their beloved hamster. "You will never understand."

"You're wrong." His voice cracked. Abruptly, he got up and walked to the door.

Then it dawned on me that he'd also lost a childhood friend, Brian, to a bottle of sleeping pills.

"Tony," I called to the closed door, wishing to retract the harsh words that had flown out of my mouth. I called again, but his footsteps had descended the staircase. Too exhausted to get up, I lay in bed, listening to the evening creeping in, engulfing us with our individual grief.

Later that night, I called Rei's home phone. Ignoring my questions, Xiao Lin kept repeating flatly, "How could he, how could he do that?" After hanging up, I booked a flight to California.

In the foyer of Eternal Peace Funeral Home, a photo of a respectable professor greeted me. His remote, closed smile had nothing in common with that crooked grin that I'd known all my life.

Then I felt my chest tightened—I didn't possess a single photo of Rei. Of the few college-era pictures I still had, he was the photographer. After our ferry trip to Ellis Island, he mailed me a closeup of my animated face, my hair flying in the wind. Why didn't I ask any passerby to take a picture of us? The need to preserve our moments together had never occurred to the young and foolish me. Now, what could I hold on to, what could I remember him by?

In Rei's abstract smile, I desperately searched for him: the skinny kid with a sword, the white-knuckled lad who enjoyed a roller coaster ride, the passionate lover in my rumpled bed, the pleading young man with a viselike grip on a park bench, the grinning man who said, "I find you again," the man drowning in sorrow when I rejected him again, the brother with vein-popping rage against my wrongdoer, and with the hidden anguish behind my closed door. . . A kaleidoscopic range of images spun—Rei at different ages, with different expressions, from different angles, and under different lights. If Agent Wright had asked me to help a forensic artist to sketch him, I would have been at a total loss. But the most agonizing thing was this: with each passing hour, the distinct features of Rei's face became more blurred, like an impressionist painting or reflections over a shimmering pond, his essence evaporating like an open bottle of perfume with fewer and fewer identifiable molecules left.

". . . a brilliant mind at his prime . . ."

". . . devastating loss to our field . . ."

I overheard snippets of whispers between two sorrowful men, presumably Rei's colleagues. Decades from now, would Rei become one of those one-line footnotes in some obscure textbook? I shuddered, recalling his reference to Galileo in our last conversation. He should be exalted as a martyr for sciences, too, and at the very least, a tragic hero who had devoted himself to his misguided beliefs.

In the crowd, two men appeared conspicuously out of place. One stood near the entrance, critically regarding the photo of a stereotypical professor and the grieving congregation, while the other milled around with a blank face, eavesdropping on conversations. Loud and clear, their manners screamed "Agent Wright."

Then I spotted a dazed woman towered by men engrossed in their conversations. Vacant-eyed and sickly pale, Xiao Lin was leaning on the arm of a skinny boy almost as tall as she. My heart jerked at the sight of his intense, obsidian eyes and dense hair. Bracing myself, I walked over and folded Xiao Lin into my embrace. She made a hoarse, hiccup sound before draining her tears onto the lapel of my black jacket, while the boy stoically looked on.

Later, Xiao Lin told me that Rei had suffered from an anxiety attack after his last Shanghai trip three months ago. After two trial medications (which caused mental fogginess), he seemed to tolerate his newest medication reasonably well. The day before his last, Rei had attended a meeting with the vice provost. Lawyers for the university had been evasive in answering her many questions, citing the ongoing internal and FBI investigations.

On his last night, Rei had paced in his study after an incoming phone call. Xiao Lin brought him the evening pill with a glass of water and asked about the call. "A wrong number" was all he said, avoiding eye contact. She hesitated. The call had lasted at least five minutes, and night calls were usually from Shanghai. But Rei looked bone exhausted, so she decided not to press.

At sunrise the next morning, a security guard doing rounds saw a man jump off the top of the physics building where Rei had worked for many years. Twenty minutes later, a phone call woke Xiao Lin up.

Rei hadn't left any notes.

On the red-eye flight back to Boston, I pressed my palm on the oval window. Outside, the clouds were black, dense, and velvety, like young Rei's hair. I lay my hand there for a long while, but all I could feel was the night chill creeping into my bones.

Random snippets of our conversations over the years bubbled in my mind, and his crooked smile sparkled brightly in darkness. My eyes smarted. I realized that I had to tackle another task: to document the true Rei for future generations, one electronic fragment at a time. I must sculpture him in three dimensions—before those images in my mind could fade away.

For my sanity, I needed to honor Rei's life. It wasn't futile to feed a dying funeral pyre with the last twigs foraged from a December field, even the fire was bound to burn out. Unlike the unheard sound of a fallen tree in a forest, the memory of the flicking orange flames could thaw the freezing heart of the fire-tenderer.

More glass clinking around the banquet table. So, my family was toasting yet another happy occasion that my mind couldn't register. As the night dragged on, my random thoughts scattered like shooting stars while I hid with a mechanical smile behind my teacup.

Apparently, I was losing my tenuous grip on my clan and was in danger of becoming an outsider in my own hometown. After each round of tireless toasting, I grew soberer; the satiated faces of my laughing kin became ruddier. Those faces were like variations on the theme of my losses. And I pondered my own mortality on what I hoped would be the distant horizon.

A few days before, at the Border Control of Pudong International Airport, a stout officer had asked me in a stern tone, "What's the purpose of your visit: business or pleasure?"

For a split second I was paralyzed. He looked familiar. Could he be the same security guard at Fudan University decades ago, the man who chased after Rei and me? The question he posed, a simple binary, suddenly became extreamly tricky. I hesitated. Was it for pleasure—to celebrate the Mid-Autumn Festival with my father? Or for business— unresolved family business? I wished for more options, such as "All of the Above" or "None of the Above." How about "bereavement"? Many travelers would have checked this box. Then a realization hit me like a lightening bolt : 2012 had been a year of mourning for the Hong family;and for me, three consecutive and compounding mourning.

Meanwhile, the man's stare intensified like a searchlight from a prison tower. Reflexively, I assembled my lips into an approximation of smile and declared, "For pleasure, sir. To visit my family."

He scrutinized my face once again and compared it with my passport photo, which had been taken a decade earlier. Poker-faced, he scrolled his mouse up and down, hammered his keyboard a few times with his fat fingers, then paused. I clenched my fist with anxiety. Just before my hands went numb, he stamped my passport with a thud, waved me off, then trained his eagle eyes on the next person in line.

Now, the thought of that insignificant encounter made my palms sweaty again. The teacup in my hand became icy. And I felt like a Shackleton explorer, trudging and leaning into an Antarctic gust—I had lost my tribal protection and banished my traitor father to the outer space of my universe.

The loss had been insidious. When Grandpa died on the train forty years before, a strong bulwark was obliterated. When Mother passed away six months before, a pillar of my fortress collapsed. When Rei exited from this world without bidding his final goodbye, I heard the dark force pummeling my front door. With Grandma gone, even the beaded curtain in the entryway was ripped apart and scattered on the crumbling floor.

I couldn't see it, the evil beast, but I could sniff its bloody stench in the air and feel its hot breath on my skin. Any moment now, a blood-soiled paw could land on my shoulder, and sharp fangs would sink into my jugular vein if I turned my head the wrong way.

Yet, the fiery Hong blood was still pulsating through my arteries.

I would put up a fight, even if I were armored with nothing but my grief. Even if I could scratch only a single scale off the beast with my fingernails.

24

MY PARENTS

At midnight, our hostess ushered out the last batch of banquet guests. While the crowd was dispersing, Binbin almost tripped over the entrance steps. Embarrassed, he slurred, "No—worries. I'm—I'm going to haul a Didi."

Ixin insisted on giving me a lift. He said, Didi—the Chinese equivalent of Uber—was "unsuitable for a girl at this hour."

It had been ages since anyone (I believe it was Tony) called me "a girl". Still, I was touched by his concern. Thus, when the valet brought out Ixin's car—a top-of-the-line Mercedes-Benz—I ran my finger on its masculine hood ridge and murmured my obligatory homage: "What a beauty!"

Ixin beamed like he had invented the model.

At the curb of a luminous high-rise near the Drum Tower, Ixin dropped off his family. The sleepy-eyed Yuanyuan blew me a kiss; Chun waved like a Rose Parade queen. When they strutted toward a carpeted entrance banked with topiary box-woods, a doorman held the gilded door with a professional bow.

On the southbound ride, I complimented Ixin's alcohol tolerance—he had remained sober throughout the evening. He chuckled, patting his nascent beer belly, "In China, deals are often done in banquet rooms, not boardrooms. To be the last man standing, every businessman has a trick or two."

When I praised Yuanyuan's accent-free English, Ixin said, "Ah, she's been taking private lessons on conversational English." Then, he sighed. "You should see her calendar. Olympic math, Ballet, piano, polo. . . Chun has enrolled our daughter in every class that might give her the slightest edge."

"Wow! Does Yuanyuan have a free minute left?" I said, suddenly feeling inadequate as a mother.

"Nowadays, every kid does that." He said with a frown, "What can we do? Let her lose at the starting line?"

Ixin was a decade younger than me. Growing up, we mingled only during our family gatherings. After an awkward silence, he inquired about my father's health.

"Couldn't be better. He's already remarried, even before Mother's ashes cooled."

"We know." Ixin slammed the brakes; a delivery boy on a moped had run a red light and cut in front of us. Unfussed, he continued, "My mother has forbidden us to speak of him."

"Ha! No wonder."

In front of Grandma's building, Ixin volunteered to pick up my family upon their arrival. A pang of anxiety hit me: I had yet to confirm our meeting point for the past two days. Instead of confessing my communication difficulty with Tony, I politely declined Ixin's offer. Before he made a nifty U-turn and sped away, he lowered the window to shout, "Hey, if you change your mind, call me anytime!"

It was almost 1:00 p.m. Boston time by the time I finished checking my voicemail, the call logs, and email. Still nothing.

After the fifth ring, I slumped into the armchair with a sinking heart. *Why has Tony stopped answering his cell phone?* In despair, I set the alarm for four hours—right before my family would have to leave for Logan Airport.

Tossing and turning in Grandma's sagging bed, I rewound the evening in my mind. Other than Ixin, no one had mentioned my father. I wished I could write him off, too.

Two days before, my father had replied to my WeChat message (of declining to brunch with him): "Smooth sailing. See you at the Mid-Autumn Festival dinner."

Seeing his message, I visualized him mopping his sweaty brows, muttering to that Tian woman, "Phew, another bullet dodged." Immediately, I punched my response in fury, "Sorry, a last-minute change. Tony and the kids will meet me in Nanjing instead."

Five minutes later, he texted back, "Have a nice trip to Yellow Mountain!"

His delayed response wiped out the minuscule satisfaction I'd squeezed out of my petty revenge. How did we arrive at this miserable junction? I almost wept. The urge to confront him on Mother's behalf had sizzled out long before. All I wanted from him was a quasi-honest explanation for his betrayal.

Now, even the flimsy explanation would be unnecessary. At some level, I'd already known how his affair started. Yet I chastised myself. *How did I miss so many glaring clues in the past?*

Stupidly, I'd never viewed my parents as an unhappy couple. To me, their strained union was as self-evident as the east-rising and west-setting sun. Growing up, the only mystery was how these two people became my parents in the first place. Finally, after our family trip to visit my ailing *nainai* in Suzhou, I probed Mother and pried out the story of their courtship.

In spring 1962, twenty-one-year-old Ting-Fang boarded a Nanjing-bound train to attend the funeral of Hao-Ran, her grandfather. After claiming her window seat, she spread the *People's Daily* on the tray table.

As usual, the domestic good news plastered on the front page made her grumble under her breath. It was an open secret that millions of farmers had perished in the recent Three-Year Famine. Reflexively, she glanced at her bulging rucksack on the overhead rack. Hidden inside were five kilos of soy and two liters of cottonseed oil—a small miracle that she pulled off in a black market on short notice. Two days prior, she had tried to persuade the bookkeeper in her tractor factory to advance her wage.

"Can't do that," he said, shaking his slick hair. Then he took a ten-yuan bill out of his flabby wallet. "But I'm willing to give you a personal loan—"

"How nice of you!" Ting-Fang exclaimed, reaching for the bill.

"Wait." Clamping the money with his knobby fingers while examining her breasts with his x-ray vision, he said slyly, "If my wife finds this out, she will kill me... How are you going to thank me?"

"Deduct the amount plus a 10 percent interest from my next paycheck. Thanks." She snatched the bill from his grasp and fled, ignoring his repeated calling from behind.

All these lecherous men! With disgust, she flipped the pages to the international section. Predictably, headlines flashed with the follies of the evil American imperialists: the failed Bay of Pigs invasion in Cuba, the misadventures in the jungles in Vietnam, an exposed price-gouging scheme of the US steel industry . . .

She sifted through the inflammatory words carefully. Even the tiniest bit of buried foreign news might have profound effects in the isolated Middle Kingdom. For instance, after the falling out of the two revolutionary brothers, sporadic surplus from the Soviet Union vanished altogether.

Just the previous morning, after hearing the rumor of a batch of cotton from Albania—one of China's last socialist allies—she'd shuffled in a long line outside of a fabric store. Eyeing the ugly, liver-brown fabric through the window and clutching three years' worth of fabric coupons she'd accumulated, she mentally calculated the minimal yardage she would need to sew pants for her growing siblings back home. Then she sighed, looking down at her layer-thick knee patches. Never mind, she would have to mend new holes with another piece of scrap. Then, three hours later, a cashier put up a "Sold Out" sign on the door and scurried inside; women near the entrance cried out in dismay.

Something glinted under the rising sun—the safety pin holding the mourning band on her sleeve. An idea emerged. If she gathered all the black bands at the funeral, would it be enough to sew a short skirt for her baby sister, or a pair of boxer shorts for her brother? She took out a pen and started to draw on the newspaper margin.

A shadow fell on her sketch; she looked up. A young man with round-rimmed glasses was squinting at the faded number above her seat. Then, taking a ticket out of his breast pocket, he cleared his throat, "Excuse me, comrade, is it possible that you're sitting in my assigned seat?"

"Oh! Pardon me." She stood up, ready for a seat exchange.

He motioned her to sit down, mumbling, "Doesn't matter to me."

"Thank you." she said, noticing his gesturing hands—as refined as those of a concert pianist.

"Not at all." His face colored as if he'd been caught doing something naughty.

Two men took the seats opposite theirs. The double-chinned man with an air of authority tapped out a cigarette for himself, a second for his hunchbacked companion, then tapped out a third to offer to Ting-Fang's seatmate. To her delight, "Xiao Huang", the shy young man, gently declined the free cigarette.

Between puffs, the two smokers carried on a serious discussion in cryptic jargon. Occasionally, they frowned, then turned to Xiao Huang for clarification. Xiao Huang leaned forward with a slight bow, then explained some technical details.

The group seemed to be rehearsing for a worrisome inquiry regarding a procedure delay due to some unexpected tiny air bubbles in a large-diameter lens. Their apprehension about a certain mysterious man was palpable. Intrigued, Ting-Fang eased down the newspaper that she was pretending to read and stole a furtive glance.

The boss noticed her eavesdropping. At once, he ground out his cigarette on the metal tray and demanded, "What's your name, comrade?"

"Hong Ting-Fang."

"Where do you work?"

"The No. 1 Tractor Factory in Shanghai."

"What do you do there?"

"I'm a saleswoman."

"A saleswoman," the man repeated, allowing the hunched sidekick to catch up with his busy notetaking. "Why are you traveling alone?"

"I'm heading home for my grandfather's funeral," Ting-Fang said, pointing to her mourning band. She was surprised by the sharp yet unobservant eyes of the man.

The boss nodded his grave face into a triple-chin. Then he interrogated Ting-Fang about her extended family.

As the rapid-fire questioning continued, Xiao Huang's face turned from pink to crimson. His nervous pen-twirling rattled the normally self-assured Ting-Fang. Soon her palms grew sweaty.

After the sidekick struck a match to light the last cigarette for the boss, both men got off at Suzhou station to restock. Xiao Huang, still red-faced, whispered to Ting-Fang, "Sorry for our rudeness. My boss' professional sensitivity overrides etiquette."

"Of course, of course." She admitted, "I shouldn't have paid any attention to your conversation, but—"

"No, *we* are the ones who should have been more discreet." He looked around nervously. (Years later, my mother learned that their dreaded meeting was with the Ministry of Defense.)

Watching the boss and his sidekick puffing on the platform, she said, "Too bad this stop is only five minutes. If it were five hours, I'd like to tour this 'Heaven on Earth.'"

"A five-hour visit won't do Suzhou any justice. Trust me, you need at least three days." He blushed again, adding, "I grew up here."

His reddened, delicate face aroused the hidden gambler in her. Fixing her gaze on his eyes behind the glasses, she ventured, "Well, in that case, perhaps you could show me around your hometown someday. In exchange, I'll be your tour guide in Nanjing." She laughed drily, knowing that most men would be turned off by her bold, impromptu proposal. "I believe you've learned pretty much everything about me by now."

After he realized that the young woman with dazzling eyes wasn't teasing, a shy smile crept up on his face. "Sounds like a fair deal," he said, extending his musician's hand, "I am Huang Qiu-Yu."

"I'm still Hong Ting-Fang." She laughed again, grasping his hand. A zap made her flinch.

"Sorry, static," Xiao Huang said reflexively.

"You don't need to apologize for everything!" She chuckled for the third time, then concurred with a sigh, "Isn't it awful—another dry spring?"

"I hope a good storm will arrive soon, to break the drought spell."

Ting-Fang's bright eyes dimmed. In the preceding three years of "natural diasters", the entire nation had sustained itself on an ultra-low-calorie diet. Forget about pork, chicken, belt fish, and eggs. She could count on one hand the occasions when tofu (by then a luxury item that required coupons too) appeared in her factory cafeteria. Her mother wrote to her that her bed-ridden grandfather had been refusing food—so that his meager rations could be passed to his only grandson.

Their talk stopped after the boss reclaimed his seat. Yet a continuous current looped between their adjacent knees. Whenever the two chain smokers stepped out at stops, words flew out again.

At Zhenjiang, the last stop before Nanjing, Ting-Fang wrote her address on the ripped margin of the newspaper and slid it over. Without a word, Xiao Huang tucked the folded paper into the shirt pocket over his heart.

At Nanjing station, she wished her travel companions a pleasant journey and walked toward the door. Then she heard the snickering.

"Xiao Huang, did that girl steal something from you?"

"Ha, ha, ha, look at his red face!"

Ignoring the burning sensation on her back and squaring her shoulders, she exited the train.

The day after the funeral, she received her first letter from poor Xiao Huang who must have endured relentless teasing for the remainder of his trip.

> *Comrade Ting-Fang,*
>
> *It's such a delight to have talked to you on the train. Thank you for your good wishes. Our meeting in Beijing turned out better than anticipated. . .*
>
> *My condolences for your family's loss . . .*
>
> *I wish to visit Nanjing in a happy circumstance and take up your offer to be my local guide.*
>
> *Solute with revolutionary love,*
>
> *Huang Qiu-Yu*

Ting-Fang slid the letter into the inner jacket of Volume 3 of Mao's compiled books and replied immediately, affirming her standing offer.

Soon, the correspondence between my parents accelerated to a daily basis. Burning with revolutionary love, astonishingly, even a monotoned engineer could produce some third-rate poems—hot enough to melt the thick armor of Mulan. Soon, the romance blossomed between the two least romantics in Shanhai.

In the endless maze of carnival mirrors at the Dashijie Funhouse, Ting-Fang waved at hundreds of versions of herself; the familiar figures—chubby, thin, giant, dwarf, and distorted in every possible plane—waved hilariously back at her. She laughed until doubling over with tears. Around her, the only unlaughing person was Xiao Huang. Pointing at the convex and concave segments of the mirrors, he was busily explaining the optical principles. Finally, a handsome couple at the far end of the hall greeted them—their own flawless reflections side by side, smiling with adoration at each other in that perfect world.

My mother was drawn to my father's thoroughgoing mind, his gentle manner, and his attentiveness. My father, growing up among languid and indecisive women, found my mother's boldness refreshing.

A year later, they took a trip to the People's Square, with two witnesses in tow. In the municipal hall, a Soviet-style concrete block erected on a former British horseracing track, they handed in red-stamped letters from their respective companies. Afterwards, as was customary in the sixties, the newlyweds went to the People's Studio on Nanjing Road for their wedding photo.

Even though the black-and-white photo was gone with the tin box, I could still see the image in my mind: my parents in their unisex Lenin uniforms, their eyes sparkling with the yearning of happy years ahead. And that cursive Mao quotation embossed on the scalloped bottom: "*A Revolution is not a Dinner Party.*"

That night, after my mother joined her two suitcases with my father's, the ensuing duty to the party was performed on his dormitory bed.

Another year later, I was born in Huashan Hospital in Shanghai.

My birth was a mixed blessing. Naming me after my maternal clan bruised the proud new father's ego, but he didn't object loudly enough to overrule the big-lunged Hongs. Over time, this initial hairline fissure continued widening to the size of an unnavigable strait.

Busy couples should have no business bringing a child into the world. After her maternity leave, my mother boarded me with my grandparents and visited me on her trip layovers. This sensible child-rearing arrangement lasted until the housing authority took over Grandpa's house when I was eight.

Mother explained to me once why she couldn't afford a nanny. She'd been sending a quarter of her paltry salary home to help raise her younger siblings—a tradition since her college years.

In fact, money was the reason that both Mother and Aunt No. 2 attended teachers' college— at the time, the only type of university that was not only tuition-free but also provided a small living stipend.

After college, my mother was assigned to a vocational school affiliated with the tractor factory in Shanghai. By chance, she discovered that salespeople received travel subsidies on top of the standard meager salary. Immediately, she requested to be switched to sales, much to the ecstasy of the manager, who had great difficulty retaining staff to cover the poorest regions.

At the time, selling goods to collectives was merely an exercise of reallocating state assets in a planned economy. Even if Mother couldn't sell a single tractor in a backwater province, no one could fire her. Nevertheless, before each trip Mother would study the agriculture of her target area, the same way a general would study the topography of a potential battlefield.

Once she arrived at the commune, she spent days observing the local farming practices before the evening town hall meeting. Often, in a one-room village school with a dim kerosene lantern flickering in the engulfing darkness, she wrote down a few simple math problems on the blackboard. Then she asked kids running among the crowd to "help her out." When an older kid in rags shouted out the correct answer, she patted the kid's lice-infested head with a smile and a "Good job." In a teacher's voice, she slowly explained the math—the carefully constructed cost–benefit analysis and the tailored installment plan—to the skeptical audience. Soon, the commune elders realized that with improved productivity, their investment in a tractor or combine harvester could be paid off in just a few seasons. One by one, they put down their homemade pipes to applaud the tall, smart woman from the big city.

Back then, performance-based bonuses didn't exist. For decades, Mother's salary remained flat; the only thing that increased was her quota. Every quarter, she brought home enamel mugs and hand towels with her factory logo—a hammer and a sickle crossing over a tractor. Soon, everyone in our clan possessed at least a pair of these regifted prizes. The stack of her citation certificates for being a "model worker" grew thick in the mahogany chest until, years later, I used the heavy-duty paper for origami projects.

Mother seldom smiled. From my vantage point now, the reason couldn't be more obvious: she was born thirty years too early. She did everything better, faster, and more cost-effectively. Worse, she held everyone to her own impossible standard. How could she smile? In a society where collective wisdom always trumped individual talent, a society that favored obedience and cronyism, a woman with true grit always ruffled the wrong feathers.

At dinner, we often laughed at her caricatures of her "Mapijin" coworkers and their outlandish acts. Somehow, one by one, those "brownnosers" were promoted by her equally incompetent boss, while she languished at the rank of an associate sales manager for the poorest region, watching her youth being trampled away by the wheels of the trains, dusty long-distance buses, and smelly animal carts.

Gradually, she stopped entertaining us with her excellent parodies. Repetition was pointless.

Once she had attained middle age, her delusions evaporated, and her cantankerousness was condensed in the few remaining remarks she reserved for her factory. Inevitably, the excessive bile spilled over from work to her family.

The mysterious forces that had attracted the two opposite atoms would eventually repel them once they became close enough. As time passed by, even the happy memories of their courtship became distorted images in the funhouse mirrors, simultaneously real and absurd.

My parents must have realized their mistake by the time I reunited with them in 1972. Witnessing no affection between them, I'd assumed that they weren't the type who wore their emotions on their sleeves. A more plausible explanation: their love had already worn out.

To be fair, few loves could be as everlasting as a diamond. Most love is glass, bursting into irrevocable shards under force. My parents' love was more like a fragile silk scarf—faded and threadbare, spared from the trash bin solely due to its owner's sentimental inertia, and destined for the mothballed trunk in a cobwebbed basement of memory.

What I witnessed countless times was Mother's litany of criticisms of my father. His past virtues were lampooned as his defects: his mild manner was now passivity; his attention to detail was old-maid fussiness; his civility equaled obsequiousness. She could cite ample anecdotes to prove her point. Often, my father and I bowed our heads at dinner, fastidiously plowed our chopsticks in our rice bowls, and exchanged occasional glances. I sometimes prayed for a knock on the door or breaking news on the radio.

Once, Mother's rants even carried on well into the night. I dry-coughed in my room, which eventually put a stop to her needling. The following dinner, my father said, "I'd like to bring Mei with me to visit my mother next Sunday."

Mother vetoed it. "NO. She didn't finish her chores last week. Let her learn her lesson for ignoring her responsibility."

One summer, my father bought me a stack of ship model kits. For weeks, I cut, folded, and glued. One evening, fighting a particularly unruly flag, I ripped it with a pair of forceps. Then, a light tap on my sweaty shoulder. My father whispered—as if the finicky flag would fly away if it heard him— "No need to use that much force." His warm breath tickled my earlobe. I forced back a giggle and my flustered heart calmed down.

Eventually, I made a flawless destroyer model. Even the minute details—of the radar, sailors on its deck, and the helicopter on its pad—looked perfect. My father loved it, too. After he applied two layers of waterproofing varnish, added a wooden plank, and retrofitted it with a propeller, we took it to a park for its maiden voyage. Alas, instead of charging forward, my *Intrepid* cruised in circles in the pond, like a confused cat chasing its tail. "Don't be sad," he said. "All the *Intrepid* needs is just a little bit of wood shaving to alter its center of gravity. Let's rebalance it next Sunday."

On the crowded bus home, I held the destroyer above my head like a trophy.

A few days later, I got home from school and immediately noticed the empty space on the bookshelf: the *Intrepid* wasn't there. The apartment reeked of astringent bleach. In the kitchen, Mother was preoccupied with her post-trip cleansing routine.

For the first time in my life, I mustered enough courage to confront her. "Mother, where is my ship?"

"Don't get too close," she said, raising her rubber-gloved hand as if to block a hardy head louse attempting to jump out of the boiling pot. Then, she pointed at a plastic bag on top of an overflowing trash bin outside the window. "You haven't noticed? It's covered with mold!"

On rare occasions, Mother asked me to cast a symbolic vote to break a tie. What choice did I have? When the frozen glacier split underfoot, I had to jump to the bigger mass and abandon the iceberg. Afterwards, I desperately searched for my father's eyes behind his thick glasses, seeking proof of our mutual sympathy in his gentle smile—as feeble as a struggling January sun through clouds.

My father spent more and more time at work, seeking warmth outside our igloo. To minimize their contact, he set up his travel schedule opposite hers—I'd always assumed he wanted to ensure that at least one parent would be at home.

Unlike Grandpa or my father, I didn't turn out to be a major disappointment to Mother. Still, I had inherited undesirable traits from these weak men. On the basketball court, I couldn't pass the ball fast enough to avoid any aggressive player. Mother's frustrated grunts from the audience only made me shrink smaller. To purge these defects out of me, she shoved me cycle after cycle through furnace, yet I could never be smelted into steel.

Gradually my physical resemblance to Mother took root, and the light in my father's eyes faded. When he glanced in my direction, he seemed to be wary of something two feet behind me. When I eagerly showed him my report cards, he said "well done" with an approving smile—the same way he praised his secretary for a typo-free document. Even after I said that I craved the food in his cafeteria, he still wouldn't bring me to his institute, citing the tightened security.

Achingly, I watched the iceberg drifting farther and farther away, and then lost the diminishing dot to the open sea. Missing the father who whispered in my ear, the one who presented his glass *tanghulu* with a shy smile, I wished for another magic moment, a portal for me to reenter his closed heart.

I held on to that hope long after it had gathered mold like that destroyed destroyer. And I never imagined that he would stop loving Mother altogether, and me, the collateral damage.

In the darkness, the wall clock ticked away second by second. Then, a quote from the old, trustworthy Hegel emerged in my head: "*Genuine tragedies in the world are not conflicts between right and wrong. Those between two rights are.*"

My parents' tragedy was only a question of *when*, not *why*. They had squandered their chance by her habitual jabbing with a dull knife dipped in fermented love, and his inevitable yet still cruel decamping. If he had to carry the burden of betrayal to his grave, then so should she, the accomplice.

Unlike us, men need lots of love. A profound sorrow washed over me as I remembered Mother's deathbed riddle. Not only was it her regret for her miscarriage of happiness, but also a piece of motherly advice, warning me not to repeat her mistakes.

I started to sweat. Could Tony have a lover? On quite a few occasions, he had opted to stay at Jay Peak or Sugarloaf for weekend ski trips after his territory calls. When he returned home, blissfully exhausted from "a great powder day," was there any unfamiliar perfume on his shirt? Or lipstick stains? I couldn't recall, because it had never crossed my mind to check for such telltale signs of a tryst.

25

A MISTAKE ON
THE SKI SLOPE

Groggy-eyed, I shut off the mercilessly screeching alarm.

Five p.m. Boston time. Dialing Tony, I mentally rehearsed my explanation for the last-minute change of plans. Even though I'd forgiven my father, hanging out with his mistress-turned-second-wife on the upcoming holiday was out of the question. Ashamed of my narrow-mindedness, I was nonetheless hell-bent on denying Aunty Tian the pleasure of meeting my beautiful children.

Yet the calls remained unanswered! So bizarre! With less than four hours before their flight, where the heck could my family be? Weren't they supposed to unplug TV and computers, and cross-check the packing list that I prepared for them: passports, universal power adapters, chargers, neck pillows . . . ? Something must have gone wrong.

Only four days had passed since I left Boston. Yet even a short stay in China could bring out full-on paranoia in a rational person. I had been tormented by nightmares every night. In one, Tony's Jeep crashed onto the guardrail of I-93; I floated along endless corridors in a hospital, swinging one door open after another, only to find mummy-wrapped bodies in beds. . . A mean voice hissed from the intercom: "Listen carefully. If you want to see them alive, at midnight, drop a duffel bag stuffed with three million dollars into the trash bin—the one chalk-marked with a white cross behind the liquor store near the rotary." I cried out, "How can I come up with three million on such short notice?"

In the most disturbing dream last night, Tony and I were watching *The King of Masks*—a Chinese movie we saw on our first date. In a scene near the climax, the old man, a virtuoso of the mask-changing art, peeled off one mask after another in rapid fire, until his true face was revealed: a malicious, grinning face—Tony's face! Gasping for air, I woke up.

Keep calm, I commanded myself. *There must be a perfect explanation for Tony's unresponsiveness.*

I tried to objectively assess the situation. I needed to evaluate facts, a complete set of unmanipulated data. But I had at my disposal only limited observations: Tony's interaction with his nuclear family, his extended family, his close friends and acquaintances.

"Tony, Tony, Tony." I muttered his name, my thoughts as heavy as his weightlifting dumbbells. Do I really know you, my dear husband?

Our love was a mistake, literally.

On Martin Luther King Day sixteen years earlier, my roommate Yolanda and I took a shuttle bus to Killington, Vermont. I had never skied before, and neither had Yolanda, a new transplant from Miami. But, with a New Year's resolution still fresh in my mind, I decided to pounce on a Ski Mart promotion: "*Buy one Killington day pass, get one for your buddy at 50% off.*" At least, I figured, the mountain air would reinvigorate my sagging spirit in the middle of a particularly brutal New England winter.

Two months prior, a subleasing ad in our cafeteria caught my eye. In one picture, a stained-glass window splashed red, green, and blue sunlight onto the top floor of a three-decker in Savin Hill. I tore a tab off because I needed to out of my claustrophobic place—the dirty-beige carpet reminded me of Wolfgang. I called the number, and Yolanda and I became fast friends since that day. (Later, she told me that she took the job as a Spanish interpreter at our medical center solely to flee her jealous boyfriend, a control freak with a violent gang past.)

At the ski rental shop nestled at the foothill, a ponytailed staff member scanned my driver's license and whistled. "Happy birthday!"

"Your birthday is today?!" Yolanda screamed. "I just assumed you were named after your birth month!"

"Actually, my name is M-E-I, not the corrupted M-A-Y. In Chinese, mei means the winter plum blossom." I sighed, remembering Grandpa who named me after the January bloom in his courtyard.

"Aha!" Seizing this opportunity, she pried. "How old are you, sister?"

"Thirty-two." I said with a wince, dreading the many lonely winters yet to come, as unstoppable as an avalanche. "All downhill from here."

"Nonsense. We're going to party tonight, oh yeah, baby!" She high-fived me, shaking her booty with a salsa movement. Even without flaunting, her voluptuous shape was as envy-worthy as J-Lo's. Behind the counter, the ponytailed dude pumped my skis in the air and hooted, his eyes glued to her gyrating hips. I frowned. Viewed from behind, my butt could pass as a boy's.

A group lesson in the ski clinic later, I cracked the formula for skiing: 90 percent boredom (shivering in long queues for the lift to the beginner's slope), 5 percent thrill (fighting for your life to avert disastrous falls or collisions), and 5 percent embarrassment (scrambling on all fours to arise from the well-trodden slush). Nevertheless, a few hours in, both Yolanda and I managed to plow down Cruise Control—an easy, blue slope—without a single fall.

Around noon, faces flushed, we toasted our success in the food court with burnt coffee. Refueled with overpriced burgers, we refastened the clips of our still-damp boots and shuffled back to the lift line. To our delight, the morning crowds had thinned considerably.

The gondola ride to the peak was breathtaking. Under a lukewarm sun, layer upon layer of long mountain ranges—fur-coated with hunter green, smoky brown, and grayish blue—kept unfolding, fifty miles in every direction. The crisp air was perfumed with balsam fir and white pine. I felt a sudden jolt of confidence: if I jumped into the sky, I could land and float effortlessly on the white powder rimmed with evergreens.

Back on the slope, to my horror, I regressed. Fighting the out-of-control skis, my legs shook like noodles. On turns, no matter how hard I dug into the edges, I kept falling. After thwacking the icy slope with my bony butt, I blinked back tears, dumbfounded. Time and again, strangers stopped mid-slope to retrieve my skis, which kept detaching and flying away the second I fell. Watching my struggle to clip my boots back into the rebellious skis, a sympathetic old gentleman shook his head and told me, "You really should get your ski bindings readjusted at the rental shop."

Just then, Yolanda whizzed by, chiming in, "Are you okay?"

"Yeah, yeah. You go ahead, I'll catch up." Bravely, I waved her and my rescuer off. A gust of wind bit my exposed nose. Every muscle in my body cramped up, even muscles I'd never been aware of. Nevertheless, I clenched my jaw and pushed on. A cumbersome trip to the ski shop would be a colossal waste of time. I was determined to squeeze the maximum return on my pricy ticket, even with a 25 percent discount.

At closing time, the ponytailed dude in the rental shop glanced at my skis and laughed. "Birthday girl, those awesome skis aren't the ones I rented to you! I would gladly trade up, but they belong to a person taller and heavier than me." Grimacing to suppress another bout of chuckles, he said, "How did you manage to fly down here in one piece?"

Thus, my afternoon misery was demystified. Staggering back to the mountain, I tucked the gear under my armpit, like a dog with its tail in between its hind legs; the wrong skis kept scraping my bruised rib cage with each step. Outside the food court, sure enough, a lonely pair of skis was leaning against the rack: a similar red-on-blue graphic pattern, but a different logo, and nearly two feet shorter!

"Hey, did you have fun with my skis?" A tall and fit young man holding a can of Coors Light grinned at me, his eyes twinkling with mischief.

My cheeks burned. "I . . . I'm so sorry! It's lame, but I didn't know any better."

"I can vouch for her," said Yolanda, flashing her irresistibly sunny smile. "This is our virgin ski trip."

The stranger eyed me up and down with a poker face and took a deliberate swig of his beer. Then he asked, "Are you okay?"

I nodded, too embarrassed to speak.

"I've been waiting for you the whole afternoon." He rattled his near-empty can. "See, My third beer."

"I feel terrible. Listen, can I pay for your afternoon portion of the ticket and your beers?"

"Hmm, interesting proposition," he said with an ear-to-ear grin. "How about you pay for my dinner instead?"

Unable to read him, I hesitated. Just then, Yolanda, a quicker thinker, elbowed me in my sore rib. "Lucky you," she announced. "We're celebrating Mei's birthday in Chinatown tonight. You're welcome to join us."

"Nice. Count me in." He extended his hand. "I'm Tony."

By then, we had missed our shuttle bus back to Boston. So, we gratefully accepted Tony's offer of a lift. As he led the way to the parking lot, Yolanda mouthed to me, "He's into you!"

I shrugged.

In the front passenger seat of a red Jeep, a man in a Red Sox baseball cap was reading *Sports Illustrated*. As we climbed into the back seats, he retracted his day laborer's stocky legs from the dashboard and started sneezing. Tony turned to me, "By the way, thank you for the free beers. You see, this guy Jeff lost a bet on when you would return."

"Excuse me, ladies, but perfumes don't agree with me." Teary-eyed, Jeff blew his nose noisily into a tissue. "Boy, did I underestimate some people's perseverance or what!"

"And stupidity, too," I said, volunteering my bruised ego as a peace offering.

We all roared.

The four-hour ride in congested traffic was crammed with jokes, many at my expense. But it wasn't half as painful as it sounded. Observing Yolanda's blatant attempts to flirt with Jeff was entertaining enough. Even more amazingly, he didn't take any of her bait.

The contrast between the two men—friends since their college years, as we found out—was almost comical. Unlike the ruggedly handsome Tony, Jeff emitted a pale aura of a lumpy flour sack, or the Pillsbury Doughboy sitting in a dingy bar on Dot Ave and waiting for any newcomer to poke his soft belly and make him say, "Hoo hoo!" On a closer look, the furrow between his eyebrows gave an impression of him brooding over a private nuisance, something as pesky as jock itch.

"What do you ladies do for a living?" Tony asked.

When I said that I was a struggling biomedical researcher, he chuckled. "Why not switch to Big Pharma then? By coincidence, I'm a drug rep for a pharmaceutical company in Cambridge. Hey, *any* drug you make," he said, winking at me via the rearview mirror to imply the illicit type, too, "I can sell. Fifty-fifty, partner?"

"Wow, you just read my mind," I laughed.

In fact, I'd been contemplating a career change for a while—ever since Dr. K, my former advisor, traded bench work for an editorial job at a prestigious journal after the birth of her second child. Still, I couldn't shake off the indelible image of her climbing ladders with a watermelon belly. If she, a superior scientist with a sterling pedigree, remarkable talents, and a great work ethic, couldn't make it in academia, what would be my chance? Most likely, I would languish in various labs with no tenure potential, another professional postdoc like Wolfgang. Now Tony's joking tipped my balance. *I'll never be Madame Marie Curie the Second,* I reasoned with Mother in my head. *This isn't a sell-out; it's about surviving and thriving.*

At the East Ocean Restaurant, agitated fish glared from the overcrowded tank; customers stared back, unfazed. My usually good appetite, whetted by my arduous misadventure on the mountain and then nonstop laughter, was further stimulated by the aroma wafting out of the kitchen. I ordered an obscene amount of food as if it were our last dinner.

Between mouthfuls, Tony peppered me with questions about the crispy fried coconut milk. After the main entrees arrived, the dish of steamed sea bass with black bean sauce became the clear winner. Within minutes, only a fish skeleton and a few ginger shreds remained on the plate.

Frowning at the garlic frog legs, Yolanda broke a crispy piece off the seafood bird's nest and plopped it into her mouth. "So crunchy!" She licked her lips while beaming Tony a beguiling smile. By then, she had deemed Teflon-coated Jeff to be non-husband material. With a bubbly personality, she effortlessly extracted vital intelligence from Tony, the still-eligible bachelor. Based on her skillful excavation, I quietly reconstructed a successful American story.

In the 1930s, Tony's Napolitano grandparents left their hill village to work at a second cousin's deli in North End, Boston. Altogether, six relatives shared a shoebox-sized walk-up behind Hanover Street. To escape the summer heat, half-naked kids played in narrow alleys where rats scurried among olive oil tins and wine crates.

During the postwar boom, Tony's family moved to a three-decker in East Boston. I could easily picture the tomatoes and peppers flourishing in their gelato-cart-sized patio. Every summer, ever-expanding throngs of cousins colonized Constitution Beach. Hands cupped on brows, boys squinted at the airplanes taking off across the narrow bay as water dripped down their tanned legs. Shrieking girls dipped their toes into the icy sea while their mamas gossiped on vibrating towels anchored by coolers filled with cold-cut sandwiches and Italian slush. Nearby, their *nonni* combed the beach with metal detectors, while their fully clad *nonne* watched their bocce-playing sons with pride.

After the Boston school-busing crisis in the seventies, Tony's family followed the urban exodus to Saugus, where Split-level ranches had mushroomed from former apple orchards. Gradually, Pickups and minivans filled up the driveway, land-locking a fifteen-foot Boston Whaler. The two-car garage became the graveyard for plastic Christmas trees with dead string lights, an energy-guzzling freezer packed to the brim, splintered hockey sticks, three busted Hoovers, and box after box of bolts, nuts, canning jars, and used toys and clothing waiting to make their way to the Salvation Army. One by one, instead of going to church on Sundays, the boys mowed their half-acre lawn or hung out with girls in a mall adjacent to an exhausted granite quarry.

"No shit! My family does the seven-fish feast on Christmas Eve, too!" Yolanda exclaimed. The two exuberant faces at the table made me wonder: *Where would Tony put down his own roots?*

Meanwhile, Jeff remained silent. (Only later did I learn that his father, a longshoreman, had died in an accident on the job when he was young.)

When the brisk waiter brought out a check and started cleaning our table, Tony rescued the last piece of salt-and-pepper squid. Chewing with a deadpan face, he said, "Hey, Mei, I still can't believe that you've never tried Pu Pu platter. It's the quintessential Chinese dish in America!"

"Yeah, right, and these fortune cookies are a paragon of Chinese culture." I cracked mine open. *"You'll meet someone very special,"* it read. Before I could pocket the strip, Yolanda peeked over my shoulder and winked.

With a snort, Tony folded up his fortune slip and tossed it onto his plate. "Mei, thanks for an authentic Chinese meal. I have to confess, I seldom venture out of the comfort zone of Kung Pao chicken." He said, turning to Jeff. "Remember the time we tried to order it in Beijing?"

Jeff thwacked his thick thigh and insisted, "You've got to tell them the story."

Five years prior, Tony and Jeff had seized an opportunity to visit China through a small grant from the international business program at their college. After the Great Wall in the morning and the Forbidden City in the afternoon, they hunted for a cheap dinner. They lucked out in an unassuming restaurant off the main road in Qianmen. One dish, made of chopped red and green pepper, peanuts, and cubed chicken meat, exceeded their expectations from the picture on a laminated menu.

The next evening, they couldn't locate their serendipitous find. Eventually, they settled for a hole-in-the-wall buried deep in the same neighborhood. The waiter spoke in rapid Mandarin, gesturing to scribbles on a smudged blackboard. Undeterred, Tony took out a Sharpie and drew a deconstruction of the desired dish on the back of a creased city map: peanuts; a "+" sign; a pepper next to a knife; a "+" sign; a chicken. To enact his artistic rendition, he pantomimed with a frenetic chicken dance, repeating, '*Chicken, chicken.*'"

The waiter alternated between cackling and frowning. Then, he whacked his forehead and exclaimed, "Ah, yes, yes, yes!" Nodding like a pecking chicken, he flew into the kitchen.

"Nice job!" Jeff gave Tony a high-five.

At the neighboring table, raucous men were engrossed in a drinking game involving complicated hand gestures. After shots of *erguotou* (the legendary firewater), the laughing loser slammed down his emptied cup on the table. Chopsticks darted in and out of a boiled pig's head, with eyes, ears, and bristles in plain sight.

The waiter reappeared, beckoning Tony with curved fingers.

The kitchen floor was covered with sticky cardboard. Animal offal, soiled cleavers, shears, and suspicious-looking devices were heaped on chopping boards. Huge cauldrons bubbled with pinkish-gray foam, giving off an offensive stench of animal fat. Above the industrial sink twirled a flytrap strip, glinting green and blue. A man in a blood-splashed apron perched on a stool, clutching a lit cigarette with a hand missing two fingers.

Entering an unlit alley behind the kitchen, a pungent odor assailed Tony's nose. His hair stood on end before his eyes could adjust to the darkness. He wished to throw away his few lousy dollars and run, but his legs couldn't decide which way to turn.

With a flourish, the waiter yanked away a tarp and revealed stacked cages. Pointing randomly at a pitiful, lean bird among the huddling flock in the far corner, he turned to Tony with a broad smile.

"What the heck? You look like shit." Jeff said as Tony retook his seat.

"You've no idea, but customers have to pick their personal victims back there."

"Oh yeah? I hope *laowai* isn't on that fucking blackboard!"

Just then, the waiter brought out a *tapas*-sized plate of fried peanuts. Before they could come up with a way to explain that this bar food wasn't exactly what they had ordered, the waiter plunked down another plate. After adjusting a knife to the exact angle to the stuffed green bell pepper as appeared in Tony's drawing, he smiled triumphantly.

Unimpressed, Jeff rubbed it in. "Next time, use your lipstick to ask for a red pepper instead."

"You try next time."

Then arrived the finale: a naked bird sticking his spiny neck out of an oily film in a soup tureen.

"Christ, you can't tell the difference between a chicken and a pigeon?" Jeff laughed till he was wheezing. He drummed his fist on the table.

As if to protest its wrongful death, the pigeon bobbed its puny head, splashing hot, greasy droplets toward Tony.

Tony said, "Sorry, birdie. Should have taken a drawing class instead of underwater basket weaving last semester." The truth was, fixated on escaping from the slaughter-yard, he didn't even glance at the poor creature in the dark.

Before Tony could finish his story, Yolanda had collapsed onto the table in a laughing fit, Jeff dabbed away tears, and I almost bent my chopsticks. I knew exactly the type of establishment that the two clueless Americans had stumbled upon: a seedy watering hole infested with tattooed night owls, places that I wouldn't set foot in. Recalling my own mishaps in New York years before, I said, "Well, one country's delicacy is often another country's nightmare. Kudos to you, for seeking an authentic experience abroad!"

"A toast to adventure," Tony said, tipping his Tsingtao beer to Jeff.

"And to the quest for the best Kung Pao Chicken!"

"Cheers!"

When our impatient waiter circulated back again, I handed him my credit card and waved off the objection from the rest of the table. "In Chinatown, do as the Chinese do. So . . . the birthday girl pays for her own party."

"Happy Birthday!" Tony sang out with a grin. "How do we get invitations to your next birthday party?"

"By being on my good side," I said.

As everyone was zipping their ski jackets to head out, I discreetly unfolded Tony's balled-up fortune slip. *Learn to forget about your past.*

A week later, Tony called. "Hey, could I take you out to an Italian restaurant tonight?"

"Me?" For a split second, I was certain that he'd mistaken me for Yolanda, who wasn't home. Being monopolized by her during my "surprise" birthday party, Tony had only brushed his sight over me during the lull of their lively chatting. Then a faint hope bubbled up. "But why?"

"Guilty conscience."

"Ha!" I laughed dryly, tamping down my jumpy heart to its resting position. "Please elaborate."

Tony did a convincing impersonation of grumpy Jeff: "*That poor girl was black-and-blue by the end of the afternoon. Then we fleeced her in the evening.*" He whistled. "Thank God you're well built. Otherwise, I might end up paying your medical bills. You know, this being America."

"Relax! When bad things happen, we Chinese only blame our own bad luck or stupidity. Besides, I have insurance, and a big discount if I see doctors at Tufts," I said giddily. "However, I never say 'no' to Italian food."

"Great. I'll pick you up in an hour."

Is this a date? I rushed to the mirror. No time to fix my limp hair, so I put on lipstick and my dating regalia: a pushup bra and the only pair of jeans that sort of flattered my boyish hips.

"TONY! TONY! Where've you been all this time?" At the entrance to a neighborhood restaurant in East Boston, a matronly hostess opened her arms and welcomed Tony in a strange, accusatory tone.

"He-e-llo, Zia Maria!" Tony double-kissed her, leaving a small smudge on one of her heavily made-up cheeks. Maria squeezed Tony's arm and said with a proprietary smile, "Look at you! Pumping iron lately? Or is it just lots of pushups in bed?"

"Zia Maria, *now* you're talking!" Tony slapped her wide waist affectionately, eliciting a cluster of husky squeals. Steering her toward me, he said, "Meet Mei. Hey, use some Listerine before talking to this nice lady, would you?"

"Naughty, naughty boy," Maria spanked Tony playfully while titling her head to give me a good once-over. "Wait till I tell your mama!"

Assuming that she was measuring me up for a report, I flashed my most charming smile.

"Ouch!" Guarding his behind with both hands, Tony pretended to beg: "Please don't tell the nuns."

Following Maria's wriggling rump through a narrow aisle, we settled into a booth in the back. Once Maria was out of earshot, I whispered, "Is she really your aunt?"

"Not that I know of," Tony laughed. "A royal pain in the butt that she is. Jeff can't stand her."

Noticing his lingering, mischievous grin, I said, "She sounded so . . . so familiar with you."

"Well, eons ago, she caught me and her daughter Cindy frolicking among laundry piles in her basement," he said, brushing the fraying edge of a worn menu.

"Was Cindy your girlfriend?"

"She thought so, but so did quite a few girls in the Saugus High class of '88." He straightened his face and studied the menu with hooded eyes. "FYI, compared with touristy restaurants in the North End, the portion size here is huge."

"Not a problem for me," I feigned a laugh with the appropriate amount of cheerfulness. *Quite a few girls.* What a shameless boast of a smooth operator! The faux leather upholstery suddenly turned stiff and sticky under my thighs. I considered my excuses for leaving, but on second thought, decided to feast first.

A cross between a railway dining car and a rustic Tuscan *cucina*, the narrow restaurant with a wall mural of red, ochre, and orange hues effused cheesy, festive vibes. Braided garlic and copper pans hung close to heads and gesturing hands of oblivious diners. The low metal ceiling amplified the loud conversations of jolly locals. A burst of combustive laughter induced a faint headache. At once, I felt at home, like in one of the Hong gatherings.

After we placed our orders, to my surprise, a long waiting line had snaked outside the window. (At the time, this homely, hidden gem had yet to be discovered by the Food Network crowds yet.) Although the hodgepodge decor inspired low expectations, the perfect golden calamari and supersized *primi* of gnocchi in pesto sauce blew me away. Then I wolfed down the homemade Bolognese pasta piled on a deep plate large enough to baptize a baby. While the hearty food and generously poured Chianti revolted against my belt, I said with a burp, "So, what do you recommend for dessert?"

"Oh my, are you trying to bankrupt me?" Tony said, feigning horror. "I've never seen such a small girl with such a shocking appetite!"

"Apparently, you've never watched the Coney Island hotdog contest. The champion is always the skinniest Japanese boy."

"Or the hungriest Chinese girl."

I was taken aback. Even though I'd never experienced starvation, generational memories had been passed down to me through my mother's mitochondrial DNA. Like a siren's whisper, every cell in my body was coded with this secret message: You never know when your next meal will be.

Small girl. With the last bite of tiramisu melting in my mouth, I savored Tony's word choice. *Small* was a titillating modifier that my countrymen would never attribute to me. Then I remembered that upon arrival in New York, I was instantly downsized from a Chinese "L" to an American "S." In China, a diminutive stature was regarded as part of the femininity package. Ha! I chuckled. I could tap into this elusive quality, after all.

For the rest of the evening, I babbled on a sugar high. Then, I caught myself laughing with abandon. What had just happened? In front of this stranger whom I had been ready to write off only two hours before, I was utterly at ease, free from pretense or self-censorship.

On the surface, we had little in common. Tony was six years younger than me, but his skin was weathered from skiing in winter, surfing in summer, and golfing in between; cooped up in labs year-round, I was wrinkle-free. He was the youngest among a gang of three brothers and a sister; I was an only child. Then, his string of laughter struck me like a lightning bolt: even a third-generation Italian American could be tethered by deep roots of family and food, just like the Chinese.

"Want to watch a Chinese movie next Sunday night?" Tony asked casually on our way out. "I heard the Coolidge Corner Theater is showing an interesting one."

Now, that sounded unequivocally like a date! Perking up from the postprandial stupor, I said, "Sure! I'd love to be your Chinese culture ambassador."

"Good. I look forward to your lectures," he laughed, "but, no quizzes, please."

"Don't laugh. I just came back from Sunday River," Tony said. Except for the two goggle-shaped pale ovals around his eyes, his wind-burnt face looked painfully raw.

"What? I can't believe anyone would ski in this weather."

"Hey, two feet of champagne powder was dumped on the mountain overnight!" He beamed. "Jeff and I were stoked, being among the first skiers up there on the slopes."

"I see. You're a diehard."

"You bet." He checked his compass watch. "Let's go. *King of Masks* starts in half an hour."

"*King of Masks*?" I laughed at the sight of his red and flaky nose. "You know, you could have used a mask yourself."

"Nah, ski masks always fog up my goggles," he said with a shrug. "Who has time to defog on a perfect powder day?"

In the movie, a young orphan girl from Southwest China disguises herself as a boy, hoping to get adopted by an old master of mask art. As the gorgeous scenery rolled on and the plot began to twist, I felt obliged to point out a few confusing double entendres in the dialogue. Tony appeared to be engrossed. So, I waited.

In the darkness, our hands bumped inside the jumbo popcorn tub wedged between our seats. A familiar yet long-absent charge startled me. My finger lingered; his hand froze for a millisecond, then scooped up a fistful of puffed kernels.

Licking the buttery flavor off my finger, I pondered whether I should intentionally brush my hand against his.

Before I could make up my mind, the movie had raced toward its happy ending: our little heroine rises to the occasion to save the day, and she calls the old master her grandfather.

My attention drifted again. I thought of Grandpa and his tragic ending. But that story would be impossible to tell on a first date.

🌸

Please call me, I prayed after our chaste kiss and goodbye hug. I waited and waited. But Tony seemed to have evaporated into thin air.

When I finally mastered the courage to call, I only reached his voicemail. "Hey, please leave your message after the beep!" He withheld his name in his cheerful, clipped greeting, never mind a promise to call back at all.

Just as I was about to give up hope, he returned my call, explaining that he'd been away at a conference in Rome. His apology sounded sincere, so I invited him over for an impromptu dinner. Good thing that Yolanda happened to be in Miami for her parents' ruby anniversary. Otherwise, she'd probably roll her eyes and say, "Get a grip, girl!"

After a quick survey of our fridge, I rushed to the Vietnamese grocery store on Dot Ave and loaded up on fresh ginger, bell pepper, chicken, shrimp, and Thai basil. For the rest of the afternoon, I cooked up a storm. At the last minute, I dashed to the nearest liquor store and bought the most expensive Barolo there, hoping it pairs well with Asian food.

"It's amazing!" Tony couldn't stop praising my rendition of his beloved Kung Pao chicken. "Better than the dish from Beijing!"

I beamed, thanking Grandma silently.

After dinner, we sat on the futon to watch a cooking show on the Food Network. Twirling his wine glass with exaggerated gaiety and patting my shoulder, Tony said, "Thanks for everything!"

Pretending not to notice his hand resting on me, I said, "This nerdy chef reminds me of my father."

"Oh yeah? Is he a great chef, too?"

"No. But, see this guy gazes at you over his sliding glasses before pushing them back up? My father does the same."

Tony laughed. An intoxicating scent suffused the few centimeters between us. Leather, sunshine, pine forest, the A-to-Z molecules of the anti-nerd danced in the air. I edged toward the source of the aphrodisiac—his inviting chest. His hand nudged me closer. Emboldened, I stole a quick kiss. He closed his eyes and murmured dreamily, "Mmm, delicious. The taste of Kung Pao Chicken?"

"Oh, cut it out." I clamped my fingers over his parted lips. He snatched my hand, pinned it behind my back, and leaned in with a mischievous grin. As light as a teasing feather, his dry lips touched mine and departed just as quickly. My lips pursued, wanting more. One thing led to another, and soon we were horizontal on the futon.

To my surprise, his certain prowess, as slyly alluded to by Aunty Maria from the Italian restaurant, was overrated. Despite his athleticism, he was rather shy and passive. His chuckling was nervous, like a boy before his Tetanus shot. I found it refreshingly sweet and endearing, considering he had grown up in a hypersexualized society.

That night, I made my womenfolk proud by affirming an ancient proverb: The way to a man's heart is through his stomach.

❧

"*Welcome!*" exclaimed Gloria, a short, stout matriarch with an ample bosom. Apparently, Aunty Maria's report had piqued her interest. And I was summoned.

Raucous laughter erupted from the dining room, darkened with heavy curtains. Lording above an oblong table with extra leaf extensions was a poor reproduction of the *Last Supper*, from which a miserable Jesus cast his reproachful gaze upon the merry crowd. In a candlelit alcove, the Virgin Mary wept over her lifeless son on her lap. As I was awkwardly offering my cheeks for the double kissing from the entire tribe, the biologist in me rushed to recall the transmission modes of the Black Death.

Soon Gloria initiated grace. Like a proper Catholic girl, I lowered my head and crossed my hands, praying for her approval.

When Tony poured wine into Gloria's glass, she smiled indulgently at her youngest. Then, raising her glass, she shouted, "Praise the Lord!"

The supper's religious undertone curbed my ordinarily voracious appetite. I cut the undercooked veal into dainty diamonds according to its grill pattern and complimented the dish with every twelfth bite.

Noticing Tony's generous second helping of the roasted lamb with garlic and rosemary, I asked Gloria for the recipe, even though I couldn't stand the lamby smell. She replied with a guarded smile, "Later."

After supper, Gloria fussed in the kitchen, allocating leftovers into Tupperware and marking her children's names on pre-printed labels with her church's name.

"Thanks, Mom. Got to go." Tracy said, grabbing her favorite eggplant parmigiana and pecking two hurried kisses on Gloria's flushed cheeks. "I love you!"

"Sweetheart, don't forget to bring the Rubbermaid back next Sunday." Gloria said, returning the kisses vigorously. "*Mmm*, love you more!"

I was dumbfounded. In Gloria's household, the word *love* was frivolously peppered around like commas or periods in conversations; kisses were dispensed more casually than Hershey's chocolate from a jumbo-sized bag for Halloween trick-or-treaters. The easy-flowing love here seemed to have nothing in common with the hard currency I had to earn and hoard in my youth.

Soon, the remaining offspring and their entourage formed a line to squeeze out of a bottleneck created by Gloria's stretched arms as she bestowed her endless kissing and hugging and *I-love-you*'s. When it was my turn in the papal procession, she brightened and said, "I hope to see you again soon, sweetheart!" I beamed.

During the Sunday love feasts, Gloria's adoring eyes lingered the most on Tony. So, I was surprised by what I overheard on Christmas Eve, right after my first seven-fish extravaganza.

"Remember the time you brought that injured chickadee home? You asked me for rags to line the shoebox? When the poor thing stopped twitching and your brothers threw it into the trash, you cried so, so hard. Then you took it out and we said our prayers and buried it under the crabapple tree . . ." Slowly, the faraway smile departed from Gloria's face. She murmured, "What happened to my angel, my sweetest baby? Sometimes, I wonder if your heart has turned into a stone!"

Tony only stared at her swollen ankles drooping over her fleece slippers.

Wringing her hands, Gloria pleaded, "Just let it go. We're all sinners. Come to the midnight mass with me, *ple-ee-ease!*"

"When are you going to open your eyes, Ma? Brian wasn't a sinner." Tony's gaze sharpened into two lancets. "Father Gabriele was."

Her doughy face sagged.

Her devastation moved me to say, "Gloria, I can go with you."

Tony glared at me and said, "Get your coat. We're leaving."

On the way to Tony's place in South Boston, frozen rain pelted his Jeep. Christmas choruses jammed the airways. "*Run run Rudolph, Randolph ain't too far behind. Run, run...* Tony shut off the stereo and cranked up the defogger. The always-congested stretch of I-93 was deserted that night, with only a lonely semi a quarter mile ahead. The silence was suffocating, so rubbed his shoulder. Reluctantly, he opened his pursed lips.

Years earlier, Brian and Tony were altar boys in their parish church. One summer, Father Gabriele selected a few boys for a lake retreat in Canada. Fortuitous tonsillitis saved Tony from the fateful trip, but Brian had never been the same afterward. A decade later, he succumbed to a bottle of Tylenol and a fistful of Zoloft.

"Nowadays, just the sight of that church makes me want to puke. . . Father Gabriele died from colon cancer two years after his transfer to Springfield. He must be burning in a special hell for priests like him." Tony started laughing, "Poetic justice!"

His hollow cackle chilled me to the bone. My thoughts drifted to a dark labyrinth with blind tunnels, a place I'd resisted revisiting all these years. I couldn't afford to become the type of fragile American lying on therapists' couches year after year while trying to figure things out—or, worse, perishing like Brian. *No, thank you, I'm fine.*

Tossing away the invisible thread, I redirected our conversation. "You know, Orientals view life quite differently. Sometimes, we consider suicide honorable—if it's to preserve one's dignity."

I proceeded to tell one of my grandfather's stories: the origin of the Dragon Boat Festival.

More than two millennia ago, Qu Yuan, a noble poet, jumped into a river to protest scheming villains who had tarnished his name. Fishermen rowed their boats up and down the river in search of him, all in vain. To lull fish away from nibbling at the corpse of their beloved poet, they threw wrapped rice cakes into the water. Even today, the Chinese still eat *zhongzhi*, rice cakes wrapped in reed leaves, in memory of Qu Yuan.

Tony reached for my cold hand and raised it to his lips for a princely kiss. "What a beautiful story." He said, then smiled to the twinkling stars, "Thank you, Grandpa."

26

THE HYBRID ADVANTAGE

Jump out now! This must be the epiphany of the proverbial frog as the water started to simmer in the pot. But, lacking an amphibian's reflex, all I could manage was to keep redialing Tony's cell phone.

Déjà vu. Now I recalled Tony's two-week disappearance after our first official date, and his agonizing procrastination before marrying me. Patience had never been my forte. Oh, heaven help me, must I relive that kind of torment again?

Once Tony and I became steady, I called Mother to warn her that I might marry a *laowai*, the very bottom of her meticulously crafted totem pole.

But my preemptive strike was unnecessary. Unknown to me, as I was sliding dangerously toward spinsterhood, she had reclassified me into the category of bananas languishing in markdown bins, with more black spots creeping up each passing day. "I won't object to you marrying any man," she sighed, "as long as you are certain."

Of course I was certain. Around Tony, a Peter Pan in his relentless chase for virgin snow and endless waves, I began to view my mundane surroundings with the marvel of a girl catching the first snowflake on her palm. And I was certain that I could make him happy, too.

However, dating a younger man came with its inherent complications.

Month after month, I sat on my hands, dropping hints, angling, and waiting. The background ticking of my biological clock crescendoed into the ominous soundtrack of a Hitchcock movie.

I had to act fast.

Subscribing to the theory that men with satisfied stomachs are most susceptible to persuasion, I labored for days for our potential last supper. As Tony was picking at his Kung Pao chicken, I cleared my throat and delivered the marriage proposal/ultimatum.

Pausing a plump peanut at the tip of his chopsticks, he struggled. "Are you sure it . . . it's a good idea?" Less skilled in the game of brinkmanship, he gulped his wine; his face seemed to be colorless under the afternoon light refracted by the stained glass. "You know, we are *quite* different."

Why does everyone ask me if I'm sure? Annoyed, I raised my glass with an exaggerated gravitas before my sermon. "Let's say that you marry a woman from a similar background. Now, imagine again you and your wife in your seventies, dozing on and off in front of the TV. What could you talk about during the commercials—anything other than aches, pains, and constipation? Versus you and I—we will never run out of topics. Being different is great! It spices up lives. It's something worth celebrating."

"Seventies! Aren't you optimistic!" He chuckled; his Adam's apple jittered like a squeamish mouse. "I can hardly see myself past thirty."

Emptying his wine glass, he stood up and walked toward the street-facing window. Two pigeons fluttered their wings and took off from their perch on the fire escape, stirring up dusty feathers accumulated in the tandem DirecTV dishes.

"Sure, it won't be easy." I said, sidling up to him. "But think of it this way: Marriage is like a rollercoaster ride—the more challenging the course, the more fun." I immediately regretted such a hasty metaphor. Yet its effect on my target was encouraging.

Across the street, an old Puerto Rican man was watching his chihuahua peeing on a hydrant. So, I joked, "By the way, I couldn't care less about the default position of the toilet seat."

He didn't laugh at my bonus concession. Instead, a wispy cloud of darkness swept across his face.

I was beyond flabbergasted. What was his endgame—after dating me for almost eighteen months by now and being green-lighted by both sets of parents—without any intention of marriage? It was long overdue—to put down our roots, to flourish and bear fruit!

In the fading sun, a defiant goldenrod flashed from a cracked sidewalk. In the near distance, the bell from St. Peter's church rang out at six o'clock. I drew in a desperate breath. Time for the nuclear option.

"Remember the *Hybrid Advantage*? I hope you didn't cut any class in Biology 101." I glided my clammy hand over his warm loins. "Just think of the beautiful and intelligent babies we could make," I murmured.

Tony's eyes gleamed, then became dreamy.

Massaging his back, I continued, "Don't worry, I feel a good vibe. We'll be a great team."

He shifted his gaze to a vacant parking lot. Then he planted an absent-minded kiss on my forehead and countered, "It'll work as long as you keep me on a long leash. Just so you know, I still plan on spending most of my free time outdoors, doing things I love."

"Okay." Locking our eyes, I firmed up the deal with a solid handshake. Inwardly, I screamed. *Always have faith in the magic of food and family!*

A compact Subaru zipped through Dot Ave, its subwoofer blasting out with Snoop Dogg's *Tha Dogg Pound*. Tony's eyes followed the red car until it made a nimble turn around a scrawny tree and disappeared into a side street. His expression was indecipherable. When he noticed me observing him, he quipped, "What? Got cold feet already?"

"Not me!"

"Let's do it." He laughed heartily. "No rain check!"

After we announced our engagement during Gloria's Sunday supper, the wall clock struck; Jesus above us seemed to blink in startlement. A cacophony of congratulations erupted. Tony's brother Andy laughed, "Hey, Mei, do you have any idea what you're getting yourself into?"

"Never mind him, the family clown," Tracy said, resting her reassuring palm on my wrist while giving Andy a disgusted look.

Leo, Tony's father, remained impassive; a stroke had left him with a perennially damp bib from constant drooling.

Looping her marshmallow arms around me, Gloria blinked away tears and smiled. "Welcome to our family!" Her happy voice was laced with a discernible tremble.

Later, Tracy explained that Gloria's sadness was for the loss of Cindy, her favorite.

I instantly understood Gloria once I met Tony's unofficial high school girlfriend (and a third or fourth cousin, depending on the sides) upon her visit on Easter. Clearly, the younger, curvy woman had grandchildren-bearing hips. After Cindy noticed my engagement ring, she nodded with a martyr's smile at Tony and soon took her leave.

Not long after graciously conceding, Gloria envisioned for us a church wedding with two hundred guests.

Tony balked, "Who needs the sanction from a bunch of criminals and hypocrites from the Vatican?"

"Tony!" Gloria gasped.

"Ma, don't you get it?" Tony jabbed at her relentlessly. "Church or secular wedding, the divorce rate is the same."

Gloria's face turned as white as a bridal gown. Lenny, her oldest son, had had a church ceremony (insisted on by her), followed by an extravagant reception at the Park Hotel (demanded by the bride). When the couple split up a year later, they still owed two installments on the wedding expenses.

Smiling awkwardly at Gloria, I wished that I could comfort her with cold facts. During my due-diligence research, I'd learned from reputable sources that the divorce rate for couples of Asian brides and Caucasian grooms (although a whopping three times higher than for the Asian-Asian combo,) is 25 percent lower than the White-White union.

Religion and statistics aside, I had to be practical. On my side, the potential wedding guests could be counted on one hand. I couldn't justify dragging my folks to the States. Passports, visas, flights, hotels, gifts, dresses, suits . . . all these hassles and costs just for the sake of them nodding politely at my in-laws' friends whom they'd never met and probably would never meet again? Most of them had a working vocabulary of only three English words: *Hello*, *Cheers*, and *Goodbye*.

So in lieu of a frivolous wedding, Tony and I pooled our savings for the down payment on a tiny saltbox house on Telegraph Hill in South Boston.

On a thunderous summer morning, we entered Boston City Hall— "the ugliest building in the world," according to an online poll. (Personally, I begged to differ. Shanghai City Hall, where my parents got married, was at least on a par.) Half an hour later, we walked out with bouncy steps, a marriage license in hand. The sky had cleared. A ray of sunlight penetrated cumulonimbus clouds, pointing down dramatically like a fat, divine finger reenacting some sort of biblical scene.

In our backyard, in front of a justice of peace and our witnesses—an exuberant Yolanda and Jeff in an ill-fitting suit—we exchanged rings and *I do*'s under an arbor of climbing roses. The raindrops on the petals shimmered when Tony kissed me and whispered, "You look beautiful in white."

"And you've never looked more handsome," I whispered back, "Hey if you like, I can wear this dress to the beach all summer."

We laughed. My wedding dress—the simplest A-line from Filene's Basement—cost $79, minus the 2 percent reward back.

A small group of guests swarmed in for hugs and photos.

Rei's absence on my big day cast a shadow of regret in my heart. When I was crossing his name off my mini-invitee list at the last minute, Tony had raised his eyebrow and asked, "But why?"

"Oh, he'll be busy this summer, visiting his sick father in China."

Tony seemed relieved with the flimsy excuse I supplied. He said with a shrug, "Oh well, then, I'll dust off my physics textbooks the next time your distinguished ex decides to pay us a visit."

The truth was, at the time, the idea of comingling Tony and Rei unnerved me as much as watching a pyromaniac reaching for a matchbox. Compartmentalizing them, I'd believed, was the best way to avert any catastrophe (from the remotely hypothetical to the unimaginable) that might derail my wedding.

Soon, Yolanda clapped her hands, and Cousin Isha and her husband Ed, the only Hong representatives who had driven down from Maine, turned on the portable stereo on the deck.

"*At last! My love has come along. My lonely days are over...*" Finger-locked, we slow-danced as Etta James soulfully belted out her signature song. Over Tony's shoulder, I saw the sun setting over the old harbor and setting the white facade of the JFK library ablaze. Soon, crimson clouds over the Blue Hill ripened into purple. Dancing with Jeff, Yolanda sang out of tune. Happiness spilled out of me like champagne bubbles. Misty-eyed, I wished the music, the dance, and the perfect summer evening would never stop . . .

27

TEAM USA

No breaking news online. I rechecked the flight status. Despite an eighty percent chance of thunderstorms in Boston, it was still a green "on-time".

Even if Tony was stuck in the evening commute with a dead cellphone, the twins should have been home for a long while now. Yet, no one bothered to pick up our house phone. In desperation, I called Jeff, our default babysitter. To my dismay, he didn't answer either.

My brain froze like our snow-blanketed backyard. It refused to churn, refused to imagine what might have happened to our kids.

After the wedding we had wasted no time procreating. Yet, month after month, no baby would settle in my barren womb. The fertility god must have been smirking and punishing me with anxieties opposite the ones in my youth.

The most terrifying thought was, *what if my dwindling, shriveling eggs have been damaged??* I had lured Tony with the promise of healthy, smart children. But chronic exposure to radioactive isotopes, UV lights, and agents in brown bottles with skull-and-crossbones labels was the standard occupational hazard for a lab researcher. The monthly return of my radiation monitoring badge provided no solace. On various occasions, I had skipped donning the clumsy lead apron during crunch time.

Cautious optimism, dashed hope, breakdown, renewed resolve. . . . After two years of IVF cycles, our precious twins finally arrived.

Holding them tight, I inhaled their scents; I caressed their soft flesh. Oh, so many tiny pink fingers and toes, nothing amiss. Even their minutest muscle twitching was mesmerizing. I wanted to kneel, to worship these miniature beings, my beautiful creation. And I would die for them if called upon. When they latched onto my breasts and suckled for the first time, tears gushed out my eyes as if from an open faucet.

Then, the objective biologist in me recognized the powerful effects of oxytocin. These crafty neurotransmitters had spilled past a floodgate in my hypothalamus, spike-released into my bloodstream, and cranked hard at my dopaminergic reward pathway. By inducing this incredible euphoria, they manipulated me into this emotional imbecile who couldn't stop weeping and smiling and loving unconditionally.

The next best thing I remembered was seeing Tony pacing in my room, each arm cradling a swaddle, grinning from ear to ear.

Only a day had passed since the doctor cut these slimy, wrinkly creatures out of my womb, yet, these budding homo sapiens were already manifesting their personalities: the baby girl wrinkled her barely-there nose, her eyes squeezed shut against the light; her five-minute-younger brother poked at the wrapping blanket, as if trying to reach his roommate of the past nine months.

"Look, Mommy is awake!" Tony told the bundles, then passed them to me with relief.

Impatiently, they burrowed toward my sore and swollen breasts. The heat and weight of their malleable bodies overwhelmed me. I could anticipate their basic needs for now, but how to protect these vulnerable beings, and guide them in the years to come?

"We'll be fine," Tony said, reading my mind. Flexing his biceps at his fledgling family, he roared, "Grow up fast, Team USA!"

❧

For a thirty-six-year-old woman, even a complication-free cesarean took an incredibly long time to recover from. Nursing one baby was exhausting, let alone two. Waking up from coma-like sleep, I felt like I was rising from the dead. A good second later, my brain registered the stinging of the stitches, the whimpering sounds, and the stench of the soiled diapers.

After Tony went back to work, Mother came to my rescue, retiring early from "a thankless job anyway."

Within three days of Mother's arrival, the twins cried less. The piled baby stuff in our living room magically disappeared. In the kitchen, rows of sterilized bottles stood like sentinels on the sparkling windowsill. She even swapped drawers to maximize the workflow and rearranged spices according to the utilization frequencies.

Appraising my surgical-clean kitchen—now as streamlined as a Ford assembly line, I felt a twinge of guilt for Mother's wasted talents. I joked, "Wow, you probably could churn out more dishes from here than a Chinese takeout during the lunch rush!"

"Piece of cake," she said, nodding with satisfaction. "When you were born, disposable diapers were unheard of. Washer and dryer, refrigerator, microwave oven, and precooked meals from stores? Science fiction."

At mealtime, she brought a food tray to my bed as if I were a sick child and she decided to spoil me at this late stage of my life. "Bed rest for a month," she insisted. "You can thank me later."

Hearing my translation of Mother's order, Tony said in amusement, "Really, a month?"

"What, you don't trust our postpartum protocol?"

"No, no, who am I to challenge ancient Chinese wisdom?" Tony raised both hands to capitulate.

Behind her back, I smiled at Tony and mouthed the words *stupid laowai!*

"Drink the fish soup before it gets cold. It's good for a new mother's milk," she demanded, then said, "Tony, I threw away your cheese in the refrigerator. It was covered with yucky mold!"

Tony bent down to rock the cribs, biting his lip to stifle a grin. Even though his favorite cheese was supposed to be moldy and stinky, he knew better than to argue with my always-right mother.

Mother also clashed with my obstetrician. She said, "Don't shower before they remove the stitches! You don't want a wound infection."

So, I dutifully sponge-bathed and washed my hair in the sink, even after I smelled whiffs of repulsive odor emanating from my body. Who would dare to disobey her? Even the leggy roses languishing on the arbor started to rebloom under her steely gaze and ruthless lopper.

Nevertheless, when this stern general first saw the twins, her face melted like warmed butter. Love at first sight. She swung them in her arms, softly humming lullabies. I felt a sting of jealousy of my own children. I had no recollection of ever receiving such luxurious affection.

One day, Gloria visited us with an armful of Tupperware: pizzelle, biscotti, lasagna, and Tony's favorite, roasted lamb. . . Even though I translated most of their conversations, to my surprise, the two grandmas somehow hit it off.

After tidying up the kitchen, I noticed that the house was unusually quiet. Glancing into our living room, I almost burst out laughing. With Paula Deen's cooking show on mute, both grandmas had dozed off on opposite ends of the sectional sofa. Their faint snoring—separated by a beat—somehow harmonized a lovely tune. Siesta, normally unobserved in the industrialized world, was another universal language they shared. At their feet, babies were sleeping in their cribs, too: Aurora frowned in a dream; Leonardo sucked his thumb with contentment.

Tiptoeing toward my camera, I woke up Mother, nevertheless. Too bad. That photo would have made the greatest Christmas card.

The twins grew up fast—faster than I could say, "Hold on, hold on, let me get my camera."

Thanks to our lucky stars, the twins were cute and smart. They rarely threw tantrums. Amazingly, they clung to each other instead of my skirt, as if they had intuited my maternal inadequacy while in my womb.

Like my father, I also discovered the babysitting function of a stack of useless lab reports and a bucket of crayons. I stored the twins' representative drawings in a shoebox, on top of their footprints at birth. Their earliest creations were crude: shoulderless, ET-like creatures with huge eyes, cradling two mini-ETs. Moving up through the years, more realistic androids emerged: four figures clutched their popsicles, grinning at orange cubes in the sky (during a Lantern Festival at Forest Hills); a frizzy-haired woman in a flowered apron arranging dotted circles (shorthand for Grandma's famous lotus rice cake) on a wonky picnic table, while two kids, a man, and a cat blissfully blew dandelions on a patch of neon-yellow lawn framed by grape vines (Tony had planted along our neighbor's chain-link fence some cuttings from his grandfather's Neapolitan original.) My favorite drawing was by Leonardo: a smiling mermaid in a seashell crown reclining against a sandcastle, her wild hair hair flowing in the wind. She was far more glamorous than the real-life model.

Mother called the twins *jingtongyulu*: my golden boy and jade girl. She never got tired of admiring their wavy chestnut hair, their amber eyes, and their freckled, milk-white skin. Watching the twins playing soccer with Tony in the yard, she once commented, "They take after their father. How wonderful!"

Even more infuriating, the erstwhile disciplinarian was borderline indulgent, forgoing the strict upbringing she'd once enforced on me. Perhaps that's what all grandmas do—grow softer as they age.

One spring evening, I came home from a long day in the lab only to find the twins sprawled on the living room floor with an open bag of orange cheese balls, watching *Mr. Rogers' Neighborhood*. "Yes, we had dinner. No, we haven't started Mandarin practice yet."

When I scolded them, they said in unison, "But our Chinese grandma said it's okay!"

Confronted, Mother waved her firm hand and said, "What's the harm of half-hour Children's show? Relax! American kids will never starve." Then she whispered conspiratorially, "Besides, the man in the cardigan has such a soothing voice."

Just as I had envisioned, Tony and I made a great team. He was the fun-loving father and the best buddy, while I aced the role of "bad cop." Or as Uncle Jeff joked: Tony the beauty, Mei the brain.

After Jeff became the assistant manager at a local ice cream factory, our freezer was overstocked with that brand exclusively. He lived in his late parents' apartment off Broadway—a five-minute stroll from us. Since Tony and I often got stuck in the brutal Big Dig traffic, it had always been a relief to return home and find Jeff chasing the twins in our backyard, huffing and puffing, and occasionally squirting his asthma inhaler.

A true Bostonian, Jeff possessed a religious fever for the hometown teams. During the maddeningly long football seasons, this invertebrate bachelor—a conclusion drawn by Yolanda and my other girlfriends—was like a beached whale on our couch. He never missed a single Patriots game, winning or losing. But how could I begrudge him, our most reliable backup babysitter?

Like Tony, the twins were natural athletes. Hockey, soccer, baseball, football, skateboard . . . they had tried it all.

Once, I saw them practicing free throws at the end of our driveway. "Can I join?" I said, walking toward them. "I was in a basketball league in college."

"No Way!"

Without a word, I picked up the ball and threw a perfect three-point shot into the hoop. "Nice!" said Leonardo.

Aurora cocked her head and said, "How did you do that?"

"See, with hours and hours of practice, even someone like Mom can excel," I said, seizing this teachable moment.

But soon afterwards they lost interest in basketball.

Despite my bonding attempts, they maintained a guarded distance from me, albeit shorter than the one between Mother and me.

On a family ski trip, Jeff and I took a break from the ski slopes. After dumping our damp boots on the stone hearth in front of the fireplace in the main lodge, we propped our exhausted legs on an empty bench and watched the mountain through a glass wall. A zigzagging figure in a red jacket whipped down the slope, his knees pistoning like a well-oiled engine; following him, two snow bunnies in pink and baby blue duplicated the leader's every move, carving clean, tight lines with elegant ease. I could even imagine their boasting, "Look, Mom—piece of cake." After the white dust settled behind them, three overlapping tracks emerged from the newly groomed snow—textbook sine waves separated by phase shifts.

"Beautiful," Jeff wheezed. "I could never get tired of looking at them in their element."

My eyes misted too.

One night, a guttural groan woke me up. Tony's contorted face was slick with sweat, his fist was clenched over his chest, and his calves were tight as steel knots.

"I don't remember any nightmares, no, not even a regular dream," he chuckled in answer to my inquiry the next morning, planting an assurance kiss on my forehead. But there was a twinge of aloofness in his kiss, like his mind had retreated into a castle where my entrance would always be denied by a polite yet resolute guard.

I brushed away my unease. Even in a fairy tale ending with "they live happily ever after," the princess still couldn't demand absolute thought-sharing from her prince. In reality, what counted was our 100 percent devotion to our growing family.

Nevertheless, our drastically different philosophies on parenting caused constant friction. Tony's laissez-faire approach made me suspect that he was trying to relive his truncated childhood through his children. I, on the other hand, hesitated to apply Mr. Sai's teaching in child-rearing. The stakes were too high, and no margin of error was acceptable.

The twins had an incorrigible habit of doing their homework on the kitchen island, where homemade cookies by Gloria and ice cream bars were within easy reach. While preparing dinner, I glanced up from time to time and barked orders: "Aurora, sit straight!" or "Stop spinning your pen, Leonardo!"

Beers in hand, Tony and Jeff watched ESPN with captions from across the open living room. Occasionally, they jumped up, fist-pumping, high-fiving, and mouthing, "*Touchdown!*" Inevitably, the twins would perk up to stare at the TV screen, shouting, "Daddy, daddy, what's happening?"

"Focus, kids! Finish your homework first!" Head shaking, I repeated my threat to lock them in their rooms upstairs.

The twins were so distractible that I never bothered to tiptoe toward them and try Mother's sneaky brush-plucking move on them. No doubt, they would fail the test. Anyway, that crude experiment had poor prognostic value. Just look at me: where were those great things I was supposed to achieve in life?

Every summer, I recruited my parents to tutor the twins. The first summer, my father constructed a solar oven out of aluminum foil in our backyard. Sadly, his passion for teaching dissipated when he presented the scrambled eggs and Aurora commented unappreciatively, "But we have microwave ovens in this country, Grandpa."

My smart kids, knowing by heart their unalienable rights to the pursuit of happiness, passively resisted any non-mandatory learning. Ten minutes into a Chinese Pinyin session, they would yawn and ask for bathroom breaks, water breaks, or snack breaks. After a Chinese chess or Go game with my father, like some tortured prisoners demanding reparation, Leonardo would pester Tony for the newest gaming gadgets and Aurora would bargain for a slumber party at her friend's house. Ask them to practice writing the Chinese characters they learned at the Chinese school? Forget about it.

Without fail, a week of mental tussling with my undisciplined kids was enough to turn my father's eyes longingly toward the phone for a rescue call from Shanghai. Eventually, even Mother shook her head and conceded defeat. "Perhaps my method won't work on American kids."

(My impartial twins treated their Italian heritage with equal indifference. After returning from a week-long Italian vacation one summer, I was too ashamed to tell my in-laws that we had subsisted on McDonald's and Pizza Hut. Pathetic, I knew. But, after roasting under the blistering Roman sun, constantly diverting the twins' attention from selfie-taking to the architectural details of the Colosseum or the Forum, who would have any energy left to fight their solid alliance?)

In recent years, Chinese had become a popular second language for some American children. Celebrities touted their kids' Chinese proficiency. Meanwhile, political pundits on TV increasingly warned about the threats from "a rising China in a multipolar world..."

Thus, I doubled down, telling the twins chasing a giant dragon in a videogame, "Stop now. You haven't practiced your ten Chinese sentences today!"

"Do we have to?" They groaned, hands still clutching their joysticks.

When they puckered their faces and struggled to meet their quotas, I sensed rebellious hormones coursing through the capillaries. I looked on stoically. *Let them be disgusted at me for now.*

Come next year, they would be thirteen and I would hold less sway over their lives. Wasting their built-in hybrid advantage would be myopic, if not criminal. It's my parental duty to pad them up for an inevitable collision of two powerful cultures, to prepare them for a possible apocalyptic future.

Since the fortuitous purchase of our saltbox in the Southie, the once needle-strewn L Street Beach had been scrubbed clean. Like the proverbial ostrich with its buried head, we overlooked the episodic, violent outburst over a shoveled-out parking space after a big snowstorm. Lucky for us, our driveway was just long enough for two tandem-parked cars. Neighborly townies smoking on their fire escapes always waved at us when we strolled toward Castle Island. More hip and/or gay couples had moved in, along with Starbucks and trendy bars on Broadway. Encouraged by the gentrification, we expanded our starter home and stayed.

Occasionally, local TV would report on drug busts in the locker rooms of South Boston High, or the abysmal dropout rate. Somehow my brain selectively ignored them . . . well, until the day Leonardo forgot his assignment on the kitchen counter. On my way to drop it off, I was sidetracked by the noise erupting from a classroom. Peering into the window, I couldn't believe what I was seeing: a young teacher was wedged between the clenched fists of two boys—taller than the frazzled woman—while the rest of the disrupted class gleefully pounded on their desks, shouting, "Fight! Fight! Fight!"

That evening, I told Tony about the disheartening drama in school. Gloria, who happened to be visiting, chimed in. "You know, there are still decent parochial schools around. Leo and I would be happy to chip in toward tuition. We've done the same for Lenny and Tracy's kids in the past."

Secretively, I relished the idea. Surely, the kids could benefit from some structure and discipline. Maybe the fabled rulers of nuns could produce miracles.

"Over my dead body!" Tony fumed, his face darkening like brooding clouds. "If you have some extra money to burn, take the senior shuttle to Mohegan Sun."

I sighed. Tony's stubbornness now left the twins with only one viable option: Boston Latin School, the highly competitive elite public school.

REPORT CARDS
AND RED BELTS

After the sixth ring, the recording in Aurora's voice would kick in. Each cheerful promise of getting back to me sounded more and more foreboding. Disheartened, I hung up for the nth time. Pacing in Grandma's chicken coop, gloomy thoughts fluttered in my mind, like wet clumps of plucked feathers.

Seismic tremors usually harbinger the inevitable eruption of Mount Vesuvius.

Earlier this year, the twins' grades had deteriorated. I could only blame myself. Distraught with the passing of Mother and then Rei, I was less vigilant.

Then came that watershed evening. After the twins nonchalantly handed me their progress reports, they beelined toward their PlayStation.

C in Foundational Reading, C+ in Math, C– in World History and Geography... The only B's were Leonardo's Exploratory Art and Aurora's Speaking and Listening. *Unbelievable!*

Heat rushed to my face when I read the teachers' euphemisms: "With more sustained efforts, Aurora could reach her full potential." "Leo has abundant, untapped intelligence and artistry..."

I stirred the ravioli with a shaky hand. *What would Mother have done if I had shown her such a sickly report?*

My children's embarrassing grades only reflected my failures. I'd failed to teach them to clutch their pens with full concentration; failed to examine their homework every night, no matter how late I got home nor how my two-hundred-pound head craved a soft pillow; failed to inspire them with biographies of Stephen Hawking, Jane Goodall, Rachel Carson, Steve Jobs, Sally Ride . . . failed to encourage them to dream big and work hard.

Tony was amused by the reports. Head still angled toward the hockey game on the screen across the room, he said, "Jesus, how did they manage C's in PE?"

"By being lazy!" I banged my slotted spoon over the pot and raised my voice. "We must ground them."

"Chill, Mei." He said, resting his hands on my shoulders, "Plenty of time for them to catch up."

"No one plays catch-up games on my watch!"

He chuckled, "Seriously? Ground them for C's?"

"Exactly! They put in zero effort."

"Come on, they are just kids being kids."

"It'll be too late when they turn Franky and Andy's age!"

Bingo! His gaze shifted from TV to the anti-fatigue floor mat under my feet.

Bringing up his brothers was my last resort. They were a quick-witted bunch, all excelled in board games or anything fun-related. Who knew what they could have accomplished in life had they lived under Mother's iron rule? Instead, Franky drifted between house painting jobs whenever his pot fund ran low. One night, Tony had to bail him out at 3 a.m. for selling two ounces of weed to an undercover cop. As for Andy, he had a lustrous record of DUIs as well as a misdemeanor caught on a Fenway surveillance camera—of him breaking a Yankee fan's side mirror with a beer bottle. Even Lenny, the most respectable eldest son, who had been managing the family deli after Leo's stroke, struggled with child support for his ex-wife and his on-again-off-again girlfriend.

"No need to blow a head gasket," Tony said, taking a can of Samuel Adams out of the fridge.

He still doesn't get it! Staring at his frowning face and unflattering shadows cast by the pendant lights, I remembered his distant boasting of coasting through schools. My rage flamed higher. *For heaven's sake, could we count on his luck to stretch over our children?*

"Listen, we must be a family of tough love. Just think of Gloria and all her 'I love you's." I air-quoted her favorite phrase and snorted, "What did that lead to? A spectacular 40 percent failure rate!" As those blistering words leapt out of my mouth, I thought gloomily that I'd been charitable toward Gloria's track record as a mother.

"Shut up! Shut the fuck up!" Tony exploded. "Never ever drag Gloria into this, you hear me?"

He grabbed his car keys, stormed out, and slammed the kitchen door. Cold air blasted in, while white foam spewing out a rattling pot and sputtering all over the range.

Tony didn't return until the next evening, haggard with a blue, stubbly chin and heavy eye bags. On his two-day-old shirt, an oily, orange smear over the breast pocket suggested that he had fallen asleep on a pepperoni pizza.

"Daddy's home!" Aurora jumped from the counter stool to hug him.

Tony stroked her silky hair and said with a tired smile, "Wow, wow, when did you grow so tall?" Then he knuckle-greeted Leonardo as usual. "What's up, buddy?"

Leonardo's tense shoulders relaxed.

After fishing in the fridge, Tony popped a beer can and gulped fast. Once his thirst quenched, he walked toward the stairs, as if I were as transparent as the water pitcher on the corner. At the landing, he paused momentarily, grabbed the handrail, and hoisted himself up the remaining steps. Two minutes later, I heard the water splashing from the shower.

Clenching my jaw, I sank a carving knife into a roasted chicken from Stop & Shop. *Fine, let me be the singular Great*

Wall for our children—massive enough to deter all the menaces on the horizon.

Two weeks after the report card incident, I sat the twins in front of my laptop.

"A PowerPoint presentation?" they grunted, eyes rolling. "Mom!"

"Look, I'm trying really hard. If you don't want my help in the future, believe me, I have better things to do. Now, pay attention," I said firmly. "Anyone who aces the quiz at the end is excused from the trash chores this week."

Despite the jazzed-up animation and special effects, the twins kept yawning through the graphs and charts of career pathways, statistics of entry-level salaries of various professions, and the median prices for housing in the metro Boston area, etc.

I clicked to the last slide. A line of *Your Dream, Your Life* sparkled over a McMansion, with the foreground of a mani-cured lawn, a three-tiered fountain, and a red Lamborghini on a circular driveway. *A mistake,* I realized. I should have chosen an image of a lit-up ski chalet in Aspen, or surfers grinning in killer waves off the North Shore of Oahu. Ignoring their smirks, I pressed ahead. "To get the life you want, count on nobody but yourselves. Now, a journey of a thousand miles starts at the first step—you must study hard for your entrance exams for Boston Latin this December."

After exchanging their bewildered looks, Aurora raised her hand. "Mother, now, explain *why* again?"

"Glad you asked." Inwardly, I was exasperated by their inability to connect the obvious dots. "In order to pursue your expensive hobbies, you need a well-paid job. For that, a useful college degree is at the minimum. And you must enter a great high school first."

"Sadly, Daddy and I can't send you to private school. And, unless my company goes public, we can't afford to move to any towns with top public schools either, like towns starting with the letter W: Wellesley, Weston, Westford, Westwood, Wayland, Winchester... Get it?"

They now looked mildly bored.

"To sum it up, your best chance to enter a decent college is by getting into the Boston Latin. But it takes only the top 20 percent of applicants." There and then, I delivered the punch line. "Wake up, kids! Your current grades won't cut it."

The slideshow and, perhaps more importantly, a carefully crafted and strictly enforced incentive program, worked to some extent. The twins' grades improved by the end of the semester. Now the probability of them getting into Boston Latin beat the odds of my company's IPO—our ticket to a W-town.

A year before the slideshow, I had announced over dinner that our most promising compound for Alzheimer's had failed a phase-three trial. Translation: my stock options remained worthless after five years of hard work. "Fingers-crossed," I said in exhaustion, "two more compounds in the pipeline."

"That's cool, Mom," Aurora chirped, "maybe your next drug could make the headlines."

"Now, that's a healthy attitude," Tony said proudly.

"That's right," I concurred. "By the way,, remember the new approach of building a human brain organoid that I mentioned before? We're making strides."

"Mom is a worry bird," Leonardo said, drawing a smiling face on his plate with a slice of beet. "She needs to learn from us how to relax."

I tried not to laugh. "Leo, eat your food instead of playing with it."

Then, six months later, our second compound went bust, too.

Nevertheless, even if the third drug became a blockbuster, I would hesitate to trade our humble abode for a white colonial in a leafy yet claustrophobic W-town. Southie had grown on us. Everything was a short drive away—our jobs in Cambridge, Gloria's house in Saugus, Chinatown, museums and the Aquarium, and the escape to the mountains or the sand dunes of Cape Cod. Plus, the kids' "lifelong" friends around the block.

Living under the same roof, naturally Tony and I resumed talking. The carpool schedule for the twins' games, crabgrass, refinancing the mortgage. . . We averted our eyes after the briefest gaze.

Unofficially, Tony had taken up residence in the small office next to the kitchen. I was relieved that the twins hadn't paid any attention. Many nights I tossed in our queen-size bed, missing his rhythmic breathing and his warm body.

On an unseasonable cold night due to a polar vortex, I heard familiar footsteps and a tap on my door. Joy bloomed in my heart. *I cried* out, "Come in."

Tony walked straight to the closet. Shaking his graying, wavy hair, he said wryly, "A puny baseboard in a north-facing room. The contractor we hired is a moron."

"It's toasty here. Stay if you like," I said with feigned nonchalance, inching to my side to make room.

He paused his hand on the closet knob, then took out a sleeping bag for camping. "Thanks. But I need to be at Montpellier for an eight o'clock appointment tomorrow morning."

I was hurt by his refusal to reclaim his spot. Then, I reminded myself, he wasn't a cruel man. Earlier this year, he folded me into his warm chest before my trip for my dying mother. Rubbing my forehead with his stubbly chin, he said gently, "Take as long as you need, okay? I'll take care of everything here." And when I was weeping uncontrollably after Agent Wright's surprise visit, he had stroked my hair and wiped away my tears. What did I do then? I battled away his hands and cried out, "You won't understand!"

Pacing in Grandma's chicken coop, I noticed that the wall calendar was stuck on the page of *August 2012, the Year of the Dragon.*

But it had been a Year of Mourning to me, with grief nesting like a set of Russian dolls.

Dragon happened to be the Zodiac sign for Mother, my twins, and myself. Traditional Chinese hold a strange superstition:

during one's birth year, which cycles every twelfth lunar year, one's personal demons would come out of hiatus to wreak havoc.

In the past, Grandma always sent me a hand-knit red belt before the Year of the Dragon. "To ward off evil," she whispered over the phone as if evil might be eavesdropping next door. "Just in case."

As a molecular biologist, I trusted only evidence-based theories. Still, decades of rational thinking could only suppress the inborn Chinese superstitions, but never eradicate them. So, I laughed and said, "Why not? Thank you, Grandma."

A beat later, Grandma chuckled too, realizing that I was merely taking out supplemental insurance to humor her.

Evil exists, of course. Now I wished that I'd asked her for clarification: *Just in case* all my scientific training proved to be a toothless scarecrow? Or, *just in case* the red belt possessed the purported magic power to shield me from the devil's sharp claws? What if the flaming red enrages the ferocious beast instead, the way a red cape swung by a matador agitates a charging bull?

Looking back, I celebrated my twelfth and twenty-fourth birthdays without a scratch. At thirty-six, I survived a high-risk pregnancy and an uneventful cesarean. Eight months before, I turned forty-eight, nearly the midpoint of life should I live to be a centenarian.

Middle age is meant to be a serpentine belt, smoothly transferring spiritual and material wealth between the decaying and the budding. Notoriously, it's also often a fatigue-failure point. This time I had no safeguarding red belt on my waist.

Before Grandma completely submerged into the twilight zone, she sounded particularly exuberant during one of my calls. "I've just finished knitting a red belt for Shu-Zhen," She announced, then volunteered, "I can knit for your twins too."

"Oh, their first zodiac year is still two years away!" I teased her, "Besides, Chinese red belts won't work for *laowai*."

"You never know. After all, they're half-Chinese." Grandma giggled, the idea of her great-grandchildren being *laowai* still tickled her. Soon her mind drifted to flavoring her bland gruel with ground nuts. And I ended the call by promising to send her a jumbo bag of Georgian pecans.

At the time, I didn't want to waste Grandma's time on my twins, who had arrived at the age of knowing everything under the sun. Her painstakingly knitted belt and the Chinese superstition would only become perennial laughingstocks.

In a race against time, Alzheimer's disease beat me. Precipitously failing, Grandma probably couldn't have finished knitting them anyway.

On my forty-eighth birthday, instead of wearing a new red belt from her, I rolled the three frayed ones into coils, pinned them in a display case, and mounted the piece of collaborative art inside my closet. Every morning, a flash of cheerful red would urge me to armor up, to venture into the world—a sometimes cold and hostile land.

A goose-bump sensation crawled all over my skin. Could my losses this year— my robust mother, Grandma, Rei, and Tony's affection, too—all be explained by the absence of Grandma's good-luck belt?

How I wished that I had encouraged Grandma to knit for us! I could have rotated her belts, wearing a proxy talisman for my twins, too!

29

MY BROKEN
SAMSUNG GALAXY

"Tony, I've been trying to get ahold of you." Staring at the flying second-hand on the clock, I rambled desperately, "Please, call me ASAP. The truth is... we can't stay in my father's apartment—" Another beep cut me off. I dialed again with shaky hands, like a junkie trying to reach his dealer for a life-saving hit. Then, at a fast clip I reiterated the logistics of reaching the Nanjing South train station.

The change of our rendezvous point shouldn't pose much challenge for Tony, a savvy world traveler. And, we had ridden on the Hu-Ning line together, twice. Besides, he could reach me easily: his company-issued iPhone had an international roaming plan. But why hadn't he called already?

Then I remembered Tony's nightmares and his emphatic denial. A premonition loomed larger with each passing second. Something had gone terribly wrong.

Pounded by monstrous waves of fear and yearning, my heart was on the verge of exploding. Pacing on the balcony and sweating profusely, I commanded myself: *Have faith. He'll call any minute now.*

I forced myself to meditate. *Inhale, hold, exhale, hold...* Eyes closed, and hands cupped over my belly, I repeated this sequence. It did nothing. Thousands of ants still chewed at my stomach.

Then, my Samsung rang. I leapt up to grasp it.

"Hey!" Tony's voice was thick and raspy, like he was fighting a cold. A thread of naked exhaustion made it sound unexpectedly sexy, too.

"Ohh—" My voice cracked. No existing words could describe the immensity of my joy. Recomposing my melting self, I said, "Did you get my messages?"

"I just got home. Saw the blinking lights."

Breathlessly, I briefed him about my father's new marital status. As I was babbling on, a loud clattering sound, like a mini avalanche, interrupted me. I glanced toward its direction. The ice maker in the kitchen, of course. But the clock above the fridge stopped me cold. The 7:30 a.m. local time meant 7:30 p.m. EST. *Whoosh*, my stomach plunged into a mushy pile. I gasped, "Aren't you supposed to be boarded by now? Your flight—"

"Listen, we aren't flying today, or anytime soon," he cut in. "Jeff had a massive heart attack. He got three stents put in at Mass General the day after you left."

"Oh my god! Is he all right now?" Recovering from the initial shock, I felt two tons lighter despite Jeff's grave condition. *Thank heavens it's not Tony or the twins, like in that awful dream.*

"He had serious complications while in the step-down unit. Now, he's back in the ICU."

"Oh my god!"

"Check your email for the latest CT scan results." Tony said, his voice seething with rage. "Jeff's had a septum defect since childhood. But his octogenarian pediatrician at the time never picked up a stethoscope to listen to his heart, just drugged him with steroids for asthma!"

"Oh, no," I murmured. An image of Jeff and his inseparable inhaler flashed in my mind. "You mean, a hole in his heart all these years and no one picked it up?"

"You know how Jeff shuns doctors like the plague. I should have pushed him."

Then, remembering what Tony mentioned earlier, I said, "Wait a minute, I can't access Gmail in China. You know that, right?"

"Shit. I forgot about all that bullshit." A distinctive can-popping sound came over the line. Then, between gulps, he said, "I'm heading back to the hospital after a quick shower. It's been touch-and-go for the past few days. But the doctors think he is finally turning the corner."

"I see. I'm so sorry for your ordeal." I released the death grip on my phone, feeling stupid for having tortured myself for a minor miscommunication between us. Then, moved by the bond between Tony and his best friend, I said, "Be strong. Hang in there for a few more days. I'm going to reschedule my return flight as soon as I hang up, I promise."

"Yes, you do that."

"Where are the twins?"

"At my mom's. Playing video games in the basement, I assume."

Silly me, why hadn't I thought of calling Gloria? After a quick round of self-scolding, I joked, "Phew! No need to worry about them starving then." In truth, they knew how to microwave mac and cheese. Mother had trained them after they turned seven, "just in case."

Tony didn't laugh. He was chewing something crunchy. *Has he been living on beer and chips since I left?* Remembering the athletic young man that he no longer was, I said helplessly, "Anything I can do?"

"Nothing, absolutely nothing. Neither can I." He burped, and then mumbled, "All *I* can do is stare at the monitors, listen to the freakin' beeps for hours on end, day and night, watch the doctors poke him, probe him, and rush him around like a sack of bruised potatoes. . . You wouldn't even recognize him now. IV lines, EKG leads, tubes, tapes, cuffs, catheter—you name it—head to toe. He. . . he just disappears behind that tangled mess. I went to the chapel the other day. But I couldn't pray either. I . . . I just couldn't . . ." His voice broke, then he blew his nose loudly.

I felt a pinch in my heart. A grainy clip from one of Gloria's old home videos flitted before my eyes. Standing on his chubby toes, a boy reaches for the cooling rack on a sun-drenched Formica counter. He greedily grabs the biggest amaretti cookie, almost the size of his pudgy palm, gobbles it up, then flashes a pure, blissful grin to the camera. A young and radiant woman appears and dusts the white powder off his cheek. Combing his fine, wavy hair with her fingers, she she bends down to kiss him . . .

How I wished that I could duplicate Gloria's act now! I wanted to wrap my arms around Tony's trembling shoulders, and sooth him with the same affection. But, hard-wired with the "Show, don't tell" philosophy on love, I couldn't make a single sound.

After an agonizing silence, he said hoarsely, "Mei, I've been thinking of your tree."

"What?"

"The Greeting Pine you wanted to show the kids, the one on top of the Yellow Mountain!" He sniffled again.

My Tony would never cry for a tree that he would miss seeing. Time stopped for the briefest moment, but every sense of mine stood on the highest alert. The phone in my hand suddenly felt like a brick of ice. Then, over the drumming of my heart, I heard a thin voice asking, "What about it?"

"Aurora googled it. It's been dead for years." His voice now raised to the pitch the savage growling of a cornered pit bull. "Don't tell me you didn't know!"

His labored breathing grew more ragged. I could visualize his strong fingers denting the sweating beer can, his rib cage expanding and lifting, his diaphragm rising and halting, struggling against a Sisyphean rock.

Cold sweat started to trickle down my spine. Gathering all the strength from the depth of my abdomen, I inhaled, then uttered through my clenched teeth, "What're you talking about?"

"Hell!"

"What do you mean?"

"Stop pretending!" He yelled. "You must have known this by now: Jeff and I are lovers. Have been. Since our China trip in college."

Black shutters blocked out my vision. Blindly, I staggered backward, hands groping in air until my calf stumbled upon something spongy. Oh mercy, Grandma's armchair! Before I could receive its full embrace, another sound erupted from underfoot, a nauseating sound. My vision returned.

Crouching down, I picked up my cracked Samsung. A smirking face seemed to peer from a cobweb of splintered glass. An eerie voice drifted out, as faint as from Mars. "Are you okay? Mei, talk to me."

"NO!" I screamed, "TOTALLY NOT OKAY!" Reflexively, my hand swung the phone away as hard as possible. The screen darkened as soon as it hit the wall.

Staring at the phone's black carcase and the sphere of debris, I hyperventilated. Yet no matter how hard I sucked in, my lungs couldn't extract enough oxygen. A fish thrashing in a muddy puddle, gasping, dying.

How could I go on? In this disorienting space warped with hidden dimensions, a realm where all the physical laws that I'd known for all my life were no longer applicable, I needed more than six senses to comprehend the simplest words, to formulate the most nebulous impression, to generate the faintest idea.

Two seconds. That was all it took for a cruel gust to knock down the fragile nest that I'd been building with my mate for years—a twig at a time, two hatched eggs inside. Something sharp stung my eyes. I blinked rapidly. Was that a mirage conjured by the King of Masks?

His hearty laughter, his teasing of my earlobe with his nose, still cold from exposure, his gentle kisses and bear hugs... Were all those moments optical illusions as in a kaleidoscope, a hologram? Of all the warm and fuzzy tenderness emanating from that unknowable stranger, which I'd attributed to love in the past, was there even a milligram of genuine affection? How could anyone act so convincingly with counterfeit currency? Even if this had been nothing but an elaborate hoax, shouldn't there be a trace amount of truth? I wanted to know—I desperately wanted to know.

A sour torrent rushed to my throat. I ran into the bathroom and emptied the residue of the previous night's banquet into the toilet. Pressing my chin against the cold porcelain rim, I cursed myself. *Fool! A pathetic, spectacular fool!*

Hatred hardened inside me, dark and dense like the poisonous pit of a peach: full of hideous holes, yet impossible to extricate without destroying the soft skin and tender flesh— the white, fragrant pulp with red, intricate veins, infused with the sun-ripened sweetness and complex flavors of our sixteen shared years.

Bitter, salty tears surged, seeking an outlet. Blurry-eyed, I zoomed into the period before the paradoxical fruit was still a green fuzzy kernel, before the bumblebee dipped its hairy legs into the yellow, sticky stigma, before the pink blossom opened its uncertain petal, and before the first tinge of rouge crept up on my cheeks at the sight of a fit, young man grinning on a mountain... Rivulets trickled down, like spring creeks swollen with snowmelt.

How could the end be so horrific, yet every step along the way had felt right?

30

THE YUAN DYNASTY VASE

A bird streaked by the window. It hopped onto a ginkgo branch, then fluttered its long, flamboyant tail. *Go away!* I shushed at it. Oblivious to my misery, the magpie tilted its head and chirped a string of cheerful notes. *Wock, wock, weer, weer!* Under the rising sun, the long shadows from the buzzing construction site were shrinking fast. A flock of wobbly kindergarteners was crossing the street with linked hands, bookended by two adults. At the sight, tears brimmed in my eyes again.

I sank into the armchair, the relic with numbered days left. It squeaked under my weight, as if scolding. True, at the sorrowful sight of a grown woman sobbing uncontrollably, Grandma would shake her silvery hair and suck her teeth to chide, "Don't waste such a gorgeous morning!" Then I heard in my head Mother's finger snapping and her impatient "Get up!"

I got up, ruthlessly denying myself the luxury of wallowing in self-pity. Back in Boston, I reminded myself, generations of mice were still scurrying in their cages in anticipation of my return to modify their fates. Unruly climbing roses were begging for the pruning shears in my gloved hands. Two unwitting teenagers were waiting, too, to be molded into citizens of the world. Most urgently, an untold story waited to be written.

I splashed cold water on my blotchy face, patted it dry, and dabbed on a bright lipstick. The woman in the mirror looked fractionally less miserable. So, I got out and hailed a taxi to the city museum. Aunt No. 2 had volunteered to bring me and my family for a visit. But, in my current state, I'd rather see the legendary vase by myself.

There were hardly any visitors today. Under the autumn sky, the yellow and hunter-green porcelain rooflines glistened against a canopy of ancient cedars. Scaling the worn marble steps toward the red Palace of Heaven Veneration, I remembered my visits during my teenage years.

After the reopening of museums in the eighties, the famous Nanjing Museum still boasted a treasure trove of 400,000 items in its permanent collection. However, I always pestered my relatives to take me to the less known city museum.

Grandma had become allergic to antiques after her reeducation stint. The worst chaperone was my uncle. On any given day, he'd rather take my younger cousins to the zoo, the water park on Xuanwu Lake, or the bustling markets near the Confucius Temple. After marching through exhibitions, he would chainsmoke under a camphor tree, brooding over the preening pigeons and giving his lazy watch a vigorous shake from time to time. When I emerged from the hall and squinted against the bright light at the threshold, he—the saddest man in the courtyard—would put out his cigarette and grumble, "What took you so long?"

For one thing, I took my time reading descriptions, large and small, of every blue-and-white porcelain vase. I took time marveling at the exquisite set of Bronze Age musical bells and intricate jade carvings that could only be appreciated through a magnifying glass. I took time sniffing the air in the intimate chambers. The faint woody aroma reminded me of Grandpa's old house. Pausing in front of *Watching the Spring and Listening to the Wind*—a painting by Tang Yin—I imagined Grandpa's eyes tracing the undulating mountain peaks, the rushing waterfall, and the two scholars conversing along the bank of a babbling spring; I could feel his warm breath on my ear as he whispered with childish delight.

Today, after meandering through three halls, finally, I arrived at the inner sanctum of the museum. The entire chamber displayed one artifact inside a bullet-proof case.

There, the Yuan vase! My scalp tingled. This must be what Mother had felt when she encountered it here a few years before.

When teenage Ting-Fang returned home from school one afternoon, the living room was teeming with excited guests. Engrossed in a heated debate, nobody paid any attention to her greetings.

In the kitchen, Grandma paused her turnip chopping and complained, "Your *bobo* has been acting crazy since this morning."

Intrigued, Ting-Fang went to the dining room, a rag and a duster in hand. She lingered at the door to the adjoining living room, diligently dusting and wiping.

"No, not me!" one white-bearded elder exclaimed. "Can't afford the risk of ending up in 'the letterhead'. I have a sick wife and a disabled son at home."

Another man dry-coughed and tapped his brass pipe on the tray to grab attention. "Brothers, if no one dares to touch it, a desperado like him is bound to unload it somewhere south. From a dark alley in Canton, it's only a boat ride to Hong Kong at night . . ."

Every man groaned.

"There is a way to secure it," Ping-An said at last, breaking the insufferable silence. "If everyone chips into a fund, we could buy it as a collective with the pooled money. Then we donate it to the government. It's impossible for the police to arrest every antique dealer in town."

"Impossible? Young man, don't be naive." The white-bearded man laughed bitterly. "It hasn't been three years since they rounded up every opium addict and locked them up in the warehouse. Remember Ashi who jumped into the river through a broken window? And the other boy died in his own puke and shit?"

"Why compare us to those lowlifes?" someone said, clicking his tongue. "Sure, the new sheriff in town dislikes us, but at least we provide some valuable services."

"Valuable services, my ass. Wait until they send you to a reeducation camp to learn to sew, like those dance girls—"

"Oh, come on!" Boisterous objections erupted.

"Brothers, brothers, stop bickering!" Ping-An spoke again, "What should we call our group? The Antique Dealers' Guild? No . . . How about the Patriotic Guild of Antique Dealers of Nanjing?"

The tongue-clicker said, "Hmm, there's a nice ring to it."

The cougher said, "Yeah, I like it too."

More men echoed their approvals.

"Large, small, doesn't matter. Those who don't want to contribute are free to leave as well, no pressure." Then, Ping-An volunteered. "I can safeguard the rescue fund tonight. Tomorrow morning, let Xiao Chui and me deal with the guy in the village."

"Great idea! Here are my lucky three to start the fund," a man said, flashing his bills for the cheering crowd.

"Five yuan from me," the cougher said, and then turned to his white-bearded friend. "Lao Qiu, I heard you made a killing today."

"Oh well, here goes my fifteen." The elder handed over his bounty reluctantly.

"Man, I've had a rotten month. Here," The tongue-clicker laid a wrinkly bill onto the pile.

"Slow down, slow down," Ping-An called out. Then he took out a piece of letterhead stationery, a fine brush, and an inkwell from a drawer. "Here, brothers, write down your names and your donation amounts."

After the guests left, Ting-Fang poked her head through the door and asked, "*Bobo*, how could anybody 'end up in a letterhead'?"

"My sneaky girl," Ping-An laughed, ruffling her smooth hair and pointing at the document filled with names. "See these vertical lines? What do they look like? The bars of a jail cell."

"Ah, these old-fashioned letterheads!" Ting-Fang complained, "Our teacher says, only the reactionaries write from right to left and top to bottom like that. We must write on horizontal lines, left to right. And use only simplified Chinese characters. On our last quiz, she deducted a full point from me for writing a character in the old way."

"That's right. Your *bobo* and his friends are behind our times," Ping-An laughed wryly, glancing at the obsolete letterhead. "Sit down, help your old man to sort this out."

"Oh my, lots of money!" she exclaimed, her eyes widening at the stack of loose paper bills. "What are you going to buy?"

"A national treasure!" Ping-An beamed brilliantly, and even the few faint pockmarks on his wide forehead glowed. "Now, tear a piece of paper from your notebook and copy down the names and amounts neatly, the way your teacher taught you."

As my mother was converting the donor list to the new format, Aunt No. 2 joined the party, sorting and tallying the bills. Meanwhile, Ping-An tap-danced in the room. Still unable to curb his exuberance, he jumped up in the air, hooting, "Ha, ha, ha... Today is the pinnacle of your *Bobo*'s entire life!"

Earlier that morning, a swarthy, rail-thin man had walked into the antique street with an awkward bundle on his back. Lowering the brim of his straw hat, he ducked into the first shop and whispered to the person behind the counter, "Huo Ji, I must speak to your boss in private."

"You are speaking to him." Xiao Chui smiled good-naturedly before leading the stranger into his back room.

After the man untied the knots of his clumsily wrapped package, Xiao Chui—as young and inexperienced as he was—fought an urge to whistle. Examining the vase, he asked, "Where did you get this?"

"Family heirloom," the man said mechanically, scanning the room with his shifty eyes. Then he lowered his gaze at his thick, dirty toenails peeking through holes in his shoes and cursed under his breath, "Fuck! If my son weren't ill, I would never even consider... parting with it."

Suspecting that the vase without provenance had been stolen, Xiao Chui hesitated. "Did your folks tell you about its age?"

"From the Qing Dynasty?"

Xiao Chui shook his head imperceptibly. *It's definitely older.*

The man's eyes lit up. He said eagerly, "Ming Dynasty? You tell me. I was too young when my *bobo* . . . died."

"Hmm, no official marking on the bottom." Xiao Chui scratched his head and said, "I have to consult an expert. Come, come with me, my colleague is only a few shops down the road."

Reluctantly, the stranger gathered his belongings and followed.

When Ping-An saw the vase, his pupils dilated.

Over fifty centimeters tall, the blue-and-white *meiping* had a powerful presence that commanded instant awe from a beholder. With a short neck, flaring shoulders, and gracefully tapered bottom, the well-balanced vase was, no doubt, a *tour de force* by a master potter. Depicted vividly on its belly was the classic tale of *Xiao He Chasing After Han Xin Under the Moonlight.* Scrolling bands of meandering vines, key patterns, and other geometric motifs decorated the rest.

Hmm, the white glaze is brilliant; yet, less translucent than in a typical Ming piece. Ping-An mused, feeling a jolt of electricity pulsing in his head. The saturated blue was robust and brilliant, yet the fluid lines diffused slightly at the edges. *This is the hallmark of Huihui Qing*—the precious cobalt blue imported from Persia via the Silk Road in the fourteenth century. He felt his pockmarks stinging now. *Yes, it must be one of the rarest Yuan Dynasty vases in existence!*

Even at this stage of his career, Ping-An had evaluated only one Yuan vase—a much smaller article in the private collection of an extremely wealthy patron. What struck him was the pristine condition of this vase, as if it had been sleeping undisturbed for centuries in a cool, dark place. He shuddered—*in an ancient tomb.*

"How did your ancestor acquire this?" Ping-An said, trying to sound casual. He was aware of the few incidents which both the tomb raiders and the involved dealers were sentenced to death.

"Hmm, many, many generations ago, one of my ancestors was an official in the imperial palace." Under the penetrating gaze of Ping-An, the man faltered. "It's also possible that my *bobo* found it in our rice field while digging an irrigation trench."

"I see. Where do you live?"

"Guanyin Mountain."

Ping-An nodded with a poker face. That village thirty miles outside Nanjing was known for clusters of ancient tombs.

"How much would you pay for it?" the man blurted, fidgeting with his fraying hat. "I need cash now."

"How much do you want it for?" Ping-An asked in an even tone.

"A hundred yuan?" After a quick glance at Ping-An's polished Oxford shoes, he stuck out his callused hand and demanded, "No, five hundred."

If the man had known anything about the rarity of his loot, in a panic, he might have dumped this "hot potato" in a ditch. Flashing his most charming smile, Ping-An said, "My friend, I'd like to give you a very fair counteroffer, but I need to free up some funds first. Everyone in the antique business knows me. Tell you what—if you trust me, you can temporarily store it in my shop; we follow proper procedures, of course. If not, leave your name and address here. I'll visit you within two days, cash in hand."

The villager brought the vase to two more dealers down the road. To his dismay, they also told him that they needed to consult Ping-An.

The next morning, Ping-An and Xiao Chui traveled to Guanyin Mountain, accessible by only a dirt road. Even though the tomb raider had left a fake name and address, they tracked him down after combing two villages.

On the bumpy wagon ride back to Nanjing, they swaddled the vase in cotton quilts and took turns cradling it with their arms and knees.

That evening, an even bigger crowd gathered in Grandpa's living room. Men clustered two and three deep around the

display table, oohing and ahhing and exchanging silly com-
ments like giddy children at a fireworks show. At the center, a
busy photographer was clicking away: the top views, the bottom
views, the panoramic in thirty-degree increments of the narra-
tive vase. And close-ups of the details.

They speculated on the future home for the vase. Since the
prestigious Nanjing Museum was under the direct control of
Beijing, Ping-An suggested donating it to the city museum.
"This way, it is more likely to stay in town for our children and
grandchildren to admire."

After the last guest left, Ping-An summoned his children.
He instructed them, "One at a time, touch the treasure for good
luck. No, no, use only your fingertips. Here, gently, like this."

When the pilgrimage round was over, he sat them down
and pointed to a figure depicted on the vase. "See this man on
the flying horse? See his official hat and light armor? He was
Xiao He, the senior advisor to Liu Bang—the first emperor of
the Han Dynasty.

"Now, right over there was Han Xin, a brilliant young man
with a humble origin and a big ego. Recognizing Han's talents,
Xiao recommended him to Liu, the future emperor.

"Then, one day in court, Liu mocked the poor manners of
Han, the country bumpkin who had sprung up out of nowhere.
Humiliated, Han decided to decamp.

"That night, when Xiao heard of the unfortunate event, he
rode his horse by moonlight to chase after Han. See here, Han
is leading his tired horse to drink from a roadside brook. And
right here, Xiao happens to turn his head over his shoulder and
spot his friend. Now, pay attention to Xiao's right hand. See
how hard he is jerking the reins to halt his horse? Children, this
scene you witness here is a famous historic moment—a reunion
of two great minds!"

"Then what happened?" The children asked in unison.

"Xiao persuaded Han to return to Liu's court with him. He
said, 'A true hero is able to rise above humiliations.' Guess what?
He succeeded. What's even more remarkable, he convinced Liu
to commission the unproven Han as commander-in-chief!

"Together, Han and Xiao squashed mighty enemies in crucial battles and helped Liu found one of the most glorious dynasties. So, you can say, it was Xiao who single-handedly paved the road to fame and fortune for Han."

"And then what happened?"

"Well, after Liu Bang became the emperor, he feared that once he died, his powerful generals would challenge his weak son for the throne. So, one by one, he killed them on fabricated pretenses. To secure his own position, Xiao became Liu's enabler. In fact, he even developed a scheme to trap and kill his friend Han. Hence the famous saying: 'It was Xiao who made Han, it was also Xiao who destroyed Han.'

"Remember, betrayal is commonplace among friends, once their interests start to conflict. . ." The light dimmed in the storyteller's eyes when he cautioned his wide-eyed children with a sigh, "So, the takeaway of the story is, never trust your friend blindly."

A dehumidifier hummed softly in a corner of the deserted chamber, accentuating the enveloping silence. The lonely Yuan vase, perched on a silk-draped pedestal inside the bullet-proof display case, beckoned me. Beams from the ceiling lights converged on and bounced off its curves, casting complicated shadows on the pearly wall behind, as if unfolding layers of petals, or projecting dreams of a time capsule.

Swells of emotions curled and crested over me. This was the vase that had cemented Grandpa's fame as the ultimate antique connoisseur of his time; yet, much later, this same vase had also smeared his posthumous reputation, causing his descendants to boil in rage and scream, *Injustice!*

Gazing at the majestic vase in awe, I was transfixed. Soon the magic of this inanimate object transported me to the era seven hundred years before I was born, to the time when an old master lifted the shutter of his kiln and cast the first human glance on his still-cooling creation. His thrill was now coursing through my veins. In a time-lapse fashion, I saw a smiling emperor bestow the vase upon a general kneeling at his feet; when the general died, his mourning family laid his beloved vase next to him in his tomb. Centuries later, a peasant dropped his dying torch in the tomb. In the pitch-darkness, his desperate, mud-caked hands fumbled on the cold, damp floor, then scooped up something huge and heavy. When he hefted it to the day-light, his face fell: there were no silver coins nor precious stones inside the dusty vase . . .Time and again, fate kept revisiting this magnificent vase, stirring up cloudy emotions in its beholders.

In a trance, I felt the accumulating weight of deposited emotions on its surface—I felt it as acutely as if sediments were silting up my own skin, layer by layer. Then, I saw the reflection of Ping-An in love: his expanding pupils, his trembling finger trailing along the intertwining floral patterns on its cool body, his glowing face, and his ecstatic smile. I saw his moving lips passing the stories to his children, the wonderment in their wide eyes, and the solemn procession of small hands along its smooth belly. . .

Muscular and refined, callused and tender, one by one, a parade of hands through time. Who would know? Maybe the DNA of Grandpa, Mother, Aunts, or Uncle was still detectable, even today.

My own fingers twitched, yearning to connect with the vase. However, a velvet rope and an airlocked glass tomb separated us, and I could only admire its sublime beauty from ten feet away.

I clicked my camera away in no-flash mode. But pictures from every angle were marred by reflective glare from the track lights. Frustrated, I stared at the vase, burning its image into gray matter.

Hand in hand, a young couple entered the hall and beelined toward us—the vase and me. The stirred air shimmered, and love was written on their shining faces. *The world belongs to the young*, I sighed, relinquishing my prime real estate and viewing the vase at an oblique angle.

Ancient Chinese master gardeners were renowned for a spe-cial art: creating new scenery by forcing viewers to move a few steps aside. As a scientist, I could appreciate this technique: the gentle unfolding of visual clues spares our inept optic nerves from being overfired and oversaturated. And only by processing multidimensional inputs can we truly see. Indeed, the young lovers' intrusion forced me to gain a different perspective.

Friendship, fame, love… A chill rippled down my spine: just like the celebrated bond between Xiao He and Han Xin, the two legendary historical figures depicted on this vase, love—in all its shapes and forms—couldn't possibly last.

Yes, the principle of homeostasis. Anytime an external stimulus causes an internal chemical fluctuation, a living organism will activate its built-in mechanisms to restore its boring but stable baseline. The same could be said about that elusive, fuzzy feeling pulsating out of a whimsical ticker the size of one's fist. Is there anything more fleeting? My face flushed. In the long river of history, even the most profound human emotion is nothing but a whimpering ripple, dying out like a sigh a second after it begins.

Yet, like a religious zealot under the banner of love, I'd trusted blindly in another mortal soul. I'd chosen to close my eyes because reality might be too scary, and the truth as ungraspable as a slippery, five-ton hippo.

Beyond the bounds of any ordinary foolishness, I'd stubbornly sown a hopeless seed between rocks on a mountaintop; I'd willed that scrawny sapling to mature and thrive in the thinnest crust of soil.

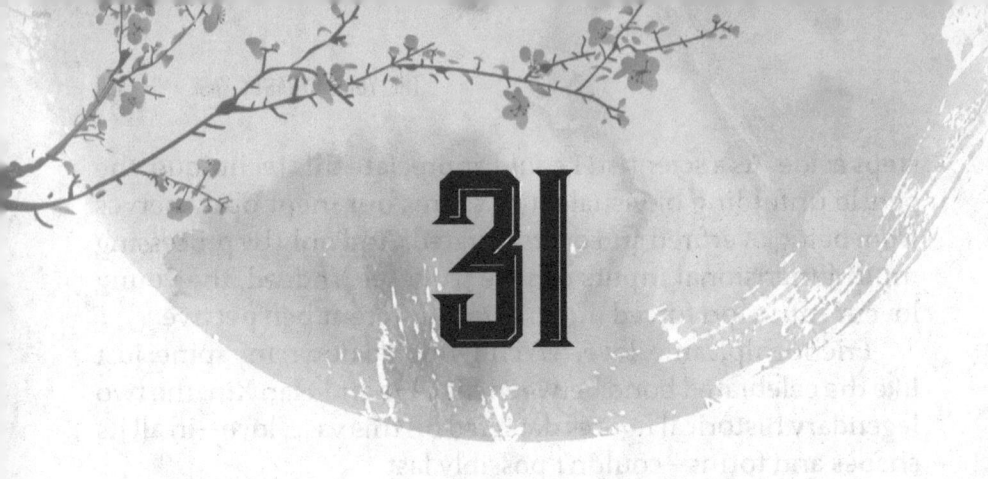

31

ONLY HEAVEN KNOWS

As usual, the Shanghai-bound train ride tied a knot in my stomach. In the blink of an eye, the newly accustomed skyline of Nanjing had flown away. Savoring the last russet eastern hill, I braced myself.

Only one thing had been settled before my flight to Boston the next day. I would celebrate the Mid-Autumn Festival with my father after all. As a matter of fact, in two hours.

The night before, I had talked to my father for almost half an hour—a record. To my surprise, he had found the missing tin box. All this time, it had been stowed in a secret compartment inside Aunty Tian's piano. She said she'd wanted to safekeep the documents and photos during the renovation of his apartment. And, somehow, she forgot to tell my father.

The news brought me considerable relief. Even though I no longer needed these props to recover my childhood memories, Binbin's prospect would be brightened.

Before ending the call, I had accepted my father's overextended olive branch to dine with him and Aunty Tian.

And then, just fifteen minutes later, the phone next to Grandma's armchair rang again. My father announced cheerfully, "I've made a 7:30 p.m. reservation for three at Ultraviolet. It's a new French restaurant."

"Celebrating a Chinese holiday in a French restaurant?"

"Why not? To tell you the truth, it's no small feat to book this place on such short notice!" He laughed smugly, hinting that he'd pulled some strings.

After hanging up for the second time, I checked out the restaurant's website. For the life of me, I couldn't understand why he would pick such an extravagant place where an average Chinese like Binbin would probably have to take out a mortgage to dine there. Perhaps he was misled by the restaurant's scientific-sounding name and its "experimental" set menu. Or maybe his new, more sophisticated wife wanted to impress me with her avant-garde taste?

Aside from the "mind-blowing" experience (exclaimed one food critic over a dish of crawfish-stuffed crab), I looked forward to celebrating the Mid-Autumn Festival with my father as an adult for the first time. I had forgiven my father for hiding the truth from me. Deep down, I still loved him and longed for his love. At our gastronomical marathon tonight, I would be civil toward Aunty Tian too, toasting her good health and longevity. I might even attempt to embrace my stepmother as a gracious American might do on the Oprah Winfrey show.

Mother would approve. She had trained me to be adaptive, not vindictive and petty. Most importantly, I had vowed to stop viewing my father through Mother's lens. Now I yearned to tell him, "Dad, I wish you abundant happiness in your second chance."

Still, I'd concealed my own thorny marital mess from my father. It was a lesser evil. How could I tell this humiliating news to anyone, especially a Chinese father?

By smashing my Samsung, I'd excommunicated Tony, de facto. What could I say to him anyway—*I can't believe it?* Facts are stubborn. Now, the only thing I couldn't believe was how I had failed to see the whistling train hurtling toward me, spewing columns of black fumes, and vibrating the dusty gravels from miles away.

For the past sixteen years, I had been protected from reality by my elephantine blind spot, inch-thick ear wax, and leather-hard hide. In the past, my folk's collective wisdom had helped me to recover from punch after punch. But, this time, I feared I might be doomed.

Even so, I decided to tap into another rich reserve—my decades of scientific training. *Baby steps*, I coached myself. *First, stop being emotional.*

Now, assess the situation objectively and logically. I shut my still-puffy eyes.

In hindsight, everything made sense. For Tony, an oblivious and stubborn wife was a godsend: an instant escape from his latent Catholic guilt, and a means to a worthy end—fulfilling Gloria's wish and passing on his genetic legacy. Nevertheless, he ended up being a tired actor trapped in an endless farce, riding a parental wagon on three wobbly wheels.

Then, watching a comatose Jeff day in and day out—the kind of agonizing, hopeless waiting that I could sympathize with—had triggered his conscience. *That's it.* When the Grim Reaper lingered in the room and the black cloak brushed his hand grasping the metal railing of the hospital bed, Tony had finally jolted awake and mustered the courage to free himself from the nightmares gnawing at him at night.

It took courage to right one's course at midlife. Still, I blamed Tony for deceiving me, for lack of prenuptial disclosure. But could I? When I proposed to him on that autumn afternoon—after bribing him with Kung Pao chicken and pouring him copious libations in that sunny apartment above Dot Ave—he had hinted that we were different kinds of people. At the time, he said, "Just so you know, I still plan on spending most of my free time outdoors, doing things I love."

Aha, there! I had failed to detect the unspoken keywords, his subtext: *with Jeff.* Desperate for a husband to fertilize my precarious eggs and to father my imaginary children, I had ignored his warning and twisted his arm to accept the vacant role in my dream. Bad luck? No, sheer stupidity!

Stop the self-loathing! I forced myself to switch to damage-control mode. With the twins in the conundrum, cutting Tony out of my life would be as feasible as operating on metastatic cancer. I squinted hard at the future, but there wasn't any glimpse of light, not even the faintest promise of the palest dawn.

No doubt that Jeff would survive—after all, he had been receiving the best possible care at the medical mecca of the world. So, I resorted to ranking the possible scenarios of our coexistence in the order of descending probability:

A divorce. Tony moves out to live with Jeff. We share custody of the twins.

A divorce. I move out, Jeff moves in. We share custody of the twins.

No divorce. Jeff stays where he is. We maintain the status quo— an equilibrium of a triangle.

No divorce. Jeff moves in. He practically lives on our couch anyway!

I winced. None of the choices was palatable.

Yet, in my numb, leaden heart of hearts, I knew that two reasonable people could work out a tolerable solution for all parties involved. Above all, we loved our children, albeit in our own ways.

But, wait a second, did I just behave like a jaded physician observing a moribund patient with detached interest and forensic precision, or a shrewd widow scheming for a new lease on life without an appropriate mourning period?

My icy lucidity at this junction of the crisis began to scare me. Perhaps, what I had fallen in love with had never been Tony per se, but the vision of building a happy life with that funny, spontaneous, athletic young man. At least, I didn't love him as deeply as I'd fooled myself into believing.

Oh, the murky depth of human affection! I winced again. Could one use an ancient measuring stick to gauge it? Could anyone love two individuals with equal intensity?

Even though it was impossible to meditate on the flying bullet train, I clasped my hands and cupped them on my lap, aiming for a mindset of cautious optimism.

The light beyond my closed eyelids darkened. And the train slowed its tempo to a stop. I opened my eyes to find our train idling at Zhenjiang Station. I spotted a tea-vending stall on the platform. An impulse propelled me to get off and fetch a rejuvenating cup.

At the counter, a girl was standing on tiptoes and loading paper cups into a tall dispenser. A neckless man in an ill-fitting Armani suit crept up behind her, laying his hairy hand on her waist. The girl almost dropped her stack. The man laughed, "Hey, do you miss me? When does your shift end?"

Blushing, the girl looked down and mumbled something in a barely audible voice.

"Come during your break, then. Room 889, the usual." Tapping his Rolex, he smirked. "Listen, don't keep me waiting this time, or my balls will explode!"

Having witnessed too much already, I turned around and sighed. Things would never change, not here, and probably not in my adopted habitat either.

The train whistled, and I jumped back on. A loose ring on my slimmed-down finger spun a quirky turn. Grandma's gold ring. Instantly, a trill of her laughter rang in my ears, and her *Just in Case*. My lips curved up reflexively. *Carry on. You'll survive, no matter what.*

Our train pulled out of Zhenjiang. Seven decades earlier, this was the place where Ping-An secured a precious cargo to rebuild our ancestral house after the inferno. And a quarter century after that, it was also here that my mother slid the paper with her address toward my father's sweaty palm, sending a shockwave to wake me—still a sleeping oocyte inside her. My throat became constricted, another tide surged. I scorned this sentimental side of me. *Enough tears already!*

I would stop grieving for my recent losses eventually, in the same way that I had stopped grieving for Grandpa—by turning him into a living part of me. Right then and there, I made another promise to Grandpa. Even though I might not avert the Hong Clan's existential crisis, I would write down the unvarnished stories of my family in brutal honesty. I hoped that my loved ones could live on, warts and all, in the memories of my twins and beyond, longer than the statues lining the public garden, or the blinking lighthouses in Broad Sound.

As we raced toward Suzhou, my father's hometown, I realized that only four days had passed since I found out about my father's secret marriage. Ironically, I'd started to appreciate his shocking revelation. This bumpy beginning of my trip had had an unintended side benefit. As the famous Mr. Sai once said, *A good fortune or a bad omen? Only heaven knows*. Without my ruminating over my parents' marriage and my own, I would have been decimated by the bombshell that Tony had dropped on me near the end of my odyssey.

Soon, the train decelerated again. To my surprise I spotted the leaning, octagonal tower perched on Tiger Hill. Just a glimpse of that ancient pagoda evoked another fleeting image— the moon over the maple bridge near the Hanshan Temple. Another tiger that had been crouching on my chest leaped away, and a synapse in my brain sparked, granting me an instant of clairvoyance. Like rain flowing into a cistern, like moonlight spilling into an open window, calmness filled my heart. For the first time in my life, I felt as serene as a Zen master at the cusp of enlightenment.

"Next stop, Shanghai Station," a computer-synthesized voice announced from overhead. Soon the train glided out of the concrete forest of the high-tech zone of Suzhou.

The sky brightened. Over the last remaining open field, a gigantic orange globe was lofting itself above the magenta horizon. What a full moon! Bold and flaming, as awe-inspiring as the yolk of a freshly laid egg. I held my breath. In that transient moment, the moon seemed to hold itself still for me, too. Then it beamed, promising perfect harmony to the universe. A surge of euphoria bathed me.

Gazing at the moon, I stroked my jade pendant and savored the story of the Moon Goddess once more.

Then, from the corner of my eye, I caught a familiar smile on the train window. No, I had to correct myself—*the unfamiliar smile of a familiar woman*.

It's that enigmatic half-smile in Tang Yin's painting—after Chang'e crash-landed on a rock and tumbled out of a lunar crater; after she rubbed her bruised forehead, wiped her tear-streaked face with her long sleeve, and staggered toward a silver palace; after she trod the icy marble floors of the empty halls with a pounding heart; after she limped after a white rabbit and wandered wide-eyed into a lush garden brimming with exotic flora and buzzing, alien insects; after she broke off a blossoming osmanthus branch and buried her nose in the sweet fragrance; after she peered down at the unsettled dust on the faraway Earth, then swallowed the last droplet of elixir that was still spinning at the base of her tongue; after she made the final quantum leap with blind faith, and, alas, transcended into a new kingdom.

A perspective shift. A mind game. A new reflex completes its loop. The Moon Goddess casts off a layer of molted skin, a coat that has become too tight. To her amazement, a pure being emerges, radiant and expansive, more magnificent than anything she could ever have imagined.

Oh, you poor thing! Now she smiles at her ghost image with overflowing tenderness, releasing and gripping her past at the same time.

THE END

ACKNOWLEDGMENTS

This book wouldn't exist without the gold mine of stories passed down from my extended family, to whom I am deeply indebted. I borrowed so much from their experiences that I can only hope they continue to invite me for Thanksgiving dinners!

Thank you, Kai, for your faith in my writing. I'll be forever grateful for your kindness and your gift of friendship.

Thank you to my beta readers and writing groups. Jessica Bird, Liesl Swogger, and Amy Johnson, without your enthusiasm and early constructive critiques, my first draft would be still languishing in a drawer. Anie Onaiza, Pia Owens, Elisabeth Sylvan, Bryan McManus, Maggie Huff-Rousselle, Kumkum Amin, and Fran Cronin, my friends, I would have aborted this project without your camaraderie. Thank you to Sandy Burton for being a true friend and providing valuable feedback from a man's point of view. Carrie Lakin and Patricia Daly-Lipe, your praise gave this writer much-needed confidence.

Thank you to Tim Weed. You are the best teacher I could ever hope for. Thank you to Tilia Klebenov Jacobs, Ursula DeYoung, Marina Werbeloff, Matthew McKay, Judy Young, Trish Ryan, Selena Lin, Julia Horwitz, Amy Heuton, and all my classmates at Grubstreet for providing an unforgettable experience. Thank you, Maya Shanbhag Lang, for your teaching of *The Caseura* at the Muse Conference. It inspired me to restructure my novel to make my heroine's journey more meaningful.

Thank you to Mike Fleming for your meticulous reading, researching, and editing. Jackie Cangro, your sharp, perceptive eyes helped me streamline the storyline. And thank you to Denise Shea, Debi Taylor, Mari Funai, Racheli Shatil, and Isabelle Bleecker for your candid feedback. Thank you to Lou Pugliese, Jolene MacFadden, and Edward Mickolus for sharing your expertise in the maddening publishing industry. I'm blessed to have met you all at the right time. Thank you to Regina Edwards, M. Ed, DTM, at Authors Roundtable of Florida Inc. for your commitment to helping Florida authors flourish.

Thank you, Autumn Skye, for your artistic rendition of my vision.

Finally, a special thank you to John for your love and all the invigorating cappuccinos every morning. Life with you has been an enriching adventure.

AUTHOR BIO

Like the protagonist in her debut novel, Wu spent her formative years in China before coming to New York City as a graduate student. After a career in biomedical research and podiatry practice, she followed her heart and pursued her dream of becoming a storyteller. At Boston's Grubstreet, she honed her fiction writing skills. She lives with her husband in Jacksonville, Florida.

Find more information about this
book and author here: